The Naked and the Deadly

THE
NAKED
AND THE
DEADLY

Lawrence
BLOCK

in men's adventure magazines

EDITED BY **ROBERT DEIS & WYATT DOYLE**

MensPulpMags.com

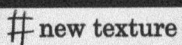

A New Texture book

Copyright © 2023 Subtropic Productions LLC

Stories and Introduction © 1958, 1961, 1962, 1963, 1967, 1968, 1974, 2023 Lawrence Block. All rights reserved.

Archival materials supplied by The Robert Deis Archive

All Rights Reserved.

Cover: Detail from "Bring on the Girls" by Bruce Minney

Designed by Wyatt Doyle

With thanks to Lynn Munroe, Gary Lovisi, and Jules Burt

NewTexture.com

 @NewTexture   @ThisIsNewTexture

MensAdventureLibrary.com   MensPulpMags.com

Booksellers: *The Naked and the Deadly* and other New Texture books are available through Ingram Book Co.

ISBN 978-1-943444-63-2

First paperback edition: May 2023

This book is also available as a deluxe, expanded hardcover with additional material

Printed in the United States of America

10 9 8 7 6 5 4 3 2 1

Men's Adventure Magazines [MAMs]

A bona fide publishing phenomenon that emerged in the 1950s and thrived through the 1970s, the tropes and aesthetic estblished by **men's adventure magazines (MAMs)** have proven so durable and have been absorbed so totally into the American consciousness that even decades after their demise, MAMs remain an incontestable—if invisible—hand behind key events and directions in entertainment and popular culture.

Incorporating the colorful, eye-catching cover paintings and pulse-pounding action/adventure fiction of pre-World War II pulp fiction magazines, MAMs added non-fiction adventures to the mix, and blurred the line between the two by frequently claiming the outrageous, high-octane fiction was also true, even when such claims were implausible, preposterous, or demonstrably false. This blend quickly became standard for the genre, and pulp "fact" ran side by side with pulp fiction.

The MAM formula cannily incorporated aspects of other popular magazines that appealed to the working-class readership they targeted, including racy "bachelor" and pin-up mags, outdoor and travel periodicals, true crime and detective magazines, and celebrity scandal rags.

The format was adopted by multiple publishers, who produced magazines of varying quality. All told, more than 160 different periodicals fit the classification. Some lasted decades, others, only a few issues—or just one. While the more lurid varieties (sometimes called "sweats" or "sweat mags") often draw the most attention (and criticism), the range and quality of MAM content is more varied than is generally understood.

Though dismissed in their time as downmarket, lowbrow entertainment, the magazines were an enduring success, enjoyed by millions of readers over three decades. MAMs published popular writers of the day, and artwork by many of the era's top illustration artists. The terse, hard-boiled intensity of the writing and the dynamic, explosive, and racy illustration art—on their covers and in their pages—are essential to their appeal, then and now. The potency of these words and images remains undiminished; their excesses still spark gobsmacked wonder, and their artistry inspires fascination on its own terms.

CONTENTS

Tricks of the Trade

by Wyatt Doyle
and Robert Deis

Hellish disasters at sea. Human monsters in swastika
and jackboots. The unvarnished realities of prostitution.
Life in an asylum's violent ward. International intrigue and
white-knuckle adventure. Party girls who turn up dead.
Randy stewardesses and sex at 12,000 feet.

The focus and subject matter of mid-century men's
adventure magazines (MAMs) were wide-ranging, and
versatile storytellers able to confidently navigate varied
genres, approaches, and authorial voices found regular, lu-
crative work in their pages. Among those talented writers
was a notable newcomer named Lawrence Block—though
his initial pieces would see print under pseudonyms.

Not the Lawrence Block you know, who is among the
most widely read, respected, and celebrated writers of
crime and mystery fiction in the world. Internationally
read and internationally honored, upon whom the Mystery
Writers of America bestowed the title of Grand Master.
A storyteller with over 65 years of professional experience
in damn near every mode of written expression, whose
essays, magazine columns, and non-fiction books focused
on the art, craft, and business of writing have endured to
inform generations. Not that Lawrence Block.

Not yet.

MAMs could be a good fit for a young writer. Block's initial pieces appeared in magazines published by Stanley Morse, whose company Stanley Publications, Inc. gained notoriety for putting out some of the extreme horror comic books that sparked the anti-comics hysteria that led to Congressional hearings and the 1954 Comics Code, which prohibited bloody violence and sex in comic books.

Morse responded by toning down his comics and amping up the blood-and-guts quotient of his magazines for adult men. He transformed the Stanley comic *Battle Cry* into a MAM of the same name and launched a number of other pioneering titles, including *All Man, Champion for Men, Man's Adventure, Man's Best, Man's Look, Man's Prime, Men in Combat, Men in Conflict, Real Men, Real War, Rugged, Rugged Men, Spur, True Battles of World War II, True Men Stories,* and *War Criminals*.

Morse would become the second-largest publisher of MAMs after Martin Goodman, who started out publishing pulp magazines and comics (including Marvel). Beginning in the early 1950s, Goodman's Magazine Management Company published a long list of popular MAMs, such as *Action for Men, Battlefield, Complete Man, For Men Only, Hunting Adventures, Ken for Men, Male, Man's World, Men, Men in Action, Stag,* and *True Action*.

MAMs published by Morse and Goodman weathered a changing marketplace across three decades, holding on until the MAM format faded away in the late 1970s.

AT THE core of all MAMs was a dedication to covering any subject thought to be of interest to American men at the time—a strategy to appeal to the largest possible readership by including a little of everything. They cast wide nets for content, offering fiction and non-fiction that played to popular and established interests and curiosities, along with pin-up photos, gag cartoons, and more. The magazines' content is best remembered today for tough, pulpy fiction, war stories, survival sagas, and "Weasels Ripped My Flesh"-style animal attack yarns, but MAM *non*-fiction was an essential and popular aspect of the magazines, and came in as many varieties as MAM fiction: celebrity gossip, biographical profiles, travel pieces, advances in technology and medicine, cryptozoological sightings and UFO-related developments…even mad-as-hell consumer advocacy had a place. As long as an idea could be reasonably tied into the broad category of *male interest*, there was room for it.

Men like sex, so MAMs included plenty of it, packing as much into the magazines as could safely pass muster with the laws, social mores, and postal regulations of the era. In a time when frank exploration of the subject could be difficult to come by, part of MAMs' appeal was as a venue where relatively adult discussions of sex and sexuality could be found—often presented salaciously, but safely within the accepted standards of the era. Publishers knew where lawmakers (and postal censors) drew the line, and even seedier MAMs with lower standards knew to toe that line or face serious legal consequences.

MAMs focused heavily on escapist entertainment and male-oriented fantasy. They offered a portal to other lives and imaginary places where excitement was everywhere and casual sex with desirable partners was easy and frequent. Directly and indirectly, they catered to male erotic fantasies from conventional to kink, making up for what they couldn't baldly say or show by emphasizing sex in every kind of content in their pages, sexualizing most situations involving women. Even an otherwise straightforward adventure like "Queen of the Clipper Ships" (pg. 24) has a prominent component of sexual threat that is the source of much of the story's tension.

THE LINE between MAM fiction and non-fiction pieces could accurately be described as *fluid*. MAM fiction was frequently presented as factual accounts, and MAM non-fiction was prone to heavy exaggeration, even outright invention.

Though MAMs were not cynical, editorial voices were presented as informed and experienced, at times judgmental. A barracks-room familiarity was typical, with readers encouraged to trust the magazines for the straight dope on everything from sex to insurance scams to international tensions, with consumer reports and fraud warnings regularly found among the hard-boiled fiction, illustration art, and pin-up photos. Exposés and accounts of historical tragedies and disasters were popular, and when the guilty party was a specific person or company (as opposed to enemy forces or fate), a bit of good old fashioned finger pointing lent a fresh edge to dusty historical accounts.

Whether the blame could be laid at the feet of money-eyed fat cats looking to save a buck or workers simply failing to do their jobs, righteous indignation proved as consistently alluring to MAM readers as accounts of wartime action or animal attack fiction. [See "The Greatest Ship Disaster in American History" (pg. 37) and "Pleasure Cruise for 137 Corpses" (pg. 53).]

Like most of these early pieces, Block's "She Doesn't Want You!" was written as *Sheldon Lord*. It is part of another notable MAM lineage: Exposés and firsthand tell-alls about taboo and forbidden subjects; in this instance, prostitution.

Since many mid-century American males were World War II veterans, Nazis were a staple of both the magazines' fictional and fact-based features. Non-fiction profiles of notable figures both heroic and notorious appeared regularly in MAMs, and Block's brief but potent look at the life and crimes of Reinhard Heydrich, Hitler's "Blond Beast" (pg. 61), appears to be his only foray into biographical sketches for the magazines.

Considering MAMs' emphasis on all things tough and manly, extreme and dangerous jobs cropped up frequently in the pages of MAMs, both as dramatic settings in short fiction and in fact-based articles. Block dipped a toe in with 1961's "Killers All Around Me" (pg. 71), written from the perspective of a mental institution employee and chronicling physical threats encountered on the job. Published as "CC Jones," Block submitted the story with the byline "CO Jones," but an editor with at least a passing familiarity with Spanish seemed to catch the author's risqué wordplay *en español* ("CO Jones" = *cojones*) and sanitized the pseudonym for print.

"Just Window Shopping" is a brief and unsettling account told from the perspective of a peeping tom, a most unreliable narrator. Despite its first-person trappings, the story is unexpectedly presented as a work of fiction and credited to Sheldon Lord, a name that until then Block had only applied to non-fiction.

IN CLASSIC pulp magazines, novels were sometimes serialized over the course of several issues before they were published in book form. By the 1950s, pulps had waned and the men's adventure magazine genre was taking shape. MAMs continued some pulp traditions, most notably, eyeball-grabbing painted covers and lots of action/adventure fiction stories. But MAMs didn't serialize novels.

Instead, MAMs published *Book Bonus* versions of novels and some non-fiction books of interest to their male readers. Typically, these were drawn from books that had already been published. Sometimes they were promoted as versions of soon-to-be-published novels, or books soon to be made into movies. Other times, they were condensed versions of existing movie tie-in novels for films that were recent hits.

Most Book Bonus stories were published by MAMs with circulations in the hundreds of thousands and budgets that allowed them to pay for reprint rights to novels and other books. Those included the top-tier MAMs like *Argosy, Bluebook, Cavalier,* and *True,* and mid-tier MAMs such as Pyramid's flagship MAM *Man's Magazine,* and Martin Goodman's popular Magazine Management MAMs. Most of the bottom tier of MAMs, with circulations of 50,000 to 100,000 or so, had budgets too slim to pay for Book Bonus reprints.

MAMs that did feature Book Bonus stories usually trumpeted them in their cover headlines, especially when they were by writers who were famous or at least well known to fans of crime and action/adventure novels. Even a short list of some of the best-selling authors who had Book Bonus stories in MAMs would include Nelson Algren, Louis L'Amour, Michael Avallone, Lawrence Block, Carter Brown, Erskine Caldwell, Brett Halliday (David Dresser), Ian Fleming, Joseph Heller, Frank Kane, Day Keene, Philip Ketchum, Alistair Maclean, Norman Mailer, Richard Matheson, Richard S. Prather, Ellery Queen, Quentin Reynolds, Robert Ruark, Mickey Spillane, and Donald Westlake.

Goodman MAMs would add a new wrinkle to the concept: Book Bonuses for imaginary books. Touted as novels soon to be published (or soon to be adapted for upcoming movies), it's doubtful that readers ever noticed these novels never *were* published—much as most didn't notice (or didn't care) that many MAM stories presented as true (and accompanied by editor's notes and photos to support that illusion) were entirely fictional. What mattered to readers was whether the story *delivered.*

For the authors of books that actually existed, Book Bonuses offered the dual advantage of an extra fee and some additional publicity. Typically, the publication of these shortened versions was arranged by the author's agent. Sometimes the agent provided the shortened version, sometimes the edited version of the text was created by the editors of the magazines.

One special aspect of MAM Book Bonus stories is that they were frequently accompanied by specially commissioned artwork by top MAM illustration artists, rather than the actual books' cover art. MAM editors usually made up their own title for the Book Bonus version to fit the high-octane, often sexually tantalizing style of the genre. Thus, the Book Bonus version of Lawrence Block's first Evan Tanner novel, published in 1966 as *The Spy Who Couldn't Sleep*, became "Great Istanbul Gold Grab" in the March 1967 *For Men Only* (pg. 294). The Book Bonus version of "The Scoreless Thai" from the 1968 Tanner novel *Two for Tanner* was titled "Bring on the Girls" in *Stag*, July 1968 (pg. 368).

UNLIKE the pulps that preceded them, MAMs usually did not have recurring characters in stories unless they were Book Bonus versions of novels constructed around characters like Mickey Spillane's Mike Hammer, Richard S. Prather's Shell Scott, Donald Westlake's Parker, and Block's Evan Tanner. The Ed London stories by Block are an exception. They are unusual because they were first published in MAMs, but didn't appear in book form until many years later.

Lawrence Block has another unusual credit in the realm of stories that connect MAMs and books. Early in their careers, Block and fellow scribe Robert Silverberg (later a Science Fiction Grand Master) both jumped on the ever-popular "sexology studies" bandwagon sparked by sex researcher Alfred Kinsey's books *Sexual Behavior in the Human Male* (1948) and *Sexual Behavior in the Human Female* (1953), generally called The Kinsey Reports.

Block would write a series of fascinating faux—but seemingly well-researched and very cogent—books of sexual studies under the pseudonym *Dr. Benjamin Morse*. They included *The Lesbian* (1961), *The Homosexual* (1962), *The Sexually Promiscuous Female* (1963), *The Sexually Promiscuous Male* (1963), *Sexual Behavior of the American College Girl* (1963), and *Adolescent Sexual Behavior* (1964).

Silverberg also wrote sexology and sex advice books under the name *L.T. Woodward*, whose books include *1001 Answers to Vital Sex Questions* (1962), *Sex and the Armed Forces* (1963), *Sex and the Divorced Woman* (Non-fiction, 1964), and *I Am a Nymphomaniac* (1965).

Excerpts from the sexology books penned by Block and Silverberg showed up as articles in MAMs, sometimes identified as Book Bonus stories, sometimes not.

Capitalizing on the sexual revolution then underway, between 1968 and 1973 Block wrote another series of sex-related books, this time under the name *John Warren Wells*. Wells' books include *Eros and Capricorn* (1968), *The New Sexual Underground* (1968), *Sex and the Stewardess* (1969), *Comparative Sex Techniques* (1971), and *Come Fly with Us* (1972), the sequel to *Sex and the Stewardess*. Portions of the Wells books were also published as articles in MAMs, sometimes with the book source identified, sometimes not. Many of those books include introductions or quotes by—who else?—the esteemed sex studies expert, Dr. Benjamin Morse.

A Naked and Deadly Introduction

by Lawrence Block

For five bucks a week, I chose Scott Meredith over
Henry Luce.

Well, in a manner of speaking. It was the summer
of 1957. After spending the month of July on Cape Cod,
where I wrote a batch of short stories before hunger
prompted me to take a horrible job in a restaurant, I quit
and headed back to my parents' house in Buffalo. I'd
bought my first car, a 1953 Buick, in order to drive to the
Cape, and I cracked it up en route to Buffalo, where I sold it
and got on a train to New York. I found a furnished room
on East 19th Street and set about looking for a job.

I had turned 19 in June, and had completed two years
at Antioch College. Antioch had (and still has) a work-
study program; students spend about half their time on
campus and the other half getting real-life experience in
jobs in their field. My first co-op job had been a year earlier, at Pines Publications, publishers of the Popular Library
paperback line and a great array of magazines. I'd spent
three months in the mail room, which gave me practical
experience as a clerk and gofer, neither of which much
appealed to me as a career choice. But Pines was a publishing company, and I knew I wanted to be a writer, and that
wasn't the worst place to start.

Two months in, the fellow in charge of promotion

and publicity told me his assistant was leaving at the end of the month, and wondered if I'd like to take his place. When I admitted I was scheduled to return to college, he assured me I should stick with my plans—and I did, but not without some reluctance. I liked school well enough, but from the jump I was impatient to Get Out There and Do Something.

What I did in August was look for something to do—and, back in Buffalo, my folks tried to lend a helping hand. Ralph Tolleris, a fraternity brother of my dad's at Cornell, was married to a woman who did something significant at Time-Life, and eventually she and I spoke over the phone. I'd spent a week responding to classified ads, and figured I'd be able to get an office job that would pay me $65 a week. Beebe Tolleris was able to offer me a job as a copy boy at *Time Magazine*. I'd work 9 to 5, Wednesdays through Sundays, with Monday and Tuesday off, and I'd make $60 a week.

I said I thought I'd keep looking.

Now it wasn't the five pre-tax dollars a week, not really. It was a deep disinclination to take a job through family connections, because what if I screwed up? What if I got fired? And so on. And yes, a path to success often started as a copy boy at *Time*, much as careers in the film business began in the mailroom at William Morris, but on the first of November I'd be back on campus in Yellow Springs, Ohio, so what was a menial job at Time going to do for me?

Next thing I knew I'd taken a test and landed a position as an editorial associate at the Scott Meredith Literary Agency. There's an interesting story that goes with it, but I tell it at length in *A Writer Prepares*, where you can find it at leisure. I got the job—and yes, the base pay was $65 a week, and if you exceeded your quota you could bring in ten or twenty dollars over that figure.

But that was the least of it. I had fallen into what I have never ceased to believe was the best possible job for anyone with career aspirations in any area of writing or publishing. By the time August had given way to September, as it so often does, I knew I wasn't going back to Antioch, not in November and very likely not ever. It was a good school and they had a lot to teach me, but I was already in the right place to learn what I really wanted to know.

I was at my desk at 580 Fifth Avenue five days a week, reading the stories of wannabe writers who paid Scott to read their work. They didn't get Scott, they got me or one of my colleagues, and it was our job to read their stories and tell them why they were unsalable, but that we'd welcome more submissions—each, of course, accompanied by the requisite fee. I'd do that until five o'clock, and then I'd go home and write stories of my own. I'd bring these to the office and give them to Henry Morrison, and he'd read them and send them to one editor or another, and most of the time they'd sell for a cent a word, sometimes a cent and a half, bringing me something like thirty or forty or fifty or sixty dollars—but the money wasn't the point. I was writing fiction! I was selling it, and it was getting published!

In addition to the stories I wrote of my own initiative, sometimes an editor would call the office with an assignment. He needed 2500 words to fill a hole in an issue that was about to go to press, say, or he had a terrific idea and needed someone to write it up. A shipwreck, or a disaster, or a Very Bad Man—generally something it would never occur to me to write, but more often than not an occasion to which I was prepared to rise.

A fellow named Ted Hecht, at a company called Stanley Publications, was the source of most of these assignments. The Scott Meredith offices were at Fifth Avenue and 47th Street, and the New York Public Library was five short blocks to the south, and I would walk there and consult the card catalog and fill out a slip to request a couple of books, and read enough to go home and write an article. That's how most of these articles came about.

But not quite all of them. The first one you'll find is "Queen of the Clipper Ships," and the byline is Sheldon Lord, the name I used on most of these pieces. But the article itself, I assure you, is one I read for the first time in a pre-publication PDF of this very book. I'd never seen it before, and I certainly never wrote it.

Now I'm unquestionably getting on in years. If I was 19 in 1957, well, you can do the math. And my memory has aged along with the rest of me, and it's among the component parts thereof that no longer function as well as they once did. There are things I don't remember all that clearly, and others I recall imperfectly. But in this instance I can say with absolute certainty that "Queen of the Clipper Ships" is not my work. It's listed in Terry Zobeck's bibliography of my work, *A Trawl Among the Shelves*, because anyone encountering it with Sheldon Lord's byline on it would certainly assume it was mine. I thought as much myself, until I finally took an actual look at it.

But it's not.

So who wrote it, only to have Ted Hecht hang someone else's pen name on it? I've no idea, and I suspect anyone who ever might have known has long since spiraled on to another incarnation. You'll note that it appears in the same issue with another shipwreck story, the *General Slocum* disaster, and slapping the same byline on both pieces is the sort of thing that can happen when an editor's in enough of a hurry to get copy to the printer. But never mind. I got $75 for "The Greatest Ship Disaster in American History," and I can but presume that the actual author of "Queen of the Clipper Ships" got as much for what he wrote, and that it didn't pain him too much to see the credit go to somebody else.

And now I'm comfortable enough seeing it here in this volume, helping to add a little heft to the book, perhaps making it that much more rewarding an experience for You the Reader. Did I write it? Well, no, but here it is, in my book, still wearing my longstanding pen name. So I think we can safely say it's mine. And, should anyone reading this be seized by the urge to reprint this stirring tale, my response would be the same as if you expressed similar interest in any of the book's other contents. I am, after all, a reasonable man. I'll listen to offers.

Ah yes. I learned a great deal from Scott Meredith...

Besides the articles—which, I have to say, would be much easier to write now, in the era of Google and Wikipedia— you'll find some of my early fiction in this volume. There are in fact three novelettes that feature a New York-based private detective named Ed London.

His origins are complex, and perhaps interesting. I left my job at Scott Meredith after a little less than a year, arranged to return to Antioch in the fall of 1958, and in the interim went home to Buffalo and wrote my first novel. (It's in print now as *Shadows*, by Lawrence Block writing as Jill Emerson; it was initially published in 1959 with a different title and pen name.) By the time I was back in Yellow Springs, I'd begun writing erotic novels for Midwood Books as—yes—Sheldon Lord, and one way or another I wrote and drank and smoked my way out of Ohio by the end of that none-too-academic year. I wound up, first in Buffalo and then in New York, making a living by writing novels.

Henry at Scott Meredith was still my agent, and the

occasional source of an assignment. One was a TV tie-in novel, a book to be published as a paperback original and capitalizing on a television show, in this case one called *Markham* and starring Ray Milland. (This was not a novelization, which would consist of turning an existing dramatic script into a prose novel; I was to take the character Ray Milland played and come up with my own story for him.)

By the time I'd finished the book, I wondered if it might be too good to sell to the low-rent house that had commissioned it. I showed it to my friend Don Westlake, who encouraged me to show it to Henry, who sent it to Knox Burger at Gold Medal, who'd already bought my first crime novel. (*Mona*, later retitled *Grifter's Game*.) Knox asked for some fixes, including changing the hero's name from Roy Markham. I picked Ed London, and made the other changes he wanted, and Gold Medal brought it out as *Death Pulls a Doublecross*. (And later it became *Coward's Kiss*. Plus *c'est la même chose*, dontcha know.)

But then I owed a book to Belmont, a book starring Roy Markham. So I had to write it, and, well, never mind. I did what I had to do, and by then Ray Milland's show was canceled anyway, but Belmont published it as *Markham* and I've since republished it as *You Could Call It Murder*.

So there I was, with a guy named Ed London who could go on to star in a series of Private Eye novels, if only I could write them. And I tried, but it never worked. I don't know why. What I did manage to write was a novelette, and it sold to *Man's Magazine*. That was a decent sale to a decent market, and in the ensuing months I managed two more Ed London novelettes, and they went to the same place. And that was as much as I ever had to say about Ed London—except for all the times I've recounted this story, which may well add up to more words (if to no more purpose) than all three novelettes and the novel itself.

And what else have we here?

"Just Window Shopping" is an early crime story, and probably one that failed to sell to one of my regular penny-a-word markets; someone evidently dug it out and sent to *Man's*, and it landed there. "Great Istanbul Gold Grab" and "Bring On the Girls" are extracts from *The Thief Who Couldn't Sleep* and *The Scoreless Thai*, both novels in my Evan Tanner series.

And there you have it. Naked? Yeah, pretty much. Deadly? You betcha.

And by Lawrence Block?

Well, mostly...

Queen of the Clipper Ships

From the pages of **Real Men**, April 1958

Artist uncredited

The crew of the *Neptune's Car* had a right to be proud of their ship. She was an extreme clipper, the largest in her class, measuring 216 feet from stem to stern. The finest Georgia pine had been used in her careful construction. Her spars were long and sturdy, stretching broad sails skyward—she had been designed to achieve the swiftest speed possible.

Proud as they were of their ship, they had even more reason to be proud of their captain. Joshua Patten was world-famed as the "Boy Wonder of the Sea." In an age when Clipper Ships were the lions of the sea and the captain was king of his ship, the eyes of the nation were on the men at the helms of the graceful Yankee Clippers. *Joshua Patten was such a man.*

Born in 1827, he was a ship's officer before his twentieth birthday. At twenty-five, he had the distinction of becoming the youngest of the Clipper Ship captains—a breed of men with salt water in their veins and cast iron in their bones.

Four years later, in 1856, Patten was pitted against Captain Gardner of the *Intrepid*, in a race that was to make history. Today, that race makes the famous annual race at Indianapolis Speedway look like a "Snowshoe Walkathon." The owners of the two ships had their fortunes invested in the outcome of the race, and the first ship to make the trip from New York to San Francisco would haul in the whole pot. It was a rich prize, and Patten had his heart set on it.

Even though Josh Patten was only twenty-nine, the years of hard work and responsibility had put lines in his face and wrinkles in his forehead. He was tall and lank, with sandy hair and a strong, prominent chin. His shoulders were slumped, but his eyes were as bright and shining as a boy's. The race was the biggest challenge in his career, but he was confident. He was confident of his ship, his crew, and his own proven ability.

He was, in fact, so sure of himself that he brought his 17-year-old bride along. His wife, Mary, was a blue-eyed blonde with a figure that was as trim as the *Neptune's Car*, in a different way, of course. She and Patten had been married just four months at the time of the voyage, and perhaps it's no great wonder that he wanted her along.

To Patten, the trip promised to be a routine one. Despite the high stakes, the fact remained that the *Intrepid* was no match for the *Neptune's Car*. But a sailor by the name of Paul Haggerty was to change everything.

Several days before the two ships weighed anchor, Patten's regular first mate had failed to show up. Haggerty was soon on hand to take his place. The shuffling, hard-drinking Irishman had been hired by Gardner of the *Intrepid* to make sure that the *Neptune's Car* reached Frisco with her topsail dragging. An ideal choice for such a role, he was a man who would do *anything* for a price. Sabotage was a little out of his line, but Haggerty had no qualms about trying his hand at it.

ON JUNE 30, the order was given to weigh anchor. The *Neptune's Car* and the *Intrepid* eased slowly down the East River. The sky was overcast and there was a light wind behind them. They drew abreast off Sandy Hook, and crew members of the two ships exchanged challenges, catcalls, and insults. Then Patten ordered the sails unfurled, and the *Neptune's Car* drew away swiftly. By eleven in the morning, the *Intrepid's* foretopsail was barely visible. By noon she was lost from sight.

Patten jubilantly turned over the helm to his newly-acquired first mate, and Haggerty repaid the trust with avid interest. He neatly steered the ship several degrees off course. It was several hours before the error was discovered, and progress was considerably cut.

Patten was furious. He righted the ship and severely reprimanded Haggerty. The saboteur skillfully apologized. "Just a mistake," he explained. "If I never made mistakes, I'd be a famous captain like yourself," he smiled. Patten was unused to flattery, and he passed over the incident.

Minutes later, Haggerty had his first encounter with Mary Patten. She entered her husband's cabin just as Haggerty was leaving it, and the two collided with an impact that sent them both sprawling to the deck. While Mary apologized, the First Mate let his eyes wander insolently over her body. "My pleasure," he said, jauntily. "Hope I bump into you again!"

As the *Neptune's Car* raced steadily southward, with a good wind at her back, a rash of "accidents" cropped up to plague the captain. On the second day out, Haggerty went to work on the spanker boom, and the sail burst loose in the middle of the night. The crew worked feverishly on the sail, with the loss of a good deal of precious time.

THAT same night, a fire broke out in the paint locker. A deckhand spotted the blaze before any great damage could be done, but time was lost in extinguishing it.

Every night was the occasion for another "mishap." First a shroud line would loosen—then a stay would become unpinned. It seemed as though nautical gremlins were plaguing the vessel, as if the Fates were determined to win the race for the *Intrepid*. Accidents are frequent aboard ship, however, and Haggerty wasn't suspected. Although Patten sensed that something was definitely wrong, he had no grounds to believe that any crewman was at fault. He merely redoubled his efforts, and the *Neptune's Car* sailed on. The *Intrepid* was still nowhere in sight.

At last another incident occurred—one which made it painfully obvious that there was a saboteur aboard. A reading of the sextant revealed that the ship was far off course, and Patten discovered that someone had magnetized the compass with the blade of a penknife. He ordered a search of the crew, but the knife was nowhere to be found. It was Haggerty's knife, of course, but it rested safely on the bottom of the ocean.

Each mishap served only to spur Patten on, renewing his vigor and determination. He worked as though possessed by demons, driving himself and his men to the limit of their endurance.

Favorable winds took the clipper's sails, and the ship made its way across the Equator and down the coast of

South America. The treacherous waters of Cape Horn lay ahead, followed by the final sprint to Frisco.

Haggerty became desperate. He drank more heavily than ever—his eyes were like those of an animal, vicious and bloodshot. He *had* to stop Patten, yet it seemed impossible. There was only one answer. *Small doses* of foul play would never do the trick—Patten was too excellent a sailor to bow to them. *The captain would have to go.*

Haggerty had another reason to get rid of Patten. With the captain out of the way, his wife might provide Haggerty excellent companionship for the cold nights at sea. He needed women, just as he needed liquor. Every glimpse of the lush, young beauty increased his desire for her. All the rum in the world couldn't decrease it.

While Patten attempted to inflame the crew with the drive to beat out the *Intrepid*, Haggerty worked against him to undermine their morale. As Patten raced the ship faster and faster, fighting desperately against the rash of mishaps, the first mate spread the rumor that Patten was an egotistical tyrant, solely concerned with the race at hand. He intimated that the captain was slowly but surely driving his men to *death*.

Finally, Haggerty pressed for a liberty stop on the coast of Argentina. This was out of the question, and Patten told him so. The first mate grew sullen and morose, and denounced Patten so roundly that the captain had no alternative but to order him below.

PATTEN was a mild man with his crew, but he did not and would not tolerate insubordination. Besides, he was beginning to associate Haggerty with the "accidents." Despite lack of proof, he finally saw the first mate for what he really was.

As Haggerty shuffled back to his cabin, he passed Mary Patten on her way to the deck. The weeks without a woman were telling on him, and he came so close to the captain's wife that he could smell her. The slim roundness of her figure and the jut of her breasts inflamed him—it was all he could do to keep from grabbing her then and there. He contained himself, however. But that night, he graduated from sabotage to a "higher level" of evil. He poured a small envelope of poison, graciously supplied by the owner of the *Intrepid* for just such an occasion, over Patten's food.

That night the ship entered the waters of Cape Horn, at the southernmost tip of South America. Those were rough, unpredictable waters, and they spelled doom for more than one clipper. On that same night the color faded from Joshua Patten's weather-beaten cheeks. He wobbled on his long legs, the poison penetrating his system, robbing him of his vitality and sapping his strength.

This weakening did not pass unnoticed by the crew, and no doubt Haggerty would have brought it to their attention if it had. Most of them attributed it to the rigors of the voyage, but one crewman laid the blame to "too much bed and not enough sleep." All were agreed on *one* point—Captain Joshua Patten was a weak man.

Patten recognized this. He knew that he was physically incapable of taking charge of the ship all by himself, but there seemed to be no other choice. The second mate was too green to take over, and all the crew was completely untrained for the job. Only Haggerty could be entrusted with the responsibility, and Patten could not see his way clear to trust the first mate with *anything*.

He didn't confide his suspicions to Mary, for he couldn't back them up. She saw only his stubborn attitude, and feared that he was killing himself. She argued with him continually as the sickness got progressively worse. Finally, she was able to convince him to place Haggerty in command.

Mary hurried to Haggerty's cabin to order him to the helm, and found him in his characteristic attire. He was stripped to the waist, with his hand gripping a half-emptied jug of rum. Seeing Mary in his cabin doorway, he put two and two together, and came up with five.

"Hi," he said. "Have a seat." He gestured drunkenly to the bed, but Mary remained standing.

"I knew you'd come around," he went on. "You're too much of a woman for the captain to handle. He's all tuckered out." He laughed and took a step in her direction, reaching out for her.

Mary started to back away, but the Irishman was too fast for her. He slammed the door and pulled her into the room. His arms closed around her waist and pressed her to him. He forced a long kiss upon her lips. She struggled, but he only gripped her tighter.

"Don't fight," he commanded. He pinned her arms behind her back and forced her down to the bunk. He kissed her again, and his rum-soaked breath filled her with nausea. Pinning her to the bed, he clasped one hand over her mouth and fumbled with the buttons on her dress with the other. She could neither move nor call for help.

THEN two things happened almost simultaneously. It was as though Providence was determined to protect the virtue of Mary Patten. First, the ship took a tremendous roll which heaved Haggerty limp upon the floor. Then, seconds later Joshua Patten himself strode into the room, his eyes blazing.

Not even Haggerty could explain his way out of the situation. He tried to put the blame on the roll of the ship, but not even a tidal wave could have had such an effect on Mary's clothing. Patten sent Mary back to her cabin, and bluntly informed Haggerty that a repeat performance would result in his death. The first mate only grinned.

Despite the incident, Patten had no choice but to turn the ship over to Haggerty. The roll which saved Mary was the initial blow of a violent hurricane, a common feature of the Horn. The poison had thoroughly permeated Patten's system, to the point of temporarily blinding him. Guiding the ship was too much for even him, and he was forced to finally admit it. Reluctantly, he turned the helm over to Haggerty's eager hands and collapsed in his cabin.

The hurricane made things easy for Haggerty. He wouldn't *have* to limit himself to sabotage any more. The storm afforded, a perfect excuse to put to port on the Argentinian coast. Such a delay would knock the *Neptune's Car* out of the race, and the *Intrepid* would win without difficulty.

Seconds after Patten had regained consciousness, Haggerty burst into his cabin with the announcement that he had given orders to turn the ship around and put to port in Rio Grande. There was, he explained, no sense whatsoever in fighting the storm. It was a shame that the race would be lost, but that was the only course.

Joshua Patten was enraged. Not only would such a move lose the race and the prize that went with it, but it would place the ship in an even more perilous position. With the hurricane at her back, the *Neptune's Car* would have the cards stacked against her. *Shipwreck and loss of life would be almost a certainty.*

Patten had his back to the wall. If he countermanded Haggerty's order, who could pilot the ship? He tried to get up from his bunk and take over control himself, but he was too weak to stand. He pulled the covers over his body and gave the order to continue on course to San Francisco.

Haggerty returned to the deck and screamed that Patten was incompetent. He ranted to the crew that the fever had damaged the captain's brain until he was no longer responsible for his words or actions. Mutiny was the only answer. Accordingly, he and several representatives of the crew presented Patten with the ultimatum: turn back willingly or submit to mutiny.

At that moment, Joshua Patten seemed an old man. His hair was touched with gray—the strength had ebbed from his body—all of his vigor was gone. *But he would not be beaten.*

He sat up in bed. He turned from one man to the other, fixing his eyes rigidly upon them. He did not say a word. Haggerty was unmoved by his action, but the members of the crew squirmed under his glance. The veins stood out on his forehead, the sweat poured from him, and his eyes burned from one man to another.

Then he spoke. First, he ripped Haggerty's arguments to shreds in cold, clear logic, demonstrating that return was tantamount to suicide. When his point had been scored, he lashed into Haggerty.

HE DENOUNCED the Irishman as a saboteur, blaming him for all the mishaps that had occurred during the voyage. Despite Patten's physical condition, the force of his personality alone won back the loyalty of the crew and set them against the first mate. They were all for lynching him from the yardarm, but Patten ordered him placed in chains in the brig for the remainder of the trip.

Then Patten played his trump card. "Mary," he announced to the astonished crew, "is to take over command." They were to follow her orders all the way to San Francisco. He stifled their protests one after the other. The fate of the *Neptune's Car* rested on the shoulders of Mary Patten!

She walked proudly to the bridge. Behind her, shuffling weakly, came her husband. Together they were to make a

32

command team that would rank as one of the most famous and competent in all the history of our merchant navy.

The storm was getting worse. The wind was shrieking so loudly that it would have drowned out a full-throated scream. The spray, breaking over the bows of the *Neptune's Car* was so thick that the violent waves were almost totally obscured.

Mary and Josh took their posts without a murmur of complaint. Mary, straining her eyes into the swirling mist, trumpeted a running description of the scene and the situation to her half-collapsed husband. And he in turn, despite his infirmity, translated the data as fast as any modern calculating machine, back into specific orders. These Mary relayed to the crew.

Mary rocked on her feet as a gust of wind tore at her, wrenching her rainproof hat from her head. She fought for balance, her long, honey-blonde hair streaming out behind her in the spray. The deck canted sickeningly as the small clipper ship ground into a hell-deep trough between two giant waves. Mary clutched frantically for the rail; and then as the weakened bow plunged headlong into the oncoming mountain of water, she was thrown backward again, collapsing with a dull, sliding thud, her body twisting down on the hard, slippery deck.

Her scream, as she rocketed across the small deck toward the rail, was like the mournful cry of a lost soul. It seemed impossible that she could survive. Josh, aware of what was happening, even with his blindness, began praying, audibly, for the peaceful flight of his wife's soul.

But at the last possible second, the ship came through the wave and across in the opposite direction. Mary's body stopped its death-slide at the peak of a long, mountain slope. And then it started back, gathering speed as it came, until her feet tangled through the legs of the captain's chair.

Half-drowned, bruised and breathless, Mary refused to quit. She struggled to her feet with a mighty effort and resumed her post, picking up her description of the high, running seas as if there had been no pause at all.

"The mast!" Joshua shouted hoarsely. "Lash yourself to the mast! For God's sake Mary, protect yourself."

Mary didn't waste breath replying. Motioning to a group of sailors feverishly working the ropes nearby, she told them to follow her husband's instructions. Moments later, tied securely to the mizzenmast, she again took up her duties.

The barometer continued to fall. Down, down, down, past the 28-inch level, the column of mercury marked the movement of one of the worst storms ever to hit any ship, *anywhere.* And with each drop, the wind grew fiercer. Sixty-foot-high waves smashed into the frame of the ship. How strong the winds were, no one knows, for there was no instrument aboard capable of recording it. But they must have been well over 125 miles per hour.

THE CLIPPER scudded along like a roller coaster, her poles totally bare, her lines singing like violin strings as they whipped taut against the mast. The long, high column of wood, taking the full force of the tremendous pressure, bent like an Indian's bow, threatening to snap in two, or even worse, to rip bodily from the deck, leaving a huge gaping hole.

Yet Mary stayed at the masthead, trying to keep from looking at the almost doubled-up wood, steeling her nerves against the shaking and shivering of the hard pole directly behind her.

"Land ho! Off the starboard bow!"

Mary stretched against the waterlogged ropes that held her, looking into the sea-drenched sky to her right.

The cold cliffs of Isle Hermite loomed up before her like a vision of doom.

"Hard a'port! Hard a'port! Hands to the tiller! Hold her! For God's sake hold her port!"

The rocks grew closer, despite their desperate efforts. The full force of the wind, and the pressure of a billion tons of water dragged them along. The boat heeled dangerously, leaning so far to one side that it almost capsized.

Another wave, this one almost cresting the mast, threatened to break over them. They plunged into it, hitting square for a moment, before plunging up again, through and over.

But the giant wave worked a miracle, even though it threatened to swamp the ship. For a brief instant, the wall of water acted as a shield against the terrible wind. The tiller bit and held. The ship turned, only slightly, but enough. When they emerged, they were moving again, clear of the threatening, barren coast of the lonely, empty island. It was a miracle!

"Mary, Mary! Are you still there!" The voice of Josh Patten broke over the howl of the storm from where he sat, still blind, lashed to his chair on the bridge.

"Aye! And still in command, sir!" The feminine voice shot back.

"God bless ye, Mary my girl! We'll lick it yet."

"God bless us all, Josh, for without His blessing we're *all* drowned."

Then, as if in reply to their courage and their faith in each other, the glass wavered and began to rise. The wind veered suddenly to the opposite quarter and slowly started to fall off. The worst was past. They had come through. The waters of the Pacific lay dead ahead.

The storm abated finally, after fourteen hours of

the worst hell any vessel has ever known. They headed
north on blue waters. Patten recovered and was feeling
in top shape when the *Neptune's Car* finally docked at San
Francisco on November 13, 1856.

The *Intrepid* could not possibly close the gap. Neither
Nature nor Haggerty could change things now, and it was
two weeks before Captain Gardner's clipper reached Frisco.
By that time Patten's men were too drunk to care, and the
Neptune's Car had been decked out in streamers. The race
was over—a saga of treachery and of Nature's violence—*a
saga of the heroism of a man and his woman.*

Attributed to SHELDON LORD

That two stories credited to the pseudonym Sheldon Lord *appear
in the April 1958* Real Men *is unusual. After all, pen names
were usually deployed specifically to* avoid *a name appearing
in the table of contents more than once in an issue. But minor
editorial blunders like this are not unusual in MAMs, and though
it was surely accidental, it's amusing that Block's Sheldon Lord
pseudonym would end up "borrowed" out from under him only
a few pages before he could use it himself: "Queen of the Clipper
Ships" by Sheldon Lord (original author unknown) appears on
page 26 of the magazine, ahead of "The Greatest Ship Disaster
in American History" by Sheldon Lord (Lawrence Block) on
page 36.   —Eds.*

The Greatest Ship Disaster in American History

From the pages of **Real Men**, April 1958

At ten o'clock on the morning of June 15, 1904, the excursion steamer *General Slocum* pulled out of her berth on New York City's East River. She was carrying 1,358 women and children to the annual picnic and outing of St. Marks Lutheran Church.

Thirty minutes later, three quarters of them, *one thousand and twenty persons*, to be exact, were dead. They were victims of a disaster that stemmed directly from the most incompetent piece of seamanship that the world has ever known.

Considering the circumstances, it was a wonder that there were any survivors at all. Had the vessel been more than a few hundred yards from shore, and travelling in an area less congested with shipping, the loss of life would almost certainly have been *complete*.

Maybe the ship was fated. Built in 1891, the *General Slocum* was just *thirteen years old* on that sunny June day. Despite legends to the contrary, she was not carrying an excessive passenger list—her certificate allowed for 2,500. However, there had been a mob scene at the pier, just before departure time. Families by the hundreds ran, pushed, shouted and fought to get aboard. But this was merely a typical last-minute rush—everyone arriving at the latest possible moment and then all trying to get aboard at once, pushing and kicking.

There were plenty of freeloaders on hand, too; both among those on board and those left behind at the dock. St. Marks, located in the heart of the city's teeming East Side, could never fill the ship entirely from its own congregation, and friends of the parishioners, as well as urchins from the surrounding slums, beat their way down to the river, hoping to find a way of participating in the pleasures of a country picnic and a boat ride.

The captain was a stickler for schedules—though from later events, it appears that *that was all* he was good for. At ten AM sharp, he cast off, ignoring the protests of those still on the dock, vainly trying to get aboard. So, luckily, several hundred picnickers were left behind. But that didn't keep them from cursing the captain then. And he deserved every one of the curses.

Ten minutes after the ship had pulled away from the pier, a fire broke out in the storeroom. A 14-year-old boy, Frankie Perditski, saw it. He ran immediately to the captain with the news.

The captain could have done any one of a number of things. He could have put to port immediately. He could have had the fire taken care of at once. Instead, he turned to Frankie with a bored expression and snapped, "Shut up and mind your own business."

Frankie shut up.

After the ship had gone another quarter of a mile, a passing dredge captain saw a puff of smoke break from the hold. He gave four blasts on his whistle to bring it to the attention of the *Slocum's* crew. But no one answered and his warning went unheeded. It was almost as if the crew was deaf and blind.

As the steamer continued on its journey, at least a half-dozen other vessels signaled, frantically blowing their whistles. No signals were acknowledged and no action was taken.

The *General Slocum* plunged ahead on the route to disaster.

Why the captain did not stop, no one will ever know. To say that he did not know what was happening is fantastic. The inevitable must have been apparent, yet he acted like an ostrich, directing the ship *straight ahead* with his own head buried in the sand.

By 11: 30, all hell broke loose. The fire had eaten away the timbers of the ship—something had to give. And it did—with a bang!

SUDDENLY, smoke streamed onto the top deck. The playing children started to cough and retch—screaming as the billowing smoke filled their tiny lungs. Seconds later, the entire storeroom burst into flame—searing tongues of fire raced throughout the ship. The result was bedlam!

On a ship where gaiety had prevailed, utter panic and hysteria took over. Adults screamed. and fainted—children ran hysterically in circles, crying like frightened animals.

The blaze tore through the ship like a tornado. In minutes the *Slocum* was a *death ship!*

The crew moved like zombies—blank-faced and wooden. It was a full five minutes before someone had the presence of mind to turn a firehose on the flames.

Before the water even reached the nozzle, the hose burst in a thousand places—*useless.*

But the captain would not beach the ship! In stolid, hard-headed stupidity, he held the *General Slocum* straight on her course to doom. The passengers shouted at him and screamed curses, but stubbornly, mule-like, he held to his course.

The ensuing scene defies description. Children screamed in convulsive frenzy, their clothing in flames and their hair burning. The smell of burning flesh filled the air. Passengers tugged at lifeboats, their fingers clawing at the sides, unable to move them from their racks. Mothers grabbed their children and, wrapping them in life preservers, leaped like flaming meteors into the river. They sank to the bottom like stones! The *Slocum* was a shrieking hell on water!

St. Marks Church was decimated that morning. Entire families were wiped out. Of the 1,358 persons aboard, 1,020 died. It was the most tragic American maritime disaster in decades.

In marked contrast to the cowardice and stupidity of the captain, there were some memorable acts of bravery and heroism that day. One young woman dashed into the flames time after time to drag children to safety, before the fire claimed her as a victim. The captain of a small cabin cruiser fearlessly rammed his boat into the smoldering hull of the *General Slocum*, in an effort to aid the victims. Men gave away their life preservers and went down with the ship. But even with these examples of selfless courage, the final results were catastrophic.

The American public was shocked and infuriated. This was no shipwreck in unchanneled waters. Nor was it a case of a battleship lost in combat. It was an excursion boat in the *middle of a river—in the middle of a city!* As long as such a thing could happen, no American could feel safe off dry land.

An investigation was launched by President Theodore Roosevelt himself, in an effort to fix the blame for the tragedy and eliminate any possibility of a repeat performance. The disclosures of that investigation were more than frightening. They were sickening.

The wreck of the *General Slocum* was more than an accident. It was inevitable. The ship was doomed before it left the dock!

The outfitting of the *General Slocum* reveals an utter lack of responsibility on the part of the owners and operators of the ship. Almost every maritime ordinance in the book was violated. The owners wanted a profit, and they would not let human lives stand in their way.

THE FIRE originally broke out in the storeroom—and no wonder. First of all, the ship was carrying a load of hay, *strictly in violation of all existing laws.* Bunched around the hay were open paint cans and oily rags. The temperature of the storeroom was far too high—in fact, the crew used to hang their wet garments there to dry, because it was the hottest room on the ship. Under such conditions, spontaneous combustion was inevitable. However, spontaneous combustion was not the only factor—the crew members smoked in the storeroom. It's anybody's guess whether the blaze was started by a cigarette butt or by itself.

The firehose rates a number one position in the Chamber of Horrors. It was at least three years past its legal lifetime, and was made of the cheapest rubber tubing available. Although a fire drill once a week was required by law, the hose on the *General Slocum* had not been used in over a year. It was there *purely for show*, and when it was used for its intended purpose, it fell apart.

The lifeboats were also showpieces. They were set out on deck nicely enough, *and they remained there*, going down with the ship. They were elaborately wired and *nailed* to the deck. Nobody could budge them. They were rotten, and would have been of little value anyway, but no one had a chance to find that out.

The real tools of what one could almost call premeditated murder, were the life preservers. *Life destroyers* would be a more accurate description. The only member of the crew who did not survive was the one who made the mistake of donning a life preserver. The others leaped overboard, but this man first slipped one of the rings around his middle. They found him later on the river bottom, nestled snugly in the death jacket.

In perhaps the most vicious method ever used to save a buck, the company owners had filled their life preservers with iron!

Most of the passengers, however, didn't get a chance to ride the life preservers to the bottom. These, also, were nailed and wired in place and couldn't be pried loose. Several times passengers pulled on the rings and were horrified to see them fall apart in their hands. The cork used was the cheapest grade available, and was more on the order of sawdust than cork. It was rotten, and the cloth that covered it was rotten too.

Incredible? Those were the facts. Life preservers were required by law to weigh sixteen ounces, and sixteen ounces of cork ran into money, even when *rotten* cork was pressed into service. So the life preservers were diabolically filled with iron—they were far worse than no life preservers at all!

Imagine jumping into the water with a bowling ball tied around your neck! That's what the mothers and children did, and the result was inevitable. They drowned.

To top it all off, the crew was totally incompetent. Able-bodied seamen drew a fairly decent salary in those days, and the ship owners found another way to cut their expenses. The crew of the *General Slocum* was composed of the sloppiest landlubbers that ever drew breath. Many of them had never been aboard ship before. They were waterfront bums for the most part—men who could get no other jobs. When disaster struck they were helpless. A good crew might have greatly lessened the effect of the fire, but the crew of the *General Slocum* was *more frightened than the passengers.*

CONTRABAND hay, a rotten hose, useless lifeboats, cast-iron life preservers, and an incompetent crew! This was the equipment of the *General Slocum.* It would have taken a miracle to prevent catastrophe. This condition was no secret. The *General Slocum* had been inspected by government inspectors, and was pronounced to be in *perfect order.*

The public was enraged. The newspapers screamed for blood, and demanded that the men responsible be punished to the limit of the law. Teddy Roosevelt swung his big stick, but he didn't speak softly. He bellowed, and he reflected the temper of the entire nation.

Perhaps the most shocking revelation of the *General Slocum* investigation was the fact that the *Slocum* was not much worse than the average steamer. Cheap, sub-standard equipment was the rule, not the exception. "The public be damned!" was the watchword of shipowners the nation over. And countless inspectors betrayed their office, pocketed their graft, and closed their eyes. If it did nothing else, the *General Slocum* disaster pointed out graphically the desperate need for nautical reform.

The years between the turn of the century and World War I were a period of mass reform. Such laws as the Pure Food and Drug Act, the Meat Inspection Act, and similar protective measures were passed. The so-called "muck-rakers," fearless writers such as Upton Sinclair, Lincoln Steffens, and Ida Tarbell, to name a few, raised a hue and cry against injustice and corruption. Crusading magazines like *Munsey's* and *McClure's* lifted their editorial voices. All these factors combined to bring the Big Stick down with a resounding .smack.

Corrupt inspectors were fired in wholesale lots. New maritime regulations with teeth in them were speedily passed. The spark that ignited the *Slocum* served to blow the shipping racket sky-high. The nation decided that such an event would not reoccur.

The barn door was firmly locked-but the horse had already been stolen; 1,020 persons were dead. Hundreds of children who survived were orphans, having lost both their parents. Laws could not change that.

Rules and regulations could not erase the memory of little children wreathed in flames.

Laws could not bring back the dead. After all the speeches and all the articles--all the blows of the Big Stick—one fact remained. *Over one thousand human beings were dead.*

Valuable lesson? No doubt about it—considering the horrifying tuition—the high cost of learning. *And the low cost of dying.*

Written as SHELDON LORD

She Doesn't Want You!

From the pages of **Real Men**, *June 1958*

You're in a room at the other end of town, and you're tired. And why not? You've got a right to be tired.

You've paid your ten dollars or five dollars or whatever the price was, and if you were lucky you got your money's worth. Now it's time to go home—the show is over. But like most men, you look once again at the girl you've just been visiting. And, like most men, you can't help wondering...

What was it like for her? All work and no play? *Or did she enjoy it too?*

Go home quick, brother. Don't even think about it—

it's better that way. Because unless you're something pretty special, the little gal didn't get any kind of a thrill outside of the keep provided by the money you gave her. And there's a helluva good chance no man in the world can give her anything *but* money. It's almost even money that you just got a smile from a gal *who likes gals!*

Surprised? You shouldn't be. If you've read your Kinsey, you'd know that an amazingly high percentage of this country's prostitutes are lesbians. They get their wages from men—*and their love from each other.*

At first it doesn't make sense. People should like their work. Veterinarians like animals, bakers like bread. So why shouldn't prostitutes like men?

When you come right down to it, there are a good many reasons. And you can't fight the facts, for this sort of thing has been going on for a good long while. Prostitution doesn't have the reputation of being the oldest profession in the world for nothing. It dates all the way back to the Greeks.

In case you didn't realize it, the Greeks gave the world more than just Socrates. The bordellos of the ancient isles were the ultimate in pleasure palaces, the likes of which the world has never seen since.

If you were an ancient Greek with enough drachmas in your jeans, you were in for a treat. The gal you sported with was no tramp from the wrong side of the tracks; when she woke up mornings, she had more perfumes rubbed into her skin than she could count. She was never too thin and never too fat. Her skin was a mixture of ivory and silk.

And she knew her trade, too. She started learning around the age of ten, and by the time she got her union card she knew every trick in the business. When an ancient Greek male tiptoed up the back stairs to his wife after an evening of "pinochle," he was a contented Greek indeed!

What do you suppose happened when all the paying customers tiptoed out of the place of "ill repute?" You guessed it, friend. That was the signal for Little Miss Ivory-and-Silk to flash a smile of her own. She didn't waste any time in finding another "companion"—with long hair and curves—and having some fun for herself.

NOR WAS this sort of thing confined to Greece. Around the turn of the century, when Chicago was the way it used to be, there was a brothel on North Clark Street with an unusual set of house rules. The last man left at three AM, and the gals retired for a beauty sleep. And if any beauty had the unmitigated gall to insist on sleeping alone, she could jolly well hustle up another job in the morning.

Just because Chicago stopped being the way it used to be, there was no reason for the lassies to change their lives. And they didn't. Rome conquered Greece, Attila conquered Rome, and Capone conquered Chicago, but you still can put down plenty of cold cash for a sweetie-pie who is a lesbian—and you'll never know it!

What's the reason for all this? That depends on the gal, of course, but there are several basic personality types.

First of all is the babe who has developed a hate for men over the years. A man seduced her in the first place, another man started her hustling, and other men—customers—give her a bad time every day. The upshot of all this is that she winds up loathing the male gender like the plague. After working hours, a man becomes about as welcome as the seven-year itch.

Louise was this type of gal—I first met her on a street a little way off the Bowery, New York's Skid Row. She must have been pretty once upon a time, but that was long ago. Like so many other prostitutes in that neighborhood, *Louise was a lesbian.* She blamed men for all her difficulties.

"Men!" she snorted. "When I was twelve years old, a man raped me in an alleyway two blocks from my house. Then I made the mistake of tellin' my old man. He called me a tramp, belted me till I couldn't sit down, and didn't speak to me for the next three weeks. After that, I couldn't wait to get out of the house."

When Louise was sixteen, she ran away from home and never came back. But men kept making life miserable for her.

"I even fell in love with one of them," she said, bitterly. "The rotten heel! He got me into this racket—wouldn't work for a living, so he let me support the both of us. First I was "entertaining" some of his friends. The guy had more "friends" than Hitler had enemies. Then I was entertaining half the town, and lover-boy was pocketing every cent. One night I found out that there were three other girls doing the same thing for him. That was when I walked out. *Men!*"

Why, I asked, didn't she quit the racket then? Why keep going with men if they were all so miserable? She had a quick answer for that one.

"Let 'em pay," she said. "They got enough from me— now let 'em pay *my way.* They think they're getting a big deal, but they don't show me a thing. *Not a damn thing!*"

That last statement holds a clue to the whole problem. A good many girls drift into prostitution and lesbianism for the same reason—to avenge a deep and abiding hatred for all men. This hatred usually goes a long way back—even to childhood. They may have started by hating their fathers, and wound up hating and despising *everything* in pants.

To these women, lesbianism becomes a means of "getting even" with men. When one gal finds physical satisfaction with another, she proves to herself that *she can exist independently of men.* She can do anything a man can do, and through her lesbianism she flaunts her self-sufficiency before the world. She requires another woman to fulfill herself, and this makes the male inadequate and superfluous.

In the same way, her hatred of men manifests itself in prostitution. She goes through the motions of enjoyment, usually fooling her partner. She feels that, in actuality, she is giving him nothing at all. She's *faking* pleasure, and thus, in her own mind, making a fool out of the man.

Shirley was like this. She was young—eighteen when I met her, and she'd already been working the streets for a year-and-a-half. She had a pretty baby face, and the type of body which one would hardly associate with a lesbian. Her curves were all there, in the right places.

Shirley's mother managed to run through four husbands in six years. Instead of swearing off men, she floated from one to another. One-third of the time she was with a man—*any man*. Another third of her time was spent in an alcoholic stupor. The rest of the time was spent in pouring out her troubles to Shirley.

"Men ruined my mother," she explained to me. "They got her so she didn't know which end was up. I felt sorry for her, and I loved her. But I made up my mind *I wouldn't let any man make a sap out of me.*"

Shirley makes saps out of men instead, and makes what she calls "a respectable living" at her trade. She's young now, and gets a minimum of ten dollars for her favors. And when *she* wants to be loved, she goes to another girl.

"No men for me!" she asserts. "That's what ruined my mother. A girl's every bit as good as a man and she won't make a tramp out of you. A man'll make a tramp out of you every time!"

There are those unkind souls who might class Shirley as a tramp, but she would argue the point. It's just business with her, *and business is business.*

Business is business, and that's where the acting comes into play. The good businesswoman not only acts as though she's enjoying every minute of it, but she makes her lover feel as though he's the best man in the world. If she's a good enough actress, he goes away feeling that he's done her a favor. There's no ego like the male ego. He'll come back again and again, anxious to pay for the privilege of making her happy.

And a lesbian can give a fantastic performance. A friend of mine kept a girl in an apartment and dressed her in mink. He loved his wife, but complained that she was cold. He wanted a woman who could give him sincere affection and satisfaction.

He had the money, and he was willing to pay the price. He didn't really feel as though he was paying, insisting that he and his mistress were the most perfectly matched couple since Adam and Eve.

He got a rude awakening. One afternoon, he dropped in unexpectedly. But someone had beat him to it. Where there should have been one head, there were two, *and they both had long hair.* After my friend picked himself up off the floor, he reclaimed the mink and gave it to his "frigid" wife. He's sadder but wiser today.

So DON'T think about it, buddy. You'll just drive yourself nuts, because no man likes to feel that his playmate is bored stiff with the whole show. It just isn't recommended for the ego. It makes a man feel about as valuable as a second appendix.

Take the gals in Germany. GIs thought they had a paradise over there during the first few years of the occupation. The Berlin Babes were built like brick bomb shelters and were about as available as flies in a fertilizer plant. And the price was ridiculously low.

But the performance left a good deal to be desired. One married serviceman had his first fling overseas, and hasn't strayed from the straight-and-narrow since he donned civvies.

"I met this gal," he recounted, "and she was a doll. A living doll! All she wanted was a bar of chocolate and a comic book. At first I couldn't believe it.

"So I went to the PX and picked up the candy and the comic, and we went to her room.

"I still can't believe what came next. She picked up the candy bar and started munching away on it, then grabbed the comic book and buried her face in it. I just stood there watching.

"After a minute or so she asked me what I was waiting for—she was ready! Then she went back to the comic book. I got the hell out of there fast!"

Admittedly, that's a rather extreme example. But one thing is certain—a good many men are paying a good many dollars for a misrepresented commodity. You just can't buy passion.

There's a third class of prostitute who take their pleasure with their own sex. These are the kind who have had so many men so many ways, that they need something different in order to enjoy *themselves.* Variety, they argue, is the spice and "seasoning" of life.

These gals have nothing against the male of the species; in fact, they'll even *enjoy* him once in a while. But they need a change from time to time, and lesbianism provides this change for them.

"I *like* men," Marcia insisted. "I've liked men from the time I was fifteen, and I'm not going to quit now. But," she said with a wink, "you can get tired of ice cream, too."

I started to protest at that point, but Marcia squelched me. "Look," she said, "a guy pays for sex and he gets sex.

51

That's all you can buy. A man hands over his money and expects to be loved, but you can't turn love on and off like a faucet. *It just doesn't work that way.*

"A good hustler can make a grandfather feel like he's twenty again, and she can make a high school kid feel more experienced than Casanova. The scrawniest, mealiest jerko in creation thinks he's Superman when he's with her. He wants love too?"

She stretched playfully. She watched me stare, her eyes twinkling with amusement. "Like what you see?"

I nodded.

"You got the price?"

I nodded again.

"You know," she said when I hesitated, "some days I just *love* ice cream."

And you know, when I finally left, I couldn't help wondering....

Written as SHELDON LORD

52

Pleasure Cruise
for 137 Corpses

PLEASURE CRUISE for 137 CORPSES

by SHELDON LORD

The burning of the Morro Castle off Asbury Park, N. J., was one of the greatest sea disasters of the entire Twentieth Century!

From the pages of **Real Men**, November 1958

The fire broke out in the ship's writing-room at 2:30 AM. While the passengers and most of the crew slept soundly, the flames raced through the ship. In an unbelievably short space of time, the whole interior was turned into a roaring inferno. Scores were trapped in their cabins without a chance—literally burned alive. Others, panicstricken, leaped overboard—only to be slashed to shreds by the ship's churning propellors!

The date was September 8, 1934. The ship was the *Morro Castle*, a fast turbo-electric vessel three days out of Havana, with 318 passengers and a crew of 240 on board.

Most of them were returning from vacations in Cuba, and the trip had been pleasant and carefree. Then the fire struck, and the ship was transformed into a floating hell.

Robert Wilmotte had been the captain of the *Morro Castle*, but a heart attack the night before cut short his career and placed First Officer William F. Warms in command. From that moment on, the gory and shameless tragedy began to unfold with relentless speed.

From the outside, the *Morro Castle* looked like a safe ship on an easy voyage. Less than four years old, she had been equipped at a cost of over five million dollars. Nothing had been spared to make the ship the last word in luxury, with paintings and tapestries on the walls and thick rugs underfoot.

But below the glittering surface, she was *an accident looking for a place to happen.*

To begin with, the owners of the ship decided to save on labor what they spent in equipping the ship. They refused to pay the minimum wages which the unions demanded, paying approximately half of the normal seaman's wage.

As a result, the crew of the *Morro Castle* was made up of raw recruits and waterfront bums—the type of men who couldn't get work anywhere else. They were underpaid, poorly fed, and completely unskilled. They went to pieces when disaster struck. The *Morro Castle* had been equipped with heavy fire-doors, but the blundering crew didn't even have the brains to keep the doors shut!

The safety equipment of the ship was hopelessly out of date; the communications system was old-fashioned and useless in time of crisis; the lifeboats were badly rusted and painted over. In addition, the ship carried a load of highly inflammable brass polish, used to keep rails and trim in tip-top shape. Such a load was against the law, and the law had been passed for a good reason. The polish was an open invitation for fire.

At 12:30 AM, a fireman smelled smoke, but didn't take the trouble to let anyone in on the discovery! The passengers went to their cabins and most of the crew retired for the night.

Then, at 2:30 AM, the fire broke out. Naturally, the door to the writing-room was wide open—if it had been shut, the fire might have been confined there and the whole tragedy averted. With the door open, the flames spread rapidly.

THE "FLOATING hotel" was nice to look at, but it was hardly fireproof. The flames leaped over the tapestries and paintings and raced along the rugs. The fire spread at an almost incredible speed, quickly enveloping the superstructure of the ship and heading toward the passengers' quarters at the stern.

To say that it was a time for action would be a classic understatement. But Acting Captain Warms was not a man of action. He was more like a headless chicken. After the fire destroyed the communications system between engine and bridge, Warms screamed his orders ineffectively into the flames.

The crew practically ignored him. They also ignored the old maxim of "Women and children first" and dashed pell-mell for the lifeboats. Like a flock of leaderless geese, they fought desperately to save their own skins.

The *Morro Castle* carried twelve large lifeboats, each capable of carrying seventy passengers to safety. Only eight of the boats were ever loosed from their chocks, and these carried a total of only ninety-eight survivors. Of that number, ninety-two were members of the crew!

The ship was travelling at a speed of twenty knots and burning like a blast furnace—even an inexperienced seaman should have realized the necessity of stopping her.

In the face of such chaos, Warms went to pieces. When he did give an order, it was invariably the wrong one. Warms stopped the port propeller and put full steam on the starboard prop, driving the ship full into the wind and fanning the flames to the cabins in the rear!

Complete terror reigned aboard ship. Over the crackling of the timbers, there echoed the shrill shrieks of hundreds of men and women. *Nobody knew what to do.* One young mother, holding her baby in her arms, clutched madly at the arm of a passing sailor.

"What should I do?" she demanded.

"Jump!" he replied. She jumped overboard—right into the whirling starboard propeller!

In the midst of the fiery bedlam, only two men kept their heads. They were George W. Rogers, First Radio Officer, and his assistant, George I. Alagna. The captain had denounced Alagna as a "dangerous agitator" because he had dared to protest against the rotten food and low pay. *He became the hero of the whole episode.*

Rogers and Alagna waited in the radio room for Warms to call for an SOS. They knew that outside assistance was essential to keep losses to a minimum, and they stayed at their post. The radio room grew hotter and hotter—paint blistered on the walls. *But the order never came.*

Warms was apparently loyal to his employers, and he carried this loyalty to the extreme. Realizing that his bosses would have to pay salvage fees if other ships were called to her rescue, he stubbornly refused to order the distress signal. The two men waited in the hot, smoke-filled radio room. As the minutes crawled by, the ship literally burned to ashes around them, *but the order never came.*

ALAGNA raced out of the radio room and searched until he found the captain. "What's the matter?" he demanded. "Why didn't you order an SOS?"

"It's not necessary," Warms snapped.

"What? *The goddamned ship's on fire!*"

"It's not necessary," Warms repeated, haughtily. "Get back to your post!" With that, he turned his back on Alagna and started to walk away.

Alagna couldn't take it any longer. "Look, you crazy _____," he screamed, "you better give that order quick before Rogers burns to death!"

Without waiting for a reply, he fought his way back through the smoke to the radio room, and Rogers began tapping out the call. The two of them stood by their posts while the shoes on their feet literally cracked and smoked from the red-hot floor beneath, not relinquishing until other ships finally sped to the aid of the *Morro Castle*. Miraculously, they survived the ordeal.

Through it all, no effort was ever made to stop the fire. After a short time, it was completely out of control, but it's doubtful whether or not the crew could have done anything even at the beginning. Although the law required a weekly fire drill, the crew of the *Morro Castle* had never had one. For all anyone knows, the firehoses may well have been inferior. As it was, they burned quickly, while the water main burst from the heat.

As the flames roared higher and higher, the *Morro Castle* steamed onward like a blind horse in a burning stable. She plunged toward her death at a speed of twenty knots.

Finally, after the fire had nearly died out by itself, the *Morro Castle* was driven to the beach. There wasn't much left of her. Her insides were a mass of twisted and charred metal, with flames licking at the bit of combustible material that remained. The paintings and rugs were only smoky memories; just a bare skeleton of a ship was left. She was beached at last on the Jersey coast, near the Asbury Park Convention Hall, a stark and horribly real monument to disaster. Sightseers by the thousands flocked to watch the fire burn itself out.

When it was all over, the nation shuddered at the total impact of the tragedy. One hundred and thirty-seven persons, most of them passengers, were dead; burned or drowned in America's worst naval disaster since the sinking of the *Titanic*.

The nation was furious. This was no commonplace occurrence, nothing at all like a shipwreck in time of war. This was the loss of a supposedly "safe, modern ship." Newspapers and magazines joined in the cry, and Congress lost no time in launching a full-scale investigation.

THE INVESTIGATION got under way almost before the last survivor had been pulled from the sea. It dragged on for weeks and weeks, and the record was filled with pages and pages of completely contradictory testimony. It seemed more like a debate than a hearing, with each team saying anything, true or false, that would put them in the right.

At one point the question of crew morale was brought up. Warms and the owners of the ship insisted that morale was high all the way through, and that the *Morro Castle* was a model of a smooth-running ship.

But the facts didn't bear them out. The men were not only underpaid—*they were overworked and undertrained.*

In a driving race to save every buck they could, the owners had adopted the practice of firing one crew when the ship docked, and signing on another when she sailed. There was no in-between period when the crew could even get the feel of the ship. No drills of any sort were ever held.

The legal minimum crew for the *Morro Castle* was 270 men. But there were only 240 in the crew, and they had to do the work of 270. Stewards had been working 16 hours a day, and a steward has to work like a dog on a passenger liner.

It's no wonder that the men of the *Morro Castle* had no great love for each other or for their ship. Fights were daily occurrences, and every man had but one goal in mind—to get off the ship as soon as he had the chance. When the fire broke out, the crew ran for the lifeboats like frightened rats.

All the way down the line, new facts were dredged up and laid upon the doorsteps of the ship's owners. All they cared for was their profit. In another short-cut to save money, they failed to fireproof the wood used in the ship's construction. To save more money, they painted over the badly-rusted lifeboats rather than replace them. It was a minor miracle that those boats which were used didn't sink to the bottom!

The men who owned the *Morro Castle* fought the investigation every step of the way. They bought every witness they could, and tried to intimidate those they couldn't buy. Alagna and Rogers, especially, drew heavy fire from the owners' attorney—but he couldn't shake their testimony. In the courtroom, as well as on shipboard, they saw their duty and they did it. The newspapers and magazines reported their testimony in detail, and the temperature of the public rose to the boiling point.

Many mysteries were never cleared up. The mysterious death of Captain Wilmotte was never brought to light, since his body was lost at sea, and it was hinted that *he never had a heart attack.* But the finger of responsibility for the disaster was pointed.

The men deemed responsible were indicted and brought to trial, including Acting Captain Warms, Engineer Abbott, the owners of the ship, and the officer in charge of examining the ship before her voyage.

The examining officer was found guilty of criminal negligence. He was fined $5,000 and given a one-year suspended sentence. Warms was sentenced to two years in prison, Abbott to four. The ship owners were fined $10,000.

But were all the guilty ones punished? How do you punish inspectors for their carelessness? How do you punish contractors who knowingly use inferior materials? How do you punish the public, when you come right down to it, for always looking the other way until tragedy occurs?

But those with glaring guilt were punished., and the heroes were rewarded. Rogers and Alagna were lauded for their courage, with Rogers even going on a lecture tour for a while, until other events pushed their names out of all the papers.

Then, to make sure history wouldn't repeat itself, new laws were passed. But even more than that, increased attention was brought to the necessity of enforcing existing laws. New laws were necessary, but they made about as much sense as the punishments and rewards.

Because no matter what laws you make, history will go on repeating itself. As long as men place their own selfishness ahead of the common good, ships will sink and planes will crash. As long as some men are irresponsible, others will die needlessly. At the same time, there will be hope—as long as there are men like Alagna and Rogers, men who will stick to their posts in the face of death.

Written as **SHELDON LORD**

They Called Him "King of Pain"

From the pages of **All Man**, May 1961

Art by ARNE ARNESEN

It was a dreary, grey day in the Nazi concentration camp. The impeccably uniformed blond officer strutted across the muddy grounds. Suddenly, he spotted a young Jewish woman prisoner. She attracted his fancy, despite her half-starved, emaciated condition. He ordered the woman brought to him and he sent the guards away. Grinning evilly, he ripped her clothes from her body and lashed out at her with his heavy boot. The woman sprawled before him. Then he spoke to her, gently. With tears of hatred and humiliation streaming from her eyes, the woman refused.

The officer's rage knew no bounds. He drove his boot squarely into her face, then bound her hands and feet. He took his cigarette lighter from his pocket. For five horrible hours he continued. When she finally lost consciousness, he revived her by splashing salt water into the burns. Finally he walked away, screaming like a madman. "No one shall refuse me!" he bellowed. "No one!"

This was Reinhard Heydrich, the beast who struck fear into the hearts of half a continent. Even Adolf Hitler stood in awe of Heydrich. His immediate superior, the notorious Heinrich Himmler, dreaded the sound of his name. When Heydrich was finally assassinated, an entire village was reduced to rubble in retribution.

As the twig is bent, so the tree is supposed to grow. But the twig which was young Heydrich was more than bent. It was warped. It was as twisted and misshapen as a pretzel with rickets.

Heydrich's father was a musician in the town of Halle, where Reinhard was born in 1904. The elder Heydrich was a quiet, peaceful man, who loved his family, classical music, and good German beer. He expected his son to follow in his footsteps, but Reinhard had other ideas. Music, he stated flatly, was fine for relaxation, but his destiny was to be a leader of men.

Without further ado, Reinhard set out to be a leader. He started with a gang of teenage hooligans who would have made the kids of *Blackboard Jungle* look like choirboys. World War I had just ended, and Germany was in a state of turmoil. The stage was set for any wolfpack, and Heydrich's wolves had a merry time. An ex-sergeant, who had been kicked out of the Kaiser's army for insubordination and perversion, taught the boys how to use firearms. He drilled them, and supplied them with the slogan, "Germany shall rule the world!"

Heydrich was appointed to the job of Torturer and Executioner for the band. He fitted the job perfectly, for he had studied torture manuals from the time he was ten. While other boys built model boats and airplanes, Reinhard made model torture racks, presses, and pillories.

His early childhood gives us a good indication of the sadism which was to emerge in his later years. He often roamed the streets in search of dogs and cats for torture— for use in some of his sadistic experiments. Once he captured a dog and broke all four of its legs so that the animal couldn't move. Then he poured kerosene on the screaming animal and set him afire. "How he screamed!" Heydrich laughed. "If only he had been human!"

It wasn't long before he got his wish. The young hoods had been holding mock trials, condemning the democratic leaders of Halle to death. This was going too far for one of the boys, and he told his father about the incident. Heydrich was livid with rage. The gang caught the boy and turned him over to the "Executioner."

"I made him scream for mercy," Heydrich said years later. "He writhed and wriggled like a worm, squealing and crying. I used red hot coals on his hands and feet; I poured boiling oil over his head. When I had finished with him, he was a driveling idiot. It was merciful to kill him, so I shot him myself. That was the only way to keep the pig quiet."

This incident happened when Heydrich was 16 years old. Within the next year, the mock-trial executions were carried out, and Heydrich boasted of personally shooting twelve Democrats in the back. The authorities were unable to prove a thing, and he was free to go.

APPARENTLY he decided that there wasn't much future in juvenile delinquency. He enlisted in the Signals section of the Merchant Marine. His sadism and perversion kept him very unpopular, but he was a relatively efficient officer. He might have stayed in the Merchant Marine—in fact, he seemed ready to settle down when he became engaged to the daughter of his commanding officer.

With the classic good looks which earned him the nickname "Blond Beast," coupled with a high intelligence and a cold, calculating mind, he lost little time in seducing the girl. But he miscalculated in one respect, and the girl became pregnant.

Her father was enraged, and demanded that Heydrich marry the girl on the spot. "Don't be a fool," Heydrich snapped. "I would never marry a girl who had premarital experience, even with me." He broke off the engagement and stormed out of the room, and was summarily discharged from the Merchant Marine.

If this bothered Reinhard, he gave no sign of it, for he was already dreaming of a position where he could fulfill the destiny he was convinced was his. Nor was it hard for him to find a place where his talents were appreciated. The day after his dismissal, he presented himself at the Hamburg office of the Nazi Party. He enlisted and passed all tests with flying colors. In no time at all he was a full-fledged member of the SS.

The SS, or *Schutz Staffeln* (Protective Guards), were the most vicious, bloodthirsty bunch under Hitler. SS officers guarded concentration camps, extracted confessions, and performed all the other brutal tasks that the average Nazi could not stomach. The entrance requirements were rigid—SS officers had to be over six feet tall, blonde, blue-eyed, and physically fit. And, as one disillusioned ex-Nazi put it, they had to be sadists. Heydrich fitted every specification, and he rapidly rose in the organization.

Whenever a dirty job had to be done, the Blond Beast was on hand to do it. Whenever a man was to be beaten, Heydrich had a whip in his hand. Even his associates were shocked by the reports of his sadism.

His off-hours were filled with equally grotesque activity. The Nazi clique in Berlin, where he was eventually stationed, was a group which literally reeked with perversion. Heydrich attended parties which began with beer and ended with every aberration known to modern man. He was insatiable, running from woman to woman, and periodically retreating into homosexuality. Nothing was ever enough for him. He always craved more power, more thrills, and more blood.

It wasn't long before Heydrich's reputation came to the attention of Heinrich Himmler, Commander-In-Chief of the SS. Himmler is responsible for more deaths than any other man in history. From 1931 on, Heydrich was Himmler's right-hand man.

Himmler decided that the SS needed something more—a security force which would serve as a high-echelon Gestapo. He looked around for a leader. "I need a strong man," he said. "I need a man who is utterly ruthless, *a man who will let no human considerations stand in his way.*" The Blond Beast was his man, and he was speedily appointed to head the SD, or *Sicherheits Dienst* [Security Service]. From then on his power became almost unlimited.

By 1933, Hitler had ascended to the Chancellorship of Germany. The Nazi Party was in control of the country. A few months later the elderly President Hindenburg died, and Hitler combined the offices of President and Chancellor, proclaiming himself the Fuehrer of the German people. Communists and Jews were speedily rounded up and jailed, and Socialists and Democrats followed in short order to the concentration camps.

As head of the SS, Himmler was placed in charge of the concentration camps and chambers of horrors. But Himmler was a weak man at heart, and Heydrich dominated him. The orders which Himmler gave were actually the orders that Heydrich formulated.

His good looks and powerful personality proved an asset once again. In order to intensify his control over Himmler, he began an affair with his superior's wife. With the skill of a Mata Hari, he uncovered the details which Himmler kept secret even from him. He continued his association with Frau Himmler until he was satisfied he knew everything he needed to know. Then he dropped her. When she sent passionate notes proclaiming her love, he told her he would show the notes to Himmler if she didn't stop pestering him.

"She disgusts me," he remarked to one of his friends. "Believe me, it was a struggle to make love to her."

The concentration camps were Heydrich's Garden of Eden. He continually invented excuses for "inspection tours"—thinly disguised opportunities for him to vent his own sadism. He was constantly on the lookout for more brutal tortures, and when a guard would balk at one of his ideas, he ordered the guard subjected to the tortures himself.

The "Sweat Box" was one of Heydrich's better-known inventions. It was a coffin-like affair, too short and too narrow for the victim to stand properly. The prisoner would be placed in the box, and red-hot air was continually pumped in. On the walls of the box were sharp steel spikes, electrically charged. When the prisoner attempted to straighten up, he would come into contact with a spike. When he jerked away from one spike, another would jab him.

There was one merciful feature of the Sweat Box. Nobody could live in it for more than an hour. And in a Nazi concentration camp, death was salvation.

On one such inspection tour, the Blond Beast spotted a young mother. Somehow, her appearance sent him into a rage. Using the polished walking stick he always carried, he began to beat the woman.

With each brutal blow he uttered a screaming curse. In minutes the ground was covered with blood. Blood sprayed from the stick, spattering Heydrich's uniform, mixing with the perspiration that poured from his face.

He stamped on her body, his boots slipping in the blood. When one of the guards attempted to pull Heydrich away, the insane officer slashed viciously at him with his walking stick, ripping his cheek open. The sight of the new wound caused him to grin, his teeth bared like an animal's.

Then he ordered the guard to be tortured and shot. "No one shall stop me!" he screamed. "No one!"

INDEED, it seemed as though no one could. In June of 1934, Heydrich aided Hitler in the infamous Blood Purge, in which over 70 of Hitler's closest followers, including Ernst Roehm, were apprehended and shot. With Roehm and his men out of the way, the power of the SS increased a hundredfold, and kept on increasing throughout the years. The SD was in the pivot position of the SS, and at its helm Heydrich became one of the leaders of Germany. He grew wealthy and lived in luxury; and more important, to him at least, he grew more and more powerful.

When a half-crazed Jew attempted to assassinate a Nazi diplomat, Heydrich gave the order for the sacking of every synagogue in Germany. When Germany succeeded in annexing Austria, Heydrich organized the wholesale arrests and executions. The Blond Beast was everywhere and did everything.

In 1939 the German army invaded Poland. France and Britain declared war immediately, and German tanks rolled in all directions. Once again, Heydrich played a prominent role. Hitler had decided that the German people needed *lebensraum*—living space. The solution was simple. Since

Germany had conquered Poland in a matter of weeks, all of Poland was available for German use. There was only the problem of a few million Poles, and Heydrich supplied an easy answer.

The Poles were destroyed. Able-bodied workers were shipped en masse to forced labor camps within Germany, where they worked twenty hours a day until they died. The others were murdered. At first, burials took time and space, but Heydrich realized that ashes took less space than corpses, so the dead Poles were cremated. He continued his reasoning further, concluding that, if the Poles were to be burned anyway, there was little point in killing them first. Millions were cremated alive.

With every incident that gave evidence of Heydrich's ruthlessness, Himmler became more wary. He had wanted a purposeful man, true, but the Blond Beast was so intent on power and destruction that even Himmler began to fear him.

"That Heydrich," Himmler once said. "Not only would be murder his own grandmother if he had to, but I suspect that he would murder her slowly!"

Himmler began to plot. He could not fire Heydrich and he didn't dare liquidate him. His only hope was to kick him upstairs to a higher position. He got his chance sooner than he expected.

In 1941, opposition to Germany was growing steadily in Czechoslovakia. The Czechs, a freedom-loving people, found German oppression unbearable. Not even Konstantin von Neurath, the tyrannical Nazi ruler of Czechoslovakia, was able to suppress them completely. It was Himmler's perfect opportunity.

Von Neurath was removed, and Heydrich took his place. Not only did he fill Von Neurath's shoes, but he exchanged the shoes for a pair of stomping boots.

Every Czech leader was either executed or imprisoned within the week. Every scientist, professor, doctor and lawyer was murdered. Heydrich was hated by every Czech alive, but the flames of discontent were virtually stifled.

Heydrich had reached the peak, but he was riding for a fall. No man so passionately hated can remain alive indefinitely, and finally Heydrich's clock ran out.

ON THE morning of May 27, 1942, Heydrich was driving from his castle to Prague. As he. slowed for a curve, Jan Kubis, a Czech patriot, heaved a bomb. The bomb landed in the back seat of Heydrich's car, the blast driving wood and metal deep into his body. Like an animal, the Blond Beast attempted to fight back, but as he drew his revolver he collapsed and Kubis fled.

Berlin was in an uproar. Hitler's personal physicians flew to Prague, and Himmler raced to his bedside. But all *Der Feuhrer's* doctors couldn't put Heydrich together again. He lingered in agony for eight days, dying at last on June 4th.

Reinhard Heydrich, the Blond Beast of the SS, was dead. Before his coffin was below the ground, Himmler swore undying revenge. He had no love for the man, but such an act could not go unpunished. And it was punished, more so than any other act before or since.

The assassin, Kubis, was quickly found and killed, but that was hardly enough. Himmler searched for a victim, and somehow settled on the town of Lidice. Lidice had been a pleasant, peaceful mining community. Himmler and his gang turned it into a living model of hell.

One morning, as the sun rose, an SS squadron surrounded Lidice. They drove off the cattle, carried off the food, and loaded the women and girls onto trucks. The women were put to work in brothels for German troops, and the younger girls were "adopted" by German families

69

and brought up as good little Nazis.

One hundred and forty-three men and boys, the entire male population of Lidice, were lined up against walls and shot. The SS troops raked the lines with machine guns until the last one was dead. Then they walked the streets for hours, bayoneting every dog, cat, and chicken they could find.

The buildings were blown up and the rubble was burned. Everything was destroyed—churches, stores, and homes. The cemetery was looted and the gravestones were smashed. When the troops left, dust and ashes were the only remains of the town.

Lidice had been obliterated. Reinhard Heydrich was a sadist at ten and a killer at sixteen.

At 38 he was dead.

Lidice has been rebuilt from the dust and ashes, but the hated memory of the Blond Beast will live forever.

Written as **SHELDON LORD**

Killers All Around Me

From the pages of **All Man**, September 1961

Art by TED LEWIN

There's no such thing as personal safety in a mental institution. When you deal with lunatics, logic, consistency, law and order fly out the window. A patient—any patient—is liable to go off the deep end at any time—day or night. The mildest-mannered little man, the calmest, sweetest, most ladylike woman, is quite apt to turn into a berserk killer at the drop of a hat.

But if it's rough anywhere in a mental institution, it's twice as rough in the violent ward. That's where we keep the proven wild ones, the men and women with long records of physical assault, murder and explosive behavior.

Even though these patients are known troublemakers, it's impossible to predict their behavior. A good 90 percent of the time, they're as quiet and happy as newborn babies. They eat, they sleep, they laugh and play games. If an outsider walked in during the peaceful periods, it would be practically impossible to convince him that he was in a violent ward.

But I know differently. I work there. For eight to ten hours a day—depending on circumstances—12.

I'm in with the confinees, joining in their games, helping them, feeding them, washing them, and generally seeing to it that they keep out of trouble. For 90 percent of the time, my job, while nothing to be gleeful about, is certainly ordinary enough.

The other 10 percent of the time is hell, pure and simple. And that 10 percent of hell comes on with no warning whatsoever. I can be playing chess with a prisoner when he'll suddenly decide that I'm trying to kill him. And then the poor son-of-a-gun will charge me with all the hate and fear of a trapped animal in his eyes. One minute he'll smile across the checkerboard; the next minute saliva will drip from his jaws and his hands will be groping for my throat.

An hour later he'll be smiling again, and we'll start a new game of checkers. I'll watch him across the board, and I'll never know when he's going to next get the urge to kill me again.

I'm not armed. I have to either stare down my berserk opponent or bop him one in the teeth. So far I've been lucky, but luck can only last so long. Eventually two hands are going to close around my windpipe and hold on until I'm dead.

There are twenty-five men in my ward, and they range from 22 to 67 years in age. They have only one thing in common—they're all sick people, and they're all liable to go berserk at any moment. Almost all of them have killed at one time or another. All of them are likely to kill again if they get the opportunity.

Charlie J. has been in my ward for over three years. To look at him, you would never expect that he was dangerous. He is 36 years old—a short slim man who keeps himself well groomed at all times. He looks like a bank teller, and that's precisely what he was for almost 14 years.

Charlie started working at a bank when he was twenty. He married a girl he had known since high school. Eventually they had children, two boys and a girl. His wife worked as a secretary for a law firm, and between the two of them they earned enough to get by. He was a quiet guy—read a lot, didn't talk much, and was a model citizen.

THEN ONE day something snapped. Only time and intensive treatment will tell us what. At any rate, Charlie didn't go right home from work that day. Instead, he went for a long walk in the park. He saw a little girl in the park-a pretty little seven-year-old with silky blonde hair. And then Charlie became the villain in one of the most shocking sex crimes ever perpetrated.

He started a conversation with the girl, and before she could scream or run away, he clasped his hand tightly over her mouth and dragged her to a wooded section of the park. There he ripped the clothing from her body and viciously raped her. That wasn't all.

When he had finished, the girl was screaming. This bothered Charlie, and he stopped the screams by pounding the girl's head against the ground. When he had knocked her unconscious, he used a penknife to dissect her alive. He cut off her fingers and toes, and slashed her body so mercilessly that identification of the corpse was almost impossible. Hours later, a patrolman discovered the body of the child. Astounded, he saw Charlie sitting against the trunk of a tree just yards away, giggling and drooling.

The town demanded the death penalty for Charlie, but the courts said that such a punishment was impossible. He wasn't responsible for what he had done. He was insane—his mind had snapped.

But it was certainly necessary that Charlie be prevented from doing a repeat performance, and that's how I got hold of him. He'll stay here until he dies.

Most of the time Charlie just sits and reads. Sometimes he plays chess or checkers. He usually wins. He's a quiet guy, a model prisoner most of the time. But not always.

One day Charlie was quietly reading. All of a sudden he stopped and hurled the book across the room with deadly accuracy. It caught me on the back of the head, and if it had been an inch or two higher I wouldn't be alive today. As it was, I was only stunned and knocked to the floor.

By the time I got to my feet, Charlie was almost on top of me. I'm no weakling, but Charlie was fighting with the strength of a madman. Somehow an insane person is twice as strong when he goes berserk. All his energies are concentrated on the battle, and he's not at all concerned with his own safety. I finally managed to kick him in the face, and his teeth fell right out of his mouth. Through it all, the other inmates went right on reading and playing checkers.

When Charlie came to, he went right back to his bunk and picked up a book. He didn't seem to remember the incident at all. An hour later he started giggling.

That's the pattern, and I've seen it repeated a thousand times. A mental patient will act as innocently as Little Lord Fauntleroy for years—then something will go haywire. There's no way in the world to anticipate such a crack-up.

GEORGE T. is that way. He's a schizophrenic, which is

a complex way of saying that he lives in two different worlds. Most of the time George sits on his bed and stares at the wall for hours on end. He won't talk to anyone; indeed, it's doubtful that he ever hears anything. His eyes are glazed like a drug addict—he doesn't move a muscle. He has to be fed with a spoon and carried to the bathroom like a baby.

When he's like this, George is easy enough to take care of. I just leave him alone in his private dream world, staring at the mysteries that he finds in the wall. But there's another side to his personality—the "Hyde" half of the Jekyll-and-Hyde arrangement—and when it comes to the forefront I feel like hopping a fast jet to the Orient.

If George just stared forever at the wall, he wouldn't be in the Violent Ward. But periodically he goes through the same process that got him committed in the first place.

George was one of the more extreme mental casualties of the Korean War. He broke down in battle, and it was an extreme breakdown. Instead of being shipped to a stateside hospital at once, he was kept in confinement for a few weeks and then returned to active duty.

It was a mistake. As soon as George got a gun in his hand, he went berserk. He looked stupidly at the gun for a moment—then he began taking potshots at his fellow soldiers. Two men were dead and four more wounded before George was subdued. They shipped him stateside at once. He's been staring at the wall ever since.

In the four years that I've been working here, George has come out of his trance five minutes. Each time he's become a violent, vicious killer. Once he seized another inmate's arm and snapped it at the elbow. Several times he charged me and fought like the madman he is, before I was finally able to lay him out and heave him back on his bunk.

One time was too close for comfort.

It was meal time and I was spoon-feeding George. It's a strange sensation—feeding a full-grown, able-bodied man three times a day—but a man can get used to almost anything. As I lifted a spoonful of succotash to his lips, his face broke into a smile. Then and there, I should have sensed that something was amiss.

Instead, I was amazed and pleased at the thought that George might be coming out of his illness. "Mr. Jones," he said, calmly, "I can feed myself."

I handed him the spoon. Instead of proceeding to feed himself, he sat staring at it for a moment. When I finally realized that he was not recovering, but was moving into the alternate stage of his schizophrenic personality, it was too late. He was off the bed and on me in a flash. I went down like a ton of bricks.

George straddled me, with his eyes gleaming and the spoon clutched in his fist. A spoon may seem like an innocent enough article, but prison guards know what deadly weapons can be fashioned out of them. In the hands of a man like George, a spoon all by itself is enough. It can kill a man easily.

I WAS SPRAWLED on my back, and George's knees dug into my chest. I could hardly breathe. His eyes almost seemed to glow with insanity. I shouted for help, but the pressure on my rib cage allowed only a weak cry. Before I could get off another call he drove his left hand into my mouth, and salty blood washed over my tongue. He left his hand there to prevent my shouting any more. I couldn't even whisper.

Then his right hand descended to my throat, slowly. He pressed the tip of the spoon against the skin, right over the jugular vein. It didn't seem at all like a spoon. It seemed a helluva lot more like a razor.

I waited for the spoon to bite into my throat. I didn't even try to get free, for I knew it was impossible. He had me pinned perfectly. I mentally went over my insurance and cursed myself for never having made out a will. I literally lay there waiting to die.

It not only *seemed* like hours—it *was* hours. Apparently George couldn't make up his mind as to just what he wanted to do with me. He didn't relax pressure for an instant, nor did he increase it. It was as though someone had stopped a motion picture in the middle of a scene.

All the while, the rest of the ward was perfectly peaceful. Most of the patients seemed completely unaware of the fact that I might die at any moment. Others watched disinterestedly, as if they were watching a television program which they had seen before. The checker games and reading continued without pause.

My life was saved as suddenly as it was threatened, and with as little reason. I stared into George's eyes, and they gradually became glazed. His grip loosened on the spoon and it dropped from his fingers, rolling from my neck and clattering upon the floor. I waited for a second until I was convinced that he had returned to his shell, then rolled him from me like a sack of flour. I tossed him back on his bunk, breathed deeply, and called for a relief attendant.

The really violent outbreaks don't come every day—if they did, I wouldn't last very long. But there are countless "minor" irritations which make the job enough to drive a guard as nutty as any of the patients.

Some of the guards actually do lose a measure of control. But these are the ones who have something the matter with them to start with. For the most part, they're sadists—men who enjoy inflicting pain. Under the pressure of constant strain, of invariable tension caused by waiting for the outbreaks they know are coming, they strike out, hitting back at the inmates with their own outbursts of unmitigated and senseless brutality.

IT WOULD be nice to say that mental hospitals are getting rid of this type of guard as fast as each can be uncovered. But it's not true.

Everyone concerned would like nothing better than that, but—it's an awful big "BUT." Who can we get to replace them? Bad as brutality is, it's still preferable to employ a guard with a streak of sadism than no guard at all. Recruitment is all but impossible.

Ask the average man in the street whether he'd take a job as guard in an asylum? Tell him the hours, the requirements, the difficulties, the potential danger, and the sickening details of his duties—*and then tell him the salary.* Don't be surprised if better than 99 and 44/100ths give you the biggest, fattest and loudest "NO" you've ever heard.

So we hire those we can get. Society demands that we have someone. The mental cases are a bigger threat to society than the guards are to the inmates. And society wins. It has to.

So we find that those with streaks of sadism, who lust for personal and physical power over their fellows—gravitate naturally to us. We take them and we're stuck with them. But we don't like them.

At least we can say that this kind of human being is in the minority, that they form a very small nucleus among the mass of other, dedicated workers. And the dedicated, high-minded men and women give their first thoughts to their patients.

One of my men, Max K., is responsible for a minimum *of four fires which took the lives of over seventy people.* His pyromania is the only thing wrong with him—he's even able to discuss his problems quite intelligently. But the son of a gun manages to get a fire started on the average of once every two weeks. They don't do more than a little damage—a pillowcase or a mattress at best—but someday he may succeed in burning the whole place down. I don't know how he gets hold of matches, but he's as clever as a bedbug. It's impossible to stop him.

Joe B. talks to the wall. Every once in a while he'll hold an extended conversation with no one in particular at the top of his lungs. Sometimes he talks in English, and other times he uses a language all his own. Maybe the wall understands, but no one else can.

There was another patient—he's cured now—who used to be a real pain in the neck. When I fed him his oatmeal, tilting the bowl so that he could swallow it directly, he would take a good-sized mouthful and spew it into my face. This is all very cute coming from a two-year-old, but it loses its charm when an adult is doing the spitting.

The fellow came back to visit a few weeks ago, and I mentioned his old habit. "It was the damndest thing," he reminisced. "I had the sensation that I was sitting across the room and some jerk was spitting in your face. It seemed hilarious!"

There are the bedwetters and the starers and the screamers—every kind of character you can think of. They'll smile at you, laugh at you, stare at you, or try to kill you. They're either pathetic or obnoxious, but I can't hate them because it's not their fault. They're sick people, and I just do my job in trying to help make them well.

Why don't I quit? I've tried, at least a dozen times. The pay is low, the hours are poor, and the work is such that I can never relax on the job. But something keeps me at it.

SOMEONE has to do the work, of course. Every day more mentally ill men and women enter hospitals from coast to coast, and there have to be men and women to take care of them.

One of the great crimes of our times—one of the greatest tragedies of *all time*—is the pitiful neglect of thousands upon thousands of mentally ill people in this country. Hospitals are ridiculously understaffed. Salaries are laughable; as a result, competent psychiatrists, nurses and staff people are almost untouchable.

Who suffers? The sick person, of course—and his family—*and society.* Thousands of mentally ill people waste away in shockingly ancient "hospitals." Many of these people *can* be rehabilitated to live normal lives, but because of neglect, they stare at the filthy walls years after year. Many doctors estimate that there are double the number of mentally-ill people walking the streets—potentially dangerous people—than there are in the mental institutions.

Once in a great while there's something terribly satisfying about my job—something that compensates for everything else.

Once in a great while a man comes back. Once in a while a man stops staring into space and returns to his senses. Then I lose a patient and society gains a responsible member. It makes me feel good to be a part of such a recovery.

So I continue to risk a pair of hands around my neck, and I go on turning my back upon madmen. Some day they may kill me, but some day they may recover.

It's the chance I take, and I think it's worth it.

Written as **CC JONES**

The Naked and the Deadly

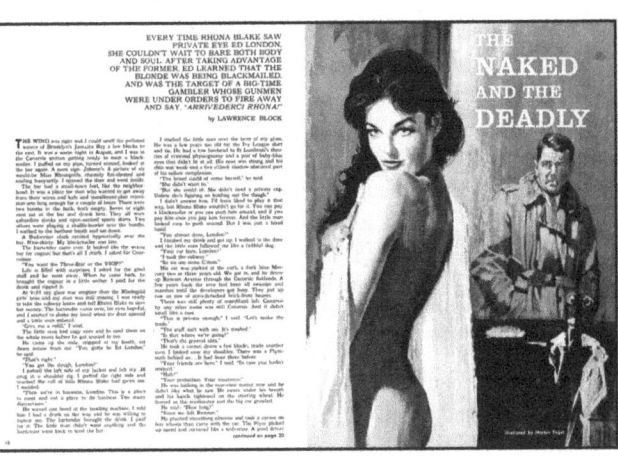

From the pages of **Man's Magazine**, April 1958

Art by MORT ENGEL

The wind was right and I could smell the polluted waters of Brooklyn's Jamaica Bay a few blocks to the east. It was a warm night in August, and I was in the Canarsie section getting ready to meet a blackmailer. I puffed on my pipe, turned around, looked at the bar again. A neon sign— JOHNNY'S. A picture of six would-be Miss Rheingolds, chastely flat-chested and smiling buoyantly. I opened the door and went inside.

The bar had a small-town feel, like the neighborhood. It was a place for men who wanted to get away from their wives and kids and installment-plan television sets long enough for a couple of beers. There were two booths in the back, both empty. Seven or eight men sat at the bar and drank beer. They all wore gabardine slacks and open-necked sports shirts. Two others were playing a shuf-fle-bowler near the booths. I walked to the furthest booth and sat down.

A Budweiser clock rotated hypnotically over the bar. Nine-thirty. My blackmailer was late.

The bartender came over. It looked like the wrong bar for cognac but that's all I drink. I asked for Courvoisier.

"You want the Three-Star or the VSOP?"

Life is filled with surprises. I asked for the good stuff and he went away. When he came back, he brought the cognac in a little snifter. I paid for the drink and sipped it.

At 9:55 my glass was emptier than the Rheingold girls' bras and my man was still missing. I was ready to take the subway home and tell Rhona Blake to save her money. The bartender came over, his eyes hopeful, and I started to shake my head when the door opened and a little man entered.

"Give me a refill," I said.

The little man had cagey eyes and he used them on the whole room before he got around to me. He came up the aisle, stopped at my booth, sat down across from me. "You gotta be Ed London," he said.

"That's right."

"You got the dough, London?"

I patted the left side of my jacket and felt my .38 snug in a shoulder rig. I patted the right side and touched the roll of bills Rhona Blake had given me. I nodded.

"Then we're in business, London. This is a place to meet and not a place to do business. Too many distrac-tions."

He waved one hand at the bowling machine. I told him

I had a drink on the way and he was willing to humor me. The bartender brought the drink. I paid for it. The little man didn't want anything and the bartender went back to tend the bar.

I studied the little man over the brim of my glass. He was a few years too old for the Ivy League shirt and tie. He had a low forehead to fit Lombrosi's theories of criminal physiognomy and a pair of baby-blue eyes that didn't fit at all. His nose was strong and his chin was weak and a five o'clock shadow obscured part of his sallow complexion.

"The broad could of come herself," he said.

"She didn't want to."

"But she could of. She didn't need a private cop. Unless she's figuring on holding out the dough."

I didn't answer him. I'd have liked to play it that way, but Rhona Blake wouldn't go for it. You can pay a blackmailer or you can push him around, and if you pay him once you pay him forever. And the little man looked easy to push around. But I was just a hired hand.

"You almost done, London?"

I finished my drink and got up. I walked to the door and the little man followed me like a faithful dog.

"Your car here, London?"

"I took the subway."

"So we use mine. C'mon."

His car was parked at the curb, a dark blue Mercury two or three years old. We got in, and he drove up Remsen Avenue through the Canarsie flatlands. A few years back the area had been all swamps and marshes until the developers got busy. They put up row on row of semi-detached brick-front houses.

There was still plenty of marshland left. Canarsie by any other name was still Canarsie. And it didn't smell like a rose.

"This is private enough," I said. "Let's make the trade."

"The stuff ain't with me. It's stashed."

"Is that where we're going?"

"That's the general idea."

He took a corner, drove a few blocks, made another turn. I looked over my shoulder. There was a Plymouth behind us... It had been there before.

Your friends are here," I said. "In case you hadn't noticed."

"Huh?"

"Your protection. Your insurance."

He was looking in the rear-view mirror now and he didn't like what he saw. He swore under his breath and his hands tightened on the steering wheel. He leaned on the accelerator and the big car growled.

He said: "How long?"

"Since we left Remsen."

He grunted something obscene and took a corner on less wheels than came with the car. The Plym picked up speed and cornered like a wolverine. A good driver might have beaten them—the Merc had enough under the hood to leave the Plymouth at the post. But the little man was a lousy driver.

We took two more corners for no reason at all and they stayed right with us. We ran a red light at Flatlands Avenue and so did they. The little man was sweating now. His forehead was damp and his hands were slippery on the wheel. They chased us for two more blocks and I dug the .38 out and let my finger curl around the trigger. I wasn't sure what kind of party we were going to, but I wanted the right costume.

The Plymouth came alongside and I pointed the gun at it. There were three of them, two in front and one in back. I had a clear shot but I held it back—for all I knew they were police. They've got a strict law for private detectives in New York State: shoot a cop and you lose your license.

But he wasn't a cop. Cops don't tote submachine guns, and that's what the boy by the window was holding. The Plym cut us off and the little man hit the brakes, and then the submachine gun cut loose and started spraying lead at us.

The first burst took care of the little man. A row of bullets plowed into his chest and he slumped over the wheel like the corpse he was.

And that saved my life.

Because when he died his foot slid off the brakes and came down on the accelerator, and we went into the Plymouth like Grant into Vicksburg. The tommy-gun stopped chattering and I hit the door hard and landed on my feet. I didn't make like a hero. I ran like a rabbit.

The field had tall swamp-grass and broken beer bottles. I zigged and zagged, and I was maybe twenty yards in before the tommy-gun took up where it had left off. I heard slugs whine over my shoulder and took a dive any tank fighter would have been proud of, landing on my face in a clump of tall grass. I turned around so that I could see what was happening and crawled backwards so that it wouldn't be happening to me.

The tommy-gun threw another spasmodic burst at me, way off this time. I got the .38 steadied and poked a shot at one of the three silhouettes by the roadside. It went wide. They answered with another brace of shots that didn't come any closer.

Some more of the same. Then the tommy-gun was silent, and I raised my head enough to see what was happening. The hoods were off the road and in their car, and their car was leaving.

So was the blackmailer's Mercury. Evidently the

collision hadn't damaged it enough to ground it, because it was following the Plymouth down the road and leaving me alone.

I waited until I was sure they were gone. Then I waited until I was sure they wouldn't be back. I got up slowly and dragged myself back toward the road. The .38 stayed in my hand. It gave me a feeling of security.

A car came down the road toward me and I hit the dirt again, gun in hand. But it wasn't the Mercury or the Plymouth, just a black beetle of a Volkswagen that didn't even slow down. I got up feeling foolish.

There were skid marks on the pavement, a little broken glass as an added attraction. There was no dead little man, not on the street and not in the field. There was no blood. Nothing but glass and skid marks, and Brooklyn is full of both. Nothing but a very tired private cop with a very useless gun in his hand, standing in the road and wishing he had something to do. Wishing he was home on East 83rd Street in Manhattan with a glass of Courvoisier in one hand and something by Mozart on the record player.

I stuck the gun back where it belonged. I found a pipe in one pocket and a pouch of tobacco in the other. I filled the pipe, got it going, headed over toward Flatlands Avenue.

The third cab I stopped felt like making a run to Manhattan. I got into the backseat and pulled the door shut. The cabby threw the flag down and the meter began ticking up expenses to be charged to the account of a girl named Rhona Blake.

I sat back and thought about her.

TWO

I SAW HER for the first time that afternoon. It was too hot to do much but sit in an air-conditioned apartment. I'd spent the morning waking up and writing checks to creditors, and in another hour it would be four o'clock and I could add brandy to my coffee without feeling guilty about it. For the time being I was feeling guilty.

The door must have been open downstairs because she rang my bell without hitting the downstairs buzzer first. I opened the door and she came inside.

"You're Edward London," she said. "Aren't you?"

I admitted it. I would have admitted to being Judge Crater or Ambrose Bierce or Martin Bormann. She had that kind of effect.

"May I sit down, Mr. London?" I pointed at the couch. She went over and sat on it, crossing one leg very neatly over the other. I sat down across from her in my leather chair and finished my coffee. She was beautiful. Her hair was ash blond, wrapped up tight in a French roll, and if there were any dark roots they were well hidden.

She was tall, close to my own height, and built along Hollywood lines. Her mouth was a dark ruby wound and her eyes were a jealous green. She was wearing a charcoal business suit but the thrust of her breasts made you wonder what business it was.

Thirty, maybe. Or twenty-five. The really beautiful ones are ageless. I watched her open a black calf purse, find a cigarette, light it with a silver lighter. She smiled at me through smoke.

"I hate to barge in on you like this," she said. "But this was the only listing I could find for you. I thought it was your office."

"I work here," I said. "It's a good-sized apartment. And I live alone, so there are no distractions."

"You're not married?"

"No."

She nodded thoughtfully, filing the information away somewhere in that beautiful head. "I don't know where to start," she said suddenly. "My name is Rhona Blake. And I want to hire you."

"Why?"

"Because I'm being blackmailed."

"When did it start?"

"Yesterday. With a letter and a telephone call. The letter came in the morning mail and told me I would have to pay five thousand dollars for...certain things."

"Do you have the letter?"

"I threw it away."

I frowned. "You shouldn't have."

"I thought it was a joke. Or maybe I was just mad, and I tore up the note. A few hours later I got a phone call. It was the same thing again. A man told me to meet him in a bar in Brooklyn with the money."

I asked her what she wanted me to do.

"Meet him and pay him. Then bring the goods to me. That's all."

I told her she was crazy. "Blackmailers operate on the installment plan," I said. "If you pay him once you'll have to pay him again. He'll bleed you white."

"I can't help it."

"You can't go to the cops?"

"No," she said quietly. "I can't."

"Why not?"

"Because I can't. Let's leave it at that, Mr. London."

So we left it at that. "Then call his bluff," I said. "Tell him to go to hell for himself. Chances are he'll throw the stuff away if he can't get anything out of it."

"No. He'll...sell it elsewhere."

"What's it all about, Miss Blake?"

"I can't tell you."

88

"Look—"

Her eyes were hard now. "You look," she said. "You don't have to know. To be perfectly frank, it's none of your business. I want you to do an errand for me. That's all. I want you to meet this man and pay him five thousand dollars and bring the goods to me. That's simple enough isn't it?"

"It's too simple."

"He won't go on blackmailing me. He'll give the material to you. I'm sure of it."

"THEN MAYBE I'll do the blackmailing. Ever think of that?"

"I've heard about you." She laughed. "I don't think I have to worry."

I knocked the dottle out of my pipe and set it down in the ashtray. I started to tell her I was a private cop, not a messenger service. But the words didn't come out. She was getting on my nerves, being cool and competent and stepping all over my masculine pride, and that was a pretty silly reason to turn down a fee.

And a pretty silly reason to send Rhona Blake out of my life.

I said, "All right." "You'll take the case?"

"Uh-huh. But I have to know more."

"Like what?"

"You could start with the identity of the blackmailer. From there you could tell me what he's got on you, and what he's going to do with it if you can't pay, and why you're over a barrel. Then you can tell me a few things about yourself. Like who you are, for a starter."

"I'm sorry. I want to keep this matter a secret, Mr. London."

"Even from me?"

"From everyone."

I went over to my desk, picked up a pencil and pad. I wrote *Rhona Blake* on the pad and looked up.

"Address," I said.

"I can't tell you."

"Phone number, then."

She shook her pretty head. "I can't tell you that either, Mr. London."

"*Mr. London.* Look," I said, "if we're going to be such close friends you really ought to call me Ed."

I didn't get a smile. I said: "How in hell am I going to get in touch with you?"

"You aren't, Ed. I'll call you."

She opened her purse again and took out an envelope filled with new money.

"Five thousand dollars," she said.

"To waste on a blackmailer?"

"To invest in my peace of mind. And how much do you want, Ed?"

"I get a hundred a day plus expenses. And if all I know is your name, I'm afraid your credit rating isn't too good. I'll take two hundred for a retainer."

She gave it to me in two bills. Brand new ones. I started to write out a receipt for $5,200 but her hand touched mine and stopped me. Her fingers were cool and soft. I looked up into the crisp green of her eyes.

"I don't need a receipt."

"Why not?"

"Because I trust you, Ed."

There were at least a dozen answers to that one. They all chased their tails in my brain, and I looked at Rhona and didn't say a word. Her hair looked as though Rumpelstiltskin had spun it out of gold. She stepped closer to me and her perfume came on like gangbusters.

"Ed—"

It was like this raw wet wind that comes just before the rain. Her hand held mine, and her eyes turned soft, and her body flowed up against mine. She came into my arms and our mouths met and that fine body of hers was taut against me and the world did a somersault.

My bed wasn't made. She didn't seem to mind. We went into the bedroom and I kicked the door shut. She kissed me, lips warm with the promise of hurried lust. She stepped back neatly and her hands made the charcoal suit melt from her body. I helped her with her bra and her breasts leaped into my hands. She gave a little shiver of animal joy and small sounds of passion tore from her throat.

It was a moment torn from Time. And we were on the bed, and her head was tossed back and her eyes were tightly shut, and her big beautiful body was a Stradivarius and I was Fritz Kreisler and Menuhin and Oistrakh and everybody else, stroking the world's sweetest music out of her.

"Oh, Ed. Oh, yes!"

She was a life-size doll who cried real tears. The room rocked. Someone took the earth out from under us and we took a Cook's tour through a brand-new world. At the end there was a monumental crescendo, and the finale came with a shake and a shudder and a sob.

HER VOICE came through a filter. "I'll call you later, Ed. I've got to go now. The blackmailer said he would call me late this afternoon and make the arrangements for the meeting. I'll tell him you'll be coming as my agent, then call you and give you the details. You can meet him tonight, can't you?"

I grunted something. She leaned over the bed and her lips brushed my face. I didn't move. She left, and I could hear her feet on the stairs. A door closed. I still didn't move.

Later, I got up and showered. I washed the sweet taste

of her body from my skin and told myself it didn't mean a damned thing. She was playing Lady of Mystery, and in that department she could give the Mona Lisa cards and spades and chuck in Little Casino. The interlude in bed was no love affair, no meeting of soul mates. It was a way to seal a bargain, a quick little roll in the hay to ensure my cooperation, an added bonus tacked onto the 200-buck retainer.

I could tell myself this. It was hard to believe it.

So I showered and got dressed and went into the living room to build myself a drink. Later she would call me. Then I would run out to Brooklyn to do the job for her.

I poured more cognac. There was a girl I was supposed to meet that night, a dark-eyed brunette named Sharon Ross. A publisher's Gal Friday, a warm and clever thing. I picked up the phone and tried to find the right way to explain why I couldn't take her to the theater that night.

"You've got a nerve," she told me. "We made that date two weeks ago. What's the matter, Ed?"

"Business," I said.

"How's tomorrow night?"

"It's out." She clicked the receiver in my ear.

So I drank the drink and crossed another Sweet Young Thing off my mental list of Things to Be Physical With. I was already giving up a lot for Rhona Blake.

She called around six. "This is Rhona," she said. "I talked to...to the man. He wanted me to come personally but agreed to meet with you."

"Sweet of him."

"Don't growl. You're supposed to meet him at nine-thirty at a place called Johnny's. It's out in Canarsie on Remsen Avenue near Avenue M. Give him the money and get the goods, Ed."

"Maybe I could get the goods without giving him the

money."

"No. The money doesn't matter. Don't do anything silly, like getting rough with him. Just...just follow orders."

"Yes, ma'am."

"Ed—"

"What?"

A long pause. "Nothing," she said, finally. "I'll...I'll call you tonight, Ed."

THREE

MY CABBY came off the Manhattan Bridge at Canal Street, then found the East Side Drive and headed uptown. It was close to eleven and the traffic was thin. We made good time. The meter was a few ticks past $5 when he pulled up in front of my brownstone. I gave him a five and two singles and waved him away.

It was still too damned hot out. I went inside, took the stairs two at a time, unlocked my door, and pulled it shut after me. I poured a stiff drink and drank it.

It was getting cute now. My client had given me five grand, and I still had that. But the little blackmailer was dead and gone, and the stuff he had on her was nowhere to be found. It was time for me to call my client, of course. Time to fill her in on all the novel developments. But I couldn't get in touch with her. She was willing to sleep with me but she wouldn't let me know where she lived.

A few minutes after twelve, the phone rang.

"Rhona, Ed. Everything go all right?"

"No," I said.

"What happened?"

I gave it to her in capsule form, telling her how I met the little man, how they waylaid us, how they killed him and tried to kill me. She let me talk without an inter-

ruption, and when I stopped she was silent for almost
a minute.

Then: "What now, Ed?"

"I don't know, Rhona. I've got five thousand bucks you
can have back. I guess that's about all."

"But I'm in trouble, Ed."

"What kind of trouble?" A pause.

"I can't tell you over the phone."

"Then come over here."

"I can't, Ed. I have to stay where I am."

"Then I'll come over there."

"No."

I was getting sick of the whole routine. "Then give me
a post office box and I'll mail you five grand, Rhona. And
we can forget the whole thing. Okay?"

It wasn't okay. She got nervous and stuttered awhile,
then told me she would call me in the morning. I told her I
was sick of phone calls.

"Then meet me," she said.

"Where?" She thought it over. "Do you know a place
called Mandrake's?"

"In the Village? I know it."

"I'll meet you there at two in the afternoon."

"Are they open then?"

"They're open. Will you meet me?"

I thought about that red mouth, those green eyes. I
remembered the poetry of her body. "Sure," I said. "I'll
meet you."

Hanging up, I hauled the .38 out of its resting place
and broke it open. I wanted a full gun handy. It looked as
though it was going to be that kind of a deal.

It was too early for sleep. I thought about the girl I'd
broken my date with: dark hair, soft curves, a sulky mouth.
Right now we'd have been out of the theater. We'd be

sitting in a cozy club somewhere on the East Side, listening to atonal jazz and drinking a little too much. And then homeward, for a nightcap and maybe a cup of kindness. But a date with a blackmailer had made me break my date with Sharon Ross. And now she was mad at me.

For the hell of it, I called her. The phone rang and rang and rang and nobody answered it.

I went into the kitchen and made instant coffee and thought about Canarsie. A tommy-gun—that was something to mull over. Only prison guards have them. They've been illegal in the States since the Dillinger era, and a hood who wants one has to shell out two or three grand for the thing. And needs good connections.

It sounded pretty complex for an ordinary blackmail dodge, and made me wonder what kind of league Rhona Blake was playing in. Triple-A, anyway.

They don't use choppers in the bush leagues.

It was late by the time I got into bed. I wedged a stack of records on the hi-fi and crawled under the covers. They played and I thought about things, and I fell asleep before the stack was finished.

THE MORNING was ragged and raw. I'd gone to sleep without flipping on the air conditioner, and when I woke up the blankets were sticking to my skin. I pried them loose and took a long shower.

I was through with breakfast by 10:30. I wasn't supposed to meet Rhona until two, but my apartment was beginning to feel like a jail cell. I looked through the bookcases for something to read and didn't come up with anything. I plucked the *Times* off my doormat, glanced through it, and tossed it into the wastebasket.

I left the apartment wearing slacks, a sport jacket, and a gun. I locked my door and headed down the stairs, and was on my way through the vestibule just as a man was leaning on my bell. I saw his index finger pressing a button next to a strip of plexiglas with *E. London* inscribed thereon. He didn't look like anyone I wanted to meet, but it was a hot day and I had a few hours to kill. I tapped him on the shoulder.

"You won't get an answer," I said.

"No?"

"No. I'm E. London, and there was nobody home when I left."

He didn't smile. "Carr," he said. "Phillip Carr, attorney at law." He handed me a card. "I want to talk to you, London."

I didn't really want to talk to him. We went upstairs anyway, and I unlocked my door again and led him inside. We sat down in the living room. He offered me a cigar and I shook my head. He made a hole in the end with an elaborate cigar cutter, wedged it in his mouth, lit it, blew foul smoke all over my apartment. I hoped it wouldn't clog the air-conditioner.

"I'll come to the point," he said.

"Fine."

"I'M HERE representing a client," Carr said, "who wants to remain nameless. He's a wealthy man, a prominent man."

"Go on."

"His daughter's missing. He wants her located."

"That's interesting," I told him. "The Missing Persons Bureau is at Headquarters, on Centre Street. They have a lot of personnel and they don't charge anything. You go down there, make out a report, and they'll find your man's daughter a damn sight faster than I will."

"He chewed his cigar thoughtfully. "This isn't a police matter," he said. "No?"

"No. We...my client needs special talents. He's prepared to pay ten thousand dollars as a reward for his daughter's return."

"Ten grand?"

"That's right."

"I don't work that way," I said. "I'm not a bounty hunter, Carr. I don't chase rewards any more than a decent lawyer chases ambulances to nail negligence cases. I get a hundred a day plus expenses. The price is the same whether I find your missing person or not."

"That's not how my client wants it."

"Then your client can find himself another boy."

"You're not a patient man," Phillip Carr said.

"Maybe not."

"You should be. Can't you use ten grand, London?"

"Anybody can."

"Then be patient. Let me show you a picture of my client's errant daughter; then you can decide whether or not you want to work for a reward. For ten grand, I'd be willing to chase an ambulance, London."

It was early in the day and it was hot as hell and my head wasn't working too well. I let him dig a thin wallet from his hip pocket. He pulled a picture from it and passed it to me.

Well, you guessed it. And I should have, but it was that kind of a day. The daughter-reward bit was as nutty as a male Hershey bar and the picture told me everything I had to know. Just a head-and-shoulder shot, the kind that made you want to see what the body looked like. A beautiful girl. A familiar face.

Rhona Blake, of course.

Carr was looking at me, a supercilious smile on his lips. I wanted to turn it inside out. But I could be as cute as he. I handed the picture back to him and waited.

"A familiar face?"

"No."

"Really?"

I stepped closer to him. "I've never seen the girl," I lied. "And the reward couldn't interest me less. I think you ought to go home, Carr."

He pointed the cigar at me. "You're a damn fool," he said.

"Why?"

"Because ten thousand dollars is a healthy reward any way you look at it."

"So?"

He made a pilgrimage to the window. I felt like walking behind him and kicking him through it. He was a smooth little bastard who wanted me to sell out a client to him, and he didn't even have the guts to lay it on the line. He had to be cute about it.

"The girl is in over her head," he said levelly. He still had his back to me. "You're working for her. You don't have to. You can be cooperative and pick up a nice package in the process. What's wrong with that?"

"Get out of here," I said.

He turned to face me. "You damn fool."

"Get out, Carr. Or I'll throw you out."

HE SIGHED. "My client's a great believer in rewards," he said. "Rewards and punishments."

"I'd hit you, Carr, but you'd bleed all over my carpet."

"Rewards and punishments," he said again. "I don't have to draw you pictures, London. You're supposed to be a fairly bright boy. You think it over. You've got my card. If you change your mind, you might try giving me a ring."

He left. I didn't show him the door.

I looked at his card for a few minutes, then went to the

phone. I dialed Police Headquarters and asked for Jerry Gunther at Homicide. It took a few minutes before he got to the phone.

"Oh," he groaned. "It's you again."

Jerry and I had bumped heads a few times in one squabble or another. We wound up liking each other. He thought I was a bookish bum who liked to live well without working too hard and I thought he was a thorough anachronism, an honest cop in the middle of the twentieth century when honest cops were out of style. We had less in common than Miller and Monroe, but we got along fine.

"What's up, Ed?"

"Phillip Carr," I said. "Some kind of a lawyer. You know anything about him?"

"It rings a bell," he said. "I could find out if this was a vital part of police routine. Is this a vital part of police routine, Ed?"

"No."

"What is it?"

"An imposition on your friendship."

"What I figured," he said. "Next time we have a vital conference, you buy."

"That could be expensive. You've got a hollow leg."

"Better than a hollow head, crumb. Hang on."

Finally, Jerry Gunther came back. "Yeah," he said. "Phillip Carr. Sort of a mob lawyer, Ed. A mouthpiece type. He takes cases for the kind of garbage that always stays out of jail. He's been on the inside of some shady stuff himself, according to the dope we've got. Nothing that anybody could ever make stick. Bankrolling some smuggling operations, stuff like that. Using his connections to make an illegal buck."

I grunted.

"That your man, Ed?"

"Like a glove," I said. "He wears sunglasses and he's oily. He's the type who goes to the barbershop and gets the works."

"Like Anastasia," Jerry said. "It should happen to all of them. What's it all about, Ed?"

"I don't know yet."

"Nothing for Homicide, is it?"

"Nothing, Jerry."

"Then the hell with it. I only get into the act when somebody dies, fella."

I thought about the corpse in Canarsie. But he never got into the files. The boys in our little poker game were too professional for that. By now he was sleeping in a lime pit in Jersey or swimming in Jamaica Bay all wrapped in cement.

"Remember," Jerry Gunther was saying, "you buy the liquor. And don't play rough with this Carr. He's got some ugly friends." "

Sure," I said. "And thanks."

I put down the phone, got out of the building, and grabbed a pair of burgers at the lunch counter around the corner. As I ate, I thought about a corpse in Canarsie and a man named Phillip Carr and a blond vision named Rhona Blake. Life does get complicated, doesn't it?

FOUR

I PICKED up my car from the garage on Third Avenue where I put it out to pasture. The car's a Chevy convertible, an antique from the pre-fin era. I drove it down to the Village, stuck it in a handy parking spot, and looked around for a bar called Mandrake's.

Rhona was right. Mandrake's was open at two in the afternoon, even if I couldn't figure out why. It was a sleek and polished little club with a circular bar, and at night the Madison Avenue hippies came there to listen to a piano player sing dirty songs. They paid a buck and a quarter for their drinks, patted the waitresses on their pretty little bottoms, and thought they were way ahead of the squares at PJ Clark's.

But in the afternoon it was just another ginmill, empty, and its only resemblance to Mandrake's-by-nightfall was the price schedule. The drinks were still a buck and a quarter. I picked up Courvoisier at the bar and carried it to a little table in the back. The barmaid was the afternoon model, hollow-eyed and sad. I was her only customer.

I nursed my drink, tossed a quarter into the chrome-plated jukebox, and played some Billie Holliday records. They were some of her last sides, cut after the voice was gone and only the perfect phrasing remained, and Lady Day was sadder than Mandrake's in the daylight. I waited for Rhona and wondered if she would show.

She did. She was a good three drinks late, waltzing in at three o'clock and glancing over her shoulder to find out who was following her. Probably the whole Lithuanian Army-in-Exile, I thought. She was that kind of a girl.

"I'm late," she said. "I'm sorry."

We were still the bartender's only customers. I asked her what she was drinking. She said a Rob Roy would be nice. She sipped at it, and I sipped at the cognac, and we looked at each other. She asked me for the story again and I gave it to her, filling in more of the details. She hung on every word and gave me a nod now and then.

"You're positive he was killed?"

"Unless he found a way to live without a head. They shot it off for him."

"I don't know what to do next, Ed."

"You could tell me what's happening."

"I'm paying you a hundred a day. Isn't that enough?"

This burned me. "I could make ten grand in five minutes," I said. "That's even better."

She looked at me. "What do you mean?"

"Nothing at all," I said. I finished my drink, put the empty glass on the table in front of me. "I had a visitor today, Rhona. A lawyer named Phillip Carr. He told me a client of his was missing a daughter. This client was willing to shell out ten grand if I dug her up and brought her around."

"So?"

"He showed me your picture, Rhona."

For a moment she just stared. Then her face cracked like ice in the springtime. She shuddered violently, and she spilled most of her Rob Roy on the polished tabletop, and her stiff upper lip turned to jello.

She said: "Oh, hell."

"Want to talk now, Rhona?"

She stared at the top of the table, where her hands were shaking uncontrollably in a Rob Roy ocean. I walked to the jukebox, threw away another quarter, and sat down again. She was still shaking and biting her lip.

"You'd better tell me, Rhona. People are playing with tommy-guns and talking in ten-grand terms. You'd better tell me."

She nodded. On the jukebox, Billie was singing about strange fruit. Husky, smoky sounds shrieked out of a junked-up dying throat. The barmaid came over with a towel and wiped up the Rob Roy.

Rhona looked up at me. The veneer of poise was all gone. She wasn't ageless anymore. She looked very young, very scared. A scared kid in over her head.

"Ed," she said. "They want to kill me."

"Who does?"

"The man who came to see you. The same men who killed my blackmailer in Canarsie last night."

"Who are they?"

"Gamblers. But not real gamblers. Crooked ones. They run a batch of rigged games. They have some steerers who send over suckers, and the suckers go home broke. The lawyer who saw you works for a man named Abe Zucker. He's the head of it. And they're all looking for me. They want to kill me."

"Why?"

"Because of my father."

"Who's your father?"

I DON'T think she even heard the question.

"They killed him," she said quietly. "Slowly. They beat him to death."

I waited while she took the bits and pieces of herself and tugged them back together again. Then I tried again. I asked her who her father was.

"Jack Blake," she said. "He was a mechanic."

"He fixed cars?"

She laughed humorlessly. "Cards," she corrected. "He was a card mechanic. He could make a deck turn inside out and salute you, Ed. He could deal seconds all night long and nobody ever tipped. He was the best in the world. He had gentle hands with long thin fingers—the most perfect hands in the world. He could crimp-cut and false-shuffle and palm and...He was great, Ed."

"Go on."

"You ought to be able to figure the rest of it," she said. "He quit the crooked-gambling circuit years ago when my mother died. He went into business for himself in Cleveland, ran a store downtown on Euclid Avenue and went straight. I worked for him, keeping the books and clerking behind the counter. The store was a magic shop. We sold supplies to the professional magicians and simple tricks to the average Joes. Dad loved the business. When the pros came in he would show off a little, fool around with a deck of cards and let them see how good he was. It was the perfect business for him."

"Where did Zucker come in?"

She sighed. "It happened less than a year ago. We came to New York. Part business and part pleasure. Dad bought his supplies in New York and liked to get into town once or twice a year to check out new items. It was better than waiting for the salesman to come to him. We were at a nightclub, a cheap joint on West Third Street, and the bus-boy asked Dad if he was looking for action. Poker, craps, that kind of thing. He said he wouldn't mind a poker game and the busboy gave him a room number of a Broadway hotel. I went back to the place where we were staying and Dad went to the game."

Billie's last record ended and the juke went silent. I was tired of wasting quarters—and we didn't need music.

"He told me about it later," Rhona said, "when he got back to our room. He said he sat down and played two hands, and by that time he knew the game was rigged. He was going to get up and leave, he said, but they were so sloppy it made him mad. So he beat them at their own game, Ed. He played tight on the hands unless he was deal-ing, and on his deal he made sure things went his way.

"He was careful about it. He threw every trick in the book at them and they never caught on. It was a big game, Ed. Table stakes with a heavy takeout. Dad walked out of the game with twenty thousand dollars of their money."

I whistled. The rigged games are usually pretty small—when you get in the high brackets, nobody trusts anybody and the games are generally honest. It's easier to rake cheap suckers over the coals than to pick the big-money boys.

"Who played in the game?"

"Two or three of the sharps. And Dad. And some oil and cattlemen."

It figured. Texans with too much money and too much faith.

"Even the oilmen didn't do badly," she said. "Dad took the money straight from the crooks. He had the time of his life. And then...then they must have figured out what happened. For a few weeks everything was fine. Then we got a note in the mail. It wasn't signed. It said Jack Blake better give back the twenty grand he won or he would get what was coming to him. He just laughed it off, Ed. He said he was surprised they had figured it out but he wasn't going to let it worry him."

"And then they killed him?"

"Yes." She finished her drink. "I was over at a friend's house. I got home and found him lying on the living-room floor. There was blood all over. I went to him and touched him and...and he was still warm—"

I picked up her hand and held on to it. Her skin was white. She took a quick breath and squeezed my hand. "I'm all right, Ed."

"Sure."

We sat there. It was pushing 4:30 and the bar was starting to draw lushes. A tough little dyke in tight slacks strode over to the jukebox and played something noisy. I looked at Rhona again.

"How do you fit in?" I asked.

"They want to kill me."

"Why?"

"They want their money back." I shook my head. "I won't buy it. You're in New York, not Cleveland. You were busy paying off a blackmailer who caught a load of lead in Canarsie. I don't buy it at all, Rhona. They wouldn't chase you that hard just because your father took them with a few fancy cuts and shuffles. They might run him down and kill him, but they wouldn't bother you."

"It's true, Ed."

"It is like hell. Where does the blackmailer fit?"

"He was blackmailing me. I told you."

"How? Why? With what?"

She thought about it. The juke was still too noisy and the bar was filling up. I was beginning to dislike the place.

She said: "All right."

I waited.

"I'm Jack Blake's daughter," she said. "I'm not a weeper and I don't throw in the towel when somebody hits me. I'm pretty tough, Ed."

I could believe it. She looked the part. Her green eyes were warm enough to throw sparks now.

"I came to New York to get them," she said. "They killed my father, Ed. Those rotten bastards killed him. They beat him and he died, and I'm not the kind of girl who can sit on her behind in Cleveland and write it off to profit and loss. I flew to New York to get something good on Abe Zucker, something good enough to put him on death row at Sing Sing. That's why they want me out of the way, Ed. Because they know I won't give up unless they kill me."

"And the blackmailer?" I asked.

"How did he fit in?"

"Klugsman," she corrected. "Milton Klugsman. He got in touch with me, told me he could prove that Zucker had my dad killed. I...I guess I let you think he was blackmailing me just to make things simpler. He called me and told me he had evidence to sell. The price was five grand."

"He might have been conning you, Rhona."

She raised an eyebrow. "Don't you think I thought of that? He could have been looking for some easy money or he could have been setting me up for Zucker. That's why I wouldn't meet him myself, why I hired you. I decided it was worth risking five grand, Ed. Five grand was just an ante in a game this size—"

She stopped, shrugged. "I guess Klugsman was telling the truth. Whatever he had, I won't get it now. He's dead. They killed him, and now they want to kill me. If I had any sense I'd get out of town until they forgot all about me."

"Why don't you?"

"Because I'm Jack Blake's daughter. Because I'm a stubborn girl. I always have been. Well, where do we go from here, Ed?"

I put a dollar on the table for the barmaid. "For a starter," I said, "we get the hell out of here."

FIVE

WE TOOK my Chevy. I drove uptown on Eighth Avenue as far as Twentieth, then cut east. There was a parking spot in front of a swanky five-story brick building on Gramercy Park. I coaxed the Chevy into it, with a Caddy in front of us and a Lincoln behind. The Chevy felt outclassed. We got out of the car, walked past a stiff doorman and into a self-service elevator.

"I didn't want a hotel room," she said as we entered her place. "I thought it would be too easy for them to find me. This apartment was listed in the *Times*. It's a sublet, all furnished and ready. It costs a lot of money but it's worth it."

"What name did you rent it under?"

"I don't remember," she said. "Not mine."

She said there was scotch if I wanted a drink. I didn't. I wandered around the living room, a brazenly modern room. Rhona sat down on an orange couch and crossed her legs.

"What do we do next, Ed?"

"Go back to Cleveland."

"And forget about it?"

"Uh-huh."

She looked away. I studied her legs, then let my eyes move slowly up her body. I remembered last afternoon, in my apartment, in my bedroom. I took a quick breath, then crammed some tobacco into a pipe and scratched a match on a box.

"He was my father, Ed."

"I know."

"I can't quit."

"Hell," I said, "you absolutely can't do anything else. You know how Zucker took care of your father? Zucker didn't go there himself, Rhona. He picked up a telephone— or he hired somebody to pick up a phone. And then a bunch of hired muscle from Detroit or Chicago or Vegas got on a plane to Cleveland and beat your father to death and flew back on the next plane. You couldn't pin something like that to Zucker in a hundred years. All you can do is take a gun and shoot a hole in his head."

"That's not such a bad idea, is it?"

I didn't answer her.

"No," she said finally. "You're wrong, Ed. Why is he scared of me? Why can't he just ignore me? He had this lawyer offer you ten thousand dollars? If he's in the clear, why am I worth that kind of money to him?"

"You must have him scared."

She swung a small fist into the palm of her other hand. A startling gesture from a girl, especially a feminine one like her. "You are god-damned right. I've got him scared," she said. "I've got the son of a bitch turning green. And there has to be evidence, Ed. Klugsman had evidence."

"Unless he was conning you."

"Then why did they kill him?"

She was right. Abe Zucker was in enough trouble to work up a sweat, enough to make him spray Canarsie with machine-gun slugs and paper Manhattan with ten-grand rewards. It didn't quite mesh yet. Something was wrong somewhere, something didn't ring true. But for the time being she was right and I had to ride with her. I drew on my pipe.

"What do you know about Klugsman?"

"Nothing but his name. And that he's dead."

"You never met him?"

"No."

"You know where he lives?"

She shook her head. "He called me on the phone, Ed. He said his name was Milton Klugsman and he told me he had the information I needed. He said he could prove who killed my father. He didn't give his address or his phone number or anything."

"The phone. Is it in your name?"

"No, it's in the name of the people I'm subletting from."

"Then how did he reach you?"

"I have no idea."

We kept running into walls and up blind alleys. I wondered if she was lying to me. So far she'd fed me enough nonsense to earn her a Pathological Liar Merit Badge, but the latest version had a plausible ring to it.

"Somebody knew you were in town. Who?"

"I don't know."

"Phillip Carr showed me a picture of you. Any idea

where he got it?"

"None."

"It was a head-and-shoulder shot, Rhona. You had your hair swept back and you were smiling, but not too broadly."

Her face clouded. "That...sounds like a picture Dad carried in his wallet. They could have stolen it when they killed him." She bit her lip. "But that doesn't make sense, does it?"

It didn't. I poked at my memory, brushed the snapshot away, and brought a different picture into focus. A face I'd seen a day ago in Canarsie. I described Klugsman as well as I could, told her how tall he was and what kind of a face he had and what clothes he was wearing. The description rang no bells for her.

I stood up, leaned over to knock the dottle from my pipe, and walked over to her. "We have to start with Klugsman," I said. "Klugsman may have had some evidence. Without it we're nowhere. I can try getting a line on him. Maybe I can find out who he was, where he lived, and who his friends were. If he had anything around the house, it's probably gone by now. But maybe he's got a friend or a relative who knows something. It's worth a try."

"You're going now?"

She seemed sad about it. She was standing just a few feet from me, her hands at her sides, her shoulders back, her breasts in sharp relief against the front of her dress. Her mouth was pouting a little and her eyes were unhappy. I looked at her and didn't want to go anywhere. I wanted to stay awhile.

"I'd better get going," I said.

"Wait a few minutes, Ed."

The voice was soft as a pillow. Her eyes were moist. She took a short step toward me, stopped. I put out my hands and caught her shoulders and she pressed against me, hard.

"Ed—"

I kissed her. Her mouth tasted of Rob Roys and cigarettes and she put her arms around me and clung to me like a morning glory on a wire fence. Her body was on fire. I kissed her eyes, her cheeks, her throat.

"I'm all alone," she said. "All alone and afraid. Stay with me, Ed."

"Sure," I said, leading her into the bedroom, decorated in various shades of green. She stood there like a statue, but who likes statues dressed? I took off her clothes and ran my hands over her body. She vibrated like a tuning fork, purred like a kitten.

The mattress was firm. I put a pillow under her head and spread that ash blond hair over it. I touched her, kissed her. She breathed jaggedly and her eyes were wild.

"Ed—"

To hell with Klugsman. He was dead. He could wait awhile...

I left her in bed face pressed to pillow, eyes closed, body curled like a fetus. I told her not to leave the apartment, not to answer the door, not to pick up the telephone unless it rang once, stopped, then rang again. That would be my signal.

"One if by land," she mumbled. "Two if by sea."

I kissed her cheek. She smiled like a Cheshire cat, happy and contented. I dressed and left her apartment.

THE FIRST stop was my own apartment. I got on the phone, cursed myself once, quietly, and called the Continental Detective Agency in Cleveland. The voice that answered sounded two years out of an expensive college. I told him to run a brief check on a man named Jack Blake, supposed to be a homicide victim within the past couple of months, and to ring me back on it.

It was simple stuff and it only took him half an hour. Jack Blake, he revealed, was a card sharp who ran a magic shop on Euclid Avenue, got beaten to death in his own home, and had a daughter named Rhona. It was she who reported all this to the police. So far it was unsolved. Did I want to know more?

I didn't. I told him to bill me and got off the phone. *I'm sorry, Rhona,* I said softly. *This time I should have believed you. I'm sorry.*

Then I got out of there and headed for the Senator, a cafeteria on Broadway at 96th, downstairs from Manny Hess's pool hall and across the street from a Ping-Pong emporium. They serve good food and run a clean place, and every small-time operator on Upper Broadway drops in for coffee-and. I went inside and got a cup of coffee and carried it to the table where Herbie Wills was sitting.

Wills, a small, gray man of forty-five, was eating yogurt and buttered whole wheat toast. There was a glass of milk standing on the table.

"Ulcers," he said. "I went to this doctor because of my stomach, he said I have ulcers. I have this very sensitive stomach, Mr. London. There are certain foods I can't eat. They disagree with me, you know."

"Sure," I said.

"Now," he said, spooning in a teaspoon of yogurt. "Can I help you, Mr. London?"

"I need some information."

"Sure, Mr. London."

Information was Herbie's livelihood. He wasn't exactly a stool pigeon, just a little man who kept his ears open and filed away everything into separate compartments of his mind. When the information market was weak he ran errands for bookies. He was a hanger-on, living in a clean but shabby room in a 98th Street hotel.

"Milton Klugsman," I said.

Herbie pursed his bloodless lips, tapped three times on the table with his index finger. "So far," he said, "nothing. More?"

I gave him a quick description. "I make him in Canarsie, Herbie. At least he's familiar with the area out there. A Brooklyn or Queens boy, then. Any help?"

"Miltie," he said. I looked at him. "Miltie Klugsman, Mr. London. This is what throws me for a moment; you said Milton Klugsman, I start thinking in terms of Milton or Milt. But I knew a Miltie Klugsman. This is all he gets called. Miltie."

"Go on."

Another spoon of yogurt, bite of toast, deliberate sip of milk. I watched him and hoped I would never get ulcers. He wiped his mouth again and shrugged.

"I do not know much," he said carefully. "Miltie Klugsman. I think he works for himself, Mr. London. I think maybe selling things, like a fence. But this is just a guess because I hardly know him at all."

"Who are his friends?"

HERBIE shrugged. "This I don't know. As a matter of fact, I hardly know Miltie Klugsman at all. You were right about Brooklyn. He lives somewhere in East New York near the Queens line."

"Married?"

"He could be. I see him once with a dark-haired girl. She was wearing a mink stole. But this doesn't mean she is his wife, Mr. London."

That sounded logical enough. "I have to find Miltie," I said. "Where does he hang out?"

He thought about it, through another spoon of yogurt,

bites of toast, two sips of milk. "Now wait a minute," he said. "Sure."

"What?"

"A diner in Brooklyn!" he said. "On Livonia Avenue near Avenue K. I don't know Brooklyn too well. The diner is one of those old trolley cars but like remodeled. I don't know the name."

"Probably something like *Diner*."

"That might be it," he said seriously. "Try there, ask around. You might even find Miltie himself."

I doubted it. Miltie Klugsman wouldn't be there unless they had plastered him under the basement floor. But I didn't tell this to Herbie.

He was a stool pigeon with a conscience. He wouldn't take the ten I gave him, insisting it was too much for the sort of information he had given me. I gave him a five finally and got out of there.

I went back to the Chevy. Some juvenile delinquent had relieved me of my radio aerial—in the morning he would go to shop class and make a zip gun out of it. Deprived of music, I headed dolefully for Brooklyn.

I went back to the Chevy. Some juvenile delinquent had relieved me of my radio aerial—in the morning he would go to shop class and make a zip gun out of it. Deprived of music, I headed dolefully for Brooklyn.

SIX

LIVONIA Avenue was filled with people. I parked two blocks from the diner—which was named *Diner* after all—and stopped in a drugstore to see if Miltie Klugsman had had a phone. He did, plus an address on Ashford Street. The pharmacist told me how to get to Ashford Street. I started in that direction, then decided to try the diner first.

It wasn't much. A ferret-faced counterman was pressing a hamburger down on a greasy grill. He turned to look
at me when I walked in. An antique whore sat at the counter near the door drinking coffee with cream.

I took a stool halfway between the old girl and a trio
of young punks in snap-brim hats, all of them trying to
look like latter-day Kid Twists. I was in Reles country,
Murder Inc.'s old stamping grounds not far from the heart
of Brownsville.

The counterman decided that the hamburger was
cooked enough to kill the taste. He surrounded it with a
stale roll, slapped it onto a chipped saucer, slid it down
the counter to the snap-brim set. He came over to me and
leaned on the counter. His face didn't change expression
when he saw the bulge the .38 made in my jacket. He
looked at me, deadpan, and waited.

"Black coffee," I said.

"No trouble. Not in here."

He talked without moving his lips. It's a trick they
teach you in Dannemora and other institutions of higher
learning. I asked him if I looked like a troublemaker. He
shrugged.

"I just want coffee," I said. The counterman nodded.
He gave me the coffee and I handed him a dime for it. He
walked away to trade a story or two with the old hooker. I
waited for the coffee to cool. The snap-brim triplets were
looking me over.

The coffee tasted like lukewarm dishwater that some
fool had rinsed a coffee cup in. I left it alone. The counterman came back, leaned over me like the Tower of Pisa.

"You want anything else besides coffee?"

"A plain doughnut." He gave me one. "That all?"

"Maybe not."

"What else?"

I sat for a moment or two trying to look like a hood trying to think. My eyes were as wary as I could make them.

"I'm looking for a guy," I said. "I was told I could find him here."

"Who is he?"

"A guy named Klugsman," I said. "Miltie Klugsman. You know him?"

Not a flicker of expression. Just a nod.

"You know where I can find him?"

"He ain't around much. What do you want with him?"

"It's private."

"Yeah?"

I pretended to do some more thinking. "I hear he buys things. I got a thing or two for sale."

"Like what?"

I shook my head. "No," I said.

"You might get a better price from somebody else," the counterman said. "Depending on what you got to sell. Miltie, now he can be cheap. You got something for sale, you want all you can get."

"I was given orders to see Miltie," I said. The hell with it—let him think I was only a hired hand. I didn't care that much about the prestige value of the bit.

"Miltie," he said. "Miltie Klugsman."

"Yeah."

"You hang on a minute," he said. "I think that guy there wants more coffee. You just hang on."

He filled a cup with coffee and took it over to the young punks. The one he gave it to had his hat halfway over his eyes. The counterman said something unintelligible without moving his lips. The kid answered.

The counterman came back. He asked me my name. I told him it didn't matter. He asked me who I worked for and I said that didn't matter either.

"I'll tell it to Klugsman," I said.

"He could be hard to find."

"So maybe I came to the wrong place." I started to slide off the stool, got one foot on the floor before his hand settled on my shoulder. I stood up and turned to face him again.

"Don't be in a hurry," he said.

"I got things to do."

"Miltie used to come in a lot. He ain't been around much. I was talking to a guy"—he nodded toward the triplets—"over there."

"I figured."

"One of 'em hangs with Miltie now and then. He says maybe he can help. If you want."

"Sure."

"Danny," he said, "c'mere."

DANNY c'mered. He was almost my height but his posture concealed the fact neatly. His fingers were yellow from too many cigarettes and not enough soap. His suit must have been fairly expensive and his shoes had a high shine on them, but nothing he wore could take the slob look away from him. It came shining through.

"You want Miltie," he said.

"That's the idea."

"He's a little hot right now," Danny said. "He's holed up a few blocks from here. I could show you."

We left the diner. Danny lit a cigarette in the doorway. He didn't offer me one. We turned right and walked to the corner, turned right again and left Livonia for a side street. The block was darker, more residential than commercial. We walked the length of the block in silence and took another right turn.

"You ever meet Miltie?"

"No," I said.

"You from New York?"

"The Bronx. Throg's Neck."

"Long way from home," he said.

I didn't answer him. We kept walking. At the corner we made another right turn.

"This is a hell of a way to go," I said.

"Yeah?"

"We just go around the block," I said. "There must be a shorter way to do it."

"This is easier."

"Yeah?"

"It gives 'em time," he said.

It took a minute. Time? Time to make a phone call, time to take the short route and come around the block to meet us. I went for my gun. I was too slow. Danny was on my left, a foot or so behind me. His gun dug into my rib cage and the muzzle felt colder than death.

"Easy," he said.

My hand was three or four inches from the .38. It stopped in midair and stayed there.

"Take out the piece," he said. "Do it slow. Very slow. Don't point it at me. I'd just as soon shoot you now and find out later who the hell you are."

I took out the gun and I did it slowly. There was a warehouse across the street, dark and silent. On our side was a row of brownstones filled with people who didn't report gunshots to the police. I let the gun point at the ground.

"Drop it."

I dropped it. It bounced once on the pavement and lay still.

"Kick it."

"Where?"

"Just kick it."

I kicked it. The .38 skidded twenty feet, bounced into the gutter. His gun was still on my ribs and he kept poking me as a reminder.

"Now we wait," he said. "It shouldn't be long."

It wasn't long at all. They came down the block from Livonia, walking fast but not quite running. They had their hands in their pockets and their hats down over their foreheads. They were in uniform. I stood there with Danny's gun in my ribs and waited for them.

"He's a cop," one of them said.

Danny dug at me. "A cop?"

"A private cop. His name is London and he's sticking his nose into things he shouldn't. They tried to buy him off but he wouldn't be bought."

"It's good we checked."

"Well," the punk said. "They said anybody comes nosing for Miltie, we should call. So I called."

I looked at my gun. It was three miles away from me in the gutter. I wanted it in my hand.

"What's the word, man?"

"The word is we got a contract."

"At what price?"

"Three yards apiece," the punk said. He was thinner than Danny, maybe a year or two older. His face was pockmarked and his eyes bulged when he stared, as though he needed glasses but he was afraid they wouldn't fit the hard-guy image.

"Cheap," Danny said.

"Hell, it's an easy hit. We just take him and dump him. Nothing to it, Danny."

"Yeah."

"It's three quick bills. And it sets us up, man. It makes us look good and it gives us an in."

They would need all the ins they could get. Danny was sloppy, strictly an amateur. You don't stand next to a person when you're holding a gun on him. You get as far away as you can. The gun's advantage increases with distance. The closer you are, the less of an edge you've got.

"We take him for a ride," Danny was saying. "Take him the same place they gave it to Miltie. Ride him around Canarsie, hit him in the head, then drive back."

"Sure, Danny."

"We use his car," he went on. "Which is your car, buster?"

"The Chevy."

"The red convertible?"

"That's the one."

"Gimme the keys."

He was much too close. He should have backed off four or five steps, more if he was a good enough shot. He was making my play too easy for me.

"The keys."

The other two were in front of us. They both had their hands in their pockets. They were heeled, but one had his jacket buttoned and the other looked slow and stupid.

"The keys!"

I let him nudge me with the gun. I felt the muzzle poke into me, then relax.

I dropped. I fell down and I fell toward him, and I snapped his arm behind his back and took the gun right out of his hand. One punk was trying to reach through his jacket button to his own gun. I gave the trigger a squeeze and the bullet hit him in the throat. He took two steps, clapped both hands to his neck, fell over, and died.

The other one—the slow-looking one—wasn't so slow

after all. He drew in a hurry and he shot in a hurry, but he didn't stop to remember that I was using Danny as a shield. He had time to get off two shots. One went wide. The other caught Danny in the chest. The punk was getting ready for a third shot when I snapped off a pair that caught him in the center of the chest. Danny's gun was a .45. The holes it made were big enough to step in.

I dropped Danny just as he was starting to bleed on me. He was still alive but didn't figure to last more than a few seconds. He blacked out immediately.

I wiped my prints off his .45 and tossed it next to him on the pavement. I ran over to the curb, scooped my .38 out of the gutter, and wedged it into my shoulder rig. That made it easy for the cops. Three punks had a fight and killed each other, and to hell with all of them. Nobody would shed tears for them. They weren't worth it.

The gunshots were still echoing in the empty streets. I looked at three corpses for a second or two, then ran like hell. I kept going for two blocks, turned a corner, slowed down. I was digging a pipe out of a pocket when the sirens started up.

I filled the pipe, lit it. I walked down the street smoking and taking long breaths and telling my nerves they could unwind now.

But my nerves didn't believe it...I couldn't blame them.

Brooklyn was cool, quiet, and dark, with only the police siren cutting through the night. I got back on Livonia, skirted the diner, got into the Chevy.

Behind the wheel, I dumped out my pipe, put it away. Then I drove along, trying to remember the directions to Ashford Street. I got lost once, but I found the place—Klugsman's address.

The building was like all the others. He must have

been small-time, I thought. Otherwise he would have found a better place to live. I walked into the front hallway. A kid, twelve or thirteen, was sprawled on the stairs with a Pepsi in one hand and a cigarette in the other. He watched me lean on Klugsman's bell.

"The bell don't work," he said. "You looking for Mrs. Klugsman?"

I hadn't known there was one, but I was looking for her now. I told the kid so.

"Upstairs," he said. "Just walk right up. Third floor, apartment three-C."

I thanked the kid, he shrugged, and I went up two flights of rickety stairs. The building smelled of age and stale beer. I stood in front of the door marked 3-C. The apartment was not empty. Gut-bucket jazz boomed through the door, records playing too loudly on a lo-fi player. I knocked on the door. Nothing happened. I knocked again.

"C'mon in, whoever in hell it is!"

The voice was loud. I turned the knob and went into the apartment where Miltie Klugsman had once lived. It was a railroad flat, three or four rooms tied together by grim little hallways. The furniture was old and the walls needed paint. The place had the general feel of a cheap apartment which someone had tried to hold together until, recently, that someone had stopped caring.

THE SOMEONE was sitting on a worn-out couch. She could have been beautiful once. She may have been attractive, still; it was hard to tell. There was a pint of blended rye in her hand. The pint was about three-quarters gone and she was about three-quarters drunk. She was a thirty-five-year-old brunette with lines at the corners of her eyes and mouth.

She was wearing a faded yellow housedress that was

missing a button or two in front and had floppy slippers on her feet. She waved a hand at me and took another long drink that killed most of the pint of rye.

"Hiya," she called. "Who in hell are you?"

I closed the door, walked over, sat on the couch.

"My name's Shirley. Who're you?"

"Ed," I said.

"You lookin' for Miltie? He doesn't live here anymore. You know the song? 'Annie Doesn't Live Here Anymore'?" Her eyes rolled. "Miltie doesn't live here anymore," she said sadly. "Miltie's dead, Ed. That rhymes. Dead, Ed."

I walked over to the record player and turned off something raucous. I went back to the couch. She offered me a drink of the blend. I didn't want any.

"Poor Miltie," she said. "I loved him, you believe it? Oh, Miltie wasn't much. Me and Miltie, just a couple of nothings."

"Shirley—"

"That's me," she said. Her face clouded, and for a moment I thought she was going to start crying. She surprised me by laughing instead. She tossed her head back and her body shook with laughter. She couldn't stop. I reached over and slapped her, not too hard, and she sat up and rubbed the side of her face and nodded her head vigorously.

"Shirley, Miltie was murdered," I said. "You know that, don't you?"

She looked at me and nodded. The tears were starting now. I wanted to go away and leave her alone. I couldn't.

"Murdered, Shirley. He had some...evidence that some man wanted. Do you know where it is?"

She shook her head.

"He must have talked about it, Shirley. He must have told you something. Think."

LAWRENCE BLOCK

She looked away, then back at me, cupped her chin with one hand, closed her eyes, opened them. "Nope," she said. "He never told me a thing. Not Miltie."

"Are you sure?"

"Uh-huh." She reached for the bottle again. I took it away from her. She came at me, sprawled across me, fingers scrabbling for the bottle. I gave it to her and she killed it. She held it at arm's length, reading the label slowly and deliberately. Then she heaved it across the room. It bounced off the record player, took another wild bounce, and shattered.

"Poor Miltie," she said.

"Shirley—"

"Jussa minute," she said. "What's your name again? Ed? I'm gonna tell you something. Ed, I'll tell you about Miltie Klugsman. Okay?"

"Sure."

"MILTIE was just a little guy," she said. "Like me, see? Before I met him I used to work the clubs, you know, do a little stripping, get the customers to buy me drinks. I was never a hooker, Ed. You believe me?"

"I believe you."

She nodded elaborately. "Well," she said. "Lots of guys, you say you were a stripper, they figure you were a whore. Not me. Some girls, maybe. Not me."

She was standing now, swaying a little but staying on her feet. She picked a pack of cigarettes from a table, shook one loose, and put it in her mouth. I scratched a match for her and she leaned forward to take the light. Her dress fell away from her body. She wasn't wearing a bra. I looked away and she laughed hysterically.

"See something you shouldn't, Ed?" I didn't say anything. "Oh," she said, continuing her story. "So I met Miltie

124

at the club. He was a good guy, you know? Decent. Oh, he did some time. You live like this, this kind of life, you don't care if a man did time. What's the past, Ed? Huh? It's the present, and what kind of guy a guy is, and all. Right?"

"Sure."

"He wanted to marry me. Nobody else, they always wanted, oh, you know what they wanted. He wanted to marry me. So what the hell. Right, Ed?"

"Sure."

"He was just a little guy. Nobody important. But we stuck with each other and we made it. We stuck together, we ate steady, we lived okay. This place is a mess now. When it's fixed up it looks better."

She pranced around the room like a hostess showing off her antiques. Something struck her funny and she started laughing again, reeling around the room and laughing hysterically. Her voice caught on a snag and the laughter changed abruptly to tears. She cried as she laughed, putting all of herself into it. I got up to catch her and she sagged against me, limp as a dishrag. I held on to her for a few seconds. Then she got hold of herself and pulled away from me.

"Poor, poor poor Miltie," she said. "I was afraid, I knew he was getting in over his head. Listen, I was just a lousy dime-store stripper, you know? I knew enough not to try to play the big-time circuit. I stuck to my own league. You know what I mean?"

"Sure, Shirley."

"But Miltie didn't know this. He wanted to do something big. I was afraid, I knew he was getting mixed up, getting in over his head. He was all tangled up in something too big for him. He was a *good* guy but he wasn't a *big* guy. I knew something like this was going to happen. I knew it."

The cigarette burned her fingers. She dropped it and squashed it beneath one of the floppy slippers. She kicked off the slippers, first one and then the other. Her toenails were painted scarlet and the paint was chipped here and there.

"He was going to get out. He was going to stick to his own league. And then—"

SHE DIDN'T break. She came close, but she didn't. The last of the liquor was taking hold of her now and she was staggering. She stepped into the center of the room, walked to the record player, put on something slow and jazzy. I stayed where I was.

"I'm still good-looking," she said. "Aren't I?"

I told her she was.

"Not a kid anymore," she said. "But I'll get by."

The music was strip-club jazz. She took a few preliminary steps to it, tossing her hips at me in an almost comical bump-and-grind, and grinned.

Then, slowly, she went into her act. We weren't in a strip joint and she wasn't wearing a ball gown. She was wearing a faded yellow housedress that buttoned down the front, and she undid it a button at a time. Her fingers were clumsy with blended rye but she got the dress open and shrugged it away. It fell to the floor bunched around her long legs. She took a step and kicked the dress away.

No bra. Just thin black panties. She had a fine body, slender waist, trim hips, full breasts with just the slightest trace of age to them. She kept dancing, moving with the music, flinging her breasts at me, grinding her loins at me.

"Not bad, huh? Not bad for an old broad, huh, Ed? Still lively, huh?"

I didn't answer her. I wanted to get up and go away but I couldn't do that either. I watched while she peeled off the panties and tossed them away. She had trouble with them but she got them off and danced her wicked dance in blissful nudity.

"Ed," she said.

She came at me, threw herself at me. Her flesh, warm with drink, was soft as butter in my arms. She looked into my eyes, her face a study in alcoholic passion mixed in equal parts with torment. She looked at me, and she squirmed against me, and then her eyes closed and she passed out cold.

There was a double bed in the bedroom. She had to sleep alone in it now. Some men with machine guns had killed the man who used to share it with her. I drew back the top sheet, put her down on the bed. I covered her with the sheet, tucked a pillow under her head.

Then I got out of there.

SEVEN

THE RIDE back to Manhattan was a long one. Every traffic light was red when I got to it.

I told myself that the picture was refusing to take shape, and then I changed my mind—it was taking shape, all right. It was taking a great many shapes, each conflicting with the other. Nothing made much sense.

Shirley Klugsman was a widow because her husband had tried to sell evidence to Rhona Blake. A man named Zucker wanted Rhona dead. He also wanted me dead, and three punks in East New York had tried to carry it off for him. And they were dead now.

I got the Chevy back into my garage and walked halfway home before I changed my mind. Then I jumped in a cab.

Rewards and punishments—Phillip Carr's phrase. They

were at the punishment stage now. They wanted me dead, and they had tried once already that night, and maybe my apartment wasn't the safest place in the world.

Besides, Rhona was alone...

The doorman barely looked at me. I let the elevator whisk me up to her floor, went to her door, and jabbed at the bell. Nothing happened. I remembered our signal, rang once, waited a minute, then started ringing. Nothing happened. I called out to her, told her who it was. And nothing happened.

She was out, of course. At a show, having a drink, catching a bite to eat. I got halfway to the elevator and my mind filled with another picture, a less pleasant one in which she was lying face-down on the wall-to-wall carpet and bleeding. I went back to her door.

On television I would have given the door a good hard shoulder, wood would have splintered, and that would have been that. This is fine on television, where they have balsa doors. But every time I hit a door with my shoulder I wind up with a sore shoulder and an unimpaired door. In Manhattan, apartment doors are usually reinforced with steel plates. You just can't trust television.

I took out the little gimcrack I use to clean my pipe. It had a penknife blade. I opened it and played with the lock. It opened. I went inside.

She wasn't there. So I sat down in the living room to wait for her, first checking the bar to see if there was any cognac. There wasn't. There was scotch, but cognac is all I drink.

Hell. This was a special sort of situation. I poured a lot of scotch into a glass and sat down to work on it.

After half an hour, I was worried. She was in too deep, playing way over her head, and she wasn't around. The room was beginning to get to me. I kept smelling her perfume and the furniture kept glaring at me.

Where the hell *was* she?

I remembered the afternoon, and the green eyes warming very suddenly, and her body close to mine. Bed, and whispers, and passion, and the happy drowsiness afterwards. And now she was gone. It was the sort of magic trick Jack Blake would have gone wild over. You just make love to this girl, see, and she disappears.

After ten more minutes of this I was morbid. I started combing the apartment in a cockeyed search for help notes or struggle signs or bullet holes. I got down on hands and knees and peered owlishly under the bed. There was a single slipper there, and a pair of stockings that had run for their lives, and a respectable quantity of dust. I checked out the closet in the bedroom. Her clothes, and not many of them. A suitcase, streamlined and airplane-gray. She had been traveling light. She was Jack Blake's daughter, coming from Cleveland with a single suitcase and a bellyful of determination, and that wasn't going to be enough.

I WENT back to the living room. The bedroom closet had been a disappointment from an aesthetic standpoint. You're supposed to open a closet door and watch a body fall out. That was how they did it on television. And all I got was a suitcase and some clothing.

There was still a closet in the front hall. I gave the knob a twist, yanked open the door, and stepped ceremoniously aside so that the body wouldn't hit me when it fell.

No body fell.

Instead there was a noise like a shotgun blast at close quarters, and there was a wind like Hurricane Zelda, and I flew up in the air and bounced off one wall into another. Then the lights went out.

EIGHT

IT WAS timeless. There was the lifting sensation, the spinning, the impact, the blackness. Then I was on my back on that orange couch and my eyes were open. I saw ash blond hair, a red mouth.

Rhona.

She was saying: "Lie still, Ed. Relax, lie still, don't try to move. My God, I came in and found you. I thought you were dead. The whole hallway was a mess. It looked as though someone fired a cannon in here. Are you all right, Ed?"

She was leaning over me, stroking my forehead with one soft hand. Her eyes were wide, concerned. Sensation was starting to come back now, with pain leading the procession. My whole body ached. I ran hands over myself to find out what was broken. Surprisingly, everything seemed to be intact. I started to sit up. There was dizziness, and I fell back on the couch and closed my eyes for a minute.

I must have blacked out again. Then I came back to life and she was lighting a cigarette for me, putting it between my lips. I smoked. I started to sit up, saw the worry in her eyes. I told her I was all right now.

"What happened, Ed?"

"A bomb."

"Where?"

"In your closet," I said. "I opened the door and it went off."

"What were you doing in the closet?"

"Looking for bodies."

"Huh?"

"Forget it."

I closed my eyes, remembering the cute little sidestep I'd executed, a nutty bit of business designed to permit the mythical corpse to fall out of the closet without hitting me.

Corny, but damn fortunate. The sidestep had taken me out of the way of the blast. If the full force had gotten me, I'd have found a body, all right.

My own.

"Ed—"

I took a breath. "Rhona, somebody had it set up for you. You were supposed to walk into the apartment and hang your coat in the front closet. They must have rigged it with a wire running to the door handle, something like that. Open the door and you yank the wire and the thing blows."

"God."

"Uh-huh. When did you leave, Rhona? Why the hell didn't you stay put?"

She was chewing on her lower lip and her eyes were focused on the floor. She said: "I got a phone call."

"You weren't supposed to answer the phone."

"I know. But it rang and rang and rang...I picked it up."

"Who was it?"

"A man. He didn't give me his name. He just said he was calling for you."

"For me?"

She nodded. "I didn't know whether to believe him or not. But he said you were in trouble and couldn't call yourself, and I thought you were the only person who knew the telephone number here—"

"Klugsman knew it, didn't he?"

"Oh," she said. "I forgot that, Ed—"

"When did he call?"

"Around midnight."

"And you left right away?"

"That's right." I put out the cigarette. "Then I missed you by less than half an hour," I said. "They must have had a man stationed right out front, ready to drop up and install the bomb the minute you left the building. It's easy enough to get into this place. The doorman is so busy being proper and distant that he doesn't pay any attention to what's going on. So the guy came in, set up shop, and left. Then I got here and waited for you." I looked at her. "Where the hell were you, anyway?"

"Times Square."

"Huh?"

"I took a taxi to Times Square, Ed. That's what the man on the phone said I was supposed to do. I went to a place called Hector's, a big cafeteria. I took a table and waited for you."

"For how long?"

"A little over an hour, I guess. It was a bore and I was scared stiff and I didn't know what was going to happen next. Then finally a man came over to me and handed me a note. He was gone almost before I knew what was going on. The note said you wouldn't be able to meet me but everything was all right and I was supposed to go back to my apartment. I got here just in time to find you."

I got up, dragged myself over to the front hall, what was left of it. There was a gaping hole in the wall directly opposite the closet door. If I hadn't stepped aside, the blast would have made a similar hole in me.

It was something to think about.

I dropped to my hands and knees and poked around in the closet. There wasn't much to look at, just enough to confirm my diagnosis of the blast. It was a simple sort of booby-trap, the kind even a child could put together. A few sticks of dynamite, evidently touched off with a blasting cap. A piece of thin copper wire was attached to the cap and to the doorknob. There was still a trace of the wire around the knob.

"God, Ed."

I got up, put an arm around her. We walked to the kitchen. She put water on for coffee. While it cooked, I gave her a quick run-down on my part of the evening. I left out the call to the Continental agency in Cleveland. She didn't have to know that I hadn't trusted her.

SHE WAS smoking too many cigarettes too quickly. She was nervous and it showed. Why not? She had a lot to be nervous about. Half the world was trying to kill her. That sort of thing tends to get on your nerves.

"It doesn't add," I said.

"What doesn't?"

"The whole thing. This morning they didn't know where to find you, Rhona. Zucker's lawyer was ready to pay ten thousand bucks just to get hold of you. A few hours later they know where you are and all they want to do is kill us both. They hand out contracts on the two of us. I'm supposed to get shot in East New York and you're supposed to get blown up in your own apartment."

"Maybe they had us followed. Or maybe somebody tipped them off."

"Who?" I shrugged. "But there's more. Why should they play around with a bomb? They could decoy you with a phone call, then drop you with a bullet on the street. Why get so fancy? Why send you on a wild goose chase to Hector's? That's the kind of play an amateur might use. A pro would be more direct. And we're up against professionals."

The coffee finished dripping. She poured out a pair of cups. I sweetened mine with a shot of scotch and let it cool a little.

"Look," I said. "Let's suppose they wanted to search the apartment. They still didn't have to get cute about it. Did you have anything here?"

"Nothing they would be interested in."

"Well, they might not have known that. But they still could have shot you down on the street and then sent a man upstairs. Or they could break in, kill you, then search. It just doesn't make any sense."

"I guess not," she said.

We sat there drinking our coffee, tossing it all back and forth and getting nowhere in particular. She started to relax. God knows how. I decided that a card mechanic has to have a sound nervous system, and she was a card mechanic's daughter. Maybe that's the sort of thing that passes down a family tree.

I told her to go to sleep. "Is it safe?"

"Nothing's safe," I said. "I don't think they'll be around tonight. It's late and we're both half-dead. I am, anyway, and you must be."

"I'm kind of tired, Ed."

"Sure. We'll get some sleep and see what happens tomorrow. It's been their play all along now. Maybe I can start something for our side, set some wheels in motion."

"I'm scared, Ed."

"So am I. But I'm tired enough to sleep. How about you?"

She shrugged. "I guess I'm all right," she said. "Uh... you'll sleep on the couch tonight, won't you?"

"No."

"Ed," she said. "Ed, listen, don't be silly. You're exhausted and you almost got killed tonight and—"

"No."

"Ed, you're crazy. Oh, you nut. Ed, Ed, you *will* sleep on the couch, won't you?"

I didn't—not on the couch...

SHE FELL asleep right away. I tossed and turned and listened to her measured breathing, and I wondered how the hell she managed it. I closed my eyes and counted fences jumping sheep, and things like that, and nothing worked. I hadn't expected it to.

It was still too tangled up to make any appreciable sort of sense. There were just too damned many inconsistencies. I couldn't figure them out.

Sleep on it, I told myself. Sleep on it, stupid. And, eventually, I did just that.

The morning wasn't too bad. She woke up first, and by the time I opened my eyes she was busy frying bacon and eggs in the kitchen. I showered and got dressed and went in for breakfast. There was fresh coffee made and the food was on the table. She even looked pretty in the morning. It seemed impossible, but she did.

The bacon was crisp, the eggs were fine, the coffee was perfect. I told her so and she beamed. "I had plenty of practice," she said. "I used to cook for Dad all the time, since my mother died."

It was around ten by the time I got out of there. First we had to go over the ground rules. This time, dammit, she would stay in the apartment. This time, dammit, she wouldn't answer the phone unless it was my signal. Same for the door.

"Ed—"

I was at the door. I turned. Her mouth came up to me and her lips brushed mine.

"Be careful, Ed."

Outside, the sun was shining. There was a different doorman on duty. He ignored me—he knew the ground rules there, by George, and the rules said that the doorman took no notice of anyone. They were strictly ornamental.

I hauled out my wallet, dug out the card I'd gotten a day ago. Just a day? It seemed much longer. I studied the card—*Phillip Carr. Attorney at Law. 42 East 37ᵗʰ Street.*

I walked to the corner to save the doorman the trouble of hailing me a cab, and to save myself the tip I'd have had to give him. I got into a taxi and told the driver to take me to Fifth and 37ᵗʰ. It was time to get rolling. Carr and Zucker and the rest of the crooked-card-game set had dealt every hand so far. Rhona and I were just throwing our chips in the center and calling every bet.

You can do that for just so long. Then it's time to deal a hand yourself.

I sat in the backseat and gnawed on a pipestem while the cabby fought his way uptown through mid-morning traffic. Phillip Carr, Attorney at Law. Okay, shyster, I thought. Let's see what happens.

NINE

THE CAB dropped me in front of Carr's building about midway between Fifth and Madison on 37ᵗʰ Street. I took an express elevator to the twentieth floor, walked along a chrome-plated hallway to a door with Carr's name on it. I walked in.

The secretary's desk was kidney shaped. The girl behind it wasn't. Her bright red hair had been painfully spray-netted until it had the general consistency of plastic. Her smile was metallic. Her sweater bulged nicely, giving a hint of flesh that the hair and the smile tried to conceal. I told her I wanted to see Carr.

"Your name, please?"

"Ed London," I said. She got up gracefully, wiggled her well-girdled hips on the way through a door marked *Private.* The door closed behind her. I picked up a magazine from a table, glanced at it, tossed it back. The door opened and the girl came out again.

"He'll see you," she said.

"I thought he would."

Phillip Carr's office had framed diplomas on the wall from every college but Leavenworth. He stood up, smiled at me, and stuck out his hand for a handshake. I didn't take it, and after a few seconds he fetched it back again.

"Well," he said. "I'm damn glad to see you, London. You were pretty hostile yesterday. I guess you've thought things over."

"Something like that."

"Cigar?"

"No thanks."

"Well," he said.

"I thought it all over. Especially what you said about rewards and punishments."

"And?"

"I've got a reward for you."

He didn't get it until I hit him in the face. He'd stood there, hands at his sides, waiting patiently for me to tell him what the reward was, while I curled one hand into a fist, and aimed it at his jaw. It was a nice punch. It picked him up and sent him sailing over his desk, and it dropped him in an untidy pile on the floor.

He came up cursing. He made a grab for a desk drawer, probably to get a gun. I kicked him away from it. He crouched, snarling like a tiger at bay, and lunged for the button that would summon the secretary. I caught him by the lapels and gave him a little push that turned his lunge into a full-blown charge. He didn't slow down until he bounced off a wall and collapsed onto the high-pile carpet.

"Take it easy," I said. "You'll have a heart attack."

"You son of a—"

I picked him up and hit him a few times. It wasn't a particularly nice thing to do. At the moment, I wasn't an especially nice guy. Try to kill someone often enough and he's bound to get riled.

I hit him in the nose, and some of the cartilage melted down and readjusted itself. I hit him in the mouth and heard a tooth or two snap. He spat them out and stared at them. I hauled him to his feet again and gave him another heave and watched him fall all over the floor.

The secretary never got in the way. Good Old Miss Girdled-Hips—she only came running when someone pressed the little buzzer. She was the soul of discretion. You could murder her boss in his office and she'd never leave her desk.

I PICKED him up again. He was breathing raggedly and bleeding profusely. I held him by the lapels and gave him my nastiest glare.

"Had enough?"

"Yes," he panted, fear in his eyes.

I felt a little foolish. Then I remembered the dynamite blast in Rhona's apartment, the tommy-gun in Canarsie, the three punks in East New York. I started to get mad again. That was dangerous—I didn't want to kill the bastard. I dumped him in an armchair and let him catch his breath.

"This time *I'll* talk about rewards and punishments," I told him. "You've got a client and I've got a client. Your client is trying to kill mine."

He didn't say anything.

"Your client is a man named Abe Zucker," I said. "He runs a rigged card game and fleeces heavy-money marks. He was doing fine. Then a man named Jack Blake came along and tried a few tricks of his own."

And, like a proud little schoolboy reciting the preamble to the Constitution, I read the whole bit to him. First he just sat there. Then he looked amused, and then he started to laugh.

I asked him what was so funny.

"London," he smirked. "You're a panic. A detective? You couldn't find sand in a desert."

"What are you getting at?"

"What am I getting at?" He laughed some more. "Abe Zucker running a card game," he said. "That's a wild one, London. Don't you know who Zucker is? Abe Zucker is so damned big he wouldn't waste his time on all the poker games in the country. That's not his line, London. It never was."

"What is?"

"Nothing just now. He got out of the heavy stuff a long time ago. He put his dough in legit stuff and kept it there. Abe Zucker is cleaner than you are, London. Card games!" He laughed again.

I kept my eyes on his face, trying to see what I could read there. If he was putting on an act he was good enough for Broadway...I believed him.

"Card games," he repeated. "Card games."

"Then straighten me out, Carr." He looked at me, the smile gone now.

"I wouldn't tell you the right time, London. Now get out of here—"

I started to leave when he added, "...you punk."

I picked him up, shook him like a rat. "Talk," I said.

"Let go of me."

"Carr—"

"You'll wind up in the river," he whined. "One word from me and every gun in the city will have you in his sights."

"I'm terrified."

"London—"

We weren't getting anywhere. He wasn't scaring me and I wasn't going to get anything more out of him. I didn't need him anymore, not now.

But he could get in the way.

I put him out with a good, clean shot to the jaw. It landed right and I got vibrations all the way up my arm to the shoulder. He sagged and went limp. I lowered him back into the chair, folded his hands in his lap for laughs. Then I opened the door and slipped through it.

The secretary was sitting in her swivel chair. I winked at her and she smiled her metallic smile at me. I wanted to reach over and pinch the place where her sweater bulged. I suppressed the impulse. I had enough problems.

THERE was a drugstore on the corner of Madison and 36th with a raft of phone booths. I ducked into an empty one, switched on the overhead fan, and dialed Centre Street. I asked the cop who answered to give me Jerry Gunther.

"I'm in a rush," I told him. "Just want some fast information. Know anything about a man named Abe Zucker?"

"I know the name."

"And?"

"Just a second. Lemme think... Yeah."

"Go on."

"He's an old-timer," Jerry said. "Was mixed up in everything big. Junk, numbers, women. He was one of the boys who managed to stay out of the papers, not just out of jail. But he was big."

"What's he doing now?"

"Nothing."

"Nothing he talks about?"

"Nothing at all," Jerry said. "He doesn't have to, Ed. He did what they've all been doing, made the money illegally and then sank it into legitimate business. He owns a piece of three hotels in Miami Beach and a couple of points in one of the big Vegas casinos. Plus God knows what else. I remember him now, Ed. I saw him once years ago—we had him up on the carpet for something. But that's ancient history now."

"Is he in New York?"

"Who knows, Ed. He's clean and nobody cares about him anymore. I think he's got a big place somewhere in Jersey. I wouldn't swear to it."

"Thanks."

"That all you wanted?"

"For the time being," I said. "I may have something for you later on."

I GOT OFF the phone, went to the counter, and picked up a couple of dollars worth of small change and a fresh pouch of tobacco. I had to wait for a booth—some fat old lady ducked into mine and she had enough dimes in front of her to talk all day and all night. Another booth emptied and I grabbed it. I dropped a fortune in silver into the phone and called the Continental agency in Cleveland.

It took a few minutes before I was connected with the op I'd talked to before. I didn't remember his name, and that had slowed things down. But I managed to get him on the line.

"London," I said. "You did a job for me yesterday. Remember?"

"I remember, Mr. London."

"Good. I want the same thing but in depth. I want you to check out Jack Blake and his magic shop. Find out what kind of business the shop was doing, what scale Blake was living on, if he was spending more than he was earning, everything. Run a line on his daughter. Find out what you can about her. Not just a surface job. The works."

141

"When do you want it, sir?"

"Yesterday," I said.

He laughed politely. "I mean—"

"I know what you mean." I checked my watch—it was a shade past noon. "When can you have it?"

"Hard to say. Two hours, three hours, four hours—"

"Give me an outside time. I don't know where I'll be. I want to be able to call you and find out what you've got."

He thought a moment. "Call between five and six," he said. "We'll have the works by then."

That left me with five or six hours to kill. I didn't want to go back to my apartment. A man's home is his castle, but mine might very well be under siege by now. Carr was undoubtedly conscious and undoubtedly sending up a hue and cry, shrieking mightily for the bloody scalp of some private eye named London. For the next five or six hours I wanted to get away from the world. My own place seemed like a ridiculous place to hide.

I settled on a movie. I sat in the balcony of a 42nd Street movie house, puffed on my pipe, munched popcorn, and watched *Ma Barker's Killer Brood* and *Baby Face Nelson*. I saw both pictures twice, and if you think that's a pleasant way to spend an afternoon, it's only because you've never tried it.

It was five when I left the show. I had a quick dinner at a cafeteria and used their phone to make another call to Cleveland. My op was on hand and he told me everything I wanted to know. I listened quietly, thoughtfully. At the end he said he would send me a bill and I told him that was fine.

Nothing was fine, though.

I stayed in the phone booth, sitting, thinking. I made two more calls, local ones. I talked a little, listened a little, hung up. I went on sitting in that booth until a stern-faced man came over and rapped on the door. I apologized to him and left.

The sun was dying outside, dropping behind the Jersey mud flats. The air was still too warm. I walked for a block or two, checking now and then to see if anybody was following me. Nobody was.

I thought about the way things can sneak up behind you from out of nowhere and slip you a rabbit punch. I thought about the way you can walk around wearing blinders, and then you can take the blinders off and still not believe what you see. But you see it, and sooner or later it sinks in and your world falls apart.

I hailed a cab and took a ride to a certain posh apartment house. I walked past a doorman, into an elevator. I rode up in silence. I got out and went to a door. I stood in front of it for a long time. Finally, I rang…I waited…I rang again.

TEN

SHE HAD never looked better. Even nude, with a white sheet under that flawless full-blown body and a pillow beneath that ash blond head, she had never looked better wearing a skirt and sweater. She flowed toward me like a hot river and she came into my arms and stayed there.

I let her kiss me. I ran my hands over her back, felt the firmness of her body, and I waited for something to happen inside me, something I was afraid of: A shadow of response, a flicker of desire.

It never came.

"Oh, Ed," she was saying. "I was so worried. You didn't call me all day. I was afraid. I thought something had happened to you; I didn't know what to think."

I didn't say anything.

"I tried calling you. You weren't at your apartment. I

143

must have called you a dozen times but you weren't there."

"No. I wasn't."

She turned coy, twisting in my arms and looking up at me. "You weren't with another girl, were you? I'll scratch her eyes out, Ed."

And then she turned kittenish again, burrowing her head in my chest and making little sounds.

I put my hands on her shoulders. I pushed, gently, easing her away. She looked at me, a question in her eyes.

They must have heard the slap in Canarsie. I hit her that hard, open-palmed, my hand against the side of her face. She stumbled and went down, started to get up, tripped, fell, then finally scrambled to her feet again. Her eyes said she didn't believe it.

"You dirty little liar," I snapped.

"Ed—"

"Shut up. I know the whole bit now, Rhona. All of it, from top to bottom. I got some of it here and some of it there and figured out the rest myself. It didn't take too much thinking on my part. It was all there. All I had to do was look for it."

"Ed, for heaven's sake—"

"Sit down." She looked at me, thought it over, plopped down on the orange couch.

"Jack Blake," I said, pacing like a caged tiger. "He was a card sharp, all right. And he stopped being a card sharp. Not to go straight, though. Just to change his line of work. He stopped cheating at cards but he found other ways to cheat.

"He opened a magic shop. It was a front, nothing more. I had a detective agency in Cleveland check the place out. Oh, the store was completely open and above board, all right. Only the place ran at one hell of a loss. Blake never made a nickel out of it."

I wanted a drink. Courvoisier, a lot of it, straight and in a hurry.

"So THE shop lost money," I continued, "and Blake lived high off the hog. A big house out in Shaker Heights. Trips to Vegas and Hawaii. You don't pull that kind of money out of a successful magic shop, let alone a losing proposition like the one on Euclid Avenue.

"So Blake had another source of income. It's not hard to figure out what it was, Rhona. The record of deposits to Jack Blake's checking account makes it obvious. The two of you were working a string of blackmail dodges. You were on a dozen different payrolls for anywhere from a hundred to five hundred bucks a month. It was a sweet little setup. And you weren't his daughter, either. That was another little lie, wasn't it?"

"You can't be serious—"

"The hell I can't. Jack Blake was never married. He never had a wife and he never had a kid. You were his mistress and his partner. His private whore."

She started to get up. She saw my eyes, and she must have guessed what I would do to her the minute she got to her feet. So she stayed where she was.

"His private whore." I liked the sound of it. "And his partner. The two of you were doing fine. Then you got hold of something that made all the little swindles look like small potatoes in comparison. You latched on to the prize pigeon of them all. You hooked a man named Abe Zucker."

I took a breath. "Five months ago Miltie Klugsman got in touch with Blake and told him he had the goods on Zucker. Zucker's been straight for years so he must have had something big on him, a rap the statute of limitations wouldn't cover. Something like murder.

"It doesn't much matter what it was. It was too big

for Klugsman and he was scared to work it on his own. He knew Blake was doing a land-office business in blackmail. They worked out a split. Klugsman couldn't have done too well with it—his widow isn't exactly living in style. But that's how it went. Klugsman held on to the evidence and Blake set up the blackmail gambit and Zucker paid. There was a healthy deposit to your father's—pardon me, your keeper's account five months ago. The first payment from Zucker was something like ten thousand dollars.

"Zucker must have thought it was a one-shot deal. When it happened a second time he figured out that it would be cheaper to arrange an accident for Blake than to pay him that kind of money for any length of time. And that was the end of Jack Blake, at least as far as this world is concerned.

"You told that part of it straight enough, Rhona. A few thugs went to Cleveland and beat Jack Blake to death."

I took another deep breath and looked at her, all prim and proper on the bright orange couch, all schoolgirl-lovely in green sweater and black skirt, and I tried to make myself believe it. It was true, all of it. But it still seemed impossible.

"JACK BLAKE was dead," I went on. "But this didn't faze you much. You could live without him, but you weren't going to let a big fat fish like Zucker wiggle off the hook. He was too profitable a source of income.

"Klugsman was anxious to give up. When Blake was rubbed out, Klugsman got nervous. He didn't want to play blackmail games anymore. He wanted out. So you got in touch with him and offered him a fast five grand for the evidence on Zucker. That would put Klugsman out of the picture and give him a healthy piece of change for his trouble. He went for it. It looked like easy money.

"But it wasn't," I said. "Zucker's hirelings were already onto Klugsman. They picked us up when I met him in Canarsie and they shot a million holes in Miltie Klugsman. They didn't kill me. Maybe they didn't care much at that point. They just wanted Klugsman.

"That left you in a bind. Zucker wanted to see you dead, too, because as long as you were alive he had a murder rap hanging over his head like a Sword of Damocles. You had to stay away from him and you had to get me to dig up Miltie's package of evidence. You were too damned greedy to take your life and run with it. You couldn't let go of that pile of dough."

"It wasn't like that—" she started.

"The hell it wasn't. It was like that all across the board. And you never came close to leveling with me. You started out as the woman-of-mystery and when that fell in you shifted gears as smooth as silk and turned yourself into the damsel-in-distress.

"You let me go to Brooklyn last night and almost get killed. You let me go up against Phillip Carr this morning. You never put your cards on the table and you never gave up the idea of bleeding that money out of Zucker." I paused. "You look great in a sweater. You look great out of one. And you put on one hell of an act in bed. But you're just another deceitful crook, Rhona. Nothing more."

Then it was quiet. Neither of us said a word. Finally, she blurted: "Ed—what now?"

"Now I call the police," I said. "I don't care what happens after that."

She uncoiled from the couch like a serpent. She flowed toward me again, and her eyes were radiating sex once more. She turned the stuff on and off like a faucet.

"Ed," she cooed. "Ed, I'm sorry."

"Stow it," I said.

"Ed, listen to me. I didn't trust you. I should have, I know it. And I'm sorry. But you don't have to call the police."

I stared at her.

"Listen to me, Ed. I didn't...didn't hurt anybody. I never murdered anyone. It's not my fault Klugsman was shot and I wasn't the murderer. It was Zucker and the men he hired. I just thought I could find a way to make a quick dollar.

"DON'T YOU understand? Ed, I never killed anyone. I never hurt you—I lied to you but I never hurt you. And, Ed, when we were in bed together I wasn't acting. I don't care what you think of me. Maybe I deserve it—"

"Maybe?"

"I know I deserve it. But I wasn't acting. Not in bed, not when we were making love—"

I wish someone had filmed all this. She would have won the Oscar in a walk.

"You could let me go," she pleaded. "You could call the police and give them everything you want on Zucker and Carr and the rest of them. I'll even help you. I'll tell you what I know. With that much, the police won't need Klugsman's evidence. You can even tell them about me, Ed, if it will make you feel better. Just give me a few hours' head start. In a few hours I can be out of town and they won't ever find me. Just a few hours, Ed," she pleaded.

"Ed, you owe me that much. We meant that much to each other, Ed."

She was as persuasive as a loaded gun. "I'd have given you that much," I told her. "Except for one thing."

"What?"

"The dynamite," I said. "Did you forget the dynamite, Rhona? You tried to kill me!"

148

That time I didn't slap her. It would have been superfluous. She reacted as though someone had belted her but good.

"The dynamite," I said. "It didn't make any sense at the time. I couldn't figure out why Zucker would use a cockeyed routine like that to get you out of the way, or how he knew where you were, or any of it. The dynamite had to be all your idea. Maybe you were afraid I would sell you out for Carr's ten-grand reward. Maybe you thought I was guessing too much about you.

"Anyway, you decided to get rid of me. And you were cute about it, too. You knew I'd come over here sooner or later. You left the apartment, figuring I'd eventually wander over to the closet. Then the dynamite would go off and I'd be out of your hair.

"And you would be in the clear. You were subletting the place under a phony name, and once I blew myself to hell you would just disappear, rent another apartment somewhere else. Nobody could tie you to me. You'd be all alone in the clear."

"Ed, I must have been crazy—"

"You still are if you think you can talk your way out of this, Rhona."

"Ed, I'm sorry. Ed—"

She was making sexy movements, slithering toward me. But I saw what she was really doing, moving toward the table next to the couch, heading toward her purse. I could have stopped her then and there, but I wanted to give her more rope to hang herself.

She got her hands on the purse. She was talking but I wasn't listening to a word she was saying. I watched her hands move behind her back, opening the purse, dipping inside.

She never managed to point her gun at me. My timing was too good. She dragged it out of the purse and I slapped it out of her hand and it sailed across the room and bounced around on the carpet. A .22, a woman's gun. They can kill you too.

Then she was beaten, and she knew it. I took out my own gun and pointed it at her, but I didn't even need it. She stayed put while I picked up the phone. It was too late to get Jerry Gunther at Headquarters. I called him at his home.

"Call downtown," I said. "Tell them to get a pickup order out for Phillip Carr and Abe Zucker. And get over here"—I gave him the address—"and make an arrest of your own."

He whistled softly. "This is going to get a lot of un-solved ones off your books," I said. "Maybe I'll let you do the buying during our next vital conference."

He said something unimportant. I hung up. Then I stood pointing the gun at Rhona while we waited for him.

ELEVEN

IT WAS Thursday, and I was having dinner at McGraw's, a favorite steakhouse of mine. I wasn't eating alone. There was a girl across the table from me, a girl named Sharon Ross.

She chewed a bit of steak, washed it down with a sip of Beaujolais, and looked up at me with wide eyes.

"The girl," she said. "Rhona. What's going to happen to her, Ed?"

"Not enough."

"Will she go to jail?"

"Probably," I said. "It's hardly a sure thing, though. She was a blackmailer, and there's a law against that sort of thing, but she's in a position to turn state's evidence and help them nail the lid on Zucker and his buddies. And, as she said, she never killed anyone. Only tried."

I shrugged. "And she's a girl. A pretty one. That still makes a difference in any case where you have trial by jury. The worst she can look forward to is a fairly light sentence. She could even get off clean, if she has an expensive lawyer."

"Like Phil Carr?"

"Like him, but not Carr. He won't be practicing much law anymore. He'll be in jail for everything the DA can make stick. And Zucker will stand trial, too."

I'D CALLED Sharon a day or two after the whole thing was wrapped up, and after she had cooled off from the broken-date routine. And, over our steaks, I had filled her in on most of the story. Not all of it, of course. She got the expurgated version. You never tell one girl about the bedroom games you played with another girl. It's not chivalrous. It's not even especially intelligent.

"I guess I forgive you," she said.

"For what?"

"For breaking our date, silly. Brother, was I mad at you! You didn't sound like a man with business on his mind, not when you called me. You sounded like a man who had just crawled out of bed with someone pretty. And I was steaming."

I looked away. Hell, I thought. When I called her I *had* just crawled out of bed with something pretty. But I didn't know you could tell over the phone.

"Ed?"

I looked up.

"Where do you want to go after dinner?"

"A little club somewhere on the East Side," I said. "We'll listen to atonal jazz and drink a little too much."

She said it sounded good. It did. We would listen to atonal jazz and drink a little too much, and then we would go back to her place for a nightcap. She wouldn't be a secretive blackmailer with a closet full of dynamite. She would just be a soft warm girl, and that was enough.

There might be explosions. But dynamite wouldn't cause them, and I wouldn't mind them at all.

Just Window Shopping

From the pages of **Man's Magazine**, December 1962
Art by WILLIAM ROSE, RUDY NAPPI,
LOU MARCHETTI, BEN WOHLBERG

I climbed over the back fence and hurried down the driveway. They probably hadn't seen me at the window, but I couldn't afford to take chances. The police had caught me once. I certainly did not want to be picked up again.

It was horrible when the police caught me. I admitted everything but that wasn't enough for them. They put me in a chair with the light shining in my eyes so that I could barely see. Then they started hitting me. They used rubber hoses so there wouldn't be any marks. They hit me so much

153

I nearly fainted.

The beating wasn't the worst of it, though. They called me names. They called me a sex fiend and a pervert. That hurt more than the beatings.

Because I'm not a pervert, you see. All I want to do is watch people. There's no harm in that, is there? I don't hurt anyone, and I never really bother anybody. Sometimes someone sees me watching them, and they get frightened or angry, but that's only once in a great while. I've been very careful lately, ever since they caught me.

And if they think I am a pervert, you should see some of the things I've seen. You wouldn't believe the things some of these normal people do. It's enough to make you sick to your stomach. Yet they are normal, and they call me a pervert, a Peeping Tom. I can't quite understand it. All I do is watch.

Ever since they caught me I have been very careful. That is why I left the window when the man looked at me. I'm almost sure he didn't see me, but he glanced toward the window and I hopped the fence and got away from there. Besides, it wasn't much fun watching at his window. The woman with him was old and fat, and I was getting bored with the whole thing. There was no sense in taking chance for that.

When I got out to the street I didn't know where to go. I used to have a perfect spot. A pretty, young prostitute over on Tremont Avenue who saw at least 10 men a night. I could spend night after night watching her. The backyard was dark and I had a perfect view. But one night she saw me watching.

She was nice about it and sensible, too. She didn't call me a pervert. But she said the men might notice me, that they wouldn't like it. She told me to stay away. It was a shame that I had to give up the spot, but at least she didn't call the police or anything.

But I couldn't watch there anymore, and I had to find a new spot. I walked down the street looking for a lighted window. I stopped at several places, but there was nothing much to see. There were just people sitting and talking or listening to the radio or reading or watching television.

Finally I found a house with a light on that looked promising. The back yard was dark, too, which was important. It's harder to see out from a lighted room when there is no light in the back yard.

I stood close to the window and watched. A man and woman were sitting on the bed, taking their clothes off. I watched them. The man wasn't bad looking but my attention was confined to the woman. I'm not queer, you understand.

She certainly wasn't beautiful. Better than average, though. Her face was nothing to write home about, her breasts were rather small, but she had beautiful legs and a generally nice shape all in all. I watched her undress and began to get excited. This was going to be a good night after all.

They undressed quickly, which is not the way I like it. It's better when they take a good long time about it. But they just pulled off their clothes and turned down the bed-covers. I guess they had been married for some time.

I was really excited by this time, and my eyes were practically glued to the window. Then the man stood up and walked over to the wall. He touched a switch, and the room was suddenly plunged into complete darkness. I was so mad I could have killed him. Why did he have to do a thing like that?

I stared through the window, but it was no use. The room was black as pitch. I couldn't understand it. How could he enjoy it with the lights out? He wouldn't be able to see a thing.

I was mad, and just about ready to go home and call it a night. But the little I had seen left me so excited that I could not stop there. I walked around, looking for another window.

By this time it was late and I had no idea where to go. Most of the people in the neighborhood were asleep by now. But I continued walking around, hoping against hope that something would turn up. I was just about ready to quit when I saw a lighted window on Bushnell Road. Never having been to that house before I decided to give it a try.

I approached the window and looked in. It was a bedroom window, with a woman sitting there. She had her back to me, reading a magazine. She was all alone.

ORDINARILY I would not have waited. Sometimes a woman will sit like that all night, just reading. But it was late and, having nowhere else to go, I waited. Besides, I had the feeling I would get a real show for my money.

As it turned out, I was right. She put down the magazine in less than five minutes, stood up and turned toward me. I was stunned when I got a good look at her. She was beautiful.

She was wearing a flower-print dress that made her look like a schoolgirl, but one good look at her would tell you she was nothing of the sort. Her body was far too mature for a schoolgirl's, with proud, full breasts that nearly ripped the dress apart. Her face was pretty as a model's, and her hair was that soft reddish-brown that drives me crazy. I was ready to watch her forever.

She started to undress. I stared at her greedily. There was no one else around, and my eyes studied every detail of her body. She undressed slowly, tantalizingly, slithering out of her dress and hanging it up in the closet. Finally she stood there nude, and it was worth all the waiting, worth all the walking that I had done that night. She was like a vision, the most perfect woman I had ever seen.

I thought I would have to go home then. I expected she would turn off the light and go to bed, and if she had I would have been satisfied. It was enough for one night. Instead, she walked to her mirror and began to examine herself.

It was the perfect view for me. I could see both her back and the mirror image of her front. She looked at herself, and I watched her. Then she began to dance.

It was not exactly a dance. She moved like a burlesque dancer, but there was nothing crude about it. She knew how beautiful she was, and she moved in rhythm, making a symphony of her body and watching herself as she did. It was something to watch.

Finally she stopped dancing. She slipped on a housecoat and stepped through a door. I guessed that she was going to the bathroom, which meant it was the end of the show. I could have left then, but didn't. I wanted to get another glimpse of her. She had to come back.

I stood silently at the window, waiting for her.

Suddenly a door opened. I whirled around to find her standing there, in the doorway, pointing a gun at me. "Don't move," she said. "Don't move or I'll shoot."

I froze in terror, staring down the mouth of the gun, which looked like a cannon to me. "I wasn't doing anything," I stammered. "Just watching you. I didn't hurt you."

She didn't say a word.

"Look," I pleaded, "just let me go. I won't bother you any more. I promise I'll stay away from here."

She ignored me. "I saw you in the mirror," she said. "Saw you watching me. I danced for you. Did you like the way I danced?"

I nodded dumbly, unable to speak.

"IT WAS for you," she said. "I liked your eyes on me. I liked the way you looked at me." She smiled. "Come inside."

I hesitated. Was this a trap? Had she called the police?

"Come here," she said. "Come inside. Don't be afraid."

I followed her into the house, into the bedroom. "I want you," she said. "I want you." She slipped out of the housecoat and tossed it over a chair.

"Come on," she said. "I know you want me. I could tell from the way you looked at me. Come here." She set the gun on the dresser and motioned for me to step closer. "I want you to make love to me," she said.

I walked over to her, and she threw her arms around me. "Take me," she moaned.

I pushed her away. "No," I said. "I don't want *that*. I just wanted to watch you. I wouldn't do *that*."

She pressed against me again. "I want you," she insisted. She opened her arms and I felt her hot breath on my face.

There was only one way to stop her. I picked up the gun from the dresser. "Don't come any closer," I warned. "Leave me alone."

"Don't be silly," she smiled. "You want me and I want you." She kept coming closer as I retreated.

That's when it happened—when the gun went off. The noise resounded in the small bedroom, and she crumpled and fell.

"Why?" she moaned. Then she died.

The police beat me. They beat me harder than last time, and they called me a pervert. They think I tried to rape her, but that's not true. I wouldn't do a thing like that.

Written as **SHELDON LORD**

Stag Party Girl

From the pages of **Man's Magazine**, February 1963

Art by HARRY SCHAARE, ROBERT MAGUIRE

Harold Merriman pushed his chair back and stood up, drink in hand. "Gentlemen," he said solemnly, "to all the wives we love so well. May they continue to belong to us body and soul." He paused theatrically. "And to their husbands—may they never find out!"

There was scattered laughter, most of it lost in the general hubbub. I had a glass of cognac on the table in front of me. I took a sip and looked at Mark Donahue. If he was nervous, it didn't show. He looked like any man who was getting married in the morning—which is nervous enough, I suppose. He didn't look like someone threatened with murder.

159

Phil Abeles—short, intense, brittle-voiced—stood.
He started to read a sheaf of fake telegrams. "Mark," he
intoned, "don't panic—marriage is the best life for a man.
Signed, Tommy Manville" ... He read more telegrams.
Some funny, some mildly obscene, some dull.

We were in an upstairs dining room at McGraw's, a
venerable steakhouse in the East Forties. About a dozen of
us. There was Mark Donahue, literally getting married in
the morning, Sunday, tying the nuptial knot at 10:30. Also
Harold Merriman, Phil Abeles, Ray Powell, Joe Conn, Jack
Harris and a few others whose names I couldn't remember,
all fellow wage slaves with Donahue at Darcy & Bates, one
of Madison Avenue's rising young ad agencies.

And there was me. Ed London, private cop, the man at
the party who didn't belong. I was just a hired hand. It was
my job to get Donahue to the church on time, and alive.

ON WEDNESDAY, Mark Donahue had come to my apartment. He cabbed over on a long lunch hour that coincided
with the time I rolled out of bed. We sat in my living room.
I was rumpled and ugly in a moth-eaten bathrobe. He
was fresh and trim in a Tripler suit and expensive shoes.
I drowned my sorrows with coffee while he told me his
problems.

"I think I need a bodyguard," he said.

In the storybooks and the movies, I show him the door
at this point. I explain belligerently that I don't do divorce
or bodyguard work or handle corporation investigations—
that I only rescue stacked blondes and play modern-day
Robin Hood. That's in the storybooks. I don't play that
way. I have an apartment in an East Side brownstone and I
eat in good restaurants and drink expensive cognac. If you
can pay my fee, friend, you can buy me.

I asked him what it was all about.

"I'm getting married Sunday morning," he said.

"Congratulations."

"Thanks." He looked at the floor. "I'm marrying a...a very fine girl. Her name is Lynn Farwell."

I waited.

"There was another girl I...used to see. A model, more or less. Karen Price."

"And?"

He stood and started walking around on my Oriental rug. He was tall, slim and good-looking and the expensive suit looked as though it had been designed for him.

"Karen Price," I prompted.

"She doesn't want me to get married."

"So?"

He fumbled for a cigarette. "She's been calling me," he said. "I was...well, fairly deeply involved with her. I never planned to marry her. I'm sure she knew that."

"But you were sleeping with her?"

"That's right."

"And now you're marrying someone else."

He sighed at me. "It's not as though I ruined the girl," he said. "She's...well, not a tramp, exactly, but close to it. She's been around, London."

"So what's the problem?"

"I've been getting phone calls from her. Unpleasant ones, I'm afraid. She's told me that I'm not going to marry Lynn. That she'll see me dead first."

"And you think she'll try to kill you?"

"I don't know."

"That kind of threat is common, you know. It doesn't usually lead to murder."

He nodded hurriedly. "I know that," he said. "I'm not terribly afraid she'll kill me. I just want to make sure she doesn't throw a monkey wrench into the wedding. Lynn comes from an excellent family. Long Island, society, money. Her parents wouldn't appreciate a scene."

"Probably not."

He forced a little laugh. "And there's always a chance that she really may try to kill me," he said. "I'd like to avoid that." I told him it was an understandable desire. "So I want a bodyguard. From now until the wedding. Four days. Will you take the job?"

I told him my fee ran a hundred a day plus expenses. This didn't faze him. He gave me $300 for a retainer, and I had a client and he had a bodyguard.

From then on I stuck to him like perspiration. He had a bachelor apartment in an expensive building on Horatio Street in Greenwich Village. I slept on a couch in his living room. It wasn't as comfortable as my big bed on 83rd Street. For a hundred a day plus, you expect a certain amount of discomfort.

Thursday and Friday were easy. We woke, had breakfast together, took a cab to his office. He went to work and I killed the morning and afternoon with a book or in a movie, and then I picked him up at his office and rode home with him. They were dull, quiet days. It was easy money.

Saturday, a little after noon, he got a phone call. We were playing two-handed pinochle in his living room. He was winning. The phone rang and he answered it. I only heard his end of the conversation. He went a little white and sputtered; then he stood for a long moment with the phone in his hand, and finally slammed the receiver on the hook and turned to me.

"Karen," he said, ashen. "She's going to kill me."

I didn't say anything. I watched the color come back into his face, saw the horror recede. He came up smiling. "I'm not really scared," he said.

"Good."

"Nothing's going to happen," he added. "Maybe it's her idea of a joke…maybe she's just being bitchy. But nothing's going to happen."

He didn't entirely believe it. But I had to give him credit. I wasn't too crazy about him—he cared too much about Money and Family and Doing The Right Thing to be the kind of buddy I would choose. But for a guy who was scared six shades of green he showed a lot of guts.

We went back to our pinochle game. The phone didn't ring any more, but now he played lousy pinochle. I won eight dollars from him before it was time for us to get dressed and go to McGraw's.

I don't know who invented the bachelor dinner, or why he bothered. I've been to a few of them. Dirty jokes, dirty movies, dirty toasts, a line-up with a local whore—maybe I would appreciate them if I were married. But for a bachelor who makes out there is nothing duller than a bachelor dinner.

This one was par for the course. The steaks were good and there was a lot to drink, which was definitely on the plus side. The men busy making asses of themselves were not friends of mine, and that was also on the plus side—it kept me from getting embarrassed for them. But the jokes were still unfunny and the voices too drunkenly loud.

I looked at my watch. "Eleven-thirty," I said to Donahue. "How much longer do you think this'll go on?"

"Maybe half an hour."

"And then ten hours until the wedding. Your ordeal's just about over, Mark."

"And you can relax and spend your fee."

"Uh-huh."

"I'm glad I hired you," he said. "You haven't had to do anything, but I'm glad anyway." He grinned. "I carry life insurance, too. But that doesn't mean I'm going to die. And you've even been good company, Ed. Thanks."

I STARTED to search for an appropriate answer. Phil Abeles saved me. He was standing up again, pounding on the table with his fist and shouting for everyone to be quiet. They let him shout for a while, then quieted down.

"And now the grand finale," Phil announced wickedly. "The part I knew you've all been waiting for."

"The part Mark's been waiting for," someone said lewdly.

"Mark better watch this," someone else added. "He has to learn about women so that Lynn isn't disappointed."

More feeble lines, one after the other. Phil Abeles pounded for order again and got it. "Lights," he shouted.

The lights went out. The private dining room looked like a blackout in a coal mine.

"Music!"

Somewhere, a record player went on. The record was "Stripper," played by David Rose's orchestra.

"Action!"

A spotlight illuminated the pair of doors at the far end of the room. The doors opened. Two bored waiters wheeled in a large table on rollers. There was a cardboard cake on top of the table and, obviously, a girl inside the cake. Somebody made a joke about Mark cutting himself a piece. Someone else said they wanted to put a piece of this particular wedding cake under their pillow. "On the pillow would be better," a voice corrected.

The two bored waiters wheeled the cake into position and left.

The doors closed. The spotlight stayed on the cake and the stripper music swelled.

There were two or three more lame jokes. Then the chatter died. Everyone seemed to be watching the cake.

The music grew louder, deeper, fuller. The record stopped suddenly and another—Mendelsohn's *Wedding March*—took its place.

Someone shouted, "Here comes the bride!"

And she leaped out of the cake like a nymph from the sea.

She was naked and beautiful. She sprang through the paper cake, arms wide, face filled with a lipstick smile. Her breasts were full and firm and her nipples had been reddened with lipstick. For a single moment she was outlined there, Nude Emerging From Cake, and she was almost lovely enough to override the coarseness of the entire evening.

Then, just as everyone was breathlessly silent, just as her arms spread and her lips parted and her eyes widened slightly, the whole room exploded like Hiroshima. We found out later that it was only a .38. It sounded more like a howitzer.

She clapped both hands to a spot between her breasts. Blood spurted forth like a flower opening. She gave a small gasp, swayed forward, then dipped backward and fell.

Lights went on. I raced forward. Her head was touching the floor and her legs were propped on what remained of the paper cake. Her eyes were open. But she was horribly dead.

And then I heard Mark Donahue next to me, his voice shrill. "Oh, no!" he murmured. "…It's Karen, it's Karen!"

I felt for a pulse; there was no point to it. There was a bullet in her heart.

Karen Price was dead.

TWO

LIEUTENANT Jerry Gunther got the call. He brought a clutch of Homicide men who went around measuring things, studying the position of the body, shooting off a hell of a lot of flashbulbs and taking statements. Jerry piloted me into a comer and started pumping.

He was as glad to see me as I was to see him. He's a good cop—and this was one of those times when a good cop was handy to have around. He's also a good friend. And he was happy to find out that there was someone in that dining room that he knew. As it stood, things were as chaotic as an anarchist's Utopia. Every man in the room was Chicken Little, running around and shouting that the sky was falling. And it was.

I gave him the whole story, starting with Wednesday and ending with Saturday. He let me go all the way through once, then went over everything two or three times.

"Your client Donahue doesn't look too good," he said.

"You think he killed the girl?"

"That's the way it reads."

I shook my head. "Wrong customer."

"Why?"

"Hell, he hired me to keep the girl off his neck. If he was going to shoot a hole in her, why would he want a detective along for company?"

"To make the alibi stand up, Ed. To make us reason just the way you're reasoning now. How do you know he was scared of the girl?"

"Because he said so. But—"

"But he got a phone call?" Jerry smiled. "For all you know it was a wrong number. Or the call had been staged. You only heard his end of it. Remember?"

"I saw his face when he took a good look at the dead girl," I said. "Mark Donahue was one surprised hombre, Jerry. He didn't know who she was."

"Or else he's a good actor."

"Not that good. I can't believe it."

166

He let that one pass. "Let's go back to the shooting," he said. "Were you watching him when the gun went off?"

"No."

"What were you watching?"

"The girl," I said. "And quit grinning, you fathead."

HIS GRIN spread. "You old lecher. All right, you can't alibi him for the shooting. And you can't prove he was afraid of the girl. This is the way I make it, Ed. He was afraid of her, but not afraid she would kill him. He was afraid of something else. Call it blackmail, maybe. He's getting set to make a good marriage to a rich doll and he's got a mistress hanging around his neck. Say the rich girl doesn't know about the mistress. Say the mistress wants hush money."

"Go on."

"Your Donahue finds out the Price doll is going to come out of the cake."

"They kept it a secret from him, Jerry."

"Sometimes people find out secrets. The Price kid could have told him herself. It might have been her idea of a joke. Say he finds out. He packs a gun—"

"He didn't have a gun."

"How do you know, Ed?"

I couldn't answer that one. He might have had a gun. He might have tucked it into a pocket while he was getting dressed. I didn't believe it, but I couldn't disprove it either.

Jerry Gunther was thorough. He didn't have to be thorough to turn up the gun. It was under a table in the middle of the room. The lab boys checked it for prints. None. It was a .38 police positive with five bullets left in it. The bullets didn't have any prints on them, either.

"Donahue shot her, wiped the gun and threw it on the floor," Jerry said.

"Anybody else could have done the same thing," I

167

interjected.

"Uh-huh. Sure."

He grilled Phil Abeles, the man who had hired Karen Price to come out of the cake. Abeles was also the greenest, sickest man in the world at that particular moment.

Gunther asked him how he got hold of the girl. "I never knew anything about her," Abeles insisted. "I didn't even know her last name."

"How'd you find her?"

"A guy gave me her name."

"What guy?"

"I forget. Some guy gave me her name and number. When I...when we set up the dinner, the stag, we thought we would have a wedding cake with a girl jumping out of it. We thought it would be so...so corny that it might be cute. You know?"

No one said anything. Abeles was sweating up a storm. The dinner had been his show and it had not turned out as he had planned it, and he looked as though he wanted to go somewhere quiet and die. I couldn't blame him.

"So I ASKED around to find out where to get a girl," he went on. "Honest, I asked a dozen guys, two dozen. I don't know how many. I asked everybody in this room except Mark. I asked half the guys on Madison Avenue. Someone gave me a number, told me to call it and ask for Karen. So I did. She said she'd jump out of the cake for $100 and I said that was fine."

"You didn't know anything about her?"

"Not a thing."

"You didn't know she was Donahue's mistress?"

"Oh, brother," he said. "You have to be kidding."

We told him we weren't kidding. He got greener.

"Maybe that made it a better joke," I suggested. "To have

Mark's girl jump out of the cake the night before he married someone else. Was that it?"

"Hell, no!"

Jerry grilled everyone in the place. No one admitted knowing Karen Price, or realized that she had been involved with Mark Donahue. No one admitted anything. Most of the men were married. They were barely willing to admit that they were alive. Some of them were almost as green as Phil Abeles. You could see the worry in their eyes, could imagine the wheels turning in their minds. A newspaper story, a parade of questions when they got home. *A bachelor dinner, dear? I thought you were with an important account from Omaha. Why didn't you tell me it was a bachelor dinner, dear? I think I need a new coat, dear. Don't you think so?*

They wanted to go home. That was all they wanted. They kept mentioning how nice it would be if their names didn't get into the papers. Some of them tried a little genteel bribery. Jerry was tactful enough to pretend he didn't know what they were talking about. He was an honest cop. He didn't do favors and didn't take gifts.

By 1:30, he had sent them all home. The lab boys were still making chalk marks but there wasn't much point to it. According to their measurements and calculations of the bullet's trajectory, and a few other scientific bits and pieces, they managed to prove conclusively that Karen Price had been shot by someone in McGraw's private dining room.

And that was all they could prove.

Four of us rode down to Headquarters at Centre Street. Mark Donahue sat in front, silent. Jerry Gunther sat on his right. A beardless cop named Ryan, Jerry's driver, had the wheel. I occupied the back seat all alone.

At Fourteenth Street Mark broke his silence. "This is a nightmare. I didn't kill Karen. Why in God's name would I kill her?"

169

Nobody had an answer for him. A few blocks further he said, "I suppose I'll be railroaded now. I suppose you'll lock me up and throw the key away."

GUNTHER told him, "We don't railroad people. We couldn't if we wanted to. We don't have enough of a case yet. But right now you look like a pretty good suspect. Figure it out for yourself."

"But—"

"I have to lock you up, Donahue. You can't talk me out of it. Ed can't talk me out of it. Nobody can."

"I'm supposed to get married tomorrow."

"I'm afraid that's out."

The car moved south. For a while nobody had anything to say. It was October, the air was cool, the night was quiet. There were noises off in the distance, produce trucks unloading. Part of Manhattan is always awake.

A few blocks before police headquarters Mark told me he wanted me to stay on the case.

"You'll be wasting your money," I told him. "The police will work things out better than I can. They have the manpower and the authority. I'll just be costing you a hundred a day and getting you nothing in return."

"Are you trying to talk yourself out of a fee?"

"He's an ethical bastard," Jerry put in. "In his own way, of course."

"I want you working for me, Ed."

"Why?"

He waited a minute, organizing his thoughts. "Look," he sighed, "do you think I killed Karen?"

"No."

"Honestly?"

"Honestly."

"Well, that's one reason I want you in my comer.

Maybe the police are fair in these things. I don't know anything about it. But they'll be looking for things that'll nail me. They have to—it's their job. From where they sit I'm the killer." He paused, as if the thought stunned him a little. "But you'll be looking for something that will help me. Maybe you can find someone who was looking at me when the gun went off. Maybe you can figure out who did pull that trigger and why. I know I'll feel better if you're working for me."

"Don't expect anything."

"I don't."

"I'll do what I can," I told him.

Before I caught a cab from Headquarters to my apartment, I told Mark to call his lawyer. He wouldn't be able to get out on bail because there is no bail in first-degree murder cases; but a lawyer could do a lot of helpful things for him. Lynn Farwell's family had to be told that there wasn't going to be a wedding. That alone was enough work for a whole team of lawyers.

I don't envy anyone who has to call a mother or father at 3 AM and explain that their daughter's wedding, set for 10:30 that very morning, must be postponed because the potential bridegroom has been arrested for murder.

I sat back in the cab with an unlit pipe in my mouth and a lot of aimless thoughts rumbling around in my head. Nothing made much sense yet. Perhaps nothing ever would. It was that kind of a deal.

The cab pulled up in front of my brownstone. I gave the driver a liberal tip, got the usual reactionary grunt, and went off into the night. I unlocked my apartment. Saturday's mail cluttered a coffee table. Nothing demanded reading—ads, bills, the usual junk mail. I threw the mail in a drawer and, after a mental wrestling match with no decision, I finally fell asleep.

THREE

MORNING was noisy, ugly and several hours premature. A sharp, persistent ringing stabbed my brain into a semi-conscious state. I cursed and groped for the alarm clock... turned it off. The buzzing continued. I reached for the phone, lifted the receiver to my ear, and listened to a dial tone. The buzzing continued. I cursed even more vehemently and stumbled out of bed. I found a bathrobe and groped into it. I splashed cold water on my face and blinked at myself in the mirror. I looked as bad as I felt.

The doorbell kept ringing. I didn't want to answer it, but that seemed the only way to make it stop ringing. I listened to my bones creak on the way to the door. I turned the knob, opened the door and blinked at the blonde who was standing there. She blinked back at me.

"Mister," she said. "You look terrible."

She didn't. Even at that ghastly hour she looked like a toothpaste ad. Her hair was blonde silk and her eyes were blue jewels and her skin was creamed perfection. With a thinner body and a more severe mouth she could have been a *Vogue* model. But the body was just too bountiful for the fashion magazines. The breasts were a perfect 38, high and large, the waist trim, the hips a curved invitation.

"You're Ed London?"

I nodded foolishly.

"I'm Lynn Farwell."

She didn't have to tell me. She looked exactly like what my client had said he was going to marry, except a little better. Everything about her stated emphatically that she was from Long Island's North Shore, that she had gone to an expensive finishing school and a ritzy college, that her family had half the money in the world. She was Lynn Farwell, 23 years young, and she wasn't supposed to be wearing a skirt and sweater today, no matter how well she filled them both. She was supposed to be wearing a wedding gown.

"May I come in?"

"You got me out of bed," I grumbled.

"I'm sorry. I wanted to talk to you."

"Could you sort of go somewhere and come back in about ten minutes? I'd like to get human."

"I don't really have any place to go. May I just sit in your living room or something? I'll be quiet."

There are a pair of matching overstuffed leather chairs in my living room, the kind they have in British men's clubs. She curled up and got lost in one of them. I left her there and ducked back into the bedroom. I showered, shaved, dressed. When I came out again the world was a somewhat better place. I smelled coffee.

"I put up a pot of java," she smiled. "Hope you don't mind."

"I couldn't mind less," I said. We waited while the coffee dripped through. I poured out two cups, and we both drank it black.

"I haven't seen Mark," she said. "His lawyer called. I suppose you know all about it, of course."

"More or less."

"I'll be seeing Mark later this afternoon, I suppose. We were supposed to be getting married in—" she looked at her watch "—a little over an hour."

She seemed unperturbed. There were no tears, not in her eyes and not in her voice. She asked me if I was still working for Donahue. I nodded.

"He didn't kill that girl," she said.

"I don't think he did."

"I'm sure. Of all the ridiculous things… Why did he hire you, Ed?"

I thought a moment and decided to tell her the truth.

She probably knew it anyway. Besides, there was no point in sparing her the knowledge that her fiancé had a mistress somewhere along the line. That should be the least of her worries, compared to a murder rap.

It was. She greeted the news with a half-smile and shook her head sadly. "Now why on earth would they think she could blackmail him?" Lynn Farwell demanded. "I don't care who he slept with… Policemen are asinine."

I didn't say anything. She sipped her coffee, stretched a little in the chair, crossed one leg over the other. She had very nice legs.

We both lit cigarettes. She blew out a cloud of smoke and looked at me through it, her blue eyes narrowing. "Ed," she said, "how long do you think it'll be before he's cleared?"

"It's impossible to say, Miss Farwell."

"Lynn."

"Lynn. It could take a day or a month."

She nodded thoughtfully. "He has to be cleared as quickly as possible. That's the most important thing. There can't be any scandal, Ed. Oh, a little dirt is bearable. But nothing serious, nothing permanent."

Something didn't sound right. She didn't care who he slept with, but no scandal could touch them—this was vitally important to her. She sounded like anything but a loving bride-to-be.

SHE READ my mind. "I don't sound madly in love, do I?"

"Not particularly."

She smiled kittenishly. "I'd like more coffee, Ed…"

I got more for both of us. She sipped hers and asked me if she made good coffee. I told her she did.

Then she said, "Mark and I don't love each other, Ed."

I grunted noncommittally.

"We like each other, though. I'm fond of Mark, and he's fond of me. That's all that matters, really."

"Is it?"

She nodded positively. Finishing schools and high-toned colleges produce girls with the courage of their convictions. "It's enough," she said. "Love's a poor foundation for marriage in the long run. People who love are too... too vulnerable. Mark and I are perfect for each other. We'll both be getting something out of this marriage."

"What will Mark get?"

"A rich wife. A proper connection with an important family. That's what he wants."

"And you?"

"A respectable marriage to a promising young man."

"If that's all you want—"

"It's all I want," she said. "Mark is good company. He's bright, socially acceptable, ambitious enough to be stimulating. He'll make a good husband and a good father. I'm happy."

She yawned again and her body uncoiled in the chair. The movement drew her breasts into sharp relief against the front of her sweater. This was supposed to be accidental. I knew better.

"Besides," she said, her voice just slightly husky, "he's not at all bad in bed."

I wanted to slap her well-bred face. The lips were slightly parted now, her eyes a little less than half lidded. The operative term I think, is *provocative*. She knew damned well what she was doing with the coy posing and the sex talk and all the rest. She had the equipment to carry it off, too. But it was a horrible hour on a horrible Sunday morning, and her fiancé was also my client, and he was sitting in a cell, booked on suspicion of homicide.

So I neither took her to bed nor slapped her face. I let

the remark die in the stuffy air and finished my second cup
of coffee. There was a rack of pipes on the table next to
my chair. I selected a sandblast Barling and stuffed some
tobacco into it. I lit it and smoked.

"Ed?"

I looked at her.

"I didn't mean to sound cheap."

"Forget it."

"All right." A pause. "Ed, you'll find a way to clear
Mark, won't you?"

"I'll try."

"If there's any way I can help—"

"I'll let you know."

She gave me her phone number and address. She was
living with her parents. I didn't bother asking for her number at work. North Shore girls don't work.

Then she paused at the door and turned enough to let
me look at her lovely young body in profile. "If there's anything you want," she said softly, "be sure to let me know."

It was an ordinary enough line. But I had the feeling
that it covered a lot of ground. She left my apartment. I
heard her footsteps going down the one flight of stairs
to the ground floor. I went to the window to watch her
emerge from the building and hop into a car parked next
to a fire plug. North Shore girl don't have to worry about
parking tickets. The car was an Austin Healey, black with
red leather seats. It fit the image.

I'm neither saint nor puritan. l can be bad, and she had
the equipment. But not at that hour of the morning. She
should have come around later in the day.

At 11:30 I picked up my car at the garage around the
comer from my apartment. The pimply attendant asked me
when I was going to trade it in. He always asks me this.
I always tell him to do something biologically impossible

to himself, and I always tip him a quarter. We didn't break the pattern.

The car is a Chevy convertible, an old one that dates from the prefin era. I left the top up.

The air had an edge to it. I took the East Side Drive downtown and pulled up across the street from Headquarters at noon.

They let me see Mark Donahue. He was wearing the same expensive suit but it didn't hang right now. It looked as though it had been slept in, which figured. He needed a shave and his eyes had red rims. I didn't ask him how he had slept. I could tell.

"Hello," he said.

"Getting along all right?"

"I suppose so." He swallowed. "They asked me questions most of the night. No rubber hose, though. That's something."

"Sure," I said. "Mind some more questions?"

"Go ahead."

"When did you start seeing Karen Price?"

"Four, five months ago."

"When did you stop?"

"About a month ago."

"Why?"

"Because I was practically married to Lynn."

"Who knew you were sleeping with Karen?"

"No one I know of."

"Anybody at the stag last night?"

"I don't think so."

More questions. When had she started phoning him? About two weeks ago, maybe a little longer than that. Was she in love with him? He hadn't thought so, no, and that was why the phone calls were such a shock to him at first. As far as he was concerned, it was just a mutual sex arrangement with no emotional involvement on either side. He took her to shows, bought her presents, gave her occasional small loans with the understanding that they weren't to be repaid. He wasn't exactly keeping her and she wasn't exactly going to bed in return for the money. It was just a convenient arrangement.

EVERYTHING it seemed, was just a convenient arrangement. He and Karen Price had had a convenient shack-up. He and Lynn Farwell were planning a convenient marriage. It was a funny world, I decided. People just did the "smart thing" nowadays. Love and hate were dead issues on the contemporary scene.

But someone had put a bullet in Karen's pretty chest. People don't do that because it's convenient. They usually have more emotional reasons.

More questions. Where did Karen live? He gave me an address in the Village, not too very far from his own apartment. Who were her friends? He knew one, her roommate, Ceil Gorski. Where did she work? He wasn't too clear. She got jobs now and then, jobs like, well, like popping out of paper cakes. Questions, answers. When the questions ran out we spent a few moments just looking at each other. He managed a smile.

"My lawyer's trying to get them to reduce the charge," he said. "So that I can get out on bail. You think he'll manage it?"

"He might."

"I hope so," he said. His face went serious, then brightened again. "This is a hell of a place to spend a wedding night," he smiled. "Funny—when I was trying to pick the right hotel, I never thought of a jail."

FOUR

IT WAS only a few blocks from Mark Donahue's cell to the
building where Karen Price had lived...a great deal further
in terms of dollars and cents. She had an apartment in a
red-brick five-story building on Sullivan Street, just below
Bleecker. The basement of the building housed the Sons
Of Palermo Social And Athletic Club. A group of ancient
Sicilians sat inside playing dominos and bocce. I went up
went three flights of stairs and knocked on a door.

The girl who opened the door was blonde, like Lynn
Farwell. But her dark roots showed and her eyebrows were
dark brown. If her mouth and eyes relaxed she would have
been pretty. They didn't.

"You just better not be another cop," she said.

"I'm afraid I am. But not city. Private."

The door started to close. I made like a brush salesman
and tucked a foot in it. She glared at me.

"Private cops, I don't have to see," she said. "Get the
hell out, will you?"

"I just want to talk to you."

"The feeling isn't mutual. Look—"

"It won't take long."

"You son of a bitch," she said. But she opened the door
and let me inside. We walked through the kitchen to the
living room. There was a couch there. She sat on it. I took
a chair.

"Who are you anyway?" she said.

"My name's Ed London."

"Who you working for?"

"Mark Donahue."

"The one who killed her?"

"I don't think he did," I said. "What I'm trying to find
out, Miss Gorski, is who did."

She got to her feet and started walking around the

room. There was nothing deliberately sexy about her walk. She was hard, though. She lived in a cheap apartment on a bad block. She bleached her hair, and her hairdresser wasn't the only one who knew for sure. She could have—but didn't—come across as a slut.

There was something honest and forthright about her, if not necessarily wholesome. She was a big blonde with a hot body and a hard face. There are worse things than that.

"What do you want to know, London?"

"About Karen."

"What is there to know? You want a biography? She came from Indiana because she wanted to be a success. A singer, an actress, a model, something. She wasn't too clear on just what. She tried, she flopped. She woke up one day knowing she wasn't going to make it. It happens."

I didn't say anything.

"So she could go back to Indiana or she could stay in the city. Only she couldn't go back to Indiana. You give in to enough men, you drink enough drinks and do enough things, then you can't go back to Indiana. What's left?"

She lit a cigarette. "Karen could have been a whore. But she wasn't. She never put a price tag on it. She spread it around, sure. Look, she was in New York and she was used to a certain kind of life and a certain kind of people, and she had to manage that life and those people into enough money to stay alive on, and she had one commodity to trade. She had sex. But she wasn't a whore." She paused. "There's a difference."

"All right."

"Well, dammit, what else do you want to know?"

"Who was she sleeping with besides Donahue?"

"She didn't say and I didn't ask. And she never kept a diary."

"She ever have men up here?"

"No."

"She talk much about Donahue?"

"No." She leaned over, stubbed out a cigarette. Her breasts loomed before my face like fruit. But it wasn't purposeful sexiness. She didn't play that way.

"I've got to get out of here," she said. "I don't feel like talking any more."

"If you could just—"

"I couldn't just." She looked away. "In 15 minutes I have to be uptown on the West Side. A guy there wants to take some pictures of me naked. He pays for my time, Mr. London. I'm a working girl."

"Are you working tonight?"

"Huh?"

"I asked if—"

"I heard you. What's the pitch?"

"I'd like to take you out to dinner."

"Why?"

"I'd like to talk to you."

"I'm not going to tell you anything I don't feel like telling you, London."

"I know that, Miss Gorski."

"And a dinner doesn't buy my company in bed, either. In case that's the idea."

"It isn't. I'm not all that hard up, Miss Gorski."

She was suddenly smiling. The smile softened her face all over and cut her age a good three years. Before she had been attractive. Now she was genuinely pretty.

"You give as good as you take."

"I try to."

"Is eight o'clock too late? I just got done with lunch a little while ago."

"Eight's fine," I said. "I'll see you."

I left. I walked the half block to my car and sat behind

181

the wheel for a few seconds and thought about two girls I had met that day. Both blondes, one born that way, one self-made. One of them had poise, breeding and money, good diction and flawless bearing—and she added up to a tramp. The other was a tramp, in an amateurish sort of a way, and she talked tough and dropped an occasional final consonant. Yet she was the one who managed to retain a certain degree of dignity. Of the two, Ceil Gorski was more the lady.

Or maybe I just see things backwards. I sat in the car and thought it over. Lynn Farwell bad to be called Lynn—she insisted on it. Celia Gorski got called Miss Gorski. I sat behind the wheel end watched while Miss Gorski left her building and walked to her subway stop. She was on her way uptown. Somebody with a camera would take dirty pictures ol her.

I waited until she was out of sight. Then I drove. over to the West Side Drive and beaded for Scarsdale.

At 3:30 I was up in Westchester County. The sky was bluer, the air fresher and the houses more costly. I pulled up in front of a $35,000 split-level, walked up a flagstone path and leaned on a doorbell.

The little boy who answered it had red hair, freckles and a chipped tooth. He was too cute to be snotty, but this didn't stop him. The suburbs are nice to visit, but they're no place to raise children.

He asked me who I was. I told him to get his father. He asked me why. I told him that if he didn't get his father I would twist his arm off. He wasn't sure whether or not to believe me, but I was obviously the first person who had ever talked to him this way. He took off in a hurry and a few seconds later Phil Abeles came to the door.

"Oh, London," he said. "Hello. Say, what did you tell the kid?"

"Nothing."

"Your face must have scared him." Abeles' eyes darted around. "You want to talk about what happened last night, I suppose."

"That's right."

"I'D JUST as soon talk somewhere else," he said. "Wait a minute, will you?"

I waited while he went to tell his wife that somebody from the office had driven up, that it was important, and that he'd be back in an hour. He came out and we went to my car.

"There's a quiet bar two blocks down and three over," he said, then added: "Let me check something. The way I've got it, you're a private detective working for Mark. Is that right?"

"Yes."

"Okay," he said. "I'd like to help the guy out. I don't know very much, but there are things I can talk about to you that I'd just as soon not tell the police. Nothing illegal. Just... Well, you can figure it out."

I could figure it out. That was the main reason why I had agreed to stay on the case for Donahue. People do not like to talk to the police if they can avoid it. And when sex is part of the picture, they will go to great lengths to avoid it. Cops aren't moralists. They are human, they cheat on their wives, they like to look at naked girls. But thil isn't quite the image they project to men who cheat on their wives and like to look at naked girls

If Phil Abeles was going to talk at all about Karen Price, he would prefer me as a listening post to Lieutenant Jerry Gunther.

"Here's the place," he said. I pulled up next to the chosen bar, a log-cabin arrangement.

Abeles had J&B with water and I ordered a pony of Courvoisier. I worked on my cognac while he made half of his Scotch disappear quickly. He lit one cigarette from the butt of the last and looked at me.

"I told that homicide lieutenant I didn't know anything about the Price girl," he said. "That wasn't true."

"Go on."

He hesitated, but just a moment. "I didn't know she had anything going with Donahue," he said. "Nobody ever thought of Karen in one-man terms. She slept around."

"I gathered that."

"It's a funny thing," he said. "A girl, not exactly a whore but not convent-bred either, can tend to pass around in a certain group of men. Karen was like that. She went for ad men. I think at one time or another she was intimate with half of Madison Avenue."

Speaks well of the dead, I thought. "For anyone in particular?" I asked.

"It's hard to say. Probably for most of the fellows who were at the dinner last night. For Ray Powell—but that's nothing new; he's one of those bachelors who gets to everything in a skirt sooner or later. But for the married ones, too."

"For you?" He finished his Scotch. "For you, Abeles?"

"That's a hell of a question."

"Forget it. You already answered it."

He grinned sourly. "Yes"—he lapsed into flippant Madison Avenue talk—"the Price was right." He sipped his drink, then continued. "Not recently, and not often. Two or three times over two months ago. You won't blackmail me now, will you?"

"I don't play that way." I thought a minute. "Would Karen Price have tried a little subtle blackmail?"

"I don't think so. She played pretty fair."

"Was she the type to fall in love with somebody like Donahue?"

Abeles scratched his head. "The story I heard," he said. "Something to the effect that she was calling him, threatening him, trying to head off his marriage."

I nodded. "That's why he hired me."

"It doesn't make much sense."

"No?"

"No. It doesn't fit in with what I know about Karen. She wasn't the torch-bearer type. And she was hardly making a steady thing with Mark, either. I may not have known he was sleeping with her, but I knew damn well that a lot of other guys had been making with her lately."

"Could she have been shaking him down?"

He shrugged. "I told you," he said. "It doesn't sound like her. But who knows? She might have gotten into financial trouble. It happens. Perhaps she'd try to milk somebody for a little money." He pursed his lips. "But why should she blackmail Mark, for heaven's sake? If she blackmailed a bachelor he could always tell her to go to hell. You'd think she would work that on a married man, not a bachelor."

"I know."

He started to laugh then. "But not me," he said. "Believe me, 'London. She didn't blackmail me and I didn't kill her."

I got a list from him of all the men at the dinner. In addition to Donahue and myself, there had been eight men present, all of them from Darcy & Bates. Four—Abeles, Jack Harris, Harold Merriman and Joe Conn—were married. One—Ray Powell—was the bachelor and stud-about-town of the group, almost a compulsive Don Juan, according to Abeles. Another, Fred Klein, had a wife waiting out a residency requirement in Reno.

The remaining two wouldn't have much to do with girls like Karen Price. Lloyd Travers and Kenneth Bream were as queer as rectangular eggs. If a naked boy had popped out of that wedding cake, Travers and Bream might have been involved. As it stood, they looked pretty clean.

I drove Abeles back to his house. Before I let him off he told me again not to waste time suspecting him.

"One thing you might remember," I said. "*Somebody* in that room shot Karen Price. Either Mark or one of the eight of you… I don't think it was Mark." I paused. "That means there's a murderer in your office, Abeles!"

FIVE

TUNING the car radio to WQXR, I listened to a Boccherini cello sonata while I wrestled with the traffic. It didn't exactly fit. Schoenberg or Webern, harsh and atonal, would have been more suitable as accompaniment to the glut of poorly-driven cars.

There was a parking place two doors down from my apartment. I wedged the car in place and went upstairs. The bottle of Courvoisier was right where it belong.ad. I pOured some into a glass.

It was late enough in the day to call Lieutenant Gunther. I tried him at home first. His wife answered, told me he was at the station. I tried him there and caught him.

"Nice hours you work, Jerry."

"Well, I didn't have anything else on today. So I came on down. You know how it is… Say, I got news for you, Ed."

"About Donahue?"

"Yes. We let him go."

"He's clear?"

"No, not clear." Jerry grunted. "We could have held

him but there was no point, Ed. He's not clear, not by a mile. But we ran a check on the Price kid and learned she's been sleeping with two parties—Democrats and Republicans. Practically everyone at the stag. So there's nothing that makes your boy look too much more suspicious than the others."

"I found out the same thing this afternoon."

"Ed, I wasn't too crazy about letting him get away. Donahue still looks like the killer from where I sit. He hired you because the girl was giving him trouble. She wasn't giving anybody else trouble. He looks like !he closest thing to a suspect around."

"Then why release him?"

I could picture Jerry's shrug. "Well, there was pressure," he said. "The guy got himself an expensive lawyer and the lawyer was getting ready to pull a couple of strings. That's not all, of course. Donahue isn't a criminal type, Ed. He's not going to run far. We let him go, figuring we won't have much trouble picking him up again."

"Maybe you won't have to."

"You get anything yet, Ed?"

"Not much," I said. "Just enough to figure out that everything's mixed up."

"I already knew that."

"Uh-huh. But the more I hunt around, the more loose ends I find. I'm glad you boys let my client loose. I'm going to see if I can get hold of him."

"Bye," Jerry said, clicking off.

I took time to get a pipe going, then dialed Mark Donahue's number. The phone rang eight times before I gave up. I decided he must be out on Long Island with Lynn Farwell. I was halfway through the complicated process of prying a number out of the information operator when I decided not to bother. Donahue had my number. He could reach me when he got the chance.

I poured more cognac in my glass and chewed on the stem of my pipe. I stacked records on the hi-fi and let the room fill up with music. I made a half-hearted attempt at getting interested in the Sunday *Times*. It didn't work.

Then I closed my eyes, gritted my teeth and tried to think straight.

It wasn't easy. So far I had managed one little trick—I had succeeded in convincing myself that Donahue had not killed the girl. But this wasn't much cause for celebration. When you're working for someone, it's easy to get yourself to thinking that your client is on the side of the angels.

In the movies, your client invariably is. I don't always have that kind of Hollywood luck. Once in a while l turn up a client with blood on his bands. There was a girl named Rhona who took me to bed one night and left a bomb for me the next day, and there have been plenty of them who have told me everything but the truth. But I'm still a patsy for the man who pays my fee. I'm on his side until be shows me the error of my ways. Donahue was my man now, and from where I sat he looked lamb-like in his innocence.

But nothing made much sense.

First of all, the girl. Karen Price. According to all and sundry, she was something of a tramp. According to her roommate she didn't put a price tag on it—but she didn't keep it under lock and key, either. She had wound up in bed with most of the heterosexual ad men on Madison Avenue. Donahue, a member of this clan, had been sleeping with her.

THIS DIDN'T mean she was in love with him, or carrying a flaming torch, or singing blues, or issuing dire threats concerning his upcoming marriage. According to everyone who knew Karen, there was no reason for her to give a whoop in hell whether he got married, turned queer, became an astronaut or joined the Foreign Legion.

But Donahue said he had received threatening calls from her. That left two possibilities. One: Donahue was lying. Two: Donahue was telling the truth.

If he was lying, why in hell had he hired me as a body-guard? And if he had some other reason to want the girl dead, he wouldn't need me along for fun and games. Hell, if he hadn't gone through the business of hiring me, no one could have tagged him as the prime suspect in the shooting. He would just be another person at the bachelor dinner, another former playmate of Karen's with no more motive to kill her than anyone else at the party.

I gave up the brainwork and concentrated on harmless if time-consuming games. I sat at my desk and drew up a list of the eight men who had been at the dinner. I listed the four married men, the Don Juan, the incipient divorcée and, just for the sake of completion, Lloyd and Kenneth. I worked on my silly little list for over an hour, creating mythical motives for each man.

It made an interesting mental exercise, although it didn't seem to be of much value. My mythical motives were fairly cute in some instances. I decided that either of the gay men could have shot Karen because they were jealous of her success with men. And Fred Klein, the one whose wife was divorcing him, could have tried to stop Karen from turning over evidence to his wife that would get her a heftier settlement. But the cutest motive of all was the one I assigned to the Lothario, Ray Powell. I decided Karen was blackmailing him by threatening to tell people that he *hadn't* slept with her!

So the hour bad its moments, even though it didn't lead to much. I stopped now and then to try Donahue's number. No answer. It was that kind of a day, all right. I couldn't even get a phone answered, let alone a question.

SIX

THE ALHAMBRA is a Syrian restaurant on West 27th Street, an Arabian oasis in a desert of Greek night clubs. Off the beaten track, it doesn't advertise, and the sign announcing its presence is almost invisible. You have to know the Alhambra is there in order to find it.

Alhambra's clientele, logically enough, consists primarily of Syrians and Lebanese who live in the vicinity. I went there for the first time a little over a year ago with a crazy oil-rich Arab who wanted me to help him kidnap one of hit escaped wives and Shanghai her back to Damascus. I passed up the case, but found myself a damn good restaurant.

The owner and maître d' is a little man whom the customers call Kamil. His name is Louis, his parents brought him to America before his eyes were open, and one of his brothers is a full professor at Columbia, but he likes to put on an act. When I brought Ceil Gorski into the place around 8:30, he smiled hugely at me and bowed halfway to the floor.

"*Salaam alekhim,*" he said solemnly. "My pleasure, Mist' London."

"*Alekhim salaam,*" I intoned, glancing over at Ceil while Louis showed us to a table. If she was remotely impressed, it didn't show. Nothing much showed through most of the dinner, as far as that went. We talked about important things like the weather. Otherwise she was quiet as a bar on Election Day.

The meal was flawless. We led off with a thick lentil soup. The main course was lamb, naturally, not skewered a la shish-kebab, but marinated in a teasing, subtle sauce and cooked slowly over hot coals, then served on a thick bed

of yellow rice. There was thin Syrian bread on the table,
a paste of almonds and vegetables on the side, and a few
other goodies.

Our waiter brought a bottle of very sweet white wine
to go with the entrée.

"I was bitchy before. I'm sorry about it."

"Forget it."

"Ed—"

I looked at her. She was worth looking at in a pale
green dress which she filled to perfection. The soft lighting
of the Alhambra made her face quite different from the one
I had seen in the harsh glare or an unshaded light bulb on
Sullivan Street. The planes and angles that had connoted
toughness before were now hallmarks of character and
beauty.

"You want to ask me some questions," she said, "don't
you?"

"Well—"

"I don't mind, Ed."

I gave her a brief run-down on the way things seemed
to shape up at that point. Sometimes it's clever to do this;
my own mind has a tendency to take short cuts and miss
obvious bits and pieces, and bouncing ideas off another
person will occasionally strike a valuable spark. This wasn't
one of those occasions. She heard me all the way through,
nodding from time to time and hanging on every word. By
the time I was done I hadn't come up with a new angle.

"Let me try some names on you," I suggested. "Maybe
you can tell me whether Karen mentioned them."

"You can try."

I ran through the eight jokers who had been at the
stag. A few sounded vaguely familiar to her, but one of
them, Ray Powell, turned out to be someone Ceil knew
personally.

"A chaser," she said. "A very plush East Side apartment and an appetite for women that never lets up. He used to see Karen now and then, but there couldn't have been anything serious."

"You know him—very well?"

"Yes." She colored suddenly. She was not the sort you expected to blush. "If you mean intimately, no. He asked often enough. I wasn't interested." She lowered her eyes. "I don't sleep around that much," she said. "Karen—well, she came to New York with stars in her eyes, and when the stars dimmed and died, she went a little crazy, I suppose. I wasn't that ambitious and didn't fall as hard. I have some fairly far-out ways of earning a living, Ed, but most nights I sleep alone."

Lines like that can stop a conversation cold. For a moment or two we both sat there feeling slightly awkward. Then one of us changed the subject, and we buzzed along for a while on small talk. It was easy and relaxed with no push and no tension, and we enjoyed it.

She was one hell of a girl. She was hard and soft, a cynic and a romantic at the same time. She hadn't gone to college, hadn't finished high school, but somewhere along the way she had acquired a veneer of sophistication that reflected more concrete knowledge than a diploma. With what she was, it would have been very easy for her to have turned brassy or bitchy or sour or stupid or coarse. She was none of these things. Surprisingly, she came across as a vital person, with quiet dignity.

We stuck to brandied coffee for two rounds, then stayed with the brandy but left out the coffee for two more rounds. Her eyes got slightly misty. During one of the little conversational lulls her face clouded completely.

"Poor Karen," she said. "Poor Karen."

I didn't say anything. She sat somberly for a moment,

then tossed her head so that her bleached blond mane rippled like a wheat field in the wind. "I'm getting morbid as hell," she said. "You'd better take me home, Ed."

The night was cold and gray. A haze blotted out most of the moon. The stars were hidden. We got into the Chevy and I drove downtown on Seventh Avenue. She stayed on her side of the car. I turned left at Bleecker, perked on Sullivan. We walked slowly to her building. The same old Italians ruminated ln the Sons Of Palermo Social & Athletic Club.

We climbed three flights of stairs. I stood next to her while she rummaged through her purse. She came up with a key and turned to face me before opening the door. "Ed," she said softly, "if I asked you, would you just come in for a few drinks? Could it be that much of an invitation and no more?"

"Yes."

"I hate to sound like—"

"I understand."

We went inside. She turned on lamps in the living room and we sat on the couch. She didn't run off to the bedroom to change into something more comfortable. It wasn't to be that sort of an evening. It would have been nice, but that wasn't part of the program for the night's entertainment.

The liquor cabinet was well stocked with expensive brands. Girls who live in Ceil's and Karen's world don't have to buy their own liquor. Men take care of that. I mixed bourbon and soda for her and poured cognac for myself.

She started talking about the modeling session she'd gone through that afternoon. "The money was good," she said, "but I had to work for it. He took three or four rolls of film. Slightly advanced cheesecake, Ed. Nudes, underwear stuff. He'll print the best pictures and they'll wind up for sale in the dirty little stores on 42nd Street."

"With the face retouched?" She laughed.

"He won't bother. Nobody's going to look at the face, Ed."

"I would."

"Would you?"

"Yes."

"And not the body?"

"That too."

She looked at me for a long moment. There was something electric in the air. I could feel the sweet animal heat of her. She was right next to me. I could reach out and touch her, could take her in my arms and press her close. The bedroom wasn't far away. And she would be good, very good.

Two drinks later, I got up and walked to the door. She followed me. I stopped at the doorway, started to say something, changed my mind. We said good night and I started down the stairs.

After I walked a flight I heard her door close. I stopped, just for a moment, and then proceeded out of the building. I put the Chevy's top down. It was cold out, but I was warm enough not to mind.

If she had been just any girl—actress, secretary, college girl, or waitress—then it would have ended differently. It would have ended in her bedroom, in warmth and hunger and fury. But she was not just any girl. She was a halfway tramp, a little tarnished, a little soiled, a little battered around the edges. And so I could not make that pass at her, could not maneuver from couch to bed.

A cute distinction. The old saying: *Treat a whore like a queen and a queen like a whore.* She was no harlot, but she was too close to that unhappy state to be treated as anything but a queen. A cute distinction, and frustrating.

I didn't want to go back to my apartment. It would be lonely there. I drove to a Third Avenue bar where they pour good drinks.

I called Mark Donahue. Again no answer. I let the phone ring a dozen times. Then I let the man behind the bar pour me a lot of cognac. He knew his job and did it well.

Somewhere between two and three I left the bar and looked around for the Chevy. By the time I found it I decided to leave it there and take a cab. I had had too little sleep the night before and too much to drink this night, and things were beginning to go a little out of focus. The way I felt, they looked better that way. But I didn't much feel like bouncing the car off a telephone pole or running down some equally stoned pedestrian. I flagged a cab and left the driving to him.

He had to tell me three times that we were in front of my building before it got through to me. I shook myself awake, paid him, and wended my way into the brownstone and up a flight of stairs.

Then I blinked a few times.

THERE was something on my doormat, something that hadn't been there when I left. It was not a summons or a charity appeal or a copy of the *New York Times*.

Not at all.

It was blonde, well-bred and glassy-eyed. It had an empty wine bottle in one hand and its mouth was smiling lustily. It got to its feet and swayed there, then pitched forward slightly. I caught it and it burrowed its head against my chest.

"You keep late hours," it said.

It was very soft and very warm. It rubbed its hips against me and purred like a kitten. I growled like a randy old tomcat.

"I've been waiting for you," it said. "I've been wanting to go to bed. Take me to bed, Ed London."

Its name, in case you haven't guessed, was Lynn Farwell.

We were a pair of iron filings and my bed was a magnet. I opened the door and we hurried inside. I closed the door and slid the bolt. We moved quickly through the living room and along a hall to the bedroom. Along the way we discarded clothing.

She left her skirt on my couch, her sweater on one of my leather chairs. Her bra and slip and shoes landed in various spots on the hall floor. In the bedroom she got rid of her stockings and garter belt and panties. She was naked and beautiful and hungry...and there was no time to waste on words.

Her body welcomed me. Her breasts, firm little cones of happiness, quivered against me. Her thighs enveloped me in the lust-heat of desire. Her face twisted in a blind agony of need.

We were both pretty well stoned. This didn't matter. We could never have done better sober. There was a beginning, bittersweet and almost painful. There was a middle, fast and furious, a scherzo movement in a symphony of fire. And there was an ending, gasping, spent, two bodies washed up on a lonely barren beach.

At the end she used words that girls are not supposed to learn in the schools she had attended. She screamed them out in a frenzy of completion, a song of obscenity offered as a coda.

And afterward, when the rhythm was gone and only the glow remained, she talked. "I needed that," she told me.

"Needed it badly. But you could tell that, couldn't you?"

"Yes."

"You're good, Ed." She caressed me. "Very good."

"Sure. I win blue ribbons."

"Was I good?"

I told her she was fine.

"Mmmmm," she said.

I think she fell asleep then. At least she stopped jabbering. My eyes were closed and my head was buried in a pillow and I was thoroughly exhausted, but for some reason I stayed awake awhile longer.

Thoughts.

I had a client, and my client had a girl he was going to marry, and I was in bed with her. A bad way for a private detective to behave, all things considered. They don't take your license away far that sort of thing, but it doesn't give you a very good name in the outside world.

Thoughts.

Not long ago I had been with girl named Ceil, and I liked her and she liked me, and I wanted her and the quite possibly wanted me. But, because she was an amateur slut in a not-too-refined way, nothing had happened. And then I had come home, and a rich bundle of fluff was on my doorstep, and because she was as socially acceptable as a black tie, there was no need for a hands-off policy, and without a word or a kiss or a caress, we wound up in the hay.

Thoughts.

The thoughts spread out and became more and more confused. Too much Courvoisier, too little sleep the night before, too wild a bedroom romp with little Lynn Farwell. Too much of everything to let a tired private cop think too clearly.

The thoughts turned gray and the grayness turned to black. I slept.

SEVEN

I ROLLED out of bed just as the noon whistles started going off all over town. Lynn was gone. I listened to bells from a nearby church ring 12 times; then I showered, shaved and swallowed aspirin. Lynn had left. Living proof of indiscretions makes bad company on the morning after.

I had breakfast in a lunch counter around the block on Third. I wolfed down a plateful of shirred eggs with chicken livers and drank three cups of black coffee. Outside, the sun was shining. It was a warm day, the kind to put down the top of a convertible.

Which reminded me.

I caught a cab, and the driver and I prowled Third Avenue for my car. It was still there. I drove it back to the garage and tucked it away. Then I called Donahue, but hung up before the phone had a chance to ring. Not that I expected to reach him anyway, since calling him on the phone didn't seem to produce much in the way of concrete results. But I didn't feel like talking to him just then.

A few hours ago I had been busy coupling with his bride-to-be. It seemed an unlikely prelude to a conversation.

My conscience was a pain in the neck. *Listen,* I told it, *she was no virgin and the two of them are no lovebirds. So quit casting yourself in the role of Wicked Seducer. It doesn't lit.*

All of which was quite true. The sex bit had been Lynn's idea all the way. Sunday morning she had barged into my apartment. and in the course of things she had managed to make it plain that she was available for fun and games if I was in the mood. Sunday night she was waiting at my door with the proverbial gleam in her babyblue eyes. Maybe she was a little bit of a nymph. Maybe she just liked bedroom games.

And the two of them were no Romeo and Juliet, no

Tristan and Isolde, no star-crossed lovers. He wanted to marry her, all right, but that didn't stop him from warming his bed with Karen Price until a month or so before the wedding was scheduled. It was the standard marriage-of-convenience routine. It came off well enough in French novels. In real life it didn't sound like heaven on earth.

I told myself this and some other things. I had a properly stiff battle with my conscience, and tried not to confuse the issue by dragging Ceil Gorski into it. A conscience is not a very powerful foe. I beat it down, inch by stubborn inch, and then I dropped the dime back in the slot and dialed Mark Donahue's number one more time.

I could have saved myself the trouble. He didn't answer.

Darcy & Bates wasn't really on Madison Avenue. It was around the corner on 48th Street, a suite of offices on the fourteenth floor of a 22 story building. I got out of the elevator and stood before a reception desk. A girl with bouffant hair and false breasts smiled metallically at me. I returned the smile. She asked me whom I wished to see.

"Phil Abeles," I said.

"May I ask your name?"

"Go right ahead," I smiled. She looked unhappily snowed. "Ed London," I finally said. She smiled gratefully and pressed one of 20 buttons and spoke softly into a tube.

"If you'll have a seat, Mr. London," she said.

I didn't have a seat. I stood instead and loaded up a pipe. I finished lighting it as Abeles emerged from an office and came over to meet me. He motioned for me to follow him. We went into his air-cooled office and he closed the door.

"What's up, Ed?"

"I'm not sure," I said. "I want some help." I drew on the

pipe. "I'll need a private office for an hour or two," I told him. "And I want to see all of the men who were at Mark Donahue's bachelor dinner. One at a time."

"All of us?" He grinned. "Even Lloyd and Kenneth?"

"I suppose we can pass them for the time being. Just you and the other five then. Can you arrange it?"

He nodded with a fair amount of enthusiasm. "You can use this office," he said. "And everybody's around today, so you won't have any trouble on that score. Who do you want to see first?"

"I might as well start with you, Phil."

I talked with him for ten minutes. But I had already pumped him dry the day before. Still, he gave me a little information on some of the others I would be seeing. Before, I had tried to ask him about his own relationship with Karen Price. Although that tack had been fairly effective, it didn't look like the best way to come up with something concrete. Instead, I asked him about the other men. If I worked on all of them that way, I just might turn up an answer or two.

Abeles more or less crossed Fred Klein off the suspect list, if nothing else. Klein, whose wife was in Reno, had tentatively made the coulda-dunnit sheet on the chance that Karen was threatening to give his wife information that could boost her alimony, or something of the sort. Abeles knocked the theory to pieces with the information that Klein's wife had money of her own, that she wasn't looking for alimony, and that a pair of expensive lawyers had already worked out all the details of the divorce agreement.

I asked Phil Abeles which of the married men he knew definitely had contact at one time or another with Karen Price. This was the sort of information a man is supposed to keep to himself, but the mores of Madison Avenue tend to foster subtle back-stabbing. Abeles told me he knew for certain that Karen had been intimate with Harold Merriman, and he was almost sure about Joe Conn as well.

After Abeles left, I knocked the dottle out of my pipe and filled it again. I lit it, and as I shook out the match, I looked up at Harold Merriman.

A pudgy man with a bald spot and bushy eyebrows, forty or forty-five, somewhat older than the rest of the crew. He sat down across the desk from me and narrowed his eyes. "Phil said you wanted to see me," he said. "What's the trouble?"

"Just routine," I smiled. "I need a little information. You knew Karen Price before the shooting, didn't you?"

"Well, I knew who she was."

Sure, I thought. But I let it pass and played him the way I had planned. I asked him who in the office had had anything to do with the dead girl. He hemmed and hawed a little, then told me that Phil Abeles had taken her out for dinner once or twice and that Jack Harris was supposed to have had her along on a business trip to Miami one weekend. Strictly in a secretarial capacity, no doubt.

"And you?"

"Oh, no," Merriman said. "I'd met her, of course, but that was as far as it went."

"Really?"

The hesitation was admission enough. "Listen," he stammered, "all right, I...saw her a few times. It was nothing serious and it wasn't very recent. London—"

I waited.

"Keep it a secret, will you?" He forced a grin. "Write it off as a symptom of the foolish forties. She was available and I was ready to play around a little. I'd just as soon it didn't get out. Nobody around here knows, and I'd like to keep it that way." He hesitated again. "My wife knows. I was so damn ashamed of myself that I told her. But I

201

wouldn't want the boys in the office to know."

I didn't tell him that they already knew, and that they had passed the information on to me.

Ray Powell came in grinning. He was a bachelor, and this made a difference. "Hello, London," he said. "I made it with the girl, if that's what you want to know."

"I heard rumors."

"I don't keep secrets," he said. He sprawled in the chair across from me and crossed one leg over the other. It was a relief to talk to someone other than a reticent, guilt-ridden adulterer.

He certainly looked like a Don Juan. He was twenty-eight, tall, dark and handsome, with wavy black hair and piercing brown eyes. A little prettier and he might have passed for a gigolo. But there was a slight hardness about his features that prevented this.

"You're working for Mark," he said.

"That's right."

HE SIGHED. "Well, I'd like to see him wind up innocent, but from where I sit, it's hard to see it that way. He's a funny guy, London. He wants to have his cake and eat it, too. He wanted a marriage and he wanted a playmate. With the girl he was marrying, you wouldn't think he'd worry about playing around. Ever meet Lynn?"

"I've met her."

"Then you know what I mean."

I nodded. "Was she one of your conquests?"

"Lynn?" He laughed easily. "Not that girl. She's the pure type, London. The one-man woman. Mark found himself a sweet girl there. Why he bothered with Karen is beyond me."

I switched the subject to the married men in the office. With Powell, I didn't try to find out which of them had been intimate with Karen Price, since it seemed fairly obvious they all had. Instead I tried to ascertain which of them could be in trouble as a result of an affair with the girl.

I learned a few things. Jack Harris was immune to blackmail—his wife knew he cheated on her regularly and had schooled herself to ignore such indiscretions just as long as he returned to her after each rough passage through the turbulent waters of adultery.

Harold Merriman was sufficiently well-off financially so that he could pay a blackmailer indefinitely rather than quiet her by murder; besides, Merriman had already told me that his wife knew, and I was more or less prepared to believe him.

Both Abeles and Joe Conn were possibilities. Conn looked best of all. He wasn't doing very well in advertising but he could hold his job indefinitely—he had married a girl whose family ran one of Darcy & Bates' major accounts. Conn had no money of his own, and no talent to hold a job if his wife wised up and left him.

Of course, there was always the question of how valid Ray Powell's impressions were. *Lynn? She's the pure type. The one-man woman.*

That didn't sound much like the drunken blonde who had turned up on my doorstep the night before.

Jack Harris revealed nothing new, merely reinforced what I had managed to pick up elsewhere along the line. I talked to him for fifteen minutes or so. He left, and Joe Conn came into the room.

He wasn't happy. "They said you wanted to see me," he muttered. "We'll have to make it short, London. I've got a pile of work this afternoon and my nerves are jumping all over the place as it is."

The part about the nerves was something he didn't have to tell me. He didn't sit still, just paced back and forth like a lion in a cage before chow time.

I could play it slow and easy or fast and hard, looking to shock and jar. If he was the one who killed her, his nervousness now gave me an edge. I decided to press it.

I got up, walked over to Conn. A short stocky man, crew cut, no tie. "When did you start sleeping with Karen?" I snapped.

He spun around wide-eyed. "You're crazy!"

"Don't play games," I told him. "The whole office knows you were bedding her."

I watched him. His hands curled into fists at his sides. His eyes narrowed and his nostrils flared.

"What is this, London?"

"Your wife doesn't know about Karen, does she?"

"Damn you." He moved toward me. "How much, you bastard? A private detective," he snickered. "Sure you are. You're a damn blackmailer, London. How much?"

"Just how much did Karen ask for?" I said. "Enough to make you kill her?"

He answered with a left hook that managed to find the point of my chin and send me crashing back against the wall. There was a split second of blackness. Then he was coming at me again, fists ready, and I spun aside, ducked and planted a fist of my own in his gut. He grunted and threw a right at me. I took it on the shoulder and tried his belly again. It was softer this time. He wheezed and folded up. I hit him in the face and just managed to pull the punch at the last minute. It didn't knock him out—only spilled him on the seat of his tweed pants. He sat on the floor for a few seconds without moving. Then he looked up at me and rubbed his face with one hand.

"You've got a good punch, London."

"So do you," I said. My jaw still ached.

"You ever do any boxing?"

"No."

"I did," he said. "In the Navy. I still try to keep in shape. If I hadn't been so angry I'd have taken you."

"Maybe."

"But I got mad," he said. "Irish temper, I guess. Are you trying to shake me down?"

"No."

"You don't honestly think I killed Karen, do you?"

"Did you?"

"God, no."

I didn't say anything.

"You think I killed her," he said hollowly. "You must be insane. I'm no killer, London."

"Of course. You're a meek little man."

"You mean just now? I lost my temper."

"Sure."

"Oh, hell," he said. "I never killed her. You got me mad. I don't like shakedowns and I don't like being called a murderer. That's all, damn you."

I CALLED Jerry Gunther from a pay phone in the lobby. "Two things," I told the lieutenant. "First I think I've got a hotter prospect for you than Donahue. A man named Joe Conn, one of the boys at the stag. I tried shaking him up a little and he cracked wide open, tried to beat my brains in. He's got a good motive, too."

"Ed, listen—"

"That's the first thing," I said. "The other is that I've been trying to get in touch with my client for the past too-many hours and can't reach him. Did you have him picked up again?"

There was a long pause. All at once the air in the phone booth felt much too close. Something was wrong.

"I saw Donahue half an hour ago," Jerry said. "I'm

afraid he killed that girl, Ed."

"He confessed?" I couldn't believe it.

"He confessed…in a way."

"I don't get it."

A short sigh. "It happened yesterday," Jerry said. "I can't give you the time until we get the medical examiner's report, but the guess is that it was just after we let him go. He sat down at his typewriter and dashed off a three-line confession. Then he stuck a gun in his mouth and made a mess. The lab boys are still there trying to scrape his brains off the ceiling. Ed?"

"What?"

"You didn't say anything…I didn't know if you were still on the line. Look, everybody guesses wrong some of the time."

"This was more than a guess. I was sure."

"Well, listen, I'm on my way to Donahue's place again. If you want to take a run over there you can have a look for yourself. I don't know what good it's going to do—"

"I'll meet you there," I said.

EIGHT

THE LAB crew left shortly after we arrived. "Just a formality for the inquest," Jerry Gunther said. "That's all."

Corpses are rarely pretty. A dead man does not look as though he is only sleeping. He looks dead. When the cause of death is a bullet that bas gone up through the roof of the mouth and out through the top of the skull, then Death itself is ugliness personified. I've seen Death often enough, natural or violent. I've looked into open caskets at men who have died in their sleep, and I've looked at what was left of a pretty woman when she went through the windshield of a smashed-up car.

I've never gotten used to it. Undertakers are supposed

to be acclimated to it, and doctors. Detectives should be. I don't work that way. Each death hurts.

"You're sure it's a suicide, then?"

"Stop dreaming, Ed. What else?"

What else? All that was left in the world of Mark Donahue was sprawled in a chair at a desk. There was a typewriter in front of him and a gun on the floor beside him. The gun was just where it would have dropped after a suicide shot of that nature. There were no little inconsistencies.

The suicide note in the typewriter was slightly incoherent. It read: *It has to end now. I can't help what I did but there is no way out any more. God forgive me and God help me. I am sorry.*

"You can go if you want, Ed. I'll stick around until they send a truck for the body. But—"

"Run over the timetable, will you?"

"From when to when?"

"From when you released him to when he died."

Jerry shrugged. "Why? You can't read it any way but suicide, can you?"

"I don't know. Give me a rundown."

"Let's see," he said. "You called around five, right?"

"Around then. Five or 5:30."

"We let him go around three. There's your timetable, Ed. We let him out around three, he came back here, thought about things for a while, then wrote that note and killed himself. That checks with the rough estimate we've got of the time of death. You narrow it down—you did call him after I spoke to you, didn't you?"

"Yes. No answer."

"He must have been dead by that time; probably killed himself within an hour after he got here."

"How did he seem when you released him?"

"Happy to be out, I thought at the time. But he didn't show much emotion one way or the other. You know how it is with a person who's getting ready to knock himself off. All the problems and emotions are kept bottled up inside."

I went over to a window and looked out at Horatio Street. It was the most obvious suicide in the world, but I couldn't swallow it. Call it a hunch, a stubborn refusal to accept the fact that my client had managed to fool me. Whatever it was, I didn't believe the suicide theory. It just didn't sit right.

"I don't like it," I said. "I don't think he killed himself."

"You're wrong, Ed."

"Am I?" I went to Donahue's liquor cabinet and filled two glasses with cognac. He wouldn't miss it. I gave a glass to Jerry. He was important enough so that he could drink on duty without looking over his shoulder. He sipped his drink. I drained mine.

"I know nothing ever looked more like suicide," I admitted. "But the motives are still as messy as ever. Look at what we got here. We have a man who hired me to protect him from his former mistress—and as soon as he did, he only managed to call attention to the fact that he was involved with her. He received threatening phone calls from her. She didn't want him married. But her best friend swears that the Price girl didn't give a damn about Donahue, that he was only another man in her collection."

"Look, Ed—"

"Let me finish. We can suppose for a minute that he was lying for reasons of his own that don't make much sense, that he had some crazy reason for calling me in on things before he knocked off the girl. Maybe he thought that would alibi him—"

"That's just what I was going to say," Jerry interjected.

"I thought of it. It doesn't make a hell of a lot of

sense, but it's possible, I guess. Still, where in hell is his motive? Not blackmail. She wasn't the blackmailing type to begin with, as far as I can see. But there's more to it than that. Lynn Farwell wouldn't care who Mark slept with before they were married. Or after, for that matter. It wasn't a love match. She wanted a respectable husband and he wanted a rich wife, and they both figured to get what they wanted. Love wasn't part of it."

"Maybe he wasn't respectable," Jerry said. "Maybe Karen knew something he didn't want known. There's plenty of room here for a hidden motive, Ed."

"Maybe. Still I wish you'd keep the case open, Jerry."

"You know I won't."

"You'll write it off as suicide and close the file?"

"But I have to. All the evidence points that way. Murder and then suicide, with Donahue tagged for killing the Price girl and then killing himself."

"I guess it makes your bookkeeping easier."

"You know better than that, Ed." He almost sounded hurt. "If I could see it any other way I'd keep on it. I can't. As far as we're concerned it's a closed book."

I walked over to the window again. "I'm going to stay with it," I said.

"Without a client?"

"Without a client."

We had one more short drink of Donahue's cognac. Men came to pick up the corpse. Jerry and I both turned away while they collected Mark Donahue's body and carried it off. Then, together, we left the apartment. Jerry sealed the place. We went outside.

At the curb Jerry said, "I'll have to tell his girl. She's not next of kin, but someone has to tell her."

"I'll do it."

"You want to?"

209

"I don't want to," l said. "But I will."

A MAID answered the phone in the Farwell home. I asked to speak to Lynn.

"Miss Farwell's not home," she said. "Who's calling, please?"

I gave her my name.

"Oh, yes, Mr. London. Miss Farwell left a message for you to call her at—" I took down a number with a Regency exchange, thanked her and hung up.

I was tired, unhappy and confused. I didn't want the role of bearer of evil tidings. I wished now that I had let Jerry tell her himself. I was in my apartment, it was a hot day for the time of the year, and my air conditioner wasn't working right. I dialed the number the maid had given me. A girl answered, not Lynn. I asked to speak to Miss Farwell.

She came on the line almost immediately. "Ed?"

"Yes—I."

"I wondered if you'd call. I hope I wasn't horrid last night. I was very drunk."

"You were all right."

"Just all right?" I didn't say anything. She giggled softly and whispered, "I had a good time, Ed. Thank you for a lovely evening."

"Lynn—"

"Is something the matter?"

I've never been good at breaking news. I took a deep breath and blurted out, "Mark is dead. I just came from his apartment. The police think he killed himself."

Silence.

"Can I meet you somewhere, Lynn? I'd like to talk to you."

More silence. Then, when she did speak, her voice was

flat as week-old beer. "Are you at your apartment?"

"Yes."

"Stay there. I'll be right over. I'll take a cab."

The line went dead.

NINE

WHILE I waited for Lynn I thought about Joe Conn. If one person murdered both Karen Price and Mark Donahue, Conn seemed the logical suspect. Karen was blackmailing him, I reasoned, holding him up for hush money that he had to pay if he wanted to keep wife and job. He found out Karen was going to be at the stag, jumping out of the cake, and he took a gun along and shot her.

Then Mark got arrested and Conn felt safe. Just when he was most pleased with himself, the police released Mark. Conn started to worry. If the case dragged out he was in trouble. Even if they didn't get to him, a lengthy investigation would turn up the fact that he had been sleeping with Karen. And he had to keep that fact hidden.

So he went to Donahue's apartment with another gun. He hit Mark over the head, propped him up in the chair, shot him through the mouth and replaced his own prints with Mark's. Then he dashed off a quick suicide note and got out of there. The blow on the head wouldn't show, if that was how he did it. Not after the bullet did things to Mark's skull.

But then why in hell did Conn throw a fit at the ad agency when I tried to ruffle him? It didn't make sense. If he had killed Mark on Sunday afternoon, he would know that it would be only a matter of time until the body was found and the case closed. He wouldn't blow up if I called him a murderer, not when he had already taken so much trouble to cover his tracks.

Unless he was being subtle, anticipating my whole

line of reasoning. And when you start taking a suspect's possible subtlety into consideration, you find yourself on a treadmill marked confusion. All at once the possibilities become endless.

I got off the treadmill, though. The doorbell rang and Lynn Farwell stepped into my apartment for the third time in two days. And it occurred to me, suddenly, just how different each of those three visits had been.

This one was slightly weird. She walked slowly to the same leather chair in which she had curled up Saturday morning. She did not wax kittenish this time. She sat down slowly, with her hands folded decorously in her lap and her feet planted one next to the other on the floor in front of the chair. I gave her a cigarette.

"I don't feel a thing," she said.

"Shock."

"No," she admitted. "I don't even feel shock, Ed. I just don't feel a thing.

A car passed outside, took a corner on two wheels and sped uptown on Third Avenue. I asked her if she wanted a drink. She didn't answer. I poured her one. She didn't drink it. I poured one for myself and nursed it.

"I wasn't in love with him" she said. "You knew that, of course."

"I gathered as much."

"It wasn't a well-kept secret, was it? I told you that much before I told you my name, almost. Of course I was on the make for you at the time. That may have had something to do with it."

She looked at her drink but didn't touch it. Slowly, softly she said, "After the first death there is no other."

"Dylan Thomas wasn't talking about dead lovers," I said.

Her eyes showed surprise. "You know the poem!" she

said. "I didn't think private eyes were literate."

"They taught me how to read in grade school. Old habits die hard."

"Yes, they do."

There was a minute of silence. Just as I was about to prompt her into speaking, she repeated, "After the first death there is no other." She sighed. "When one death affects you completely, then the deaths that come after it don't have their full effect. Do you follow me?"

I nodded. "When did it happen?" I asked.

"Four years ago. I was in college then."

"A boy?"

"Yes."

She looked at her drink, then drained it.

"I was 19 then. Pure and innocent. A popular girl who dated all the best boys and had a fine time. Then I met him. Ray Powell introduced us. You probably met Ray. He worked in the same office as Mark."

I nodded. That explained one contradiction—Ray's referring to Lynn as the pure type, the one-man woman. When he had known her, the shoe fit. Since then she had outgrown it.

"I started going out with John and all at once I was in love. I had never been in love before. I've never been in love since. It was something." For a shadow of an instant a smile crossed her face, then disappeared. "I can't honestly remember what it was like. Being in love, that is. I'm not the same person. That girl could love; I can't."

She reached out a hand for another cigarette. I gave her one, she took two drags and set the cigarette in an ashtray. Smoke rose from it in a long thin column that reached almost to the ceiling.

"He was going to pick me up and something went wrong with his car. The steering wheel or something like that. He was going around a turn and the wheels wouldn't straighten out and—

"I changed after that. At first I just hurt. All over. And then the callous formed, the emotional callous to keep me from going crazy, I suppose." She picked up a cigarette and puffed on it nervously then stubbed it out. "You know what bothered me most? We never slept together. We were going to wait until we were married. See what a corny little girl I was?

"But I changed, Ed. I thought that at least I could have given him that much before he died. And I thought about that, and maybe brooded about it, and something happened inside me." She almost smiled. "I'm afraid I became a little bit of a tramp, Ed. Not just now and then, like last night. A tramp. I went to Ray Powell and lost my virginity, and then I made myself a one-woman welcoming committee for visiting Yale boys."

Her face filled up with memories. "I'm not that bad any more. And I don't honestly feel John's death either, to be truthful. It happened a long time ago, and to a different girl."

"I don't think Mark Donahue killed himself," I said, "or the girl. I think he was framed and then murdered."

"It doesn't matter."

"Doesn't it?"

"No," she said, sadly, vacantly. "It should, I know. But it doesn't, Ed." She stood up. "Do you know why I really wanted to come here?"

"To talk."

"Yes. I've learned to pretend, you see. And I intend to pretend, too. I'll be the very shocked and saddened Miss Farwell now. That's the role I have to play." Another too-brief smile. "But I don't have to play that role with you, Ed. I wanted to say what I felt if only to one person. Or what I

214

didn't feel." She rose to leave.

"And now I'll wear imitation widow's weeds for a while, and then I'll find some other bright young man to marry. Goodbye, Ed London."

I ALMOST forgot about the date with Ceil. I'd made it the night before instead of the pass I would have preferred to make. When I got there, she said she was tired and hot and didn't feel like dressing.

"The Britannia is right down the block," she said. "And I can go there like this."

She was wearing slacks and a man's shirt. She didn't look mannish, though. That would have been slightly impossible. I asked her what the Brittanie was.

"A fish-and-chips place. Cheap, fast, easy, and good. Or don't you like fish-and-chips?"

"I love them."

"Good."

We walked down the block to a hole in the wall with a sign that said, appropriately, FISH AND CHIPS. There were half a dozen small tables in a room decorated with travel posters of Trafalgar Square and Buckingham Palace and every major British tourist attraction with the possible exception of Diana Dors. We sat at a small table and ordered fish-and-chips and bottles of Guinness.

I said, "Donahue's dead."

"I know. I heard it on the radio."

"What did they say?"

"Suicide. He confessed to the murder and shot himself. Isn't that what happened?"

"I don't think so." I signaled the waiter for two more bottles of Guinness. Then I used Ceil for a sounding board again, bringing her up to date on what had happened since I'd seen her last. I left out the little interlude with Lynn.

It might have certain relevance when placed in the proper context, but I wasn't that obsessed with telling all the facts.

"It's possible that someone—probably Conn—killed Donahue," I added. "The door to his apartment was locked when the police got there, but it's one of those spring locks. The inside bolt wasn't turned. Conn could have gone there as soon as he learned Mark was released, then shot him and locked the door as he left."

"How could he know Mark was released?"

"A phone call to police Headquarters, or a call to Mark. That's no problem."

"How about the time? Maybe Conn has an alibi."

"I'm going to check that tomorrow," I said. "That's why I would have liked to see Jerry Gunther keep the file open on the case. Then he could have questioned Conn. The guy threw punches at me once already. I don't know if I can take him a second time."

She grinned. Then her face sobered. "Are you sure it was Conn? You said Abeles had the same motive."

"He's also got an alibi."

"A good one?"

"Damn good. I'm his alibi. I was with him in Scarsdale that afternoon, and I called Donahue's apartment as soon as I got back to town, and by that time Donahue was dead. Phil Abeles would have needed a jet plane to pull it off. Besides, I can't see him as the killer."

"And you can see Conn?"

"That's the trouble," I said. "I can't. Not really."

WE DRANK up. I paid our check and we left. We walked a block to Washington Square and sat on a bench. I started to smoke my pipe when I heard a sharp intake of breath and turned to stare at Ceil.

"Oh," she said. "I just had a grisly idea."

"What?"

"It's silly. Like an Alfred Hitchcock television show. I thought maybe Karen really did make those phone calls to him, not because she was jealous but just to tease him, thinking what a gag it would be when she popped out of the cake at his bachelor dinner. And then the gag backfires and he shoots her because he's scared she wants to kill him." She laughed. "I've got a cute imagination," she said. "But I'm not much of a help, am I?"

I didn't answer her. My mind was off on a limb somewhere. I closed my eyes and saw the waiters wheeling the cake out toward the center of the room. Stripper music playing on a phonograph. A girl bursting from the cake, nude and lovely. A wide smile on her face—

"Ed, what's the matter?"

Most of the time problems are solved by simple trial and error, a lot of legwork that pays off finally. Other times all the legwork in the world falls flat, and it's like a jigsaw puzzle where you suddenly catch the necessary piece and all the others leap into place. This was one of those times.

"You're a genius!" I told Ceil.

"You don't mean it happened that way? I—"

"Oh, no. Of course not. Donahue didn't kill Karen—" I stood.

"Hey, where are you going?" Ceil asked.

"Gotta run," I said. "Can't even walk you home. Tomorrow," I said. "We'll have dinner, okay?"

I didn't hear her answer. I didn't wait for it. I raced across the park and jumped into the nearest cab.

I called Lynn Farwell from my apartment. She was back in her North Shore home, and life had returned to her voice. "I didn't expect to hear from you," she said. "I suppose you're interested in my body, Ed. It wouldn't be decent so soon after Mark's death, you know. But you may be able to persuade me—"

"Not your body," I said. "Your memory. Can you talk now? Without being overheard?"

She giggled lewdly. "If I couldn't, I wouldn't have said what I did. Go ahead, Mr. Detective."

I asked questions. She gave me answers. They were the ones I wanted to hear.

I strapped on a shoulder holster and jammed a gun into it. I covered up the shoulder rig with a sports jacket. The jacket didn't match the slacks I was wearing, but I wasn't too worried about little niceties like that. I had more important things to worry about than sartorial dissonance.

My cabby was waiting outside. I jumped into the back and gave him an address. We got going.

TEN

IT WAS a luxury apartment building in an expensive neighborhood. A prestige address. The doorman, all done up in miles of gold brocade, wanted to know who I was. I flipped open my wallet and showed him a badge that said Special Officer. It was the kind you get by sending two boxtops and a quarter to General Mills. The doorman saluted sharply and I went past him.

The door to Powell's apartment was locked. I rang the bell once. No one answered. I waited a few minutes, then took out my pen knife and went to work on the lock. Like the locks in all decent buildings in New York, this was one of the burglar-proof models. And, like just 99 percent of them, it wasn't burglar-proof. It took half a minute to open.

I turned the knob. Then I eased the gun from my shoulder holster and shoved the door open. I didn't need the gun just then. The room was empty.

But the apartment wasn't. I heard noises from another room, people noises, sex noises. A man's voice and a girl's voice. The man was saying he heard somebody in the living room. The girl was telling him he was crazy. He said he would check. Then there were footsteps, and he came through the doorway, and I pointed the gun at him.

I said, "Stay right there, Powell."

He looked a little ridiculous. He was wearing a bathrobe, his feet were bare, and it was fairly obvious that he had been interrupted somewhere in the middle of his favorite pastime. I kept the gun on him and watched his eyes. He was good—damned good. The eyes showed fear, outrage, surprise. Nothing else. Not the look of a man in a trap.

"If this is some kind of a joke—"

"It's no joke."

"Then what the hell is it?"

"The end of the line," I said. "You made a hell of a try. You almost got away with it."

"I don't know what you're driving at, London. But—"

"I think you do."

She picked that moment to wander into the room. She was a redhead with her hair messed. One of the buttons on her blouse was buttoned wrong. She walked into the room, wondering aloud what the interruption was about, and then she saw the gun and her mouth made a little *O*.

She said, "Maybe I should of stood in the other room."

"Maybe you should go home," I snapped.

"Oh," she said. "Yes, that's a very good idea." She moved to her left and sort of backed around me, as if she wanted to keep as much distance as possible between her well-constructed body and the gun in my hand. "I think you're right," she said. "I think I should go home... And you don't have to worry about me."

"Good."

"I should tell you I have no memory at all," she said. "I never came here, never met you, never saw your face, and I cannot possibly remember what you look like. It is terrible, my memory."

"Good," I said.

"Living I like very much better than remembering. Goodbye, Mr. Nobody."

The door slammed, and Ray Powell and I were alone. He glared at me.

"What in hell do you want, exactly?"

"To talk to you."

"You need a gun for that?"

"Probably."

He grinned disarmingly. "Guns make me nervous."

"They never did before. You've got a knack for getting hold of unregistered guns, Powell. Is there another one in the bedroom?"

"I don't get it," he said. He scratched his head. "You must mean something, London. Spit it out."

"Don't play games."

"I—"

"Cut it," I said. "You killed Karen Price. You knew she was going to do the cake bit because you were the one who put the idea in Phil Abeles' head."

"Did he tell you that?"

"He's forgotten. But he'll remember with a little prompting. You set her up and then you killed her and tossed the gun on the floor. You figured the police would arrest Donahue, and you were right. But you didn't think they would let him go. When they did, you went to his place with another gun. He let you in. You shot him, made it look like suicide, and let the one death cover the other."

He shook his head in wonder. "You really believe this?"

"I know it."

"I suppose I had a motive," he said musingly. "What, pray tell, did I have against the girl? She was good in bed, you know. I make it a rule never to kill a good bed partner if I can help it." He grinned. "So why did I kill her?"

"You didn't have a thing against her," I said.

"My point exactly. I—"

"You killed her to frame Donahue," I added. "You got to Karen Price while the bachelor dinner was still in the planning stage. You hired her to make a series of calls to Donahue, jealousy calls threatening to kill him or otherwise foul up his wedding. It was going to be a big joke—she would scare him silly; and then for a capper she would pop out of the cake as naked as the truth and tell him she was just pulling his leg.

"But you topped the gag. She popped out of the cake covered with a smile and you put a bullet in her and left Donahue looking like the killer. Then, when you thought he was getting off the hook, you killed him. Not to cover the first murder—you felt safe enough on that score...because you really didn't have a reason to kill the girl herself. You killed Donahue because he was the one you wanted dead all along."

Powell was still grinning. Only not so self-assuredly now. In the beginning, he hadn't been aware of how much I knew. Now he was learning and it wasn't making him happy.

"I'll play your game," he said. "I killed Karen, even though I didn't have any reason. Now why did I kill Mark? Did I have a reason for that one?"

"Sure."

"What?"

"For the same reason you hired Karen to bother Donahue," I said. "Maybe a psychiatrist could explain it better. He'd call it transference."

"Go on."

"You wanted Mark Donahue dead because he was going to marry Lynn Farwell. And you don't want anybody to marry Lynn Farwell. Powell, you'd kill anybody who tried."

WE WERE getting down to the wire now. The grin had faded almost completely. I could reed other things in his face now. He was trying to measure the distance separating us, calculating whether he could jump me before I had time to shoot him.

"Keep talking," he said.

"How am I doing so far?"

"Oh, you're brilliant, London. I suppose I'm in love with Lynn?"

"In a way."

"That's why I've never asked her to marry me. And why I bed down anything else that gets close enough to jump."

"That's right."

"You're out of your mind, London."

"No," I said. "But you are." I took a breath. "You've been in love with Lynn for a long time. Four years, anyway. It's no normal love, Powell, because you're not a normal person. Lynn's part of a fixation of yours. She's sweet and pure and unattainable in your mind. You don't want to possess her completely because that would destroy the illusion. Instead you compensate by proving your virility with any available girl. But you can't let Lynn marry someone else. That would take her away from you. You don't want to have her—except for an occasional evening, maybe—but you won't let anyone else have her."

He was tottering on the edge now...trying to take a step toward me and then backing off. I had to push him over that edge. If he cracked, then he would crack wide open. If he held himself together he might wriggle free. I knew damn well he was guilty, but there wasn't enough evidence to present to a jury. I had to make him crack.

"First I'm a double murderer," Powell said. "Now I'm a mental case. I don't deny that I like Lynn. She's a sweet, clean, decent girl. But that's as far as it goes."

"Is it?"

"Yes."

"Donahue's the second man who almost married her. The first one was four years ago. Remember John? You introduced the two of them. That was a mistake, wasn't it?"

"He wouldn't have been good for her. But it didn't matter. I suppose you know he died in a car accident."

"In a car, yes. Not an accident. You gimmicked the steering wheel. Then you let him kill himself. You got away clean with that one, Powell."

For a moment the mask slipped. That was going back far, to a murder he had probably almost forgotten. It had been a shot in the almost-dark, too, but it had been right. His face showed it. He stared at me for one moment with naked hate in his eyes. Then the mask dropped back into place. I hadn't cracked him yet. I was close, but he was still able to compose himself.

"It was an accident," he exclaimed. "Besides, it happened a long time ago. I'm surprised you even bother mentioning it."

I ignored his words. "The death shook Lynn up a lot," I said. "It must have been tough for you to preserve your image of her. The sweet and innocent thing turned into a round-heeled little nymph for a while."

"That's a damned lie."

"It is like hell. And about that time you managed to have your cake and eat it, too. You kept on thinking of her as the unattainable ideal. But that didn't stop you from taking her virginity, did it? You ruined her, Powell!"

He was getting closer to the edge. His face was white and his hands were hard little fists. The muscles in his neck were drum-tight.

"I never touched her!"

"Liar!" I was shouting now. "You ruined that girl, Powell!"

"Damn you, I never touched her! Nobody did, damn you! She's still a virgin! She's still a virgin!"

I took a breath. "The hell she is," I yelled. "I had her last night, Powell. She came to my room all hot to trot and I bedded her until she couldn't see straight."

His eyes were wild.

"Did you hear me, Powell? I had *your girl* last night. I had Lynn, Powell!"

And that cracked him.

He charged me like a wild man, his whole body coordinated in the spring. I stepped back, swung aside. He tried to turn and come toward me but his momentum kept him from pulling it off. By the time he got back on the right track, my hand had gone up and come down. The barrel of the gun caught him just behind the left ear. He took two more little steps, carried along by the sheer force of his rush. Then he folded up and went out like an ebbing tide.

He wasn't out long. By the time Jerry Gunther got there, flanked by a pair of uniformed cops, Powell was babbling away a mile a minute, spending half the time confessing to the three murders and the other half telling anyone who would listen that Lynn Farwell was a saint.

They started to put handcuffs on him. Then they changed their minds and bundled him up in a straitjacket.

ELEVEN

"I GUESS I missed my calling," Ceil said. "I should have been a detective. I probably would have flopped there, too, but the end might have been different. We all know what girls become when they don't make it as actresses. What do lousy detectives turn to?"

"Cognac," I said. "Pass the bottle."

She passed and I poured. We were in her apartment on Sullivan Street. It was Tuesday night, Ray Powell had long since finished confessing, and Ceil Gorski had just proved to me that she could cook a good meal.

"You figured it out beautifully," she said. "But do I get an assist on the play?"

"Easily." I tucked tobacco into my pipe, lit up. "You managed to get my mind working. Powell was a genius at murder. A certifiable psychotic, but also a genius. He set things up beautifully. First of all, the frame couldn't have been neater. He very carefully set up Donahue with means, motive and opportunity. Then he shot the girl and left Donahue on the hook."

I worked on the cognac. "The neat thing was this—if Donahue managed to have an alibi, if by some chance somebody was watching him when the shot was fired, Powell was still in the clear. He himself was one of the few men in the room with no conceivable motive for wanting Karen Price dead."

Ceil moved a little closer on the couch. I put an arm around her. "Then the way he got rid of Donahue was sheer perfection," I continued. "He made it look enough like suicide to close the case as far as the police were concerned. And Jerry Gunther isn't an easy man to bulldoze. He's thorough. But Powell made it look good."

"You didn't swallow it."

"That's because I play hunches. Even so, I was up a

225

tree by then. Because the murder had a double edge to it. Even if he muffed it somehow, even if it didn't go over as suicide, Donahue would be dead and he would be in the clear. Because there was only one way to interpret it—Donahue had been killed by the man who killed Karen Price, obviously, and had been killed so that the original killing would go unsolved. That made me suspect Joe Conn and never let me guess at Powell, not even on speculation. Even with the second killing he hid the fact that Donahue and not Karen was the real target."

"And that's where I came in," she said happily.

"That's exactly where you came in," I agreed. "You and your active imagination. You thought how grim it would be if Karen had only been playing a joke with those phone calls. And that was the only explanation in the world for the calls. I had to believe Donahue was getting the calls, and that Karen was making them. A disguised voice might work once, but she'd called him a few times.

"That left two possibilities, really. She could be jealous—which seemed contrary to everything I had learned about her. Or it could be a gag. But if she was jealous, then why in hell would she take the job popping out of the cake? So it had to be a gag, and once it was a gag, I had to guess why someone would put her up to it. And from that point—"

"It was easy."

"Uh-huh. It was easy."

She snuggled closer. I liked her perfume. I liked the feel of her body beside me.

"It wasn't that easy," she said. "You know what? I think you're a hell of a good detective. And you know what else?"

"What?"

"I also think you're a rotten businessman."

I smiled. "Why?"

"Because you did all that work and didn't make a dime out of it. You got a retainer from Donahue, but that didn't even cover all the time you spent before Karen was killed, let alone the time since then. And you probably will never collect."

"I'm satisfied."

"Because justice has been done?"

"Partly. Also because I'll be rewarded."

She upped her eyebrows. "How? You won't make another nickel out of the case, will you?"

"No."

"Then—"

"I'll make something more important than money."

"What?"

She was soft and warm beside me. And it was our third evening together. Not even an amateur tramp could mind a pass on a third date.

"What are you going to make?" she asked, innocently.

I took her face between my hands and kissed her. She closed her eyes and purred like a happy cat.

"You," I said.

Twin Call Girls

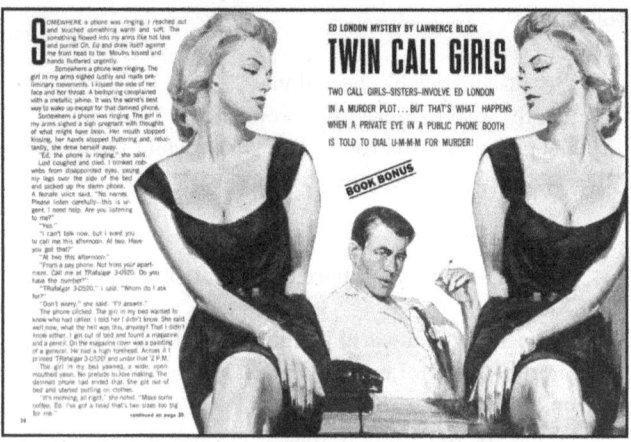

From the pages of **Man's Magazine**, August 1963

Art by MORT ENGEL

Somewhere a phone was ringing. I reached out and touched something warm and soft. The something flowed into my arms like hot lava and purred *Oh, Ed* and drew itself against me from head to toe. Mouths kissed and hands fluttered urgently.

Somewhere a phone was ringing. The girl in my arms sighed lustily and made preliminary movements. I kissed the side of her face and her throat. A bedspring complained with a metallic whine. It was the world's best way to wake up except for that damned phone.

Somewhere a phone was ringing. The girl in my arms sighed a sigh pregnant with thoughts of what might have been. Her mouth stopped kissing, her hands stopped flut-

228

tering and, reluctantly, she drew herself away.

"Ed, the phone is ringing," she said.

Lust coughed and died. I blinked cobwebs from disappointed eyes, swung my legs over the side of the bed and picked up the damn phone.

A female voice said, "No names. Please listen carefully—this is urgent. I need help. Are you listening to me?"

"Yes."

"I can't talk now, but I want you to call me this afternoon. At two. Have you got that?"

"At two this afternoon."

"From a pay phone. Not from your apartment. Call me at TRafalgar 3-0520. Do you have the number?"

"TRafalgar 3-0520," I said. "Whom do I ask for?"

"Don't worry," she said. "I'll answer."

The phone clicked. The girl in my bed wanted to know who had called. I told her I didn't know. She said well now, what the hell was this, anyway? That I didn't know either. I got out of bed and found a magazine and a pencil. On the magazine cover was a painting of a general. He had a high forehead. Across it I printed 'TRafalgar 3-0520' and under that '2 PM'

The girl in my bed yawned, a wide, open-mouthed yawn. No prelude to love making. The damned phone had ended that. She got out of bed and started putting on clothes.

"It's morning, all right," she noted. "Make some coffee, Ed. I've got a head that's two sizes too big for me."

Ceil Gorski had other things that were pretty big, too; she was a dark-roots blonde of equally good company in and out of the hay. Somebody had killed her roommate about a year ago, and Ceil had helped me crack the case. Last night she had helped me crack a bottle of cognac.

229

I made a pot of coffee which we drank in the living room. She asked about the phone call.

"Probably some crank," I said. "All cloak and dagger. That's one trouble with being a detective. You get a lot of idiot phone calls."

"And all at the wrong time, Ed. You're supposed to call her back. You going to?"

"Probably."

"And the number'll turn out to be the YWCA, or something. You lead a rough life."

I told her it had its moments.

"Like last night," she said, grinning seductively. "Last night was fun. I got pretty smashed, though. Did I do anything silly?"

"You said we ought to get married."

"Well that's not so silly." She finished her coffee. "I better get out of here. I've got a job lined up at one, and I have to look erotic by then. A photographer wants to take pictures of me in the nude."

"I don't blame him."

She was that kind of model—a little cheesecake... sometimes things that were a little rougher.

I walked her down a flight of stairs and out into the morning sun. Then I put her into a cab. A fine woman, Ceil Gorski. A little soiled around the edges, a little tarnished, but still smooth and sweet inside. Enough so that I was still angry with the voice on the telephone.

AT 2 PM I called TRafalgar 3-0520. It wasn't the YWCA. The same voice answered on the first ring, saying, "Ed London?"

"Yes. Who is this?"

A sigh of relief. "I'm in terrible trouble," she said. "Somebody is trying to kill me. I need your help. I'm

230

scared."

I started to tell her to come to my place, but she cut me off. "I can't go there," she said.

"Why not?"

"It's not safe. Listen, I'll meet you in Central Park. Is that all right?"

"It's a pretty big place. Want to narrow it down a little?"

"There's an entrance to the park at 94th Street and Fifth Avenue. There are two paths. Take the one that bears uptown. A little ways up there's a pond, and the path divides to go around the pond. I'll be sitting on one of the benches on the uptown side of the pond."

"How do I recognize you?"

"I'm blonde. Not too tall. Don't worry, just come. It never gets crowded there. I'll be alone. I'll...I'll recognize you, Mr. London."

"What time?"

"Four-thirty. Please be on time. I'm very scared."

I HAD A sandwich in the restaurant where I'd made the phone call, then walked back to my apartment. It's on 83rd Street near Third Avenue, not too far from the part of the park where I was supposed to meet my mystery woman. She still hadn't told me her name. I smoked a pipe on the way back to my place and thought about Central Park and all the wildlife that call it home... Yes, New York is a summer festival.

Any other time the setup would have worried me a little. If I had been on a case, say, the meet-me-in-the-park approach would look an awful lot like a perfect way to turn one Edward London into a sitting duck.

But I wasn't working on anything at the moment. It's a funny business—you can have six or seven clients one week and then no clients for a month. There's nothing to do but take an occasional farm-out job from one of the big agencies or sit around on your tail and improve your mind.

I had been sitting on my tail for two weeks running. Any work at all looked good by now. There might be a client on that bench in Central Park, but I would just have to go and see for myself.

I sat in my apartment until four, thumbing through Sutherland's text on criminology and listening to a stack of Vivaldi records. The reading was dull but the music sounded cool and crisp. At four I stuffed tobacco into a pipe and went outside into the dry heat of a New York summer afternoon, looking for a wench on a bench.

She had picked a quiet part of the park. I walked in through the 94th Street entrance and passed a covey of maids pushing carriages. They milled around near the entrance and gossiped about their employers. I took the path that led uptown and walked toward the pond.

The sun shined brightly now and the sky was as clear as it gets over Manhattan, a sort of steely gray with occasional hints of blue. I knocked the dottle out of my pipe and stuck the mature man's pacifier in a jacket pocket. I patted the front of my jacket. There was another pacifier there, a .38 snug in a shoulder rig. The bulk of the gun was reassuring in the loneliness of Central Park.

The pond came into view, flat, calm and stagnant. Three beer cans and two ducks floated on the water. I thought of sitting ducks. I started walking around the uptown side of the pond and then I saw her, sitting alone on a bench and not looking at me. I wanted to call her name but she had never gotten around to telling me what it was.

"Hello there," I called.

No answer and no glance. I looked at my watch. It was 4:30, I was right on time and she was the only person around. She was blonde, young and dressed nicely. I walked faster. She still did not look at me. I hurried along, worried now, and I reached her and looked at her and saw, finally, why she had not moved.

I was on time. But someone had gotten to her first, had found her before me.

Her hair was done page boy style and it framed her face in gold. She had red lips, a button nose and skin that was cool and would grow colder—because she had a little round hole in the middle of her forehead with powder burns around it.

Once she had been pretty, and once she had been frightened...and now she was dead.

TWO

I LOOKED around. The park was as still as the girl. I went through the inane formality of holding her cool and limp wrist and feeling for a pulse. There was none. There is rarely a pulse in the wrist of a girl who has been shot through the middle of the forehead. She had been dead 15 or 20 minutes. I let go of her wrist and it flopped into her lap.

If she had a purse, someone had snatched it. No identification. I did not know her name, who had scared her, who had followed her, who had killed her or why. She had wanted help, my help, but I did not get to her in time.

I didn't want to leave her on the bench. There is something ineffably discordant about a lone corpse left to cool and stiffen on a park bench. But I turned and walked back around the edge of the pond and down the path. I stopped once to look back at her. She did not look dead from a distance. She looked like a young girl sitting quietly, waiting to meet a suitor.

I walked to Fifth Avenue, down to 86th Street, east

toward home. There was a bar on Madison. I stopped there to use the phone booth. I dialed Centre Street police Head-quarters. Some sergeant answered the phone.

"There's a body in Central Park, a dead girl," I said, and quickly gave him the location. He kept trying to in-terrupt, to get my name, to find out more. But I had said everything I wanted to say. So I put the phone on the hook, had a slug of cognac at the bar and left for home...

IT WAS no time for music or for books. I put the records away and found a bottle of Courvoisier sitting silent on a shelf. I poured a short drink and swallowed it down, poured a long drink and sat with it. I lit a pipe and smoked and drank.

The day had started off with an unreal quality to it. Private detectives do not get mysterious phone calls from anonymous people. They do not keep unexplained ren-dezvous with nameless voices in secluded parts of Central Park. It had all seemed a game staged by some more or less harmless lunatic, and I had gone through the paces like a dutiful clown.

The corpse changed all of that. The girl, so neatly shot, poised so unobtrusively on the park bench, was a jarring coda to the symphony of annoyance that began with a phone call's interruption of romance. I had made my call to the police without giving my name and, conse-quently, was not involved. I had gone through the motions and had stumbled on the death of a prospective client who had not lived long enough to pay me a retainer. I had gone to her aid without believing she really existed, and when I had found her she was dead, and I never had the chance to become involved.

But I still felt involved.

The cognac disappeared steadily from my glass. I filled

it again, sat down with it again, thought again.

The phone rang. I picked it up and Ceil said, "You're hard to get hold of. Was it the YWCA?"

"No."

"Oh, you really met the girl? What was she like?"

"I met her."

"And it wasn't a gag?"

"No," I said, tired. "No gag."

"She's there now. In your apartment."

"No."

"You don't talk much, do you? We had a dinner date tonight, I think. Is it still on?"

"I'll have to take a raincheck."

"That's damned nice of you," she exploded. "You're one swell guy, Ed London."

I didn't feel like explaining. But I started to anyway, and got nowhere. The phone made a sharp little click and all at once I was talking to myself.

Well, Ceil would have to understand—later, when I was ready to explain that you never get used to death. You can meet it a thousand times in a thousand places, you can see it happen and you can cause it to happen and you can stumble upon its ultimate results, and still it's a menacing stranger—twice your size—on a dark, deserted street.

My friend on the police force have never gotten used to it. Sure, they can look at tom-up bodies without getting sick, and they can see an array of bodies after a catastrophe without waking up in the night. But this does not make them used to it.

I knew an obstetrician once who loved his work. He told me he got a kick every time he delivered a baby, as though part of himself were reborn with every birth. The thrill never wore off for him. And it is that way with death, the other end of the spectrum. The chill never wears off.

Each time it is as if a part of you dies.

At 5:30 I was still nursing my drink. Time dragged. Outside, the street was still bright. Then a buzzer sounded. Someone was downstairs in my vestibule. I got up slowly, drink in hand, and pressed the answering buzzer that would open the downstairs door. I waited and listened to footsteps on the staircase. The footsteps halted in front of my door. There was a knock.

I finished the cognac and went to the door. I turned the knob and flung open the door—to look into the face of the girl I had found dead in Central Park. I saw the blue eyes, the blonde hair, the button nose. I saw everything but the little hole in the middle of the forehead.

"You're Ed London," she said.

The same voice. The telephone voice. I froze momentarily and tried to get my breath. My head was spinning and the world was slightly out of kilter, as though some son of a bitch had tilted it like a pinball machine. I had just seen this lovely little blonde—dead; and now she stood at my door on her own two shapely feet.

"You're not you!" I exclaimed stupidly as she stepped inside my apartment.

"I don't understand."

"You don't understand!" I echoed. "That's the understatement of the year when it comes to my confusion."

SHE SCREWED up her face and looked at me as though I had lost my mind. Maybe I had. I started wondering how much cognac I had downed. Not that much, but maybe it was having a weird affect on me.

I took a deep breath and stammered, "B-but I just saw you, in Central Park, where I was supposed to meet you. Only somebody else met you first and you were dead. Shot between the eyes."

It sounded idiotic now—her standing beside me, a living, breathing doll. But she made her way through the maze of my meaningless words and something soaked in. Her mouth fell open and she gasped like a fish on a line. Her eyes bugged. She said, "Oh no! Good God," and gave a shrill little scream and fell into my arms and cried her eyes out...

THREE

I HELD the girl until she got a half-nelson on herself, then eased her into one of the twin leather chairs that give my living room the air of a British men's club. She stayed in the chair and finished her crying while I poured cognac into a glass for her. I could have used some myself, but things made little enough sense sober and I didn't want to get a load on.

I made her drink the cognac. Then I lit cigarettes for both of us, and sat down in the other leather chair and waited for her world to settle down a little.

After a long time she said, "I can't believe it, Mr. London. I can't believe Jackie's dead."

"Jackie?"

"Jacqueline Baron," she said. "She was my sister." She broke down again, suddenly regained her composure. "Not my twin sister. She was a year older. But we looked enough alike to pass for twins. My parents named her Jackie and me Jill. Jackie and Jill. Like the nursery rhyme. They thought it was cute."

"Who called me? You or Jackie?"

"She did."

"Because she was afraid?"

"Because we were both afraid," Jill said. She held the glass of cognac in her hand, stared at it a moment, then drained it. "This is very good," she said. "What is it?"

"Cognac."

"Oh. It tastes good, makes me feel warm. But I still feel cold inside. Somebody killed Jackie and now they're going to kill me. Oh, God, I'm scared."

She started to cry again. She started to cry again. She was trembling. I wanted to go to her but figured I would let her cry herself out. Nothing I could say would bring back her sister.

After a while she calmed down again. I asked if she knew who had been trying to kill Jackie and her. She said she didn't know. I asked why anyone would want them dead. She didn't know that either.

"We'd better take this from the top," I said. "When did it all start?"

"Three days ago, I think."

"What happened?"

"There was a phone call. Jackie answered. We share an apartment—shared an apartment," she added morosely. "Jackie answered it. She listened for a minute, looked frightened and slammed the phone down."

"Who was it?"

"She wouldn't say. Wouldn't tell me anything about it. Then, the next day, someone in a truck tried to run us both down. It was so frightening. We were crossing the street and a truck came speeding at us from out of nowhere. He missed us by inches. Luckily, we got across in time."

"Did you get a look at the truck?"

She shook her head. "No, I was too frightened. And I thought—then—it was just accidental. But Jackie was worried. I could tell something was wrong. When I prodded her, she told me about the phone call. Someone was going to kill us both."

"Did she say why?"

"She didn't know."

"No idea?"

"Nothing she told me about... But there's more. Yesterday, someone tried to kill me. Right on Park Avenue. A car whizzed by and somebody shot at me. Whoever it was missed. I was petrified."

"Why didn't you go to the police?" I asked.

"I don't know."

"You don't know? Someone threatened you and then tried to kill you. Twice. Why didn't you notify the police?"

"It's... We couldn't."

"And this morning Jackie called me. She wouldn't call the police either, but she called me. That doesn't make much sense."

She didn't answer. She asked for a cigarette. I gave her one and lit it for her. I knew there was a lot she wasn't telling me.

"Look at me," I said. "This is no game. Somebody shot your sister. Killed her in cold blood. Right now the police are picking her body up from Central Park and trying to figure out who the hell she is. You can't afford to sit around deciding how much you can tell me and how much you can keep to yourself. You either open up or I'll pick up the phone and call the police and you can tell it to them. Which is probably a fairly good idea at this stage."

"No, don't."

"Then you'd better start talking."

"Yes," she said. "I guess you're right."

She started talking. Jill and Jacqueline Baron lived together in an expensive apartment on East 58th Street off Park. They were self-employed. They earned a good living.

They were call girls.

"We were going to be models," she said. "You know, everybody starts out to be a model. Only we never did make it. You have to starve yourself, get so thin it's disgusting."

I didn't say anything

"But we did all right," Jill said. Her eyes turned hard, bitter. "We had all the qualifications for our chosen work... I'm not bad to look at, am I?"

She was wearing a green sheath dress that hid her figure as effectively   as Saran Wrap. She had long legs, and they were crossed at the knee now so that I could see their shape, which was fine. Her breasts pushed out at me in a way that would keep her out of bounds for the fashion photographers but undeniably in bounds for any red-blooded man between the ages of 18 and 80. And she was beautiful to boot.

"Pretty," she said. She rolled the word on her tongue and her eyes clouded. "Our looks were our downfall. It's an easy life for a lazy girl, with looks and a figure, Ed. It doesn't take any talent at all. The men come and they tell their friends about you and pretty soon you have a date every night, and every date is at least a fifty dollar bill and maybe a hundred, and no income tax out of that, either... Would you pay me fifty, Ed?"

"I wouldn't pay even if the girl were mink lined."

"But do you think I'd be worth it?"

"I'm sure you would."

SHE LAUGHED softly. She was playing Little Miss Desirable now, running her tongue over her lower lip, pouting a little, arranging herself in the chair to make herself appear as the personification of commercial lust. The act drained away her sorrow, and her fear. She got caught up in it and part of the reality of Jackie's death left her for the moment.

"It was handy," she said. "Jackie and I had good times together. We were closer than sisters, Ed. You...well, you say how much we looked alike. We've always been able to pass for twins. That was an asset in business, you know."

"Why?"

"Because we could cover each other's dates." She smiled, remembering. "If Jackie had two dates at the same time and I was free, I would take one of them and pretend I was Jackie. The tricks never knew the difference. They couldn't even tell us apart in bed."

"Handy."

"Uh-huh. Sometimes we would take a trick together. You know, a man would want to go to bed with both of us at once. A real sister act." She closed her blue eyes. "Men get their kicks in funny ways. Some need two girls in order to get their jollies. Men are all sick, Ed."

"You get a distorted picture."

"Do I?"

"Yes. You just meet the men who pay you. The straight ones, the sane ones, they're home with their wives in front of a television set with a can of beer close by. But you don't get to see that kind."

Her eyebrows went up a notch. "And you? Have you got a wife, Ed London?"

"I don't even have a television set. But let's forget my sex life for the time being." I felt like forgetting it myself; her sister had put a crimp in it with an ill-timed morning phone call and her sister's death had make me break a date with Ceil Gorski. The less said about my sex life, the better.

"Let's take it from the top," I said. "You're both call girls and you live together. That is, lived together. Someone is trying to kill you and you don't know who or why. Any ideas at all?"

"None."

"Were you blackmailing anyone?"

"No."

"Was Jackie?"

"If she was, she didn't tell me about it."

"Okay. How about men? Any boyfriends?"

"The only men in my life are customers, Ed."

It was a sort of hopeless line of questioning. All she knew was that her sister had been shot and she was next in line.

I went into the kitchen and made two cups of instant coffee. She took cream and sugar in hers. I had mine black, with enough cognac to sweeten the brew. We sat at my kitchen table and drank the coffee while I made meaning-less notes on a pad of yellow paper. I jotted down her name and her address, and made notes of the "timetable " of Jackie's murder from the first phone call to the discovery of the body. I didn't fill much of the paper—there wasn't much to write.

"Why didn't you go to the police?" I asked Jill Baron.

"You should know that by now. Call girls don't look for help from the law. The police leave you alone if you live a quiet life and stay out of trouble, but if you draw them a map of who you are and where you live and how you earn your living, you might as well hang out a sign. The crooked cops come with their hands out and the honest ones haul you off to jail."

She worked on her coffee. "Jackie didn't even want to call in a private detective. She said you couldn't trust them. But your name had been mentioned somewhere, and I heard you were honest. So I insisted we call you."

"Well, now's a good time to go to the police, Jill. Who-ever is after you is playing for keeps."

She shook her head. "But they'll just ask me questions," she said. "Questions, questions, questions, and I don't know any of the answers that count. So what good will it do me?"

Her voice broke off and her eyes dropped. I took one of her small hands in mine. Her flesh was cold.

"Ed, help me," she pleaded. "If you help me maybe we can find out what it's all about and then go to the police. It won't do any good to go to them now."

She had a point. She couldn't give the cops anything much to work on, and any protection they might give her would disappear sooner or later. Police protection is a nice theory but it can never work out the way it should. The cops don't have the manpower to guard a person closely for any length of time.

And I had a reason of my own for wanting to stay away from Centre Street—police headquarters—for the time being. I had found a body in Central Park and had reported it anonymously, leaving out my own role in the case. The police frown on this sort of thing, especially on the part of a private cop. They can say nasty things about it when a man's license comes up for renewal.

"Jill."

She looked at me.

"Think, now. Were you or Jackie ever arrested? I mean for any offense at all."

"Just a traffic ticket once. Nothing more."

"Did they fingerprint you?"

"No, I just got a ticket."

"Were either of you ever fingerprinted for anything? A government job? Anything?"

"I turned a trick with a UN diplomat once. But you don't get fingerprinted for that sort of thing. Why the questions?"

I filled a pipe and lit a match. Without prints, it was going to take them a while to identify Jackie Baron's body. A corpse without identification is a tricky thing, and although police routine always comes up with an answer, it takes time. They run through Missing Persons files, they ship the prints to Washington, they play games with laundry marks...

So we had time to dig around a little.

"All right," I said. "We'll leave the police out of things, at least for the time being."

"And you'll help me, Ed?"

I was a knight in tarnished armor, and she may have been in distress, but it would take some imagination to call her a maiden.

"I'll help you," I said.

FOUR

I PUT MY gun in the shoulder rig where it belonged, went to the window, pulled back the shade and peered across the street. A few old ladies were walking home. No one seemed to be lurking in the shadows.

"Did anyone follow you here?"

"No."

"Are you sure?"

"No."

I told her to wait there and left the apartment. I walked downstairs, then left through the rear exit where the janitor drags the garbage. There is a low fence between the yard of my building and the yard of the building behind it that fronts on 84th Street. I pushed a garbage can against the fence, climbed onto the can and dropped over the fence. I walked through that building, smiled at a curious seven-year-old boy, and came out on 84th.

The air was cooler now with the beginnings of a storm blowing up over the East River. The sky was a darker gray; in a few hours it would be completely black. I walked around the block to 83rd and headed toward my own building again, keeping my eyes open. All the parked cars were appropriately empty, all the doorways were now un-tenanted. If she had been followed, her shadow had melted.

The coast seemed clear.

I went upstairs. She was standing by the fireplace looking at some of my books. "Grab your purse," I said.

"Where we going?"

"Downtown. I'm hiding you."

We left the apartment. A cab drove up, and I gave the
driver an address in the West Twenties. As he put the taxi
in gear, Jill looked at me inquisitively.

"It's a friend's apartment," I said.

"Anyone I know?"

"Probably not. She's an actress, out of town with a
road company. She won't be back for two months."

"And you have a key to her apartment?"

"Yes."

She smiled. "How cozy, Ed. Hiding one girl at a girl
friend's apartment. Won't she mind?"

I thought of Maddy Parson—the deep, intense eyes,
the soft voice, the warmth. We were long-time friends,
much more than that. Once or twice I might have married
her, if she hadn't already been wed to greasepaint and foot-
lights. No, I thought. Maddy wouldn't mind.

"She won't be there to mind," I said.

She kept quiet the rest of the trip. Once or twice she
dabbed at her eyes with a handkerchief. The cabby took
Second Avenue downtown to 23rd Street, then cut west and
doubled uptown a block to the address I had given him.
The meter read a dollar and change, I gave him two singles
and waved him away.

"Here?" Jill said, surprised.

"That's right."

"Your actress friend can't be making much money."

"It's a tough business."

"It must be. Maybe she should try my line, Ed. Or
doesn't she have any aptitude in that direction?"

"Don't be bitchy."

She pouted. "Was I being bitchy?"

"Very."

"I'm sorry," she said. "I'll try to be good. It's just...I guess I'm cracking wise to get Jackie out of my mind, what happened to her, and oh, it isn't really working, Ed."

The apartment was a third-floor loft in an old brick building that had been condemned years ago. It wasn't legal to live there, but Maddy and the landlord had taken care of that. According to the lease she gave acting lessons in the loft and didn't live there. Maddy paid her rent the first of every month, and the landlord bought off the firemen every few months, and everybody was happy.

Jill and I climbed an unlit and shaky staircase past the machine shop on the first floor and Madame Sindra's palmist studio on the second floor. She stood in front of Maddy's door while I found the right key and opened it. We went inside. She sat down on a couch while I turned on the lights.

"Well," she said. "Now what?"

I sat down next to her. "You'll be safe here," I said.

"I know."

"And you can stay here while I try to get a line on whoever is after you. But I've got to ask you a question I already asked you, Jill. And you have to answer it straight."

"Go on."

"Were you mixed up in anything besides hustling?"

"Isn't that enough?"

"I'm serious. Ever try blackmailing a customer? Or did you ever overhear anything you shouldn't have heard? Think about it. It's important."

Her face screwed up in concentration and then relaxed. She shook her head negatively.

"Nothing?"

"Nothing."

"And Jackie?"

"If she was, I never knew about it."

"Then it can only add up one way," I said. "Somebody had a reason to see Jackie dead. But you both looked alike and you both acted alike and he couldn't tell you apart. Maybe Jackie was working some sort of deal of her own. He couldn't be sure it was Jackie he was after, or that you weren't in on it with her. So he has to kill both sisters to make sure he gets the one he wants. Do you follow me?"

She nodded but looked perplexed. "Jackie wouldn't do anything like that," she said.

"Are you positive?"

"Well—"

I got to my feet. "I want you to stay here," I told her. "Don't leave the apartment, not for anything. Don't make any phone calls. As long as you're here, you'll be safe. Nobody followed us here and nobody's going to come here looking for you. Just stay put and wait for me."

"Where are you going?"

"To your apartment."

She stared at me. "Is that safe? The police—"

"I'm sure they haven't identified Jackie's body yet. It should take them two or three days unless they get lucky. And if I spot any cops, I'll come right back. If not, I'll have a look at your place and see if Jackie left anything around of interest."

"And suppose the…the killer is waiting there?"

"That's a chance I'll take. But I'm a big boy."

She looked me up and down, the kind of look I had given her earlier. "Yes," she said evenly. "You are."

"Give me your apartment key."

She went over to her purse and gave me a brown leather keywallet. She started to hand it over; then she took it back and looked at it, frowning. "This is Jackie's," she said.

"What?"

"It happens all the time," she said. "We both have these things for our keys, same color, and we keep taking each other's—" She broke off and looked at me. Her eyes were bright, as though she were trying to put a smile on top of a scream. "I keep forgetting she's dead. I talk about her as if she's still here..." She collapsed in a chair and cried. Her shoulders heaved from her sobs.

I'm no good at that sort of scene. The reality of her sister's death was first hitting home, and for the next hour or so there wasn't anything I or anybody else could do for her.

I took her dead sister's keys and said, "Jill, I'll hurry back."

I FOUND a cab heading uptown on Eighth. We rode through dark streets, past the bright scar of light on Times Square—then east on 57th. I got out of the cab at 57th and Park and lit up a pipe in a doorway. Four college kids hurried past me, the girls tottering drunkenly on their high heels, the boys wondering if the girls would be drunk enough...

I walked up to 58th Street and found her building. It was a remodeled brownstone with a new front and an air of impressive prosperity. There were no squad cars parked outside, nobody who looked like a cop near the doorway. I crossed the street and walked into the building. A row of doorbells with name cards showed that the Baron girls lived in apartment 2-D. I buzzed. No one buzzed in reply.

The building was a walk-up. I used a key on the outer door, then climbed a flight of carpeted stairs. A finer build-ing than Maddy's no question about it. Whoring paid far more handsomely than acting.

There were three other apartments on the second floor besides the one I sought, and someone was standing in the hallway in front of one of them. I didn't want an audience when I opened Jill's door—New Yorkers are tolerant people, but there is no point in straining this inherent tolerance. I walked up to the third floor and waited. Then I went back to the second floor, emptied my pipe in a hall ashtray, and stood in front of Jill Baron's door. A good heavy door, with 2-D painted neatly upon it, and a little card beneath the bell on which someone had neatly lettered THE MISSES BARON.

The customers must have liked that.

I took out the key to the apartment, listened at the door, heard nothing. On a hunch I dropped to one knee and squinted myopically through the keyhole. The apartment was dark inside.

I stood up again, stuck the key in the lock and turned. I twisted the doorknob, pushed the door open and stepped into a black room. I was groping around for the light switch when the Empire State Building fell on my head.

It was good but not good enough. He caught me on the side of the head just above the ear and I did a little two-step and wound up on my knees. He moved in the darkness, coming in to throw the finisher. My head was rocky and my legs wouldn't behave. I managed to swerve out of the way of the blow and got to my feet, but my rubbery legs didn't want to hold me. He came at me again, a blur in the darkness, and something hard shot past my head. I ducked and swung, aiming for where his gut should be.

My aim was good but there was nothing behind the punch—the shot on the head had drained my strength. He backed away from the blow and hit me in the chest. It wasn't a hard punch but it sent me reeling.

Somehow, I got to the light switch. I flicked it on and

saw him, moving toward me and blinking at the sudden burst of light. A big man, a fast man. A chin like Gibraltar and a chest like a beer barrel. Ham-hock hands, and a leather-covered sap in one of them. He swung the sap. I dodged, caught it on one shoulder. My arm went numb and my fingers tingled. I tried to make my hand fish the .38 out from under my jacket, but my arm was having none of it. It wouldn't behave.

He moved at me, grinning. I doubled up a left hand and pushed it at him. He batted it out of the way casually and kept coming. I lowered my fat head and charged him like a bull, and he picked up that sap and let me have it right between the horns.

This time it worked. I caught a knee in the face on the way down but I barely felt it at all. I just noticed it, thinking, *Ah, yes, I've been kneed in the face*, taking note of it but not caring a hell of a lot about it one way or the other. Then I blacked out...

FIVE

IN THE movies they shake their heads, blink a few times and everything is all right again. Men have miraculous powers of recovery in the movies. A deep breath, a nod of the head and they're in perfect shape.

It's not like that, friend,

I wasn't out long. Five minutes, ten minutes. I opened both eyes and blinked in the darkness and tried to get up, which was a mistake. I fell down again. It was as though someone had cut the tendons in my arms and legs. They just wouldn't do my bidding.

This time I stayed down for a while. I took deep breaths the way they do in the movies, and I also took inventory. My head felt like a sandlot baseball after nine innings. My shoulder was aching and my arm was numb.

I got up and, this time, stayed erect. The room was dark—apparently my "friend" had shut off the lights before leaving—I managed to find the light switch for the second time that night. This time, though, I was alone. I found a chair, collapsed into it and smoked a cigarette.

There had been just the two of us, me and the man with the sap. But the room looked as if it had been the scene of a gang war. A bookcase stood empty on one wall, its contents heaped on the floor. Chair and sofa cushions were scattered around. My friend had been looking for something. Whether he had found it, I couldn't tell.

I got up a little shakily and checked out the rest of the apartment. There were two bedrooms branching off a hallway, one Jackie's the other Jill's. Each came equipped with a huge bed, which more or less figured. Each had been searched, and was a mess. I gave the rubble a quick once-over, pawing through mounds of lacy underwear that would have given a fetishist a quick thrill. I didn't find anything very interesting. I didn't expect to.

There was some aspirin in the medicine chest, and it seemed like a good idea. The aspirin bottle nestled between a tube of vaginal jelly and a bottle of oral contraceptives... Jackie and Jill were not careless lovers, it seemed. I gulped down three aspirins with a water chaser.

It was beginning to look more and more like black-mail. My man was systematic, I reasoned. He had somehow trailed Jackie to the meeting place in the park, then got close enough to her to put a gun to her forehead and shoot. Then he had doubled back to the girls' apartment for a crack at Jill. Jill wasn't there, of course, so he'd jimmied the door and rifled the room for the pictures or tapes or whatever it was that she was holding out on him.

He might have found them and he might not—I couldn't say. But it was an odds-on bet that, if he didn't find them, they weren't around. The place had been turned upside-down.

Then I came along and rang the buzzer, and he rose to the occasion by dousing the lights and hiding in the dark. I opened the door in the darkness and he was there, ready and waiting. From there on in it had been reasonably quick, if not painless.

It was too late to search the place. My friend had already taken care of that. But it made sense to straighten up a little. The way things stood, anybody who stumbled into the apartment for one reason or another was going to figure out that things were not according to Hoyle. A maid or a janitor might wander in and call the cops, and that would fix up their body-identification problem for them.

The longer it took the police, the more time I had to work. So I went through the apartment like somebody's maid, putting the books back in the bookcase, fluffing up cushions and placing them where they belonged, stuffing clothes into drawers and closets. I didn't go overboard. The place did not have to pass muster, just so long as it lost the aftermath-of-a-hurricane look.

There was a bottle of scotch in one of the closets. This slowed me down a little. Aspirin is all well and good, but it's limited. It can't get rid of the full effects of a couple of slugs on the skull. I swallowed enough of the scotch to take the edge off things, capped the bottle and stuck it back in the closet.

At which point the doorbell rang.

The cops are great when it comes to timing. They always show when you don't want them, right to the second. It didn't seem likely that they could have identified Jacqueline Baron's body that quickly. If I had been anxious for them to figure out who she was, I would have waited a week. But this time I wanted them to have trouble, so they were setting a record for speed.

The bell rang again.

I sat down softly on an overstuffed chair and waited. Maybe they would go away. Maybe they would come back tomorrow. A feeble hope at best, but somehow I couldn't see myself going to the door, opening it and saying hello to a couple of detectives from Homicide. They might get upset.

"HEY," someone yelled. "Hey, open up in there, willya?"

I got up reluctantly, walked to the door.

"Hey, Jackie," the voice yelled again. "Open up, Jackie. What the hell, open the door!"

This was no cop.

"Who's there?" I said.

"It's Joe, dammit, and where the hell is Jackie?"

A customer. A drunk customer, from the sound of things. I dug my wallet out of a pocket, opened the door, flipped open the wallet and shoved it in the man's face. He blinked and I pulled the wallet back and buried it once more in my pocket. I had given him a quick look at my driver's license but he didn't know the difference.

"Crawley, Vice Squad," I said. "Who the hell are you, chum?"

His eyes clouded, then turned crafty. He was sad because Jackie was not available and scared because I was there, holding him by the arm. "I—I made a mistake," he stammered. "I must have the wrong apartment."

He was a white-faced man with a network of blue veins showing around his cheeks. He wore an expensive suit and a Sulka tie. He was a rich drunk with a married look who looked as though he desperately wanted to be home.

"You've been drinking," I said.

"Well, a couple of beers."

"You know where you are?"

"Sure."

"This place is a cathouse, chum. You know that?"

He tried hard to look shocked. He didn't manage it at all. He looked lost and comical but I didn't laugh at him.

"Maybe I better be going," he said.

I said nothing.

"Uh—" he closed his eyes. "Maybe I ought to buy some tickets to the Policeman's Ball, officer. Do you have any?"

I told him to see a patrolman, He said yes, he would be sure to do that, and he mentioned a captain who, he said, was a very good friend of his. I must not have looked impressed. He coughed nervously, turned and hurried off down the stairs. I didn't think he would be back soon, or ever.

I gave him 10 minutes to disappear completely, then turned off all the lights and left the Baron girls' apartment. The hallway was clear this time. I walked down carpeted stairs, through the vestibule and out to the street. There was no one around. I walked two blocks without spotting a tail, stepped into a hotel lobby on Central Park South and came out on Fifth A venue without anyone behind me.

A cab was waiting for a light to turn green. I got in, the light changed and we headed downtown to a loft on West 24th Street where a blue-eyed blonde call girl was waiting for me.

SIX

I CLIMBED the two flights of rickety stairs and knocked on Maddy Parson's door. A voice asked me to identify myself, which I did, and the door opened.

Jill Baron drew back when she saw me. "You look terrible," she said. "What happened?"

We sat on Maddy's couch and I told her. Outside, the night was soundless. We were in a business neighborhood and the businesses had all shuttered their doors long ago. Once in a while a truck rumbled by, and now and then a crowd of tourists staggered along the street, fresh from one of the Greek nightclubs in the area, with Retsina in their stomachs and visions of belly dancers in their heads.

"Did he hurt you badly, Ed?" she asked.

"I'll live." I described him again, the hulking mass of him, the bulldog chin, the once-broken nose. "Try to get a picture of him, Jill. Think. Any bells ring?"

She screwed up her face and shook her head. "No bells, Ed. I'm sorry."

"Nothing?"

"I could probably think of a hundred men who fit that description. I might know the man if I saw him, but this way—" She spread her hands. "A better description might help. If you could tell me about his appendectomy scar—"

"I wouldn't be in a position to know about that."

"But I might," she said. Her face brightened. "You know, I would have given a thousand dollars for a look at Joe Robling's face. Was he very frightened?"

"A little."

"I ought to be angry at you," she said. "He was a good customer. Generally drunk, but a hundred-dollar trick who never got rough and never complained."

"He asked for Jackie."

"He always asked for Jackie," she said, a wry smile breaking through her generally somber mood. "But I took him a few times, now and then, if Jackie was busy. He never knew the difference. You don't think you scared him off for good, do you?"

"I wouldn't know."

She looked at me and pouted. "Oh, stop it," she said.

"For heaven's sake, don't go moral on me, Ed. You know what I am and I know what I am, and if we can't relax and accept it, there's something wrong with us. Didn't you ever know a call girl before?"

I've known a few. Hard little girls with something missing inside them, as empty in their own way as their habitual clients. The mythical whore with the heart of gold is a creature I have never met. The respectable prostitute is a creature of existentialist drama, nothing more. White slavery doesn't exist, not for the New York hooker. Girls stay in the business because of some inner flaw. They tell me the psychiatrists can trace it all back to Oedipal fixations and toilet training, but it doesn't much matter how it started. Yes, I've known call girls before. I've even liked a few of them. But not many, and not very much.

"You don't want to talk about my business," she said.

"No, I don't."

"What do you want to talk about?"

"Your sister."

"Oh." The somber mien returned.

"You didn't see that apartment after our unidentified friend got through with it. Either you or Jackie had something he wanted badly. If it wasn't you—"

"It wasn't, Ed."

"—then it must have been Jackie. She had something or knew something and it got dangerous for her. And now it's dangerous for you, too."

She frowned. "I don't know, Ed. Suppose it was just some...well, some nut. You meet them in my business. I know you don't want to talk about the world's oldest profession, but that much is true. The oddballs you meet!"

She closed her eyes, reminiscing. "Why couldn't it be like that? What if one of them, some man who was a customer, what if he got it into his head to kill us? A Jack-the-Ripper type."

"It doesn't add."

"Why not?"

"Look, a psycho might have his own reasons for wanting to kill a couple of hookers, I'll grant you that. But a psycho wouldn't play it so cool. He might come after you with a knife, might bust down your door and try to beat your brains in or shoot you or whatever. But I doubt if he would carefully trail Jackie to Central Park and put a neat little bullet in her forehead and then methodically search the apartment.

"He might go on a destructive rampage, just trying to rip up everything he could get his hands on. But that isn't what our boy did. He gave the place a thorough search and let it go at that. He's got a reason, Jill." I stopped for breath. "It looks like blackmail to me."

"But Jackie—"

"Tell me about her, Jill."

"She—" She stopped there, and then grimaced. "It's hard to talk about her," she said.

"I know this is tough on you, Jill, but it's necessary."

She took a deep breath, and tried again. "She liked good clothes, fancy restaurants, expensive furniture. She hated nightclubs but sometimes she had to go to them on dates. She liked the Museum of Modem Art and modem jazz—"

"Men?"

"She didn't have a sweet man. Neither of us did. I think she was seeing someone, not business, but I don't remember his name. I'm not sure if she ever told me his name."

"Did you ever meet him?"

"I don't think so. Is he important?"

"I don't know yet. Keep talking. Was Jackie having

money troubles?"

She didn't answer me.

"Was she?"

She stood up, walked across the room. Her dress was snug on her professional body. She lit a fresh cigarette, stood at the window, blew out smoke. "I know what you're thinking," she said, "but you're wrong. She couldn't be a blackmailer, she couldn't. She was my sister. We had differences, but she was still my sister, and I can't believe that of her—"

"Tell me about those differences, Jill."

"What's there to tell? The usual minor spats over nothing."

"How about money?"

"No problem at all. We kept separate bank accounts. No community property. What was mine was mine and what was Jackie's was Jackie's. I don't know what she had in the bank. I've got ten or fifteen thousand saved, and she certainly earned as much as I did, except…"

"Except what?"

"I don't know. Something was bothering her. She had a weakness for horses, phoned in bets every morning from our apartment. Possibly she was a heavy player."

"And got in deep?"

"Maybe. She didn't talk about it, but I think she owed a little money here and there. She dressed well, I told you that, and of course we both had charge accounts and credit cards and all that. She may have run up some fairly heavy tabs around town, and owed her bookmaker."

She paused, then said, "This is guesswork, Ed. A guess I don't particularly like to make. My sister was no more of a saint than I am, but I hate to think…"

Her voice trailed off. She leaned over and ground out her cigarette in one of Maddy's ashtrays. "I would have loaned her the money. I would have been glad to."

"Did she ever ask?"

"No. Never." She narrowed her eyes, remembering. "But there was something. She mentioned how nice it would be if a pile of money fell into her lap. We always talked like that; it was nothing special. But if I had only thought to offer her money, if I had only asked her—"

"Don't blame yourself, Jill."

"Why shouldn't I?" Her voice nearly broke, but she controlled it.

I stood up, took her arm. "Jackie was riding for a fall," I told her. "If you had bailed her out this time, she would have gotten in over her head some other time. Blackmail's an easy out in your line of work. You must have thought of it yourself once or twice."

"Not seriously."

"But for all you knew Jackie did think of it—seriously. She might have tried to squeeze somebody before. But this time she picked on the wrong man and he squeezed back. There was nothing you could do about it, Jill."

She drew close to me and her perfume was heady. I felt the warmth of her before her body actually touched mine. Her head was tilted and her eyes were misty and half-closed. "You 're good for me," she sighed. I was holding her arm, and she drew even closer to me.

"I'm cold and I'm scared and I'm shaky, but I'm no frail petunia, am I, Ed? But right now I wish I was. I wish I could make you believe I need to be treated like a frail petunia."

I made some sort of motion toward her, and inexplicably she now backed away from me. "You know what's worst, Ed? I feel guilty."

"Guilty? What for?"

"JACKIE'S dead, but I'm alive, and I'm glad I'm alive. I'm glad it was Jackie instead of me. That thought's been in my mind ever since you told me she was dead. I've been trying to make it go away, but I can't. Isn't that terrible, Ed?"

"No, it isn't," I told her. "That's the most normal reaction in the world."

"My God, are you good for me. I'm cold and I'm scared and I'm a no-good prostitute. And poor Jackie's on some cold slab someplace; and I'm—I'm—I know, I'm cold. She's cold but she

doesn't know it, she—Ed, for the love of God, make me warm."

I looked at her, and I told myself she was just another hooker. There were thousands of them, and none of them were worth it. That's what I told myself. But I went over anyway and put my arms around her, and she was trembling.

"I'm a stranger here," she whispered, with a pathetic attempt at coquettishness. Her voice trembled like her body, but she persevered. "A stranger who doesn't know her way around. Show me where my bed is, Ed."

I showed her...

It was very dark in the bedroom, with the barest bit of light coming in through the window from a streetlamp down the block I got out of my clothes in the darkness and found her in the bed. Her body was naked and waiting.

Her mouth was a warm well. Her arms went around me, drew me close. Her body moved beneath mine, twisting and writhing in a horizontal dance as old as time. My hands went all over her and all of her was smooth and soft and fine.

"Oh, hurry, hurry—"

I had stray thoughts. I thought how disloyal it was to Madeline Parson to embrace another girl in her bed, and

I thought, too, that this display of affection was Jill's own way of paying me a retainer instead of cash. Unhappy thoughts, those.

But she was good, very good, and the thoughts went away. One thought came back at the end, one that was almost funny. That morning her sister Jackie had interrupted something along these lines, and now sister Jill was making up for it. It was ironic.

Then that thought, too, vanished. The scene dropped off and the world went away, and there were only the two of us alone in some special bracket of space and time. We visited a special place devoid of call girls and criminals and sudden death. We went there together.

A pleasant trip. Afterward, sleep came quickly.

SEVEN

IN THE morning, no telephone intruded. The smell of coffee woke me. I yawned, rolled over and buried my face in the pillow. The room was heavy with the air of spent passion. I yawned again, opened my eyes and saw her come in with a steaming cup in her hand.

"I made coffee," she said.

I didn't say anything. She was wearing some sort of silky black thing and the sight of her brought memories in a flood. She crossed the room and sat on the edge of the bed, close enough so that I could have reached out a hand and rubbed her hip. I reached out a hand and rubbed her hip.

"But it's too hot," she said.

"What is?"

"The coffee, silly." She turned and stared. "What did you think I meant?"

"Forget what I thought. What about the coffee?"

"It's too hot." She set it down on the bedside table.

261

LAWRENCE BLOCK

"While it cools—"

While it cooled, we warmed. She slipped the night-gown off and came back to bed. She said *Mmmmm, what a way to wake up* and then she did not say anything for a very long time. The phone stayed respectfully silent.

Later she curled up beside me while I drank the coffee. She made good java. She would murmur something from time to time, and from time to time I would run a hand over her. I touched the arch of her hip, the strawberry birthmark on the side of her thigh. A large measure of reality faded away. Intimacy does that. It pushes away unpleasant things, things like Jill's profession and Jackie's death and the big-chinned murderer-at-large.

But these things came back, slowly. I finished the coffee and got out of bed. Jill asked me where I was going.

"To get a paper," I said. "I want to find out what the police know about your sister. Wait here."

It was somewhere after nine. On the second floor, Madame Sindra was holding court behind her crystal ball. A worried little woman, gray-haired and sad-eyed, was having her fortune told in words spoken with a sibilant Middle Eastern accent. Sometimes Madame Sindra came upstairs during the day and had coffee with Maddy, and then her accent was straight out of South Philly, with overtones of carny argot. It's a deceptive world.

The sky was overcast and the air thick with overdue rain. People hurried by in blankets of sweat. Later, with any luck, the sky would open up and the rains would come. I walked down Eighth Avenue to 23rd Street and picked up the four morning papers. I carried them back to the loft.

I found Jill Baron as nude as I'd left her. She wanted to know if there was anything in the papers.

"I haven't looked yet," I told her. I gave her the *News* and *Mirror*, kept the *Times* and the *Tribune* for myself. We

262

sat side by side on Maddy's couch and went through the papers looking for a report of Jackie's murder.

The *Times* didn't print the story, but the other three papers did. It wasn't an important one. There was no obvious sex angle and the body had not been identified, at least not by the time they made up the papers. There was a certain amount of color in that the victim was an attractive girl, but this was not enough to put the story on page three of the tabloids. The *Trib* buried it on page 17.

The journalistic tone varied from paper to paper but the message was the same in each story. Acting on an anonymous phone tip, police had found the body of a girl in her middle twenties on a bench in Central Park. She had been shot once at close range in the forehead and had died instantly. Her body had not yet been identified, and no clues as to the probable identity of her killer had been announced.

According to the *Mirror*, the possibility of suicide had not been entirely ruled out—the girl could have shot herself and someone could subsequently have stolen the gun, possibly the same person who later tipped the police. This seemed unlikely, though, since paraffin tests showed that the dead girl had not fired a gun.

"Then they don't know anything," Jill said.

"The papers don't. Or didn't, when they went to press. That was a while ago. The police may know a lot more."

I reached for the phone. "I'm calling them," I said.

"To tell them—"

"No. To ask them."

I asked the desk man at Centre Street for Jerry Gunther in Homicide. He was there.

"Ed London, Jerry. How's it going?"

"Well enough. What's up?"

"I just read something about a dead girl in the park.

The one who was shot in the head. Know who she was?"

"Are you mixed up in this one, Ed?"

I laughed that off. "I don't think so. I have a Missing Person to look for and she comes close to the description in the *Tribune*. Have you got a make on this girl yet?"

"Nothing. We're working on it. Think it's your pigeon?"

"I hope not. Mine is a blonde, not too tall, pretty face—"

"So's this one."

"—brown eyes, slender build—"

"This one is blue-eyed and stacked. You sure about the eyes?"

"Positive," I said. "I guess it's not my girl. I didn't think so but I wanted to check it out. I've got a hunch the girl I'm after skipped to Florida."

We said pleasant things to each other and he hung up. When it all worked itself out, Gunther was not going to rush over and kiss me. But we had been friends for a long time. He knew I played things a little cute some of the time, knew I tossed away the rule book once in a while. But he also knew I usually had a sound reason.

"No identification," I told Jill. "They don't even sound close. We've got time."

"Well, where do we go from here?"

"Good question." I dug out a pipe and tobacco, filled the pipe and lit it. "Jackie was blackmailing someone—either the guy who sapped me or whoever hired him. She could have been blackmailing him with something she knew or with something she had. The ape man turned your apartment inside out, so it must have been something she had. You follow?"

"Uh huh."

"Which leaves two possibilities," I continued. "Possibility one is that the goods were stowed in your apartment, in which case the killer has them by now. The other possibility is that Jackie parked the stuff elsewhere." I drew on the pipe. "Did she have any friends who might be holding it?"

"I don't think so."

"Any hiding place that might appeal? Think."

She thought and her eyes narrowed. She said, "Oh!"

"What?"

"She has a—a safe-deposit box. The Jefferson Savings Bank on Fifth Avenue. She took the box about a year ago because she wanted a safe place for her insurance policy. We both took out policies a long time ago payable to each other, and she kept hers in the box. I don't know what else she kept there."

"It wasn't a joint box? You don't have access to it?"

"No." She smiled. "I told you we kept money matters separate. I think there were a lot of things Jackie didn't tell me. I didn't have a key. But she had the box. I know she still has it, because they bill every year and she got a bill not too long ago."

"Did she go to the box often?"

"I don't know. I never asked her about it." She took out a cigarette and I gave her a light. "That would be the obvious place, wouldn't it? If she had something to hide—"

"Of course," I said.

She took a deep breath. "But it doesn't do us any good. Now that Jackie's dead, we can't get to the box. Unless, if we could tell them she was dead—"

"You'd still need a court order."

"Then we're stuck."

I stood up, walked over to the window. "They don't know Jackie is dead—"

"So?"

"Do you know how she signs her name?"

"Yes, but—"

"Could you fake her signature? After all, you have her keys. One of them may be the key for the safety-deposit box."

She hurried into the bedroom, came out again with her purse in tow. It was a large black bag. She dipped into it and came out with Jackie's key wallet. She sat down on the couch and inspected the keys one by one.

"Let's see—this is to the apartment, and this is the outer door and…Does this look right?"

It was a large brass key with a number on it. "That's the key," I said. "And that would be the box number. Two-zero-four-three. Now we need something with her signature on it."

"I can forge her signature," Jill said, "and she can—I'm sorry."

"What?"

"I was going to say, she can forge mine. Wrong tense." Again she repressed tears, sighed and continued. "We used to practice copying each other's signatures when we were kids. It's been a long time, but I think I can come fairly close. Not exact, though. Do you think I can get away with it?"

I NODDED. I did think so. The signature they require with each visit to a safe-deposit vault is more a matter of form than anything else. Not many people sign their name identically every time. Some do; some people have a rubber-stamp signature that never varies. But Jill could come close enough to Jackie's signature to convince everyone but the experts. Besides, they wouldn't pay too much attention to the signature. If Jackie had been blackmailing someone recently, and if she had been in recently to put the blackmail material in the box, the guards would remember someone as pretty as she. And when Jill went to the box they would think she was her sister. They didn't know Jackie was dead, no doubt didn't even know she had a lookalike sister.

So there would be no major problem.

"There are little things," I said. "You won't know your way around. Won't know which is your box or where you're supposed to take it. Jackie might even have known the guards well enough to have exchanged a few words."

"I think I can manage it."

"Are you sure?"

She looked at me bravely. "Do we have a choice, Ed?"

She stood up, dropped the keys back into her bag, took my arm and we left.

The Jefferson Savings Bank is situated on the south-east corner of Fifth Avenue at 43rd Street, a glass-and-steel triumph of functional architecture over aesthetic values. There is something about modern architecture which does not inspire my financial trust. I keep my money in a bank built 50 years ago, one which looks as though it has been standing forever. A bank should look like a bank; this one didn't.

We went inside together. It wasn't immediately apparent where they kept the safe-deposit vault, but it would have been somewhat out of character if we had wandered around asking directions. Then I saw a sign at the head of a staircase and nudged Jill. We walked down the stairs together, broke an electric eye beam, went up to a long desk. A little old man looked up at us over the desk and smiled at Jill.

"Miss, uh—"

"Baron. Jacqueline Baron."

"Yes," he said. She told him the number of the box. He got a card from a drawer, wrote the time and date on it, and gave it to her. I held my breath while Jill signed her sister's name. He glanced at the signature, set the card aside, walked around the desk and unlocked a swinging iron gate. Jill turned, smiled sweetly and entered the restricted area.

I watched her go into the vault room and hand her keys to the guard. He fitted his key into the double lock, then used her key. He withdrew the box and pointed toward a row of cubbyholes. She went into one of them and closed the door.

The guard came back. *A roomful of secrets,* I thought. *Untaxed bills, stolen goods, all those things along with more mundane items like wills and birth certificates and government bonds. If these walls could talk...*

The door of the cubbyhole opened. Jill came out with her purse over her arm and the metal box in one hand. The guard hurried back with her and locked the box away, going through the two-key ritual a second time. He led her to the gate, unlocked it, stood aside to let her pass. She winked quickly at me and I took her arm. We climbed the stairs, broke the electric eye beam once more.

On the street she said, "I have to believe it now. Jackie was a blackmailer!"

"What did you find?"

"I'll show you. But not here. Can we go someplace?"

We walked over to Sixth Avenue and up a few blocks. There was a small, run-down tavern at the comer, with one man behind the bar and two drunks in front of it. Otherwise the place was empty. We took a booth in the back and sat together, facing the door.

The bartender came back and asked us what we wanted. We said coffee would do, and he recommended a luncheonette down the street. I ordered cognac for both of us. He went away and came back with two shots of brandy. I paid him and he left us alone.

I pointed to her purse. "Well, what did you find?"

She reached into the purse and pulled out a long white envelope, a short fat manila envelope, and a thick roll of bills. The bills were secured by a doubled-up rubber band. I riffled them. There were thirty or forty, most of them hundreds with a sprinkling of fifties.

"Three or four thousand here," I said.

"Three thousand. I counted."

I reached for the white envelope. "That's the insurance."

I opened it. The policy had been written by the Ohio Mutual Insurance Company. It had been drawn about a year and a half ago and the face amount was $50,000.

"You've come into a lot of money," I said.

"If I live to collect it."

I opened the brown envelope. There were a dozen pictures inside, black and white glossies. The precise scenes varied in form but the game was the same in each. There were two persons in each photograph, a man and a woman. Both were nude and busy; and this photographic record of their activities would have sold well in the back room of a 42nd Street pornography shop. The prints were good and clear, the composition fine.

The girl was Jackie, and a look at her showed that the resemblance between the Baron sisters was just as striking when the girls were unclad. She was a dead ringer for her sister. A very dead ringer, now.

And the man was no stranger, either. When I had seen him he had clothes on, which constituted an improvement. He wasn't beautiful. When I had seen him, for that matter, he had a sap in his hand and had been swinging it at my skull.

"The man," I said, feeling my scalp. "I recognize him."

"So do I," Jill murmured.

EIGHT

I PICKED up my glass and drank the brandy. They do not stock fine cognac in the Sixth Avenue joints. But it went down anyway and the warmth spread.

"His name is Ralph," Jill said. "That's all I know."

"A customer of Jackie's?"

"Not a customer." She lowered her eyes. "I think I told you she was seeing somebody. I couldn't remember his name then. Seeing his picture, I remembered. His name is Ralph. I saw him with her…oh, maybe three times altogether. I never talked with him but I saw him. He came over to take her out. Where they went, I never knew."

"When was this?"

"The first time was maybe two months ago, and then again two or three weeks after that."

"Did she talk about him?"

"Not much. Jackie wasn't that much of a talker."

I tapped the stack of pictures. *More of a doer*, I thought. But I didn't say it. *De mortuis nil nisi bonum*— speak well of the dead.

"What did she say?"

"That she had started seeing him. That he wasn't a customer but a friend. The first time I got a little bitchy, I think. I don't remember it very well. I was slightly stoned and I'm not too good at remembering things that happen when I drink."

"Give it a try. It's important."

She closed her eyes and thought it over while I drank her brandy. The bartender looked our way to see if we wanted more. I shook my head and he looked the other way again.

"I asked her if she was taking a pimp," Jill said suddenly. "I remember now. And Jackie…slapped me. Not hard, but slapped me. "

"Did she say anything?"

"She said she was thinking about marrying him, but I don't believe she really meant it."

"Was this the first time you met him?"

"Yes."

"Did she ever say anything about it again?"

"No. Maybe she felt I disapproved of the whole thing, I don't know. I met him one more time, but we just said hello and passed like ships at night. She never mentioned him again, or marriage." She paused. "He was the man in the apartment?"

I nodded.

"I don't understand," she said. "She might blackmail a customer. But her boyfriend—"

I thought about that and it started to make more sense than she thought it did. Jackie met Ralph, then either fell in love with him or pictured him as a good prospect for marriage and a way out of her debt-ridden state and call girl routine. She was in hock up to her eyeballs and she needed an out in the worst way—this made more sense than the love bit, which sounded out of character. So she played him hard, and she gave away something she usually sold at a good price.

And then some roof fell in on her. Maybe he had a wife somewhere. Maybe he wasn't interested in marrying her. One way or another, she turned out to be the sucker and she had the money worries without any help from Ralph in the offing. So she decided to make him pay through the nose for the free samples. She set up a date, rigged a camera or hired a cameraman, and took a flock of pictures. Then she used them to put the squeeze on Ralph.

That was a mistake. It changed everything, turned the whole world upside-down. Ralph paid her off—this was what the three grand in the safe-deposit box represented.

But he didn't pay her enough and she kept squeezing; but he was willing to take only so much. He shot her, turned her apartment upside-down looking for the pictures, and would kill Jill if he got a chance, since she was the only possible link to him and Jackie.

I knew the killer now. I had his picture and his first name. The rest would take some finding, but the police were the ones who could pull it off.

"I have to make a phone call, Ed," Jill said. "My answering service. And I want to use the little girl's room." She started to leave, then called back. "Ed, I could use a drink now. Will you order me a highball?"

She scooped up her purse and left the table. I sat there with an insurance policy, a roll of bills and a stack of dirty pictures. I looked at the pies again—solely for investigational purposes, of course—and put them in their envelope and tucked the envelope into my jacket pocket. I put the policy in its envelope and pocketed the roll of bills. Then I went to the bar and got myself a fresh brandy and a rye and ginger ale for Jill.

When she came back to the table, she sipped her drink and smiled at me. We talked some more until we finished our drinks. Then we rose to leave. I gave her the insurance policy and the money. She didn't ask for the pictures.

"What are you going to do now?"

"Call the police."

"Why?"

"Why not? They can run down Ralph a lot faster than we can. And the sooner we level with them, the easier it will go. Do you know how many laws we've broken in the past 20 hours?"

"I'm used to breaking laws," she said.

So was I, but I never felt too secure about it. I've played it loose and thrown out the book when unavoidable, but I don't play games with the police unless absolutely necessary. I live in a comfortable apartment and I drink good cognac and pay my bills on time. It's hard to do this if they lift your license.

"Ed, wouldn't it be better if we could give them Ralph's full name? Wouldn't that make it simpler all around?"

"Sure it would."

"Jackie had a little black book," she said. "It's one of the tools of the trade, along with a bottle of Enovid and a strong stomach. I know where she kept hers."

"Where?"

"In the apartment, and in a place where Ralph probably couldn't find it."

"Would his name be in it?"

"Of course. And if I could go there—"

"We could go to the police first," I said. "Then we could hunt down the little black book."

Jill made a face. "Let's do this my way," she said. "Please, Ed? Please?"

WE DID it "her" way. Actually we wound up doing what I had really wanted to do in the first place, although I had managed to argue the other side fairly convincingly. You don't play private cop unless you've got a kind of a hero complex, a strong wish to do things on your own. I wanted to get out from under, sure, but I also wanted to be able to walk up to Jerry Gunther with the whole thing tied up in a neat package. I had been playing with the case on my own, and it only seemed fitting and proper to finish it up the same way instead of running to Gunther at this stage of the game.

While I paid the bartender, Jill went to the ladies room to play games with her make-up. I got impatient.

It wouldn't take forever for Homicide to figure out who Jacqueline Baron was, and once they did, we couldn't get to the apartment without running into an army of cops. She came out and we left the bar. We flagged down a vacant hack, then took off for her place.

The cab crawled through traffic like a salmon bucking the current on its way upstream to spawn. The cabbie kept swearing at the traffic and each time he would excuse himself to Jill. The ride took forever. She was tense and jittery toward the end and I could understand why. We were coming down the stretch now, on the heels of the fiend who had killed her sister and threatened her own life.

The cab stopped outside her building. Her key opened the outer door. Then she turned toward me and said, "Wait here for me, Ed. I'll be down in a minute."

"I'll come up with you."

"No. Wait here. If the police are there, Ed, it's sensible for me to come walking in; it's my home. But if you're with me and they find out you're a private detective, they'll start asking a lot of questions we can't answer."

She had a point, but I said, "What about our friend Ralph?"

"He's already been here and searched the place," she said. "Why would he come back?"

I shrugged. "All right."

Her feet led her hurriedly up the flight of carpeted stairs. I stayed in the hallway at the foot of the stairs, poised to ward off imaginary intruders. No intruders appeared. I reached for a pipe and listened as her key entered the lock upstairs and the door opened. I hauled out a pouch of tobacco and her door swung shut. I opened the pouch and started to fill the pipe and Jill screamed, "Ed..."

The scream was shrill and brittle. I dropped the pipe and the tobacco and dug my .38 out of the shoulder rig, simultaneously charging up the staircase. I was halfway up when a gun went off. The apartment had thick walls and a heavy door but that shot echoed loud and long through the building, and another scream followed its shattering concussion.

Her door was locked. I put the mouth of the .38 to the lock and shot it to hell and gone, gave the door a kick and watched it fly open.

Jill was standing in the center of the room. She had a little gun in her little hand. Her dress was torn, her hair messed up. She was through screaming and she stood staring downward with wild and stricken eyes.

He was on the floor. Ralph, the mystery man, he of the bulldog jaw and the descending blackjack. He was on his back with his legs tangled awkwardly under him and his hands clutching out at nothing and a fountain of blood still gushing from the raw red wound in his throat.

She turned, saw me. I went to her and the gun spilled from her fingers and clattered on the floor. She put her head against my chest and wailed. I held her and her wailing stopped. After a while, she pushed me away, sucking in gulps of air. She looked ready to keel over. I led her to a chair and she sagged into it.

She said, "I should have...I should have let you...come with me. I didn't think—"

"He was waiting for you."

She managed to nod. "I came in. I closed the door... turned around and...he was pointing a gun at me. I tried to grab it and he grabbed at me and he tore my dress and—"

"Take it easy."

"I can't take it easy. I killed him. Good God, I killed him!"

I calmed her down. A cigarette helped. She smoked it greedily. Then I asked her how it had happened.

275

"I fought with him. I didn't even fully realize what was happening. I just knew he was trying to shoot me, and I screamed. I must have deflected the gun... It went off and—"

Ralph lay dead, a bullet wound in his throat. I looked at Jill. The intruder had torn her dress and her bra in the struggle. Her body was visible to the beltline. She pulled the dress together in unnecessary modesty.

"It's over now," I said. I crossed the room and picked up the phone.

NINE

IT COULD have been worse. Jerry Gunther could have been off and some other Homicide cop could have taken charge. But it was bad enough as things stood.

"I thought you were a friend of mine," Jerry sneered.

"I am."

"A friend is somebody who plays cute with me? A friend withholds evidence?"

I didn't say anything. Policemen were moving around the room, measuring things. A photographer took pictures. Other cops made chalk lines across the carpet.

"I'm not a stupid cop, Ed. Am I?"

"No. Jerry—"

"You should have called me when you found the girl in the park. You should have called me when the sister showed up at your apartment. You should have called me when you ran up against Traynor the first time. You should have—"

The dead man was Ralph Traynor. It said so in Jackie's address book and on a batch of cards and papers in his wallet. He lived somewhere in Brooklyn.

"You should know better, Ed."

I gave Jerry my side of it. I told him that my first aim

was to keep the girl free and clear and save her from publicity and the killer. "You would have spotlighted her," I said.

"I would have stuck her in a cell."

"And we never would have gotten anywhere. You know that and I know it, dammit. My way worked."

"It did?"

"Yes, Jerry. You have the killer. He's dead, but he would have been just as dead in a year after a trial and a batch of appeals. The state comes out a few dollars ahead and the case is closed out that much faster." I took a breath, smiled. "I know I played it cute. Maybe I was wrong. My reasons seemed good at the time."

He sighed, then punched me in the arm to show that we were still friends. I took Jill by the arm and went down the stairs behind Gunther. A police car was parked in front alongside a fire hydrant. Jerry's uniformed driver was at the wheel.

Jerry got in next to the driver and Jill and I sat in the back. The driver didn't use the siren. We drove moderately across town, then went down to Centre Street on the East Side Drive.

It took time for them to get our statements. I gave them mine as quickly as possible in a little room with Gunther and a police stenographer. I took it from the top, starting with the first phone call the day before and concluding with the arrival of the law. I left out little things like the interlude with Jill at Maddy Parson's apartment. Certain facts don't belong in a police report.

Jill took a little longer with her statement. The stenographer typed them both up and we signed them.

"You can both go now," Jerry said. "We'll be getting a report from ballistics and a rundown on Traynor pretty soon. So far everything checks out."

Jill nodded. She got to her feet and turned to me.

"Are you coming, Ed?" There was invitation in her voice. I thought of the part of the statement that I'd omitted. That diverting interlude.

"I'll stick around for the ballistics report," I said. "But how about dinner?"

"Wonderful," Jill said. "I haven't eaten in 24 hours. Just coffee this morning. Before, I was too scared to think about it. Now I'm suddenly starving."

Looking at her, thinking about another interlude, I felt hungry, too.

Jill said goodbye to Jerry, and we watched her go. Afterward we sat for a few minutes without saying anything. Then Jerry commented on Jill's looks. He poked me in the ribs. "Hearty appetite, tonight," he smiled. Then, serious again, he said, "Ed, you certainly fall into some bizarre cases."

"I guess so."

"But it all works out. Ballistics should confirm what we've already pretty well established. Jacqueline Baron was shot with a slug out of a .25 calibre automatic, probably foreign made. The gun that finished Traynor was an Astra Firecat. It fits."

"A little gun."

"Uh-huh. Easy to hide in a pocket. No bulge under the jacket, like the cannon you're wearing." He tapped me over the heart. "No gun for deer hunting, but good enough at close range. And he got close enough to the Baron girl to leave powder burns on her forehead."

"I know," I said. "I saw them." I lit my pipe. "A peculiar gun for a man like Traynor to use. A little gun would get lost in those big mitts of his."

Jerry grinned. "Sure. Chances are he'd have bought himself a Magnum, if he had the choice to make. But when it comes to picking up an unregistered gun, you take what you can get. We had a little old lady who shot her husband with a Super Blackhawk. The recoil on that thing must have knocked her into the next room. And then a hulk like Traynor uses a little job like the Astra. Those foreign guns—the thing is you can get 'em sent to you through the mail, Ed." He frowned. "Traynor's gun did a job though. Killed the Baron girl, then killed him."

He had things to do. I went outside and walked around the corner to a lunch counter. A group of uniformed patrolmen sat around eating. I had a pair of hamburgers and two cups of coffee.

When I finished, I went back to Headquarters. The ballistics report had confirmed what everyone already took for granted. The same gun had killed both Jackie Baron and Ralph Traynor. I was not surprised. They also knew a little about Traynor. A master mechanic, he owned his own collision shop on Pitkin Avenue. He was married. Someone was going over there now to tell his wife. I did not envy the man on that particular assignment.

Gunther passed me in the hallway. He said, "Go home now, Ed. We have everything we need. We'll want you and Jill Baron for the inquest in a day or. two. Let her know, will you?"

I said it would be my pleasure.

It was raining when I got outside, but I didn't feel like springing for another cab. I had run up enough expenses, especially since my client had thus far paid me nothing in negotiable cash. There had been other compensations, of course.

TEN

SOMETHING stank.

I spent a long time sitting at my window watching the rain come down on 83rd Street. There was a drink at

279

my elbow but I somehow never got around to touching it. There was a pot of coffee on the stove, and I left that alone, too. I looked at the rain and at 83rd Street and I added up everything, and something still stank.

The packet of pornographic pictures was still in my jacket pocket. Gunther had not wanted them. They were evidence, but with Traynor dead there would be no trial, just the formality of an inquest to tie up what loose ends remained so the file could be marked closed.

I took out the brown envelope and opened it. I spilled the black-and-white glossies into my lap. Then, one by one, I examined them again.

An odd sensation. Pornographic photos, sure to arouse the libido of any vicariously-oriented lecher. But this was a special case; both subjects engaged in such lively activity were lively no more. The nubile blonde was dead, and the massive man was dead, and neither would again have the chance to play bedroom games.

A very odd sensation.

I reached for my drink, took a small sip of the cognac. A little bell rang somewhere in the back of my mind. I tried to ignore the bell but it fought to be heard with the tenacity of an alarm clock on a cold morning.

I looked at the pictures again. Three of them had similar scratches, little seemingly meaningless spots...

Outside, it went right on raining.

At a quarter after four I called Centre Street and got through to Jerry Gunther. "I was wondering about Traynor," I said. "Get anything more on him?"

"A little. Listen, it's over, Ed. And you're out of it anyway. What's your interest?"

"I've got to type up a report for my client."

He didn't argue. They had found a little more about Traynor, not a hell of a lot but enough. He was in good

shape financially, though not rich. He had been seeing
a lot of Jackie Baron, and his wife knew he was playing
around—but not with whom. She had been thinking of
divorcing him, had even gone to a lawyer to ask what a
divorce would entail. She wanted to get rid of him, but she
also wanted to gouge him for every nickel she could get.

"That made him a good blackmail prospect," Jerry
Gunther said. "With those pictures in her lap, Mrs. Traynor wouldn't have to take a plane to Reno. She could get a
New York divorce and a nice piece of alimony. But Traynor
wasn't rich enough to pay forever. He forked over money
once or twice, which accounts for the dough you found in
Jackie's safe-deposit box. Then she squeezed too hard and
he decided to kill her instead."

"Did you check his bank account for large
withdrawals?"

"Ed," he said exasperatedly, "we're not working on this
case. We're closing it. Something eating you?"

"No. Just routine, Jerry."

I thanked him. He said what the hell, call him anytime,
he was just a public servant. I told him I might take him up
on that sooner or later.

I took him up on it 20 minutes later, after two cups
of coffee and a lot more thought. I got him on the phone
and heard him growl something to somebody else; then he
asked me what the hell I wanted now.

"A favor."

"Shoot."

"Has Jackie Baron's body been released yet?"

"No."

"It's still at the morgue?"

"Yes. The sister hasn't claimed it yet, probably won't
until tomorrow, I guess. Why?"

"Call the morgue for me. Tell them I have permission

to look at the body."

He didn't say anything at first. Then he spoke softly. "Ed, you 're onto something."

"Partly."

"Tell Papa."

"I'll tell Papa as soon as there's something to tell. I'm just stabbing in the dark right now. I don't know anything for sure."

"You think there's something funny?"

"There could be. Make the call for me, will you?

He swore at me a little, but said he would make the call. I hung up, finished my coffee end put on my trench coat. Every private cop has to have a trench coat; it comes with the license. I added a slouch hat to keep the rain off my head and checked myself in the mirror to make sure I looked true to form. I did. Then I went outside and ducked around the corner to pick up my car.

The pimply attendant asked me where I was going on a day like this.

"To the morgue," I said.

He laughed. He thinks I'm a great comic.

THE LITTLE man at the morgue had thick glasses and no jaw. He was not a lovely man and he had an ugly job. I showed him identification and he checked my name with the little note on his clipboard. Then, flashing a ghoulish smile, he said: *This way, Mr. London.*

I followed him past the slabs on which reposed bodies covered with sheets.

"Here we are," he said finally. "Miss Jacqueline Baron. We didn't know who she was, you know, until a few hours ago. That's dreadful, isn't it?"

"What is?"

"To be dead and unknown. I'd hate that. People should

have serial numbers." He clucked his tongue. "Do you want to see the girl?"

"Yes."

He nodded, drew the sheet down as far as her neck. They had performed an autopsy. It wasn't pretty.

"All the way," I said.

He took the sheet off and we stood viewing the body like a pair of necrophiliacs in paradise. I tried not to look at the chinless man's eyes. His job might have unwritten compensations for him, and I did not want to think about them.

I looked at the body, at the legs. Smooth white skin everywhere. No scars, no blemishes. Nothing but clear flesh frozen in the gray permanence of death.

I turned away. The little man covered her with the sheet and joined me. We walked to the exit. He asked me if I had known the girl. I said I had seen her once, not mentioning that she had been dead at the time. He did not say anything more.

At 7 PM I parked in front of the building on 58th Street. I went up the stairs for Jill Baron. She was ready, and she looked better than ever. "You're on time," she said. "Let's go, I'm starving."

We drove to a steakhouse on Third Avenue, one of the dark quiet restaurants where newspapermen go when they sell a magazine story. A waiter brought us rare sirloins and baked potatoes, then drinks and coffee. We talked trivia all through dinner. She kept smiling at me, a smile ripe with promise. I smiled back. A good meal shared together in pleasant surroundings. A prelude to an intimate evening.

Afterward I said something about a club downtown where they played good jazz. She took my arm, stepped up close and let me smell her perfume. "We don't have to go anywhere," she said.

"I thought you'd want to celebrate your deliverance

from terror."

"I do." Her voice turned husky. "But we can celebrate at my place, can't we?"

I smiled. Who was I to argue with a woman?

We drove back to her apartment.

She poured drinks and we sat on the couch and imbibed them. Traces of chalk marks remained on the carpet, and a throw rug did not quite hide the stain of Traynor's blood.

"I won't be living here much longer," she said. "I may even leave New York. One thing is sure... I'm getting out of this business, Ed."

I didn't say anything.

"I can't say I hated every minute of it because I didn't. It was easy and profitable. But it does things to a girl, makes her start hating herself. Jackie wasn't a blackmailer, not at heart. The work changed her. It must have. I don't want to turn into something that would fill me with self-loathing. It's important to like yourself, Ed."

We finished our drinks. On cue we turned to each other. Her face was flushed from the drink and her lips tasted of it. She snuggled up against me and whispered sweet somethings.

The bedroom was neat and clean, the bed turned down. She moved to turn off the light. I told her to leave it on.

"You want to see me naked, Ed?" A narcissistic smile showed I had scored 100 percent with an apt remark.

"Yes, from head to toe."

"I'm glad," she murmured. "I like that."

We kissed. She undressed slowly, sensuously. We stretched out on the bed. She lay back, her eyes closed, her arms at her sides. A nude goddess, waiting.

I touched her cheek, her shoulder. My hand moved

over silken flesh. My finger touched the strawberry birth-mark on the side of her thigh and she quivered beneath my touch.

The birthmark. The one that had been scratched from the negatives of the pornographic photographs. *The one that was nowhere to be seen on the body in the morgue!*

Her eyes opened and she looked at me. There was the shadow of a question on her face but she kept it back, wait-ing. I took my hands away from her body.

"It was a nice try, *Jackie*," I said. "It almost worked."

Her mouth made an *O* and her eyes bugged. She was already out of her clothes. Now she jumped out of her skin.

ELEVEN

SHE WASN'T talking. She lay naked on the bed with beads of sweat already starting to emerge upon her forehead. Her eyes were trying to say that she didn't know what I was talking about. Their message didn't convince me.

"I've been calling you Jill," I said. "But you're not Jill. Jill's in the morgue. She's there because you put a gun to her forehead and killed her!"

She stared at me, her breasts heaving with emotion.

"You're not Jill. You're Jackie. And some of the things you told me about Jackie were true. Jackie had money worries. Jackie was a gambler and Jackie owed a lot of tabs around town. Jill had money in the bank but Jackie didn't. Jackie owed money."

I stopped for a breath. "So Jackie killed Jill," I said. "You needed money, fast. A long time ago you and Jill took out policies naming each other as beneficiaries. If Jill was eliminated, then you got the money you needed in a hurry. So you thought it all out and decided to kill your sister."

"You're insane—"

"No. You figured it all out and somewhere along the line you saw a way to do it better. It was one thing to kill Jill—then you got the money and paid your debts. But it was even neater to kill her and assume your sister's identity. Then your debts would be written off completely. You could start fresh with no one mad at you. You could be Jill."

I looked at her coldly. "Probably Jill was a nicer girl, anyhow."

The room was quiet. I looked at her naked body and looked quickly away. Flesh in and of itself is no stimulant. She kindled no desire, not after I'd proved to myself that she had killed her own sister, and Ralph Traynor.

"There was more to it than that," I went on. "You might have had a lot of trouble figuring out a good way to kill Jill. But it became infinitely easier when you made it look as though Jackie had been murdered. Jill didn't have any reason to work a blackmail dodge. Jill had money in the bank. But you had plenty of reason to be a blackmailer, and if you made your sister look like a blackmailer nobody would look your way if she got herself murdered. They would just look for the person she had been blackmailing.

"You probably started to play a little blackmail at the beginning. Figured on squeezing some money out of Ralph Traynor. Hell, you're not the sentimental type. You wouldn't have put Traynor on the free list because you liked his looks. You started seeing him because you thought you could blackmail him. You had a set of blackmail pics taken and were ready to start showing them to him; but then you realized he couldn't come up with the big money you needed."

Jackie had a pack of cigarettes on the night table. I took one and lit it. "That was one thing I wondered about," I continued. "Traynor made a good living but he wasn't rich. I could see him coming up with three thousand dollars

286

in a pinch, but I couldn't see how you figured on getting any more than that from him. But you never blackmailed him at all. You had the pictures taken, and when you saw the prints and thought about the money you needed, you got the idea of killing Jill.

"And you went right ahead with it after you put a pile of money and the pictures in your safe-deposit box That set the stage. Jill never suspected a thing. Maybe she noticed you were a little nervous. Probably not. You 're a good actress, Jackie."

She looked at me. Her face showed no expression whatsoever, as though she was waiting patiently for me to finish spouting my nonsense and to return to reality. I took a final drag on the cigarette and ground it out in an ashtray.

"A damned good actress. Maybe you have to be a good actress to be a good whore. Anyway, yesterday morning you got away from Jill and called me. You were all mystery on the phone. You were willing to risk my writing the whole thing off as a gag because you wanted things to work out just right. And you wanted to make sure you had me playing ball with you. If I didn't call you back, you'd just postpone the murder a day or two and phone some other private eye.

"But I cooperated. You were there when I called you back and you arranged a meeting with me at 4:30. Then, about an hour ahead of time, you took Jill for a walk in the park. She thought the two of you were just going out for some fresh air. You went to the spot where you were supposed to meet me, took the automatic from your purse and blew your sister's brains out."

For the first time, she shuddered. It was a momentary reaction, a quivering of the upper lip, a brief outbreak of gooseflesh over her naked body. It passed quickly. Maybe now, hearing it from me, the enormity of the whole diabolical plot was beginning to sink in.

"You stuck the gun back in your purse and left the park, Jackie. Maybe you hung around long enough to make sure I discovered the body. Maybe not. Either way, you had plenty of time to double back to my apartment and wander in like a little lost lamb. You staged that part beautifully. You hadn't told me anything about sisters over the phone and as far as I knew there was only one of you, and that one was dead on a park bench. You came into my arms with a whole load of shock value working for you, and then you let yourself fall apart in tears when I told you your sister was dead. You played the scared act to the hilt and made it look as though you were in a hell of a lot of danger."

SHE SAT speechless—mouth agape, looking ludicrous in her nudity.

"And that worked, too. If the non-existent blackmail victim had only been after your sister, I would have taken the whole thing straight to the police and they would have picked it to pieces. But the killer was supposed to be after you, too—and I had to catch him and keep you in the clear at the same time. I stowed you at Maddy's, and you got busy setting up a frame for Traynor.

"You were cute about it," I went on. "You never did get around to blackmailing Traynor, so he still thought he was your loving boyfriend. As soon as I left Maddy's you got on the phone and called him, told him to get over to your apartment. Or maybe he was there all along—it's the same either way. You told him some pest was on his way over and that he should knock the pest out and leave him there.

"Traynor didn't know anything about murder. All he knew was that he was crazy about you, the poor fool. So he waited in the dark until I came in, and he slugged me. Then he turned your apartment upside-down to make it look as though it had been searched. I don't know what you told him to get him to go along with that. It must have been good."

She laughed. "Ralph would do anything for me," she said. "He didn't need a reason."

"Sure. Anyway, he knocked me out and gave me a good look at him in the process. I believed your story right off the bat, but this made it perfect. The whole blackmail pattern was fixed now. I had to believe in Traynor because he damn well existed and I had an aching head to prove it. I went back to Maddy's with my head in a sling and you let me coax a little more information out of you. About Jackie being in debt, and about Jackie having a boyfriend—all of that. If you gave me all of it at once I would have tried to pick holes in it, but you were too smart for that. You made me pry it out of you and I swallowed it whole."

"You said I was a good actress, Ed."

She was smiling now. I had her pegged and she knew it, but she could still manage a smile. God knows how.

"I didn't get a chance to look for holes in your story, not that night," I said. "You kept me busy in bed. More acting, Jackie."

"That wasn't *all* acting."

I ignored the line. "A repeat performance in the morning," I said. "And then the safe-deposit box—hell, that was something. You let me talk you into impersonating Jackie, and what it amounted to is that you impersonated yourself. No wonder you didn't have any trouble with the signature. It was your own signature.

"You did a good job there, you know. You had to look uncertain enough to make me think you were Jill and confident enough not to make the guard suspicious. You got the money and the pictures from the box and you were home free, or close to it."

SHE MOVED a little on the bed, a coldly calculated but subtle and seductive maneuver that made her breasts jut out. She wanted to make me conscious of her body, but didn't want to act whorish about it.

She could have saved herself the trouble. Her body was now about as exciting to me as Jill's, stretched out on a slab in the morgue. She stretched like a cat and ran her tongue over her lower lip and not a single spark flew.

"We went to the bar and looked at the pictures, Jackie," I continued. "Then you got up to make a phone call. You didn't call your answering service. You called Traynor, told him to get to your apartment right away. I don't know what reason you gave him, but you pulled the strings and he performed on schedule. You worked a stall act at the bar to give him time to get there, dawdled in the john, all of that. Then we got to your apartment to look for Jackie's address book. You made me wait downstairs. What would have happened if I went up with you?"

"I knew you wouldn't, Ed."

"The hell you did. You hoped I wouldn't but you had it all figured out if I did. I was lucky I stayed downstairs."

Her eyes went innocently wide.

"Because you would have killed me. You would have used your gun on me and then you would have used my gun on Traynor to make it look as though we shot each other. That would have been a little tricky to pull off but you would have done it if necessary. Then with both of us dead you could try your story on the police.

"It might have worked too. But it wasn't as sure a thing as it could have been, and that was why you wanted me to stay downstairs to back you up. However, you would have made your play either way."

"Oh, no, Ed. That's not true!" She put her heart into it. "I never could have killed you, Ed."

"No?"

"Ed, I—"

I told her to save it. "You went upstairs and let yourself in," I continued. "Traynor came over to kiss you and you screamed your head off. His face must have been something to see just then. You had him running around in circles anyway, and a good loud scream must have rattled the hell out of him. But he didn't have much time to worry about it. You took out the gun and shot him. Then you gave out with another scream.

"This afternoon I thought about that part of it. The door was locked when I got upstairs. I had to shoot it off. Why would you lock the door when you were ducking into the apartment for a minute? When would you get a chance to close the door with Traynor waiting to kill you?

"You did it to stall. It gave you a few extra seconds to tear your dress and build the scene. By the time I shot my way through the door you were into your act, and from then on everything was set up. It couldn't miss, could it?"

She didn't answer.

"The gun checked out, the same weapon used for both killings. I backed your story every step of the way. You ran one hell of a lot of risks but things broke right for you each time. And by the time you left Headquarters you were clear. There would be a coroner's inquest, maybe a few more questions that you could answer with your eyes closed. Then Jill's body would be buried with your name on the headstone. You'd be Jill, with no debts and whatever money she had had, plus $50,000 worth of insurance money."

She didn't answer. Her hands moved down over her own naked flesh in a calculated movement that was supposed to look unconscious and automatic. I remembered making love to her, the flavor of her embrace, the touch of her body.

"You almost made it," I said.

"What tipped you off, Ed? The birthmark?"

"Partly. That clinched it, of course. As soon as I got the idea that it was you in the photographs, I knew you had lied to me. And that was the trouble with the whole gambit, Jackie. It was all built on a pyramid of lies. As soon as one of them broke down, the whole thing collapsed. All the little inconsistencies that I had glossed over came back in spades. Every loophole showed up bright and clear."

"Then I should have gotten those pictures back. I could have said I wanted to bum them—"

"I would have figured it anyway."

"How?"

I thought for a second. "It was too pat," I said. "You timed everything so perfectly, Jackie. So damned perfectly. Traynor was always at the right place just at the right time. Somebody had to be calling his signals.

"And another thing—the powder bums on Jill's forehead. That was too neat and cute. If she knew Traynor was after her, she wouldn't have let him get that close. She would have run or tried to fight or something. The death scene looked as though it had been the handiwork of someone she knew, someone she wasn't afraid of." I frowned. "Someone like her sister."

"I... I wanted to make it fast."

"Uh-huh. You should have walked away and fired three or four shots into her. It would have looked better that way."

"I wanted Jill to die quickly. I didn't want it to hurt her."

"Sure. You're an angel of mercy and an angel of death all rolled into one. *There was a little whore and she had a little bore right in the middle of her forehead.* You should have

292

stuck to the other nursery rhyme."

"What rhyme?"

"The one about Jackie and Jill going over the hill," I said. "Get dressed."

"You're turning me in?"

"What do you think?"

But she wasn't through yet. Her lush body flexed and her lips curled in a sensual smile. "Look at me," she said.

I looked.

"I'm well off now financially, Ed. I'm not good at arithmetic but I'm sure you can figure it out. I'll bet it's a lot of money, right?"

"It's a lot of money."

"And there would be more than money, Ed." Her hands touched her breasts. "I have a good clientele."

I wonder if she thought it would work. Probably not. But it was all she had left and it didn't hurt to try.

I stood up. She swung her legs over the side of the bed, got to her feet and came toward me. "Get dressed," I sneered. "I can't stand the sight of you."

She blinked. Maybe no one had ever told her that before. She stood still. I pushed her aside, walked past her and picked up the phone. I started dialing. I was making more work for Jerry Gunther, but I had a hunch he wouldn't mind.

Great Istanbul Gold Grab

From the pages of **For Men Only**, March 1967

Art by MORT KÜNSTLER

The Turks have dreary jails. The plural might be inaccurate, for all I truly knew, there might be but one jail in all of Turkey. Or there could be others, but they need not be dreary places at all.

But, whatever the case, there was at least one dreary jail in Turkey. It was in Istanbul, it was dank and dirty and desolate, and I was in it. The floor of my cell could have been covered by a nine-by-twelve rug, but that would have hidden the decades of filth that had left their stamp upon the wooden floor. There was one small barred window, too small to let very much air in or out, too high to afford more than a glimpse of the sky. When the window turned dark, it was presumably night; when it grew blue again, I guessed that morning had come. But, of course, I could not be certain that the window even opened to the outside. For all I knew, some idiot Turk alternately lit and extinguished a lamp outside that window to provide me with this illusion.

I never saw another prisoner, never heard a human sound except for the Turkish guard who seemed to be assigned to me. He came morning, noon, and night with food. Breakfast was always a slab of cold black toast and a cup of thick black coffee. Lunch and dinner were always the same—a tin plate piled with a suspicious pilaf, mostly rice with occasional bits of lamb and shreds of vegetable matter of indeterminate origin. Incredibly enough, the pilaf was delicious.

It was the boredom that was stifling. I had been arrested on a Tuesday. I'd flown to Istanbul from Athens, arriving around ten in the morning, and I knew something had gone wrong when the customs officer took far too much time pawing through my suitcase. When he sighed at last and closed the bag, I said, "Are you quite through?"

"Yes. You are Evan Tanner?"

"Yes."

"Evan Michael Tanner?"

"Yes."

"American?"

"Yes."

"You flew from New York to London, from London to Athens, and from Athens to Istanbul?"

"Yes."

"You have business in Istanbul?"

"Yes."

He smiled. "You are under arrest," he said.

"Why?"

"I am sorry," he said, "but I am not at liberty to say."

MY CRIME seemed destined to remain a secret forever.
Three uniformed Turks drove me to jail in a jeep. A clerk
took my watch, my belt, my passport, my suitcase, my
necktie, my shoelaces, my pocket comb and my wallet. He
wanted my ring, but it wouldn't leave my finger, so he let
me keep it. My uniformed bodyguard led me down a flight
of stairs, through a catacombic maze of corridors, and
ushered me into a cell.

There was nothing much to do in that cell. I don't
sleep, have not slept in sixteen years—more of that later—
so I had the special joy of being bored, not sixteen hours
a day, like the normal prisoner, but a full twenty-four. I
ached for something to read, anything at all. Wednesday
night I asked my guard if he could bring me some books or
magazines.

"I don't speak English," he said in Turkish.

I *do* speak Turkish, but I thought it might be worth-
while to keep this a secret.

The pattern changed, finally, on my ninth day in jail,
a Wednesday. I had my usual breakfast, and performed
a brief regimen of setting-up exercises. An hour or so
after breakfast I heard footsteps in the hallway. My guard
unlocked my door, and two uniformed men came into my
cell. One was very tall, very thin, very much the officer.
The other was shorter, fatter, sweaty, and moustached1 and
possessed an abundance of gold teeth.

Both carried clipboards and wore sidearms. The tall
one studied his clipboard for a moment, then looked at me.
"You are Evan Tanner," he said.

"Yes."

He smiled. "I believe we will be able to release you very shortly, Mr. Tanner," he said. "I regret the need to have dealt so unpleasantly with you, but I'm sure you can understand."

"No, I can't, frankly."

He studied me. "Why, there were so many points to be checked, and naturally it was necessary to keep you in a safe place while these checks were made. And then you acted in such a strange manner, you know. You never questioned your confinement, you never banged furiously on the bars of your cell, you never slept—"

"I don't sleep."

"But we did not know that then, don't you see?" he smiled again. "You did not demand to see the American ambassador. Every American invariably demands to see the ambassador. If an American is overcharged in a restaurant, he wants to bring the matter at once to his ambassador's attention. But you seemed to accept everything—"

I said, "When rape is inevitable, lie back and enjoy it."

"What? Oh I see. But that is a sophisticated reaction, you understand, and it called for explanation. We contacted Washington and learned quite a great deal about you. Not everything, I am quite certain, but a great deal." He looked around the cell. "Perhaps you've tired of your surroundings. Let us find more comfortable quarters. I must ask you several questions, and then you will be free to go."

In an airy cleaner room a floor above, the taller man sat beneath a flattering portrait of Ataturk and smiled benevolently at me. He asked if I knew why they had arrested me so promptly. I said that I did not.

"You are a member"—he consulted the clipboard—"of a fascinating array of organizations, Mr. Tanner. We did not know just how many causes had caught your interest, but when your name appeared on the incoming passenger

297

list it did line up with our membership rosters for two rather interesting organizations. You belong, it would seem, to the Pan-Hellenic Friendship Society. True?"

"Yes."

"And to the League for the Restoration of Cilician Armenia?"

"Yes."

He stroked his chin. "Neither of these two organizations is particularly friendly to Turkish interests, Mr. Tanner. Each is composed of a scattering of—how would you say it? Fanatics? Yes, fanatics. The Pan-Hellenic Friendship Society has been extremely vocal lately. We suspect they're peripherally involved in some acts of minor terrorism over Cyprus. The Armenian fanatics have been dormant since the close of the war. Most people would probably be surprised to know that they even exist, and we've had no trouble from them for a very long time. But suddenly you appear in Istanbul and are recognized as a member of not one but both of these organizations." He paused significantly. "It might interest you to know that our records indicate you are the only man on earth to hold membership in both organizations."

"Is that so?"

"Yes."

"That's very interesting," I said. "Would you care to explain these memberships, Mr. Tanner?"

I thought this over. "I'm a joiner," I said finally.

"Yes, I'm sure you are."

"I'm a member of...many groups."

"Indeed." He referred to the clipboard once more. "Our list may not be complete, but you may fill in any significant omissions. You belong to the two groups I mentioned. You. also belong to the Irish Republican Brotherhood and the Clann-na-Gaille. You are a member of the Flat Earth

Society of England, the Macedonian Friendship League, the Industrial Workers of the World, the Libertarian League, the Society for a Free Croatia, the Confederacion Nacional del Irabajadores de Espana, the Committee Allied Against Fluoridation, the Serbian Brotherhood, the Nazdoya Federovka, and the Lithuanian Army-in-Exile," He looked up and signed. "This list goes on and on. Need I read more?"

"I'm impressed with your research."

"A simple call to Washington, Mr. Tanner. They have a lengthy file on you, did you know that?"

"Yes."

"Why on earth do you belong to all these groups? According to Washington, you don't seem to *do* anything. You attend an occasional meeting, you receive an extraordinary quantity of pamphlets, you associate with subversives of every conceivable persuasion, but you don't do much of anything. Can you explain yourself?"

"Lost causes interest me."

"Pardon?"

There seemed no need for a reply.

"It seemed quite obvious to us that you were an *agent provocateur*," he continued. "We contacted your American Central Intelligence Agency, and they denied any knowledge of you, which made us all the more certain you were one of their agents. We're still not certain that you're not. But you don't fit any of the standard molds. You don't make any sense."

"That's true," I said.

"You don't sleep. You're thirty-four years old and lost the power to sleep when you were eighteen. Is that correct?"

"Yes."

"In the war?"

"Korea."

"You were shot through the head? Is that what happened?"

"More or less. A piece of shrapnel. Nothing seemed damaged—it was just a fleck of shrapnel, actually—so they patched me up and gave me my gun and sent me back into battle. Then I just wasn't sleeping, not at all. I didn't know why. They thought it was mental—something like that."

"I see. Continue."

"Well, they kept knocking me out with shots, and I would stay out until the shot wore off and then wake up again. They couldn't even induce normal sleep. They decided finally that the sleep center of my brain was destroyed. They're not sure just what the sleep center is or just how it works, but evidently I don't have one any more. So I don't sleep."

"Not at all?"

"Not at all."

"You are in good health, Mr. Tanner?"

"Yes."

"Is it not a strain on your heart, this endless wakefulness?"

"It doesn't seem to be."

"And you'll live as long as anyone else?"

"Not quite as long, according to the doctors. Their statistics indicate that I'll live three-fourths of my natural life span, barring accidents, of course. But I don't trust their figures."

He frowned. "How do you live?" he asked.

"I receive a disability pension from the Army. For my loss of sleep."

"They pay you one hundred twelve dollars per month. Is that correct?"

It was. I've no idea how the Defense Department had

arrived at that sum. I'm certain there's no precedent.

"You do not live on one hundred twelve dollars per month." He narrowed his eyes at me. "Why are you in Turkey, Mr. Tanner?"

"I'm a tourist."

"Don't be absurd. You've never left the United States since Korea, according to Washington. You applied for a passport less than three months ago. You came at once to Istanbul. Why?"

I hesitated.

"For whom are you spying, Mr. Tanner? The CIA? One of your little organizations? Tell me."

"I'm not spying at all."

"Then why are you here?"

I hesitated. Then I said, "There is a man in Antakya who makes counterfeit gold coins. He's noted for his counterfeit Armenian pieces, but he does other work as well. Marvelous work. According to Turkish law, he's able to do this with impunity. He never counterfeits Turkish coins, so it's all perfectly legal."

"Continue."

"I plan to see him, buy an assortment of coins, smuggle them back into the United States, and sell them as genuine."

The man looked at me for a long time. Finally he said, "One moment, please." He used a phone on his desk and called someone. I looked up at Ataturk's portrait and listened to his conversation. He was asking some bureaucrat somewhere if there was in fact a counterfeiter in Antakya and what sort of things the man produced. He was not overly surprised to find out that my story checked out.

To me he said, "If you are lying, you have built your lie on true foundations. I find it frankly inconceivable that you would travel to Istanbul for such a purpose. There is a profit in it?"

"I could buy a thousand dollars worth of rare forgeries and sell them for thirty thousand dollars by passing them as genuine."

He was silent for a moment. "I still do not believe you," he said at length. "You are a spy or a saboteur of one sort or another. I am convinced of it. But it makes no matter. Whatever you are, whatever your intentions, you must leave Turkey. You are unwelcome in our country, and there are men in your own country who are very much interested in speaking with you.

"Mustafa will see that you get a bath and a chance to change your clothes. At three-fifteen this afternoon you will board a Pan American flight for Shannon Airport. Mustafa will be with you. You will have two hours between planes and you will then board another Pan American flight for Washington, where Mustafa will turn you over to agents of your own government." Mustafa, who was to do all of this, was the grubby little man who had brought my pilaf twice a day and my toast each morning.

We stopped at the clerk's desk. I was given back my belt, my necktie, my shoelaces, my pocket comb, my wallet, and my watch. Mustafa took my passport and tucked it away in a pocket. I asked him for it, and he grinned and told me he didn't speak English.

We left the building. The sun was absolutely blinding. My eyes were unequal to it. We walked along toward a 1953 Chevrolet, its fenders crippled, its body riddled with rust. We sat in back, and Mustafa told the driver to take us to the airport. He leaned forward, and I heard him tell the driver that I was a very deceptive spy from the United States of America and that I was emphatically not to be trusted.

They all see too many James Bond movies. They

expect spies everywhere and overlook the profit motive entirely. A spy? It was the last thing on earth I would ever become. I had no intentions of spying for or against Turkey or anyone else.

I had come, quite simply, so that I could steal approximately three million dollars in gold...

IT HAD begun some months before in Manhattan at the junction of two streams—a girl, and a most noble lost cause. The girl was Kitty Bazerian, who rolls her belly in Chelsea nightclubs as Alexandra the Great. The noble lost cause, one of the noblest, one of the most utterly lost, was the League for the Restoration of Cilician Armenia.

Kitty and I met at a wedding in Greenwich Village. My friend Owen Morgan was being married to a girl from White Plains. Owen is a Welsh poet with no discernible talent who had discovered that one could make a fair living by drinking an impressive amount, spouting occasional poetry, and seducing every sexy female within reach. He startled me by asking me to be his best man, an office I had never before performed. So I stood up for Owen and passed him the ring at the appropriate time, and afterward Kitty Bazerian danced at his wedding.

She was small and slender and dark, with fine black hair and huge brown eyes. She stood demurely, garbed in a wisp of diaphanous fluff, and someone said, "Now Kitty Bazerian will dance for us," and the house band from the New Life Restaurant began to play, and her body sang in the center of the improvised stage, music in motion, silk, velvet perfection, adding a wholly new dimension to sensuality.

Afterward I found her at the bar, dressed now in skirt and sweater and black tights, which was about right for Owen's wedding.

"Alexandra the Great," I said.

"Who told you? They promised not to say."

"I recognized you myself."

"Honestly?"

"I've watched you dance at the New Life. And at the Port Said before that."

"And you recognized me right away?"

"Of course. I never knew that Alexandra the Great was an Armenian."

"A starving Armenian right about now. I already had too much to drink and I'm starving."

"May it never be said that Evan Tanner let an Armenian starve. Why don't we get out of here?"

We did. I suggested an Armenian restaurant in the Village. She asked me why I was so very hipped on Armenians. I told her I was writing a thesis on Armenia.

"You're a student?"

"No, I'm just writing a thesis."

"I don't...wait a minute, you're Evan *Tanner!* Sure, Owen told me about you. He says you're crazier than he is."

"He may be right."

"And you're writing about Armenians now? You ought to meet my grandmother. She could tell you all about how we lost the family fortunes. She makes a good story out of it. According to her, we were the richest Armenians in Turkey. Gold coins, she says; more gold coins than you could count. And now the Turks have it all." She laughed. "Isn't that always the way?"

I don't remember what we had or how it tasted. There was a good red wine with the meal, but we got drunker on each other than on anything else. It does not happen often for me, the special magic, the perfect harmony. It happened this time.

And outside afterwards, a breeze playing with her marvelous black hair, she said, "I live with my mother and my grandmother, so that's out. Do you have a place we can go to?"

"Yes."

"But Owen said something about you not sleeping. I mean—"

"I don't, but I have a bed."

"How sweet of you," she said, taking my arm, "to have a bed."

It was about a week after that when I finally did meet Kitty's grandmother. Kitty had told me several times that I would enjoy the old woman's story, and she became especially enthusiastic when I showed her my membership card in the League for the Restoration of Cilician Armenia. She had never heard of the group—rather few people have, actually—but she was certain her grandmother would be delighted.

"She has some pretty grim memories," Kitty said. "She was the only one of the family to get away. The Turks killed everybody else. I have a feeling she got raped in the bargain, but she never said anything about it exactly, and it's not the kind of subject you discuss with your grandmother."

KITTY LIVED in Brooklyn, just across the bridge, in a neighborhood that was largely Syrian and Lebanese with a scattering of Armenians. We walked from the subway. It was early after. Her grandmother sat in front of the television set.

Kitty said, "Grandma, this is Evan Tanner. He wanted to see you."

She was a gnomish little woman, her still-black hair parted absurdly in the middle, a strange light dancing merrily in her brown eyes. She was smoking a Helmar cigarette and had a tall glass of a dangerous orange liquid beside her. This was her life—a chair in front of a television set in her daughter's house. It was extraordinary, her eyes said, that a young man would come to see her.

In Armenian I said, "I am not Armenian myself, Mrs. Bazerian, but I have long been a great friend of the Armenian people and their supporter in their heroic fight for freedom."

Her eyes caught fire. "He speaks Armenian!" she cried, "he speaks Armenian!"

"I knew she would love you," Kitty told me.

"Kitty, make coffee. Mr. Tanner and I must talk."

And the old woman's story was a classic. It had happened in 1922, she told me. She had been but a girl then, a girl just old enough to seek a husband. "And there were many who wanted me, Mr. Tanner. I was a pretty one then. And my father the richest man in Balikesir..."

Balikesir, a town about a hundred miles north of Smyrna, was the capital of Balikesir Province. She had lived there with her mother and her father and her father's father and two brothers and a sister and assorted aunts and uncles and cousins. Her father's house was one of the finest in Balikesir, and her father was the head of the town's Armenian community. A fine house it was, too, not far from the railroad station, built high upon a hill with a view for miles in all directions. A huge house, with high columns around the doorway and a sloping cement walk down to the street below. Of the five hundred Armenian families in Balikesir, none had a finer house.

"The Greeks were at war with the Turks," she told me. "Of course, we were on the side of the Greeks, and my father had raised funds for the Greeks and knew many of their leaders. There were thousands of Greeks in Balikesir, and they were good friends with the Armenians. Our churches were different, but we were all Christians, not heathens like the Turks. At first my father thought the Greeks would win. The British were going to help us, you see. But, then, no help came from the British, and my father learned that the Turks would win after all."

It was then that the gold began to come to the house in Balikesir. Every day men brought sacks of gold, she said. Some brought little leather purses, some brought suitcases, some had gold coins sewn into their garments. Each man brought the gold to her father, who counted it carefully and wrote out a receipt for it. Then the man left, and the gold was put in the basement.

"But we could not leave it there, you see. The bandits were already at the gates of Smyrna, and time was short. And my father had in his hands all the gold of all the Armenians of Smyrna."

"Of Balikesir, you mean?"

She laughed. "Of Balikesir? Oh, no. Why, there were only five hundred families of our people in Balikesir. No, they brought all the Armenian gold of Smyrna as well because they knew that Smyrna would fall first and they knew, too, that my father was a man who could be trusted. Just a few sacks would have held all the gold of Balikesir, but the riches of Smyrna—that was another matter."

Her father and his brothers had worked industriously. She recalled it all very well, she told me. One afternoon a man had come with news that Smyrna had fallen, and that very night the whole family had worked. There was a huge front porch on their house, wooden on the top, with concrete sides and front. That night her father and her uncle Poul broke through the concrete on the left side. Then the whole family carried the gold coins from the basement and hid them away beneath the porch.

They made many trips, she told me. They carried big sacks and little sacks, and once she had dropped a cloth purse, and the shiny coins had scattered all over the basement floor, and she had to scurry around picking them up and putting them back into the purse. Almost all the coins were the same, she saw a bit smaller than an American quarter, with a woman's head on one side and a man on horseback on the other, and the man, she remembered, was sticking something with a spear.

British sovereigns, of course. The head of Victoria and the reverse was St. George slaying the dragon. That had been the most common gold coin in the Middle East.

At last all the coins were in place, Kitty's grandmother explained, and they filled the space beneath the porch to capacity. And then her father and her uncle mixed cement and carefully patched the opening in the concrete by the light of a single lantern. After the cement set, they rubbed little bits of gravel into it to give it an aged appearance and they dusted it with dirt from the road so it would be the same shade as the rest of the porch cement.

Until then the Turks in Balikesir had been peaceful. But now, once they had heard of Ataturk's victory a hundred miles to the south, they suddenly grew courageous. The next morning they attacked, overrunning the Greeks and Armenians. They burned the Greek quarter to the ground and they butchered every Greek and Armenian they could find. The violence in Balikesir had not made the history books. Smyrna, sacked at the same time, overshadowed it.

Kitty's grandmother, however, had been only in Balikesir and had seen only what took place in Balikesir. She spoke calmly of it now. The burnings, the rape, the endless murder. Children pierced with swords, old men and women shot through the head—screams, gunshots, blood, death.

She was one of the few to survive, but her words indicated that Kitty had been right: "I was young then, and

pretty. And the Turks are animals. I was ravished. Can you
believe this, to look at me now, that men would want to
have me that way? And not just one man, no. But I was not
killed. Everyone else in my family was killed, but I escaped. I was with a group of Greeks and an old Armenian
man. We fled the city. We were on the roads for days. We
were crowded together aboard a ship. Then we were here,
New York, America."

"And the gold?"

"Gone. The Turks must have it."

"Did they find it?"

"Not then, no. But they must have it now. It was years
ago. And no Armenian went back for it. I was the only
one of my family to live, and only the people of my family
knew of the gold. So no Armenian found it, and so the
Turks must have gotten it all."

I took the subway back to my apartment and sat down
at my typewriter and wrote up everything I could recall
of Kitty's grandmother's story. I read through what I
had written, then roamed the apartment, pulling books
from the shelves, checking articles in various pamphlets
and magazines. A broadside of the League for the Restoration of Cilician Armenia alluded to the confiscation
of the wealth of the Armenians of Smyrna. But I could
find no records anywhere of the discovery of the treasure
of Smyrna. It was taken for granted by everyone that
the Turks had found the gold, but no one knew this for a
certainty.

And there were no records anywhere to indicate that
the gold had been cached in Balikesir. There was one woman's memory—and she claimed to be the only survivor who
had known of the cache.

The night I told Kitty. "I think it's still there." I said
and explained to her.

"Figure that a British sovereign is worth ten or twelve dollars today. Figure they had about half the actual volume of the hiding place filled with gold. Judging by the size of the porch as she described it and just estimating roughly, yes, it would be a lot of money."

"How much?"

"A minimum of two million dollars. Possibly twice that much. Say three million dollars maybe."

"Three million dollars," she said.

The next morning I went downtown and applied for a passport.

IT HAD all seemed magnificently simple then. I would fly to Istanbul and find some way of getting to Balikesir. I would work my way through the city—the present population is 30,000—until I found the house Kitty's grandmother had described to me.

As it turned out, there was only one slight matter I hadn't counted on—how was I to know the damned Turks would arrest me?

Mustafa was poor company. He stayed with me like a summer cold straight onto the plane.

We sat in the tourist section. Evidently the Turkish Government intended to reroute spies as economically as possible. The ride to Shannon was long, choppy, uncomfortable, and supremely dull, and it was made even more uncomfortable and dull by the fact that I would never be able to return to Turkey. The Turkish Government would revoke my visa and never grant another, and the U.S. Government could probably cancel my passport. It was unfair.

And throughout all of this there would be interrogation—endless interrogation. Why had I gone to Turkey? Who was I representing? What was I plotting? Who? What? Where? When? Why?

I simply could not return to the United States. I simply could not land in Washington.

I looked over at Mustafa. We would be landing at Shannon. Shannon Airport in Ireland. Ireland. Not Turkey, not the United States of America. Ireland. And we would have two precious hours between planes. We would get off this plane, Mustafa and I, and we would wait in Shannon Airport for two hours before it was time to board our flight for Washington. I would have two hours to rid myself of Mustafa.

I almost shouted at the beauty of it. I knew people in Ireland! I received mail from Ireland every month; almost every week. I was an active member of the Clann-na-Gaille and the Irish Republican Brotherhood. If I could find some of those people—any of them—I was safe. They would be my sort of people, my spiritual brothers. They would hide me, they would care for me, they would *conspire* with me!

I closed my eyes, tried to bring the map of Ireland into focus. Now what was the city right near Shannon?

Limerick.

Of course, Limerick. And I knew someone in Limerick. I was sure I knew someone in Limerick. Who?

It was Dolan, PP Dolan, Padraic Pearse Dolan, named for the greatest of the Easter Monday martyrs who had proclaimed the Irish Republic from the steps of the Post Office in O'Connell Street. And he didn't live in Limerick City but in County Limerick, and I remembered his whole address now: PP Dolan, Illanaloo, Croom, Co. Limerick, Republic of Ireland.

If only I could get rid of Mustafa.

I looked at him, sitting contentedly while the music was piped into his ears. Dream on, I told him silently. You'll get yours, little man.

We finally landed at Shannon, taxied, stopped. I walked

at Mustafa's side into the small one-story airport. Our
luggage had been checked through to Washington, so there
was no real customs check. We stood in one short line, and
a pleasant young man in a green uniform checked our passports. Mustafa handed both passports to him, and the man
returned them, and Mustafa took them both and pocketed
them. He seemed very pleased with himself. He had my
passport, after all, so where could I go?

Indeed, where *could* I go? Mustafa led me to a bench,
and the two of us sat side by side upon it. I looked around.
There was a door that led to the Shannon Free Shopping
Center. There was a booth where two, beautiful, green-clad
girls dispensed travel folders. There was a men's room.

Of course!

I stood up. Mustafa rose to his feet at once and glared
at me. "The men's room," I said. "The toilet. I have to use
the toilet." He understood every word, of course, but we
were both still pretending that he didn't. In desperation I
pointed at the men's room door.

"I can't go anywhere," I said. "You've got my bloody
passport. Come along if you want."

And, of course, the little bastard came along.

The men's room was a long narrow affair. I walked the
length of it, and my Turkish shadow stayed at my side. I
paused in front of the last stall and asked him if he wanted
to come in with me. He smiled and took up a position directly in front of the stall. I closed the door and bolted it.

So he thought I was James Bond, did he? Fine. Just for
that I was going to *be* James Bond.

I sat down on the throne and slipped my shoes off. I
shrugged out of my jacket and hung it on the peg. I placed
the shoes side by side, toes pointing outward, right where
they would most likely be if I were doing what I had osten-
sibly come to do. I hoped Mustafa would be able to see the

tips of the shoes.

I crawled under the partition, around the next toilet, under the next partition, around still another toilet, into another stall, all the way down to the end. I did this as quickly and as silently as possible, squirming on my belly like a pit viper, and certain that I was going much too slowly and making far too much noise.

I was in the very last stall when I heard the outside door open. I stopped breathing. A man came in, used the urinal, left. I wondered if Mustafa was still standing there like a soldier. I peeked out at him, and there he was, a cigarette dangling from his lower lip, his eyes focused stupidly upon my shoes.

I slipped out of the stall, lowered my head and charged.

He barely moved at all. At the last moment he turned lazily around just in time to see me hurtling through the air at him. His mouth fell open, and he started to take a small step backward, and I sailed into him, my head ramming him in the pit of his soft stomach, and down we went.

I was ready for a war. I had visions of us bouncing one another off plumbing fixtures, hurling karate chops at one another, fighting furiously until one of managed to turn the tide. But this was not to be. I had never realized just how great an advantage surprise can provide. Mustafa collapsed like a blown tire. We fell in a heap, and I landed on top, and he did nothing but gape at me.

"You are doomed," I said. "I'm a secret agent working for the establishment of a free and independent Kurdistan. I've poisoned the entire water supply of Istanbul. Within a month everyone in Turkey will perish of cholera."

His eyes rolled in his head.

"Sleep well," I said, and I slammed his head against the floor again, but infinitely harder this time. His eyes went glassy, and their lids flopped shut, and for a moment I was afraid that I had actually gone and killed him. I checked his pulse. He was still alive.

I dragged him back into the stall where I'd left my shoes and jacket and I stripped off all his clothes and used strips of his shirt to tie him up and gag him.

I took my passport arid Mustafa's passport from his pants and put them both m my pocket. I stuffed his clothes in a trash can and poked them down to the bottom. I kept expecting him to emerge from the men's room and chase after me, but he stayed where he was, and I hurried through a pair of big glass doors to the outside.

There were taxis, but I didn't dare take one. Someone might remember me. I wouldn't leave a trail. I asked a stewardess where I could get a bus to Limerick. She pointed at an oldish doubledecker bus, and I headed toward it.

When the bus reached Limerick, I jumped off, walked to the nearest clothing shop and ducked inside. Fifteen minutes later I was outside again, wearing a pair of gray, woolen trousers, a bulky tweed sport coat and a black wool sweater. Tucked under my arm was a package containing my American suit.

I stopped inside a pub and asked if I could take a bus to Croom. The pubkeeper said there wasn't one until the following morning, but that I could rent a bicycle at a shop named Mulready's down the street and ride to Croom myself in less than an hour. Mr. Mulready, the proprietor would even give me proper directions on how to get there.

I couldn't stay any long in Limerick—it was becoming too dangerous. A rented bicycle at Mulready's was the only answer.

It was dark and raining when I pedaled into Croom. I parked my cycle in front of a pub and went inside. l asked the bartender if he knew where PP Dolan lived.

I followed the tortuous directions, made all the correct turns, and found the house. It was a small cottage, gray in the dim light. A television antenna perched on the thatched roof, and smoke trickled upward from the chimney.

I staggered to the door, hesitated, tried to catch my breath, failed, and rapped on the door. I heard footsteps, and the door was drawn open. I looked at the little man in the doorway: he was more a leprechaun, short, gnarled, with piercingly blue eyes.

"PP Dolan?"

"I am."

"Padraic Pearse Dolan?"

He seemed to straighten up. "Himself."

"You've got to help me,' I said. The words flowed in a torrent. "I'm from America, from New York, I'm a member of the Brotherhood—the Irish Republican Brotherhood—and they're after me. I was in jail. I escaped when we reached Ireland. You have to hide me." And, gasping for breath, I dug out my passport and handed it to him.

He took it, opened it, looked at it, at me, at it again. "I don't understand," he said gently. "The picture's no likeness of you at all. And it says that your name is…let me see"—he squinted in the half light—"Mustafa lbn Ali. Did I say that properly? Nora, do make Mr. Mustafa Ali some tea."

I had made two mistakes, it seemed. When I changed my summer suit for proper Irish clothing. I had transferred only one passport and the wrong one at that. My own passport remained in my suit. And my suit, had somehow been separated from me. I had carried the parcel into the pub, but I hadn't had it with me when I left Mulready's cycle shop. I'd left it either at the pub or with Mulready, suit and passport and all.

"My name's not Mr. Ali," I said. "I took his passport by mistake. He's a Turk. He was my jailer in Turkey. He was

315

taking me back to America when I escaped."

"You were a prisoner, then?"

"Yes." His face seemed troubled by this, so I added, "It was political, my imprisonment."

This eased his mind considerably. Nora, his daughter, came over to us with the tea. She was a slender thing, small-boned, almost dainty, with milk-white skin and glossy black hair and clear blue eyes.

"Your tea, Mr. Ali," she said.

"It's not his name after all," her father said. "And what would your name be, sir?"

"Evan Tanner."

"Tanner," he said. "Forgive me if I seem to pry, Mr. Tanner, but what led you to come here? To Croom and to my house?"

I told him a bit of it. He became quite excited at the thought that I was an American member of the Brotherhood and that I had heard of him. "Do they know of me, then, in America?" he mused. "And who would have guessed it?"

But it was Nora who seized on my name. "Evan Tanner. Evan Michael Tanner, is it?"

"Yes, that's right—"

"You know him, Nora?"

"If it's the same," she said. "And Mr. Tanner, is it you who writes articles in *United Irishmen?* Oh, you know him, Da. In last month's paper, the article suggesting that honorary representatives of the Six Counties be given seats in the Dail. 'Wanted: Representation for Our Northern Brethren,' by Evan Michael Tanner, and wasn't it the article you admired so much, and saying what a grand idea it was, and wouldn't you like to shake the hand of the man that wrote it?"

He looked wide-eyed at me. "And was it you who wrote

that article, Mr. Tanner?"

"It was."

He took the tea from me. "Nora," he said, "spill this out. Bring the jar of Power's. And mind who you tell!" He shook his head sadly. "It's a hell of a thing to say," he explained, "but there are spies and informers everywhere."

The four of us, Dolan, Nora, his son Tom and I, listened to the latest developments in the Evan Tanner case on the kitchen radio. It seemed that Mustafa had seen a good number of James Bond movies, and they had served to supplement his account of my escape. According to the radio report, I was a dangerous spy of unknown allegiance being returned to America after attempting to infect all of Turkey with a plague of cholera. In the Shannon lavatory I had crushed a small pellet between my fingers, liberating a gas that temporarily paralyzed Mustafa's spinal column. Though he fought valiantly, he was in no condition to prevent my knocking him unconscious and trussing him up.

"It looks bad," I said: "Sooner or later they'll turn up the suit and spot the passport. Once they trace me to the bicycle shop, Mr. Mulready will be able to tell them that I went to Croom. And if they follow me this far, they'll be sure to find me."

"Don't talk nonsense. And don't be worrying about your suit, either. Most likely it's still unwrapped in Mulready's waiting for you to come back for it. If you left it there, it's still there now. And if you left in the pub, sure they'll take it to Mulready's, knowing you'll have to return a rented cycle to the cycle shop sooner or later. Tom can go for it tomorrow, and you'll have it in your hands without the gardai ever knowing of it."

"If they're already there and see him—"

"Tom will be looking for them, and if they're there, he will leave without being seen. Don't bother yourself about it, Mr. Tanner. Tom Dolan showed me to my room. It was reached through a trapdoor in the second-floor ceiling. Tom stood on a chair, moved a lever, and a flap dropped from the ceiling, releasing a rope ladder. I followed Tom up the ladder and into a long, narrow room. The ceiling, less than four feet high in the center, sloped to meet the floor on either side. A mattress in the center of the room was piled generously high with quilts and blankets. Tom lit a candle at the side of it and said he hoped I wasn't the sort who grew nervous in cramped quarters.

"To shut up tight," he said, "you haul in the ladder and then catch hold of that ring in the panel with the stick. Draw it shut and fasten it, you see, and it cannot be opened from below. Will you be all right here?

"It seems comfortable."

He clambered back down the rope ladder and tossed it up to me, then raised the panel so that I could catch it with the hooked stick. I locked myself in, blew out the candle, and stretched out on my mattress in the darkness. It was still raining, and I could hear the rain on the thatched roof.

AFTER about half an hour I yawned, stretched, and went downstairs. The turf fire still burned in the hearth. I sat in front of it and let myself think of the gold in Balikesir. My mind was clearer now, and I felt a good deal better physically, with the effects of the whiskey almost completely worn off.

The gold. Obviously I had gone about things the wrong way. It would now be necessary to approach the whole situation through the back door, so to speak. I would stay in Ireland just long enough for the manhunt for the notorious Evan Michael Tanner to cool down a bit. Then I would leave Ireland and work my way through continental Europe and slip into Turkey over the Bulgarian border.

I would set up way stations along the route, men I could trust as I had trusted PP Dolan.

Europe was filled with such men. Little men with special schemes and secret dark hungers. And I knew these men. Without asking an eternity of questions, without demanding that I produce a host of documents, they would do what they had to do, slipping me across borders and through cities, easing me into Turkey and out again.

I was so lost in planning that I barely heard her footsteps on the stairs. I turned to her. She was wearing a white flannel wrapper and had white slippers upon her tiny feet.

"I knew you were down here," she said. "Is it difficult for you to sleep up there?"

"I wasn't tired. I hope I didn't wake you?"

"I could not sleep myself.

"Not on my account."

"Will you have tea?"

"Oh, don't bother."

"It's no bother." She made a fresh pot of tea which we drank in front of the fire.

"It must be grand to be able to go places, just to go and do things. I was going to take the bus to Dublin last spring, but I never did. It's just stay home and cook for Da and Tom and care for the house. It's only a few hours to Dublin by bus. Can you ever go back to your own country, Evan?"

"I don't know," I said slowly.

"You could stay in Ireland, though." Her eyes were very serious. "I know you're after gold now, but if you didn't get back to America, you could always come to Ireland."

I realized, suddenly, that she had put on perfume. She had not been wearing any scent earlier in the evening. It was a very innocent sort of perfume, the type a mother might buy her daughter when she wore her first brassiere.

She put her hand on mine. "You *could* come back to Ireland," she said slowly, earnestly. "Not saying that you will or won't, but you *could.*" Her cheeks were pink now, her eyes bluer than ever in the firelight.

We kissed. She sighed gratefully and set her head on my chest. I ran a hand through her black hair. She raised her head and our eyes met.

"Tell me lies, Evan."

"Perhaps I'll come back to Ireland, and to Croom."

"You're the sweetest liar. Now one more lie. Who do you love?"

"I love you Nora."

We crawled through the trapdoor to my little crow's nest between ceiling and roof. I retrieved the ladder and the panel and closed us in. No one would hear us, she assured me. Her father and brother slept like the dead, and sounds did not carry well in the cottage.

She would not let me light the candle. She took off her robe in a comer of the room, then crept to my side and joined me under all the quilts and blankets. We told each other lies of love and made them come true in the darkness.

She left me, found her robe, opened the trap door, and started down the ladder. "Now," she said, "now you'll sleep."

The next morning after breakfast, I was alone again. I sat down with a pad of notepaper and a handful of envelopes and began writing a group of cryptic letters. It would be well, I felt, to leave as soon as possible and it would probably not be a bad idea If some of my perspective hosts on the continent had a vague idea that they were about to have a clandestine house guest on their hands. The intended recipients ranged as far geographically as Spain and Latvia, as far politically as a Portuguese anarcho-

syridicalist and a brother and sister in Romania who hoped
to restore the monarchy. I didn't expect to see a quarter of
them but one never knew.

I made the letters as carefully vague as I could. Some
of my prospective hosts lived in countries where international mail was opened as a matter of course, and others
in more open nations lived the sort of lives that made
their governments inclined to deny them the customary
rights of privacy. The usual form of my letters ran rather
like this:

> *Dear Cousin Peder,*
>
> *It is my task to tell you that my niece Kristin is celebrating
> the birth of her first child, a boy. While I must travel many miles
> to the christening, I have the courage to hope for a warm welcome
> and shelter for the night.*
>
> *Faithfully,*
> *Anton*

The names and phrasing were changed, of course, to
fit the nationality of the recipient and the language of each
letter was the language of the person to whom it was sent.

I couldn't mail the letters from Croom, of course, and
wasn't sure whether or not it would be safe to mail them all
from the same city, anyway. But at least they were written.

When Nora came back to the cottage she kept blush-
ing and turning from me. "I'm to have nothing to do with
you," she said.

"All right, then."

"Must you accept it so readily?"

I laughed and reached for her. She danced away, blue
eyes flashing merrily, and I lunged again and fell over my
own feet. She hurried over to see if I was all right, and I
caught her and drew her down and kissed her. She said
I was a rascal and threw her arms around me. We broke

apart suddenly when there was a noise outside, and the door flew suddenly open. It was Tom. His cycle—or mine, or Mr. Mulready's—was in a heap at the doorstep.

He was out of breath, and his face was streaked with perspiration. "The old woman at the pub found your suit," he said. "Went to the gardai. They traced you to Mulready, and the fool said you were bound for Croom, and there's a car of them on the road from Limerick. I passed them coming back."

"You passed them?"

"I did. They had a flat tire and called for me to help them change it. Help them!"

"I'll leave the house."

"And go where? In Limerick City they say that more are coming over from Dublin, and detectives from Cork as well. Go to your room and stay quiet. They'll be on us in five minutes, but if you're in your room they'll never find you."

PERHAPS IT was only five minutes that I crouched in the darkness by the side of the trapdoor. It seemed far longer. I heard the car drive up and then the knocking at the door. I caught snatches of conversation as the two policemen searched the little cottage. Then they were on the stairs, and I could hear the conversation more clearly. Nora was insisting that they were hiding no one, no one at all.

The other garda was tapping at the ceiling. "I stayed in a house just like this one," he was saying. "Oh, it was years ago, when I was on the run myself. What's the name here? Dolan?"

"It is."

"Why, this is one I stayed in," the garda said. "A hiding place in the ceiling, if I remember it. What's this? Do you hear how hollow it sounds? He's up there, I swear it."

The garda was evidently working the catch to the panel. I had secured the hook on the inside, and although he opened it, the panel would not drop loose. Finally, he'd loosened the panel slightly, enough so that his fingers could almost get a purchase on it. He tugged at it, and I felt the hook straining. It was old wood. I didn't know if it would hold.

"You're wasting your time," Nora said desperately.

"Oh, are we?"

"He was here, I'll not deny it, but he left this morning."

"And contrived to fasten the hook up there after himself, did he? I hope you don't expect an honest Irish policeman to be taken in by a snare like that, child."

"And did I ever meet one?"

"Meet what?"

"An honest Irish policeman—"

At that unfortunate moment the hook pulled out from the wood, and the panel swung open all the way, the garda following it and falling to the floor with the sudden momentum. The other reached upward, caught hold of an end of the rope ladder and pulled it free. I was in darkness at the side of the opening.

The policeman who had forced the panel was getting unsteadily to his feet. The other turned to him and drew a revolver from his holster. "Wait here," he said. "I'll go in there after him."

"Take care, Liam. He's a cool one."

"No worry."

I watched, silent, frozen, as the garda climbed purposefully up the rope ladder. He used one hand to steady himself and held the gun in the other. His eyes evidently didn't accustom themselves to the dark very quickly, for he looked straight at me without seeing me.

I glanced downward. The other garda stood at the

bottom of the ladder, gazing upward blindly. Tom was on his left, Nora a few feet away on the right, her jaw slack and her hands clutched together in despair. I glanced again at the climbing garda. He had reached the top now. He straightened up in the low-ceilinged room, and he roared as his head struck the beam overhead.

I took him by the shoulders and shoved. He bounced across the room, and I threw myself through the opening in the floor, like a paratrooper leaping from a plane. Between my feet, as I fell, I saw the upraised uncomprehending face of the other garda.

"Up the Republic!" someone was shouting. It was days later when I realized that it was my voice I had heard.

It was neither as easy nor as glorious as the assault upon Mustafa, but it had its points. The garda dodged to one side at the last possible moment. Otherwise my feet would have landed on his shoulders, and he would have fallen like a steer. Instead, I hit him going away, caromed into the side of him, and he and I went sprawling in opposite directions. I scrambled to my feet and rushed at him. He was clawing at his revolver, but he had buttoned the holster and couldn't open it. He had white hair and child-blue eyes. I swung at him and missed. He lunged toward me, and Tom kicked him in the stomach just as Nora brought her shoe down on the base of his skull. That did it; he went down and out.

I barely remembered the trapdoor in time. I rushed to it, threw the rope ladder upward and saw the end of its strike the upstairs garda hard enough to put him off stride. I swung the panel back into place. He got his balance and lunged for it, and his fingers got in the way. He roared as the panel snapped on them. I opened it, and he drew out his fingers, howling like a gelded camel, and I closed the panel again and held it while Tom fastened the catch in place.

"It won't hold him," Nora said.

"I know."

"If he jumps on it—"

"I know."

But he wasn't jumping on it. Not yet. The prostrate policeman was starting to stir, and the one in the attic room was kicking at the panel. Sooner or later he would leap on it with both feet and come through on top of us. I raced down the stairs and out the door. Their car, a gray Vauxhall sedan with a siren mounted on the front fender, was in front of the cottage. They had left the keys in the ignition, reasoning, perhaps, that no one would be such a damned fool as to steal a police car.

I wrenched open the door, hopped behind where the wheel should have been. It was the wrong side, of course. I got behind the wheel and turned the ignition key, and the car coughed and stalled. I tried again, and the motor caught.

I put the accelerator pedal on the floor and went away.

I had no particular idea where I was going until a road sign indicated I was headed for a town called Rath Luire. I had never heard of it and didn't know whether it lay north, south, east, or west of Croom. When I reached the town and passed through it I found the same road went on to Mallow and ultimately to Cork. This was better than returning to Limerick, but it wouldn't get me to Dublin, or to London, or to Balikesir. I was driving a stolen police car in hazardous fashion with no real destination in mind, and somehow this struck me as a distinctly imperfect way to proceed.

A few miles past Mallow I took a dirt road to the right, drove for a mile or so, and pulled off to the side of the road.

I got out of the car. A trio of blackfaced sheep, their

sides daubed with blue paint, wandered over to the heaped-stone fence and regarded me with interest. I walked around the car and got back inside. There was a road map of Ireland in the glove compartment. I opened it and found out approximately where I was. I was approximately lost.

I walked back to the main road. My side road had also been headed toward Cork, with a branch cutting off toward Killarney and points west. Thus, whoever found the car might conclude that I was headed in that direction, had car trouble, and continued toward either Cork or Killarney on foot. I didn't know how well this would throw them off the trail or for how long, but it was something. For my part, I started walking toward Mallow. I'd gone less than a mile when a car stopped, and a youngish priest gave me a lift the rest of the way.

I mailed about half of my letters in Mallow. A copy of Cork *Examiner* had my picture on the front page. I pulled my cap farther down on my forehead and hurried to the bus station. There was a bus leaving for Dublin in a little over an hour, the ticket clerk told me.

It was almost nine o'clock when the bus reached the terminal in Dublin. The whole trip was only 150 miles or so, but we'd had many stops and several waits. I left the bus and found the terminal crawling with gardai. Several of them looked right at me without recognizing me.

A pair of James Bond movies were playing in a theater a few doors down from the remains of the Nelson monument. The IRA had dynamited the top of the monument a few months earlier, and the city had blown up the rest of it but hadn't yet put anything in its place. A tall man with glasses and a black attaché case was looking at the monument, then glanced at me, then looked at the monument again. I went into the cinema and sat in the back row for two and a half hours, hoping that Sean Connery could give me some sort of clue as to what I might do next. I had a pocketful of American money that I didn't dare spend, a handful of English and Irish pounds; I did not have a passport, or a way of getting out of Ireland, or the slightest notion of what to do next.

James Bond was no help. Near the end of the second picture, just as Bond was heaving the girl into the pot of molten lead, I saw a man walking slowly and purposefully up and down the aisle, as if looking for an empty seat. But the theater was half empty. I looked at him again and saw that he was the same man who had looked alternately at the Nelson monument and at me. There was something familiar about him. I had the feeling I'd seen him before at the bus station.

I sank down into my seat and lowered my head. He made another grand tour of the cinema, walking to the front and back again, his eyes passing over me with no flicker of recognition. I couldn't breathe. I waited for him to see me, and then he walked on and out of the theater while I struggled for breath and wiped cold perspiration from my forehead.

But he was there when I came out. I knew he would be.

I tried to melt into the shadows and slip away to the left, and at first I thought I had lost him. When I looked over my shoulder, he was still there. I walked very slowly to the corner, turned it, and took off at a dead run. I ran straight for two blocks while people stared at me as if I had gone mad, then turned another corner and slowed down again. A cab came by. I hailed it, and it stopped for me.

"Just drive," I said.

"Where, sir?"

I couldn't think of the answer to that. "A pub," I managed to say. "Someplace where I can get a good dinner."

The cab still had not moved. "There's a fine restaurant

just across the street, sir. And quite reasonable, as well."

My man came around the corner. He didn't have his attaché case now, I noticed. I tried to hide myself, but he saw me.

I said, "I had a row with my wife. I think she's following me. Drive around the block a few times and then drop me off at that restaurant, can you?"

Ten minutes later he dropped me in back of the restaurant. As I opened the door I glanced over my shoulder and saw the tall man with glasses. He was still trying to catch a cab. He saw me, and our eyes met, and I felt dizzy. I pushed open the door of the restaurant and went inside. When I looked back, I saw him crossing the street after me.

The headwaiter showed me to a table, I ordered a brandy and sat facing the door. I had never before felt so utterly stupid. I had escaped and then, brainlessly, I had returned to precisely the place where the tall man was waiting.

The door opened. The tall man came in, looked my way, then glanced out the door again. His face clouded for a moment and he seemed to hesitate. Perhaps, I thought, he was afraid to attempt to capture me by himself. No doubt I was presumed armed and dangerous.

Could I make a break for it? Surprise had worked twice before, with Mustafa and the two gardai. But I couldn't avoid the feeling that the third time might be the charm. This man was prepared. He was walking toward my table—

Still, it seemed worth a try. I looked past him as though I did not see him, my hands gripping the table from below. When he was close enough I would heave it at him, then run.

Then over his shoulder I saw the gardai—three of them, in uniform—coming through the doorway. If I got past him, I would only succeed in running into their arms.

The tall man with the glasses stumbled, fell forward toward me. His right hand broke his fall, his left brushed against my right side. He said, "Mooney's, Talbot Street," then got to his feet and swept past me.

And the gardai, solemn as priests, walked on by my table and surrounded him. One took his right arm, the other his left, and the third marched behind with a drawn pistol. They marched him out of the restaurant and left me there alone.

I could only stare after them, I and all the other patrons of the restaurant. It was late, and most of the other diners were about half-lit. At the doorway the tall man made his move. He kicked backward at the garda with the pistol, wrenched himself free from the grasp of the other two, and broke into a run.

Along with other diners, I pressed forward. I heard two short blasts on a police whistle, then a brace of gunshots. I reached the door and saw the tall man rushing across the street. A garda was shooting at him. The tall man spun around, gun in hand, and began firing wildly. A bullet shattered the restaurant window, and I dropped to the floor. A fresh fusillade of shots rang out. I peered over the window ledge and saw the tall man lying in a heap in the middle of the street. There were sirens wailing in the distance. One of the gardai had taken a bullet through one hand and was bleeding fiercely.

And no one was paying any attention to me.

Mooney's, Talbot Street, he had said. I didn't know what he meant, or who he was, or who he thought me to be. Why had he followed me? If the police were following him, why should he follow me? What was Mooney's? Was I supposed to meet him there? It seemed unlikely that he would ever keep the appointment.

Then I found in my right coat pocket, where he must

have placed it when he fell, a metal brass-colored disc perhaps an inch and a half across. Stamped upon it were the
numerals 249.

At that point it was easy enough to figure out the
what, if not the why. I worked my way back to O'Connell
Street and found Talbot Street, just around the corner from
the cinema. Mooney's was a crowded pub halfway down the
block. I found the checkroom and presented the brass disc.
As I had expected, the attendant handed over the black
attaché case, and I left a shilling on the saucer. I closed myself in a cubicle in the men's room and propped the attaché
case upon my lap. It was not locked. I opened it.

On top was an envelope with my name on it. I drew a
single sheet of hotel stationery from it. The message was
in pencil, written in a hurried scrawl:

    Tanner—
    *I just hope you're who I think you are. Deliver the goods to
the right people and they'll take care of you. The passports are
clean. Big trouble for everybody if delivery isn't made.*

SIX HOURS later I was in Madrid. Esteban Robles lived on
Calle de la Sangre—Blood Street—a dim, narrow two-
block lane in the student quarter south of the university .

I found Robles on the third floor of a drab tenement
permeated with cooking smells. His room resembled the
cell of a slovenly monk—a desk piled high with books
and newspaper clippings and cigarette stubs, another heap
of books in a corner, four empty wine bottles, a pan of
leftover beans and rice, and a narrow cot that sagged in the
middle. The floor was incompletely covered with linoleum,
its pattern obscured by years of dirt. Robles himself was a
young fellow with the body of a matador and the bearded
face of a protest marcher. I knew him as a fellow member
of the Federation of Iberian Anarchists. It was a danger-

ous thing to be in Spain, and I had trouble convincing him that I was not an agent of the Civil Guard.

"But what do you want here?" he kept demanding. "But why do you come to me?"

"I have to go to Turkey," I explained.

"Am I an airplane? This is not safe. You must go."

"I need your help."

"My help?" He glanced again at the door. "I cannot help you. The police are everywhere. And I have nowhere for you to stay. Nowhere. One small bed is all I own, and I sleep in it myself. You cannot stay here."

"I want to get out of Spain."

"So do I. So does everyone. I could make a grand fortune in America. I could become a hairdresser. Jackie Kennedy."

"Pardon me?"

"I would set her hair and make a fortune."

"I don't think I—"

"Instead, I rot in Madrid." He fingered his beard. "I could set Jackie Kennedy's hair and make a fortune. Lady Bird Johnson. Are you a hairdresser?"

"No."

"I have had no breakfast. There is a cafe downstairs, but you cannot go. They will shoot you in the street like a dog. Can you speak Spanish?"

We had been speaking Spanish all along. I was beginning to suspect that Robles was mad.

"There is a cafe," he said. "They know me there. So they will give me credit." He glanced at the door again. His fear was so genuine that I was beginning to share it.

"I have no money," he said.

I gave him some Spanish money and told him to get breakfast for both of us. He snatched the notes from me, glanced again at the door, lit a cigarette, smoked furiously, dropped ashes on the floor, and was gone like a shot.

I closed the door and wished that it had a functioning lock on it. I went to the window and drew the shade. It was badly torn. Through the hole in the shade I looked into a room in the building next door. A rather plump girl with long black hair was dressing. I watched her for a few moments, then left the window and sat on Esteban's bed and opened my black attaché case. A gift of Providence, I thought. An ideal survival kit for a hunted man. It had everything I might need—money, passports, and documents so secret I had no idea what they were.

Along with the unsigned and unintelligible note, the attaché case had contained a heavy cardigan sweater with a London label, a change of underwear, a pair of dreadful Argyle socks, a safety razor with no blades, a toothbrush, a can of toothpowder made in Liverpool, and a Japanese rayon tie with a fake Countess Mara crest. There was also a Manila envelope holding banded packages of British, American, and Swiss currency—two hundred pounds, one hundred fifty dollars, and just over two thousand Swiss franks. Another larger envelope contained three passports. The American passport was in the name of William Alan Traynor, the British in the name of R. Kenneth Leyden, and the Swiss for Henri Boehm. Each showed a rather poor photograph of the tall man.

A third Manila envelope, carefully sealed with heavy tape, held the mysterious documents. These, evidently, were the "goods" that I was to deliver to "the right people." I had attempted to slit the tape with my thumbnail in the manner of James Bond opening a packet of cigarettes. This proved impossible, so I had laboriously peeled off the tape in the privacy of the Dublin lavatory and had a look at the contents of the parcel. It had made no particular sense to me then; now, in the equally dismal atmosphere of Esteban Robles' dirty little room, it remained as impenetrable as ever.

Half a dozen sheets of photocopied blueprints. Blueprints for what? I had no idea. A dozen sheets of ruled notebook paper covered with either the mental doodling of a mathematician or some esoteric code. A batch of carefully drawn diagrams. A whole packet of confidential information, no doubt stolen from someone and destined for someone else. But stolen from whom? And destined for whom? And indicating what?

When I first opened the case it had scarcely mattered. I had packed everything away and taken a taxi to the Dublin airport. I used the American passport to buy a ticket to Madrid and paid for it with American money.

By flight time I took my attaché case from the locker, lodged the envelope of unidentifiable secret papers between my shirt and my skin, and incorporated the currency with my own small fund of money. I tucked my two extra passports (and Mustafa lbn Ali's) into a pocket, combed my hair to conform to Traynor's passport photo.

At the time, never having met Esteban Robles, I had no idea he was a lunatic.

The packet of secret papers bothered me. If I had known just what they were, I might have had some idea what to do with them. Knowing neither their source nor their destination nor their nature, I was wholly in the dark.

In a sense, I felt a sort of debt to my anonymous benefactor, the tall man who had been shot down by the Irish police. However invalid his assumptions of my identity, however suspect his motives, he had done me a good turn. He had provided me with three passports to spirit me out of Ireland and away from the manhunt that sooner or later would have caught up with me. He had endowed me with a supply of capital that would help me on my way to Balikesir. But who was he? And which side was he on?

He was not on the Irish side; that much was obvious. All right, then, suppose he was an enemy of Ireland. Why would he be spying on Ireland? What precious information could the Irish possibly have that he or his employers would want? And who could his employers be? The British? The Russians? The CIA? The answer was unattainable without a knowledge of the nature of the documents, and they remained as impenetrable as ever.

I was getting nowhere. I gave it up, put everything back in the attaché case, closed it, and stretched out on Esteban's unsanitary bed until its owner returned.

"Ah." He scratched at his beard. "It is not safe for you here. It is not safe for either of us. We must leave."

"We?"

"Both of us!" He spread his arms wide as if to embrace the beauty of the idea. "We will go to France. This afternoon we rush to the border. Tonight, under the cloak of darkness, we slip across the border like sardines. Who will see us?"

"Who?"

"No one!" He clapped his hands. "I know the way, my friend. One goes to the border, one talks to the right people, and like that"—he snapped his fingers soundlessly—"it is arranged. In no time at all we are across the border and into France. I will go to Paris. Can you imagine me in Paris? I shall become the most famous hairdresser in all of Paris."

"I don't know," I said. "I'm not sure it sounds like the best of all possible plans. It might be dangerous for us to travel together."

"Dangerous? It would be dangerous for us to separate."

"Why?" He spread his hands. "Why not?"

I reached under the bed for my attaché case. I wanted to escape this madman. The case was not there.

"Esteban—"

"You look for this?" He handed it to me. I opened it and checked its contents. Everything seemed to be there.

"You see, ' he said solemnly, "it would be very dangerous for us to be separated. Every day at four o'clock the Guardia Civil come to check on me to make sure I am still here. I am subversive."

"I believe it."

"But they do not feel that I am dangerous. Do you understand? They only check to see who it is whom I have been seeing and what correspondence I have received and matters of that sort. I always tell them everything. That is the only way to deal with these fascist swine. One must tell them everything, everything. Only then can they be sure that I'm not dangerous."

If they thought the foul little lunatic was not dangerous, then they did not know him as well as I did.

"So if they come today, I must tell them about you. The names on your three passports, and the papers with the letters and the numbers upon them, and—"

"When will the Guard visit you?"

"In a few hours. So you see that it is good you came to me. In all of Madrid, it was to Esteban Robles that you came. Is it not fate?"

In all of Madrid, it was to Esteban Robles that I came. Of all my little band of conspirators, of all my troupe of subversives and schemers and plotters, I hid sought out the Judas goat of the secret police. And now I had to take the madman with me to France.

We took a train as far as Zaragoza, a bus east to Lerida, and another bus north to Sort, a small village a few miles from the frontier. The rest of the way was easy—I bribed a farmer who was passing through Sort in his donkey wagon to let Esteban and me hide under the hay in the back of the wagon while he crossed the border at Andorra. The border officials there suspected nothing and the farmer kept riding into France, taking us as far as Foix.

It was almost impossible to explain to Esteban that we were not going to Paris together. He insisted that brothers such as we could not be separated and he ultimately began to weep and tear at his hair. I did not want to go to Paris. There was a man I had to see in Grenoble, near the Italian border. I tried to put Esteban on a Paris train, but he would have no part of it. I had to come with him, he insisted. Without me he would be lost.

And so we boarded a train to Paris, Esteban and I. We got on the train at Foix, only I got off it at Toulouse and took another train east to Nimes and a bus northeast to Grenoble.

M. Gerard Monet must have already received the cryptic note I'd sent him from Ireland. I went to his home. His wife said that he was at his wine shop—it was not quite noon—and told me how to find him. I walked to the shop and introduced myself as Pierre, who had written from Ireland. He put a finger to his lips, walked past me to the door, closed it, locked and bolted it, drew a window shade, and took me behind the counter. He was a dusty man in a dusty shop, his hair long and uncombed, his eyes a brilliant blue. "You have come," he said. "Tell me only what I must do. That is all."

"My name is—"

He held up one band, corded with dark blue veins. "But no, do not tell me. A man can only repeat what he knows, and I wish to know nothing. My father was of the movement. My great-grandfather fell at Waterloo. Did you know that?"

"No."

"For all my life I have been of the movement. I have

watched, I have listened. Will anything come of it? In my
lifetime? Or ever? I do not know. I will be honest with you,
I doubt that anything will come of it. But who is to say?
They tell me the days of the Empire are over for all time.
The glory of France, eh? But I do what there is for me to
do. Whatever is requested, Gerard Monet will perform
what he is capable of performing. But tell me nothing of
yourself or your mission. When I drink, I talk. When I
talk, I tell too much. What I do not know I can tell no one,
drunk or sober. You understand?"

"Yes."

"What do you require?"

"Entry to Italy."

"You have papers?"

"I don't know whether or not they're valid. I'd rather
slip across the border, if that can be arranged."

He picked up the telephone, put through a call, talked
rapidly in a low voice, then turned to me. "You can leave in
an hour?"

"Yes."

"In an hour my nephew will come to drive you to the
border. There are places where one may cross. First we
shall lunch together."

"You are kind."

IN DOWNTOWN Milan I picked up a copy of the Paris edition
of the *New York Herald Tribune* and learned what all the
fuss was about. The passports were a dead issue, worthless
now, a liability. Someone Had connected me to the tall man
who had been shot down in Dublin. The paper didn't spell
it out but explained that the fugitive Evan Michael Tanner
had stolen important government documents in Ireland
and was thought to be making his escape through continental Europe. They knew I had. left Dublin under the false

American passport and knew I had changed money under the British one at Madrid.

In an alleyway I destroyed the other two passports. I broke the cases open, tore the printed matter into scraps, and tossed the scraps to the winds. I was about to do the same to the remaining passport, the one for Mustafa Ibn Ali, but it seemed to me that there might be a use for it sometime, perhaps in Yugoslavia. One never knew.

The newspaper article described the black attaché case I was carrying, so I bad to rid myself of that, too. I didn't know where to throw it away, so I sold it in a secondhand store for a handful of lire. The money was scarcely enough to matter, but I was getting to the point where money mattered, even small amounts. I caught a train for Venice without incident.

Ljudevit Starcevic had a small farm outside of Udine. He grew vegetables, had a small grape arbor, and kept a herd of goats. When an independent Yugoslavia had been carved out of the Austro-Hungarian Empire at the close of the First World War, he bad joined Stefan Radic's Croat Peasant Party. In 1925 Radic abandoned separatism and joined the central government. Starcevic did not. He and other Croatian extremists fought the central regime. Some were killed. Starcevic, who was very young at the time, was imprisoned, escaped, and eventually wound up in Italy.

He was astonished when I spoke to him in Croat.

He lived alone, he told me. His wife was dead, his children had married Italians and moved away. He lived with his goats and saw hardly anyone. And he wanted—desperately—to talk.

He fed me a dish of meat and rice. We sat together and drank plum brandy and talked of the future of Croatia.

He wanted to know I if I planned to start a revolution.

"I will not start a revolution," I said. "Ah." His eyes

were downcast.

"Not this time."

"But soon?"

"Perhaps."

His leather face creased in a smile. "And now? What do you plan this trip, Vanec?"

"There are men I must see. Plans to be made."

"Ah."

"But first I must cross the border."

"On Tuesday two men must do the work of three. They cannot cover the space of three. Believe me, I know how to get you to Croatia."

Clouds filled the sky all Tuesday afternoon. The night was black as a coal mine, moonless and starless. Around eight o'clock old Starcevic and I set out for the border. I carried a leather satchel he had given me. In it was a loaf of bread, several wedges of ripe cheese, a flask of plum brandy, and the inevitable mysterious documents that were my last souvenir of Ireland.

When we approached the border, Starcevic drew me down in a clump of shrubbery. "Now we must be very quiet," he whispered. "In a few moments the border guard will pass us. You see that tree? If you climb it, you can get over the fence."

He fell silent. I waited, my eyes on the tree and the fence beyond it. The tree did not look all that easy to climb. There was a branch that extended over the fence, and I saw that it would be possible to move along the branch and jump clear of the fence. It would also be possible to make a very attractive target on the branch, outlined against the sky.

After a few moments we saw the sentry pass. He was tall enough to play professional basketball. He wore high laced boots and a severely tailored uniform and carried a rifle.

We waited five long minutes. Then Starcevic touched my shoulder and pointed at the tree. I ran to it, tossed my leather satchel high over the fence, and shinnied up the tree. I climbed out onto the proper branch and felt it bend under my weight, but it held me, and I moved out until I was clear of the boundary fence. I had the horrible feeling that a gun barrel was trained on me and I waited for a shot to pierce the night. No shot came. I caught hold of the branch with my hands, let my feet swing down, then let go and dropped a few yards to the ground. I found the satchel, snatched it up, and started walking.

So that was the Iron Curtain, I thought. A stretch of barbed wire one could pass over simply by shinnying up a tree. A hazardous obstacle for James Bond and his cohorts but child's play for that great Croatian revolutionary, Evan Tanner.

By dawn Wednesday I had reached the Slovenian city of Ljubljana. There a displaced Serbian teacher took me into his house, fed me breakfast, and took me to a friend who let me ride to Zagreb in the back of his truck. The ride was bumpy but quick. In Zagreb, Sandor Kofalic fed me roasted lamb and locked me in his cellar with a bottle of sweet wine while he rounded up a Croat separatist who provided me with a travel pass that would let me ride the trains as far as Belgrade.

In Belgrade I had dinner with Janos Papilov. I waited at his house and played cards with his wife and father-in-law while he went to hunt up transportation. He came back with a car, and late at night we set out. He drove me sixty miles to Kragujevac and apologized that he could go no farther. Like the others I had met, he did not ask where I was going or why I was going there.

Two nights later, I was in Tetovo in Macedonia. And

there I felt safer than ever. The whole province of Macedonia is peppered with revolutionaries and conspirators. The ghost of the IMRO, the Internal Macedonian Revolutionary Organization, has never been entirely laid to rest. In the years before the First World War the IMRO had its own underground government in the Macedonian hells, ran its own law courts, and dispensed its own revolutionary justice. Its spies and agents ran amok throughout the Balkans. And, though generations have passed since the cry of "Macedonia for the Macedonians" first echoed through that rocky would-be nation, the IMRO lives on. It may be found in every hamlet of Macedonia. It is listed even now on the US attorney general's list of subversive organizations.

Of course I am a member.

IN TETOVO I stopped at a cafe for a glass of resinous wine, asked directions to the address I had, and headed for Todor Prolov's house.

It was a smallish hut at the end of a drab and narrow street off the main thoroughfare, on the southeast edge of downtown Tetovo. Broken panes of glass in the casement windows had been patched with newspaper. Two dogs, thin and yellow-eyed, slept in the doorway and ignored me.

The girl who opened the door had an opulent body and blonde hair like spun silk. She held a chicken bone in one hand.

"Does Todor Prolov live here?"

She nodded.

"I wrote him a letter," I said, "My name is Ferenc."

Her eyes, large and round to begin with, now turned to saucers. She grabbed my arm, pulled me inside. "Todor," she shouted, "he is here! The one who wrote you! Ferenc! The American!"

A horde of people clustered around me. From the center of the mob, Todor Prolov pushed forward to face me. He was a short man with a twisted face and unruly brown hair and a pair of shoulders like the entire defensive line of the Green Bay Packers. He reached out both hands and gripped my upper arms. When he spoke, he shouted.

"You wrote me a letter?" he bellowed.

"Yes."

"Signed Ferenc?"

"Yes."

"But you are Tanner! Evan Tanner!"

"Yes."

"From America?"

"Yes."

A murmur of excitement ran through the group around us. Todor released my arms, stepped back, studied me, then moved closer again.

Again his hands fastened on my biceps. "And now the big question," he roared. "Are you with us?"

"Of course," I said, puzzled.

"With IMRO?"

"Of course."

He stepped forward and caught me in a bear hug, lifting me up off my feet and leaving me quite breathless. He set me down, spun around, and shouted at the crowd.

"America is with us!" he roared. "You have heard him speak, have you not? America will aid us! America supports Macedonia for the Macedonians! America will help us crush the tyranny of the Belgrade dictatorship!"

Behind me the streets had suddenly filled up with Macedonians. I saw men holding guns and women with bricks and pitchforks. Everyone was shouting.

A child rushed by me holding a bottle in his hand. There was a rag stuffed into the neck of it. The rag smelled of gasoline.

I turned to the girl who had opened the door for me. "What's happening? What's going on?"

"But of course you know. You are a part of it."

"A part of what?"

"Our revolution," she said.

The street had gone mad. There were so many guns going off that they no longer sounded like gunfire. It was too much to be real, more like a fireworks display on the Fourth of July. To the north a row of houses was already in flames. A police car roared past us, and men dropped to their knees to fire at it. One shot burst a tire. The car swung out of control, plowed off the street into a shop front. The police jumped out, guns ready, and the men in the street shot them down.

The girl was at my side. "They're crazy," I said. "They'll all be killed."

"Those who die will die in glory. But America will help us."

I stared at her.

"You said America would help. You told Todor—"

"I told him I was behind his cause. That is all."

"But you are with the CIA, are you not?"

"I'm *running from* the CIA."

Two blocks down the street a canvas-topped truck careened around the comer and pulled to a stop. Uniformed troops spilled from it. Some of them had machine guns. They crouched at the side of the truck and began firing into the crowd of Macedonians. I saw a woman cut in two by machine-gun fire. She fell, and a baby tumbled from her arms, and another blast of gunfire tore the child's head off.

Shrieking, a young girl heaved a homemade cannister bomb into the next of soldiers. The gunfire ceased. Two of the soldiers staggered free of the truck, clutching at their wounds, and a ragged volley of shots from the rooftops cut them down.

A police van had piled up at the barricades closing the south end of the block. A trio of uniformed troopers had taken up positions behind the barricade and were firing at us. Two had rifles, one a Sten gun. I grabbed up a brick from the ground and heaved it at them. It fell far short.

Their fire came our way. I ran forward, toward the source of the firing. A youth ran beside me, pistol in hand. More shots rang out. The youth dropped, moaning, wounded in the thigh.

I grabbed up his pistol.

I kept running. The Sten gun swung around and point-ed at me. I fired without aiming and was astonished to see the policeman spill forward, a massive hole in his throat. His blood washed out of him and coated the piled-up bed-steads and furniture of the improvised barricade. One of the other police fired at me. The bullet brushed my jacket. I ran toward him and shot him in the chest. The third one shoved a rifle in my face and pulled the trigger. The gun jammed. I clubbed him aside and kicked him in the face. He was reaching for another gun when I lowered the pistol and blew off the back of his head.

A cheer went up behind me. The rebels had fired a public building in the center of town. I grabbed up the Sten gun of the first cop I had killed and pushed forward with the crowd. For four blocks almost every house we passed was in flames. In the middle of the city, we pressed in around the police station. A small force of police and soldiers had barricaded themselves inside the stationhouse. They were firing into the crowd from the windows and lobbing grenades down amongst us. I saw the girl who had been at Todor's house putting the torch to the front door. The flames leaped. A band of men were heaving Molotov cocktails into a second story window. The blaze spread in several places, and the crowd dropped back out of range to let the fire have its head.

We shot them down as they came out. There must have been two dozen of them, not counting the ones who never got out the door.

In the public square, Todor proclaimed the Independent and Sovereign Republic of Macedonia. For a thin fraction of a moment I actually thought the revolution would succeed.

The Independent and Sovereign Republic of Macedonia, while unrecognized by the other independent and sovereign nations of the earth, did endure in fact for four hours, twenty-three minutes, and an indeterminate number of seconds.

I WAS cloistered with Todor and Annalya. Annalya was his sister, with blonde hair and huge eyes and hourglass body. The three of us were to plan the course of the revolution.

"You shall not return to America," Todor insisted. "You shall stay here forever in Macedonia. I will make you my prime minister."

"Todor—"

"I will also make you my brother-in-law. You will marry Annalya. You like her?"

"Todor, what do we do when they send in the tanks?"

"What tanks?"

"They used tanks in Budapest in fifty-six. What can your people do against tanks?"

While he tried to think of a reply to this dismal bit of news, Annalya and I left him. We ran around town, planning the defense of Tetovo. We ranged barricades around the entire town, blocking off every road in and out of it and concentrating the bulk of our defenses across the main road on the north and the smaller roads immediately to either side of it. I was fairly certain the initial assault would come from that direction. If we were properly prepared, we might be able to break even in the first attack.

After that, when the tanks came down and the fighter planes dived overhead, was something I did not want to think about.

"Ferenc?"

"What?"

"Do we have any chance? Tell me the truth."

"There is no chance, Annalya."

"I thought not. We will all be killed?"

"Perhaps. They may not want a massacre. The Russians got a fairly bad press after Hungary. They may just kill the leaders."

"Like Todor?"

I didn't answer her.

"It would be horrid if we lost and they spared him."

"I do not understand."

She smiled. "My brother wishes to be a hero. He is a hero already. He has fought like a hero and he will fight like a hero again when the troops arrive. It is only fitting that he die like a hero. Do you understand?"

"Yes."

"Where will the worst of the fighting be?"

"In the center."

"Then I must be certain that Todor is here," she said. "In the center. May it please God that he dies before he learns that we are defeated."

I went eastward on foot, walking toward the emerging sun. The night had been very cold, but the morning was warm in the sunlight, the air very clean and fresh. The hillside was green, but a deeper and much darker green than the fields of Ireland. I was in no hurry and had no special fear of being noticed. My clothes were the same peasant gear worn by the men working in their fields or walking along the road. I knew that they wanted me in Yugoslavia—the last moments in Tetovo, when Annalya and I had huddled together in the storm cellar waiting for a car to spirit us out of town, the army loudspeakers kept demanding that the villagers turn in the American spy.

It was Annalya who decided that I had to escape and who dragged me away from the fighting, brought me and my leather satchel to relative safety in the cellar, and finally got us a ride south and east of Tetovo.

"You wanted to make sure your brother was killed," I said. "Why are you making sure that I get away?"

"For the same reason."

"I don't understand."

"Todor had to die in battle," she said. "And you must escape. It would be bad for us if the enemy captured you. This way you are our American, mysterious, romantic. The government will know you were here with us and will be unable to lay hands on you. And our people will know you will return some day and resume the fight. So you must escape."

She accompanied me to the farmhouse but refused to go to Bulgaria with me. She felt she would be safe where she was and that she could not leave her people. Her place, she said, was with them. And, in that farmhouse, while other men drank bitter coffee in the kitchen, she asked me to go upstairs with her and make love to her. In a passionless voice she at once offered herself and insisted that her offer be accepted.

It was both loving and loveless—and better than I had thought it would be. Until the moments our bodies joined, it was impossible to think of the act, let alone experience anything resembling desire. But then I was astonished by the urgency of it all. And I was more astonished yet at her cries at a moment of what might have been passion. "A son! Give me a son for Macedonia!"

I did my best.

IT TOOK quite a while to reach Sofia, but the city held refuge for me in a priest in The Greek Orthodox Church. I was sent to him by an IMRO member who was also a member of an organization called the Society of the Left Hand.

My lack of knowledge of the Society of the Left Hand greatly inhibited conversation. I dared not espouse any particular political viewpoint lest it should develop that Father Gregor did not happen to be in sympathy with that point of view. Father Gregor's housekeeper produced an excellent shashlik, and his cellar yielded up a commendable bottle of Tokay wine.

"Ah, it is good. More wine?" He refilled our glasses. "At nine o'clock there is a broadcast of Radio Free Europe. Do you often hear it?"

"No."

"For my part, I never miss it. And just as that program concludes there is a broadcast of Radio Moscow, also beamed to Sofia. This is another program I always enjoy hearing. Do you listen to Radio Moscow?"

"Not often."

"Ah. Then, I think it shall be a treat for you. The juxtaposition of these two radio programs is a delight to me. One is dashed from one world to another, and neither of the two worlds reflected has much in common with the world one sees from Sofia."

The program came on and I heard my own named mentioned. I almost dropped my wine glass.

"Yet another act of Russian provocation has threatened the peace of the world," the announcer proclaimed. "This time the crime is espionage, a black art that seems to have been invented in Moscow. The criminal band operates under the leadership of Evan Michael Tanner, an American citizen corrupted by the communist lies and tainted by communist bribery. Through stealth and subterfuge this traitor to the peace of the world managed to get hold of the complete dossier of the British air and coastal defenses. The key defense secrets of this gallant European nation are even this minute moving behind the Iron Curtain toward the tyrant's home base in Moscow.

"Yet there is still hope for mankind. Tanner, it has been learned is on his way to a small city in northwestern Turkey, there to make contact with his superiors. Will he be intercepted? Free men everywhere, peace-loving men throughout the world, can only pray that he will..."

British air and coastal defenses—but how could they have been stolen in Ireland? And if they had been stolen in England, why on earth would the tall man have run to Ireland with them? And for whom had he been working? And why? And—

Gradually, as the announcer shifted to another point, I managed to work out at least a part of it. The only way it made any sense was that the Irish themselves had stolen the British plans. Then the tall man or some other member of his gang had filched the plans a second time in Dublin. That would explain why it was the gardai rather than some branch of British Intelligence that had picked up the tall man's trail, arrested him, and eventually shot him dead.

The Radio Moscow program had an added kicker.

"Continuing their program of harassment, agents of the American Central Intelligence Agency once again launched a desperate attempt to undermine the security of one of the peace-loving socialist republics of Eastern Europe. This time our sister nation of Yugoslavia was the victim. Playing on racial friction and decadent economic drives, CIA operatives under the direction of Ivan Mikhail Tanner sparked an abortive fascist coup in the Province of Macedonia. With tons of smuggled weapons and the tactics of Washington-trained terrorists, these social fascists were able to overcome the efforts of the fine people of several Macedonian villages. Through the efforts of people in the surrounding territory, and with the aid of crack government troops from Belgrade, the Washington-inspired uprising was quickly brought under control and the wave of terror ended forever."

I poured myself a fresh glass of wine. It was beginning to look as though there would be quite a delegation waiting for me in Balikesir. The British, the Irish, the Russians, The Turks, the Americans—and, of course, the nameless band that had stolen those plans in the first place.

After the programs were finished, Father Gregor smiled and said, "I noticed that one man was mentioned on both programs, though in different contexts. A Mr. Tanner. Did you notice that?"

"Yes."

"Do you find this amusing?"

"I—"

He smiled gently. "May we halt this masquerade? Unless I am very much mistaken, which, I admit, is of course a possibility, I believe that you are the Evan Michael Tanner of whom they speak. Is that correct?"

I didn't say anything.

His eyes glinted brightly. "At any rate, I know that you are you. Are you really going to Ankara? Or was the report correct?"

"I'm going to a small town. As they said."

"Ah. You have friends there?"

"No."

"May I ask you a delicate question?"

"Of course."

"You need not answer it, and I need not add that you have the option to answer it untruthfully. Is there, perhaps, the opportunity for you of financial profit in Turkey?"

I hesitated for some time. He waited in respectful silence. Finally, I said that there was an opportunity for financial profit.

"So I suspected. I presume you would prefer not to tell me your precise destination in Turkey?"

Did it matter? The rest of the world already seemed to know. I said, "Balikesir."

Father Gregor got to his feet and walked to the window. While looking out it he said, "In your position, Mr. Tanner, I would have a great advantage. I am, as you no doubt know, of the Left Hand. I would be able to enlist the aid of other members of the Left Hand. If I were attempting to bring something into Turkey, they might help me. If, on the other hand, I were bringing something out of Turkey, they again might be of assistance."

I said nothing.

"Of course, there is a custom in the Society. I would be expected to give the Left Hand a tithe of the proceeds of the venture. A tenth part of whatever gain I realized."

He put his hands together." It would be possible to assemble a dozen very skillful men in Balikesir at whatever time you might designate. It would be possible to supply the material you might need for a proper escape. It would be possible—"

"A plane?"

"Not without extreme difficulty. Would a boat do?"

"One that could reach Lebanon."

"Ah. It is gold, then?"

"How did—"

"What else does one sell in Lebanon? For many items

351

Lebanon is where one buys. But if one has gold to sell, one sells it in Lebanon. One does not get the four hundred Swiss francs per ounce one might realize in Macao, but neither does one get the one hundred thirty francs one would obtain at the official rate. I suspect you might realize two hundred fifty Swiss francs an ounce for your gold. Is that what you had anticipated?"

"For a priest," I said, "you're rather worldly."

He laughed happily. "There is only one thing."

"Yes."

"It would be necessary for you to join the Society of the Left Hand."

"I would have to become a member?"

"Yes. You are willing?"

"I know nothing about the Society."

He considered this for a few moments. "What must you know?"

"Its political aims."

"The Left Hand is above politics."

"Its general aims, then?"

"The good of its members."

"Its nature?"

"Secret."

"Its numerical strength?"

"Unknown."

We sat looking at each other.

"You wish to join?"

"Yes."

"That is good." He went to another bookshelf, brought down a Bible, a ceremonial knife, and a piece of plain white cloth. I covered my head with the white cloth, gripped the knife in my right hand, and rested that hand atop the Bible.

"Now," said Father Gregor, "raise your left hand…"

I ENTERED Balikesir in the afternoon three days later on the back of a toothless donkey. With the British air and coastal defense plans between my skin and my shirt, with the leather satchel abandoned in Bulgaria, with my face unshaven and my hair uncombed and my body unwashed, and with Mustafa lbn Ali's passport clenched in my sweaty hand.

For the remainder of the afternoon I wandered slowly through the downtown section. There could not possibly have been as many agents of various powers as I fancied I saw, but it certainly seemed as though the city was swarming with spies and secret agents of one sort or another.

I had to dodge them all. But I also had to slip in and out of the streets of the city until I found that house high on a hill at the edge of town, the big house with the huge porch that Kitty Bazerian's grandmother may or may not have recalled correctly. Then I had to break into the porch, remove the gold, accept help from the Society of the Left Hand, and, hardest of all, manage to avoid having the Left Hand walk off with every last cent of the proceeds.

Because I did not trust them an inch.

There was a moon three-quartets full that night. Around nine I began hunting for the house, and it took me until an hour before dawn to find it.

The house needed painting badly. Some of its windows were broken, a few boards loose on its sides. I approached it very cautiously and came close enough for a quick examination of the porch. The floorboards seemed to have remained undisturbed for a long period of time, and the concrete sides were uniformly black with age. There was one part where the porch might have been broken and re-cemented years ago—perhaps when the gold was originally hidden away there, or perhaps later when someone else had beaten me to the punch and removed the treasure. There was only one sure way to find out, and it was too close to dawn for me to make the attempt.

I drifted downtown again. I wasted the day wandering through the markets, killing time in a filthy movie house, sitting over cups of inky coffee in dark cafes. At night I returned to the house. I had purchased a crowbar and small flashlight at the market and had walked around all day with them hidden in the folds of my clothing.

In the darkness I went up onto the porch and worked at the boards. It was hellish work—I had to be silent, I had to be fast, and I had to be prepared to melt into the shadows at the approach of a car or a pedestrian. I finally cleared out a large enough area so that a man could slip through. I turned on the flashlight and looked inside.

The beam was weak. But it was enough. I was looking—wide-eyed, suddenly breathless—at the gold of Smyrna!

I spent the rest of the night beneath the porch.

There were sacks and boxes and little leather purses, and everything was stuffed with gold coins. The great majority were British sovereigns with the head of Queen Victoria, but there was a scattering of Turkish pieces and a handful of pieces in each lot from other nations. Counting this treasure was out of the question. Instead, I incorporated the small bags inside the larger gunny sacks and tried to calculate the total weight of the treasure.

My guess placed it somewhere between 500 and 600 pounds. I was sitting in the exhilarating presence of somewhere around a quarter of a million dollars in gold.

The Society of the Left Hand made 1 contact in the market a day later. A furtive little man with smallpox scars on his chin flashed me one of the secret signs—a particular arrangement of the fingers of the left hand that Father Gregor had taught me. I returned the sign. He nodded for me to follow him and I did.

He led me up on street and down another until we reached a large old house in the Arab section.

"We have rented this house," he said. "You will come inside?"

I went inside and met my four companions. There were three others, I was told. One waited in the harbor at Burhaniye with the boat they planned to use. Two others had left to make arrangements for a car. Had I found the gold? I said I had. Would we be able to get it out? I said we would.

They were all delighted.

"We will. help you," the scarred one said. His name was Odon; the others had not volunteered their names. "And we will be content with a tenth of the proceeds."

He was the least convincing liar I had ever met in my life.

"Where is the gold?"

I explained its approximate location.

"And how much is there?"

I told him my estimate.

"We will go tonight," Odon said. "We will purchase a car. One of our men has a Turkish driver's license and a passport to match it. There is no chance we will be questioned. We will go to the house and load the gold into metal strongboxes. You understand? We have the boxes in the garage. Come, I will show you."

There were two dozen steel strongboxes in the garage on top of a huge workbench. The bench overflowed with rusted hardware and tools—long rattail files, rusted padlocks, nuts, bolts, washers.

"Have we enough boxes?"

I calculated quickly. "Yes. They'll hold the gold."

"Good. We will fill them at the house. You understand? Or, for safety's sake, you will go beneath the porch and fill them. Then, when you are ready, the car will return for them, and we will all go at once to Burhaniye. Before dawn we will all be on our way."

That night clouds concealed the face of the moon. It was a bit of good luck. After midnight we drove to the house. Odon stayed in the car with two of the others. Another pair remained at the house—we were to stop for them before making the run to Burhaniye. I scurried onto the porch, opened up my little rabbit hole, and dropped down into my burrow. Another man passed the strongboxes down to me one at a time.

"Shall I wait with you?"

"No," I said. "Go back to the car. Come for me in an hour."

I had finished packing the boxes by the time the car returned. Odon came to me from the car and suggested that I hand them up one at a time, and he would trek them back to the car.

That would make it a little too easy. I hopped out of my burrow. "I'm too exhausted to lift another thing," I said. "Send one of the other men to do the lifting. I'll wait in the car."

They brought the boxes out quickly enough, one man handing them up, two others relaying them to the car. Odon placing them in the trunk, but they made enough noise to wake corpses. He drove well, at least. He put the gas pedal on the floor, and we were back at home base in no time at all.

Odon stuck the car in the garage. "Get the others," he told one of the men. "And hurry. We have to be on that boat before dawn. There's no time."

l got out of the car. I passed the hardware bench, scooped off a curved linoleum knife. As I walked around the car I stuck the knife into the left rear tire, pulled it out fast, and pocketed it. The tire did not blow but went down fast, almost instantaneously. I let one of the others discover it.

Odon cursed rather colorfully. "We have to get another car," he said. "Damn it to hell, somebody go out and steal a car. We have to—"

An argument developed. Two of the men utterly refused to make the trip in a stolen car. Another pointed out that they could get a tire in the morning and they could use some sleep for the time being.

"And if in the meanwhile someone runs off with the gold?"

The wait-until-tomorrow crowd carried the day. Odon locked the trunk and closed the garage door. We all trooped inside the dingy house. A cupboard yielded up a bottle of rather poor brandy. We drank and sang and drank and danced and drank, and one by one we dropped off to sleep until at last all of us were sleeping peacefully.

All but one of us.

With such an abundant supply of tools around the locked trunk was not much of an obstacle. I was busy for almost an hour. Then I slipped back into the house. They were all still asleep.

I CONTRIVED to be obviously awake before them. Odon sent a man out to buy a tire. He came back with it and put it on the car.

It was an easy drive. The ship, a trim little cutter, lay at anchor, with a thick-set man on board. He came down to greet us. The harbor officials were taken care of, he reported. They would look the other way. We need only load the ship and be off.

Odon took me aside. He handed me a sack full of padlocks. "You must lock the strongboxes," he said. "It is only fitting, as you are the man who will receive the greater share of the gold and you must be assured that we do not try to cheat you. If the boxes are not locked we might take more than our share during the voyage. Do you understand?"

"But I trust you, Odon."

He very nearly blushed. "No matter," he said.

I went to the trunk and Odon opened it with his key. I locked each box in turn and handed the boxes one by one to Odon's men, who carried them to the ship and came back for more. By the time I was handing over the final box, all of the men had managed to work their way onto the boat. Only Odon was left, and just as I passed him the final box, a man called his name from the shin.

"Ah," he said, "there seems to be trouble on board. Wait right here, I'll be back in a moment."

"I'll go with you."

"Oh, it's not necessary. Ah, what's that down there?"

I looked where he pointed. He had picked up the tire wrench and he telegraphed the blow so completely that it took a certain amount of effort to let him hit me at all. He dropped the tire iron, tucked the strongbox under his arm, and ran to the ship.

They had been kind enough to leave the keys in the ignition. I turned the car around and drove back to Balikesir, found the house, pulled into the garage, and closed the door.

They would not open those strongboxes until they reached their destination, which would take a day at the least. They wouldn't open the boxes because they would not trust one another enough before they got back to Sofia and split it into their unrightful shares.

I could see them all, gathered in Father Gregor's comfortable house, ceremoniously unlocking or breaking open the padlocks, lifting the lids of each box in turn, and finding some six hundred pounds of rusty hardware, by my own admittedly rough estimate.

I had presented my unofficial resignation from the Society of the Left Hand the only organization from which I had ever resigned.

The gold was where I had left it, piled under a tarpaulin in the farthest corner of the garage. I used a variety of tools to open up the door panels of the Chevy and packed the door solid with gold coins. I stowed more of them under the seats, inside the cushions, under the trunk lining, and on top of the hood liner. It took several hours to pack the car properly. A certain amount of rattling was perhaps inevitable, but one expected rattles in a ten-year-old automobile.

I found a razor and some soap. I got out of my clothes, bathed, shaved and put my filthy clothes on again.

The Turkish passport and the Turkish driver's license were in the glove compartment.

According to the speedometer, I logged about eight hundred miles all told. I drove nonstop for almost two full days. I had no trouble at the border. The Customs guards checked my car well enough, but they had no particular reason to take the doors apart so they didn't.

I STAYED at a good hotel in Beirut and put my car in the hotel garage. I told the bellhop that I was interested in finding a reliable gold merchant, and I tipped him a sovereign. Within an hour a young Chinese came to me. Did I have gold to sell? I said that I did. Would I accept fifty dollars an ounce? I said that I would not.

"How much, sir?"

"Sixty."

"That is high."

"It is low. You would pay sixty-five if I insisted. Tell your boss that I do not bargain. Tell him sixty dollars an ounce."

"How much gold, sir?"

"Six hundred pounds."

He did not wink, he did not blink, he remained wholly inscrutable. He left, he returned. "Sixty dollars an ounce is acceptable," he said.

I went to a very modern office in a very modern downtown building. A Chinese in a London suit sat across the desk from me and worked out the details with me. I was a very difficult bargainer at first. After the fun and games in Turkey I had given up trusting anyone. But we worked out the arrangements. Several of the Swiss banks maintained major branches in Beirut. I need only open an account in one of them, a numbered account, and the Chinese would deposit funds in my account equal to sixty dollars an ounce for my total consignment of gold. His company had a warehouse where we would have sufficient privacy. I drove the car there, and several of his employees unloaded the gold from the car according to my directions. It was all weighed and tallied before my eyes; the gold weighed out at five hundred seventy-three pounds and four ounces.

"You wish payment in Swiss francs?" the Chinese in the London suit asked.

"I would prefer dollars."

"Of course."

The rest was mechanics. I fully expected someone to attempt to cheat me out of the whole bundle, but no one did. We went to the Beirut offices of the Bank Leu. I opened a numbered account. No one, I was assured, would ever know of the existence of the account or the balance in it without my express permission. No government on earth could obtain such information. I and only I could make withdrawals from the account.

We concluded the transaction. The Chinese merchant took all the gold away—and I had on deposit precisely $371,520.

There was only one thing left to do. After dinner, and after I had spent about an hour resting as completely as possible on my most comfortable bed, I left the hotel and took a taxi a few blocks farther down the street. I got out of the cab in front of the American Embassy.

A young man sat behind a large desk in the hallway. I stood in front of his desk for several minutes before he raised his neat head from the pile of papers in front of him.

He asked if he could help me.

"I hope so," I said. "You see, I've lost my passport."

"I don't suppose you remember the number?"

"I'm afraid not."

He sniffed. "Your name?"

I paused, perhaps for dramatic effect.

"My name is Evan Michael Tanner," I said. "I suggest you tell your boss the name. Evan Michael Tanner. You go tell him Evan Michael Tanner is here, and you see what he says."

He reached for a buzzer and rang for the guards. We waited for them to come for me. It didn't take long. Exactly two hours later, handcuffed and under heavy guard, I was loaded upon a jet plane at Beirut airport. Its destination—Washington.

THE JAIL cell in the basement of CIA headquarters in Washington was far more comfortable than the dank dark room in Istanbul. It was well lighted and very clean. There was a bed, a small dresser, and a shelf of paperback books. The books were mostly spy novels, I discovered.

The meals were good. Actually, there was no single

dish that was as good as the pilaf I had had in Istanbul, but there was a great deal of variety in the cooking. The only aspect of the two weeks I spent there that became absolutely unbearable was the endless routine of questioning.

"Who are you working for, Tanner?"

"I can't tell you."

"Why?"

"Those are my instructions."

"We're more important than your instructions, Tanner."

"No, you're not."

"We're the US Government."

"I'm working for the Government."

"Oh, you are? That's very interesting, Tanner. You're working for the CIA?"

"No."

"For whom, then?"

"I can't tell you."

"The US Government?"

"Yes."

"I think you're crazy, Tanner."

"That's your privilege."

"Suppose we give you a phone. You call somebody and make contact, okay? And then they can come and spring you, and we'll all be happy. How does that sound, Tanner?"

"No."

"No? Why the hell not?"

"I was instructed not to make contact."

"So, what the hell are you going to do? Sit here forever?"

"Sooner or later I'll be contacted."

"How? By voices talking to you in the night?"

"No."

"Who gave you those papers?"

"I can't—"

"Shut up. Why did you turn them over to us?"

"Those were my instructions."

"Really? I thought you couldn't give us a thing, Tanner."

"I was told to deliver the papers to the CIA if I could find no other alternative. It would have been better to deliver them to my superiors, but I could find no way to get into the country except through the American Embassy, and that meant delivering the papers to you."

"Tanner, would you like to know something? I'll tell you something—we almost believe you. Almost. Why don't you help us out?"

"How?"

"Give us one name. Just one little name, Tanner, and maybe you'll be able to get out of here."

"I can't."

"A phone number, then."

"No."

You know something? They're probably beginning to worry about you. Why not let me call them for you?"

"No."

"Give me the initials, Tanner. Just the initials."

"No."

"It's all a big lie, isn't it? You a communist, Tanner? Or just a nut?"

"No."

"Well, how the hell will you get out?"

"My superiors will have me released."

"How will they find you?"

"They'll find me."

And they did.

I had been in the jail cell for over three weeks, and one morning after breakfast a guard came and turned the key in my cell door. One of the CIA men was with him. "They've come for you, Tanner. Get your things."

What things? All I had were the clothes I was wearing.

"And follow me. They found out you were here, finally. God knows how. I guess we've got a leak we don't know about."

Two men in dark suits were waiting in the front lobby. One of them said, "Phil Martin," and extended a hand. I shook it. The other said, "Klausner, Joe Klausner," and I shook his hand.

"The Chief just heard about you," Martin said. "It took us a long time. You've been here three weeks?"

"About that."

"Christ."

"It wasn't so bad."

"I'll bet," Martin said. "The car's out front. The Chief wants to see you right away. There's a bottle in the car if you want a drink first. You look as though you could use it."

There was a half pint of blended whiskey in the glove compartment. I took a long drink, capped it, and put it back. The three of us sat in the front of the car with me in the middle. Phil was driving.

"The Chief is very anxious to see you, Tanner," Phil said. "He didn't know you were one of ours. He suspected it when we got rumbles about the bit in Macedonia. Dallmann had contacts in Macedonia. Dallman's dead, you know."

"I know."

"Well," Phil said.

We rode the rest of the way in silence. Phil dropped us in front of a shoe repair shop in a slum. Joe and I entered a building by the door to the right of the shop and climbed three flights of squeaking stairs to the apartment on the top floor. He knocked. A deep voice invited us inside. Joe opened the door, and we went in.

Joe said, "Here's Tanner, Chief."

"Check."

Joe left and closed the door. The Chief was a round-faced man, bald on top, with fleshy hands that remained in perfect repose on the desk in front of him. The desk was empty of papers. There was a box labeled IN and another labeled OUT. Both were empty. There was a globe on the desk and a map of the world on the wall behind him.

"Evan Michael Tanner," the Chief said. "It's a pleasure to meet you, Tanner."

We shook hands. He motioned me to a chair, and I sat down.

"Dallmann's dead," he said. "I suppose you knew?"

"Yes."

"Shot down in Dublin, ironically enough. It must have happened just after he passed the papers to you."

I nodded.

"I suspected you might be Dallmann's man when we first began to get reports on you, but I wasn't sure. I became somewhat more certain when we received reports of the incident in Macedonia." He smiled for the first time. "That was excellent work, Tanner. That was one of the neatest bits of work in years."

"Thank you, sir."

"It may well turn out to have been the biggest wedge driven in Yugoslav hegemony since the end of the war. They were astonished when that revolt broke out. Astonished. The last thing anyone expected was a blowup in Macedonia. I suppose that was why you made your first trip to Istanbul?"

"That's right."

"And of course that fell in. Brilliant work of yours,

picking up Dallmann in Dublin afterward. And then having the nerve to carry through with the Macedonian plans. Most men would have settled for the British papers and brought them straight home. Dallmann would be proud of you, Tanner."

I didn't say anything. Dallmann—the tall man—must have guessed I was on his team from the Istanbul fiasco.

The Chief looked down at his hands. "Strange situation in Ireland," he said. "The Irish filched that set of plans out of London as neat as anything. The British didn't even know who had them. But we knew and we couldn't let them stay in Irish hands. Irish security isn't the best in the world, you know. And those plans were fairly vital. Dallmann took them away in a matter of days. Another power could have done the same thing. Oh, sorry I had to put you through three weeks of CIA interrogation. Understand you didn't tell them a thing."

"I had to give them the plans."

"Well, that was all right. Couldn't be helped. What are your plans now, Tanner?"

"I'll go back to New York."

"Back to business as usual, eh?"

"Yes."

"Good. Very good." He thought for a moment. "We might have a piece of work for you now and then."

"All right."

"We're hell to work for. I don't know exactly what sort of arrangement you had with Dallmann. Doesn't much matter now, does it? But we're very hard masters. We give you an assignment and that's all. We give you no contacts. We don't smooth the way for you a bit. If you get caught somewhere, we never heard of you and you never heard of us. We can't even fix a parking ticket for you. And if you get killed, we drink a toast to your memory and that's all.

No group insurance. No full-dress funeral with burial in Arlington. Understand?"

"Yes, sir."

"So you might hear from us some time. If something comes up. Sound good to you?"

"Yes, sir."

"You'll find your own way out. Walk a few blocks before you catch a cab. Might as well go straight back to New York. Don't ever try to contact me. I suppose you know that much, but I'll say it anyway. All right?"

"All right."

"How are you fixed for money?"

"I could use the plane fare. I'm out of ready cash."

"Besides that."

"I'm all right." I thought for a moment. "I managed to...uh...pick up a little for myself this trip."

He gave me two hundred dollars for the plane and incidental expenses. We shook hands a third and final time, and I let myself out.

Bring on the Girls

From the pages of **Stag**, April 1968

Art by BRUCE MINNEY

It wasn't a cell exactly. When one speaks of a prison cell, one implies rather a sort of room in a sort of building, with perhaps a barred door and window. A stone or cement floor. A cot, a dangling light bulb, a pot of some sort in which various bodily functions may be performed.

Not like this idiot contrivance in which I was presently trapped, a rude box eight feet square and four feet high, constructed entirely of bamboo, and suspended from the limb of a tall tree, with its bottom about five feet from the ground.

You couldn't call it a cell, then. What you could call it was a large birdcage. And it was the only sort of birdcage to be found for miles around. Birds are not caged in dense teak forests far in the north of Thailand.

I had been in the cage ever since the guerrilla patrol captured me four days previously. I had never lived through longer days. My bamboo cage seemed to have been devised as a special form of Oriental torture. One could not stand up. One could crouch, and there was barely enough head-room to crawl about.

I could just manage to peer through the bamboo sides at the guerrilla encampment surrounding me. I did this, at one time or another, from every side of the cage. I saw any number of huts, cooking fires, rifles, machetes, sharpened stakes, and Siamese guerrillas. I saw various articles of my clothing—I was quite naked in my cage, like a bird plucked free of feathers—being worn by various guerrillas.

There was a small hole in the center of the floor through which a bowl of wormy rice was passed to me twice a day if they remembered. Now and then someone would also pass me a cup of greasy water, and now and then I would void whatever had to be voided through the same aperture.

It might not have been so bad if I could have slept. But when I was eighteen years old, a piece of North Korean shrapnel had been rudely deposited in my brain, and in the course of this, something called my sleep center had been destroyed. I have not slept in seventeen years.

During the first day in my cage, I tried to attract atten-tion by making noise. I called out now and then in Siamese, which I speak moderately well, and in Khmer, which I don't. No one ever went so far as to answer me, but when-ever I made any noise, someone came over and raised one side of the cage, sending me sprawling over to the other side. I learned my lesson. I stopped talking.

My silence was met by silence, with no interrogation

369

whatsoever. I had decided at first to try convincing them that I was not an American agent named Evan Michael Tanner and then I decided to convince them that I was. Both of these decisions were quite irrelevant. No one asked me anything, not name or rank or serial number, nothing at all. I stayed where I was and waited for something to happen, but it didn't.

Until late one afternoon someone finally spoke to me. A hand poked a rice bowl through the central hole in the bottom of the cage. I sent the bowl back empty, received a cup of tepid water in return, drank the water, returned the cup, and a soft, sad voice said, "Tomorrow."

Or perhaps the voice said, "Morning." Siamese, like so many other languages, makes no distinction between the two concepts.

So I said, "*Tomorrow*? Or *Morning*?" In any case I repeated the word.

"Upon the rising of the sun." Well, that cleared things up.

"What will happen then?"

"Upon the rising of the sun," he said mournfully, "they will kill you."

His words filled me with hope.

Not, let me add, because I thought he was right and hoped for death as a respite from life in a cage. Consider: not We *will kill you* but They *will kill you*. Thus implicitly disassociating himself from any personal involvement in the act, either active or passive.

"They will kill you at sunrise," he said again. "There was talk of getting you a woman," he went on mournfully. "Usually when a man is condemned to die, he is first given a woman. It is the custom.

"But," he continued, "there will not be a woman for you. It was decided that you are a capitalist imperialist dog and a white devil, and that your seed must not be mingled with the love juices of our women. It is what they decided."

They again.

"I have never had a woman," he said.

"Never?"

"Never in all my days. I have, however, spent many hours thinking about such a thing."

"I can imagine." It gave me an idea.

"There is nothing on earth to match the embrace of a woman," I said. "No other sensation is its equivalent. The soft, sweet texture of female flesh, of hungry lips. The taste of a woman, the subtle but pungent aroma of a woman..."

I went on in this vein for quite a while. It had the desired effect.

"Stop," he said at last. "Please stop."

"It is unfair that you have never known such joy. If only I were free, I would do something about it."

"What would you do?"

"I would help you find a woman."

"You could do this?"

"With ease and with pleasure."

He hesitated for a moment. "It is a trick," he said suddenly. "It is a capitalist imperialist trick, a trick."

And he went away.

I slapped a mosquito and said something obscene in Siamese. At sunrise they were going to kill me. I had to get away, and they were not going to let me get away, and my little virginal friend had decided that he did not trust me.

"You would really get me a woman?"

He had returned. It was darker now, and his voice was more urgent now, and I could guess what he had been spending his time thinking about. Capitalist imperialist trick or no, I was his one chance, just as he was mine.

"I will."

"I have decided to trust you, my friend."

"Good."

"I shall help you. We will escape."

"Good."

"I go now. When the camp sleeps, I shall return. I go now, my friend, my good friend."

I celebrated by slapping another mosquito.

I wondered if my little friend would come back and whether his help would make much difference one way or the other. The cage could only be opened by lowering it to the ground, which in turn could not be done without making a hell of a racket and waking the entire camp.

I wondered if the Land Rover still worked. But even if it were still operable, which was doubtful, I couldn't count on it to take me anywhere.

Was there anything of value in the car? Nothing much, really. The extra clothing I had brought would have been appropriated by the guerrillas. They probably would have left the butterfly-collecting equipment alone. The spreading board, the killing jar, the butterfly net, designed to cover my presence in the jungles and rubber plantations of Thailand, and all quite wasted now.

I closed my eyes and cursed. Then I stopped cursing and started thinking. Of the two thinking turned out to be the more productive. By the time night had fallen and my little Thai friend had crept soundlessly to my cage and whispered his presence, I had it all figured out…

MY FIRST meeting with Tuppence—Miss T'pani Ngawa—took place at a PAUL meeting held on a rainy Thursday night in a storefront church on Lenox Avenue at 138th Street.

PAUL is the Pan-African Unity League. That night

there was a brief report on the slaughter of Ibos in Nige-
ria, a somewhat more extended lecture on conditions in the
Congo, and, finally, a report by Miss Ngawa on social and
economic progress in Kenya.

When the meeting ended, she and I went out for
coffee. We had an immediate common bond. I was the only
Caucasian at the meeting, and she was the only African. All
the others in attendance were American Negroes.

"The Back-to-Africa bit," she said. "Bwana and simba
and the bloody drums in the bloody jungle, like it is all
something else, you dig?"

Tuppence, being a highly unorthodox combination
of things, spoke an English all her own. She was the only
child of a Kenyan mother and an American father. Her
father, one Willie Jackson, had been an African Nationalist.
The Army sent him to North Africa during the Second
World War, where he rather promptly deserted and headed
south. He changed his name to Willie Ngawa, married
Tuppence's mother, and conceived Tuppence.

Tuppence grew up learning English and Swahili and
sang the folk songs of Kenya. She went to college in London, began singing with a jazz group there, and ultimately
came to New York, where she got a more or less steady
gig with a local jazz quartet, and concurrently developed a
reputation as an African folk singer

I received Tuppence's history a little at a time over a
period of several hours after leaving the PAUL meeting.
We drank several cups of coffee in a chrome-and-formica
diner on 125th Street, and wound up, happily enough, at my
apartment on 107th Street. We sat on my couch drinking a
Yugoslav white wine.

We finished one bottle and got most of the way
through a second, when Tuppence said, "You dig baby,
Bwana Evan? Do you now?"

"Ah, the natives are restless."

"They are indeed. Do you think you might extinguish that barbaric cacophony"—we had been listening to a Miles Davis record—"and put on something tribal?"

I changed the jazz record for a Folkways recording of Kenyan and Ugandan chants, dances, and work songs. Tuppence bounced off the couch, kicked off her shoes and began to dance.

"Native girl dance for you, Bwana Evan." Her white eyes rolled in her dark face. "Native girl make you hot with passion, wild with lust. Native girl turn you on, baby. You better believe it."

I don't know whether or not her dance was an authentic example of Kenyan tribal folk-dancing. I rather think not. It seemed a combination of African dance and current American styles, with the limbs loose, the hips shaking, the buttocks twitching. Through it all Tuppence's lips showed a smile of eternal female knowledge, and her huge eyes twinkled.

So she danced, and we looked at each other, and something clicked neatly and finally into place, and we both knew that the evening was going to end properly. Because the special magic was there. It is not often present, and without it there is really no reason on earth why a man and woman should bother having anything to do with one another.

The record went on, and Tuppence went on dancing, and I moved around the room turning off lights until only the shallow glow of one small lamp illuminated the room. My couch is one of those clever contrivances that turns into a bed when the occasion demands it. The occasion demanded it, so I pulled the proper levers. Then Miss T'pani Ngawa changed the leitmotif of the dance slightly, incorporating within the structure of basic African tribal

374

rhythms certain dance patterns generally associated in times past with Union City, New Jersey.

Which is to say that she took off all her clothes.

"Bwana approve?"

"Bwana approve."

"Ah! What Bwana doing?"

"Bwana going to integrate you," I said.

"Oh, wow—"

THAT WAS how it began. A month went by as months usually go by, and then Tuppence dropped in one afternoon and told me she was leaving the country.

"A State Department tour," she said. "Deluxe treatment all the way. Manila, Tokyo, Hong Kong, and Bangkok. This chick is going a long way from Nairobi, baby."

"It sounds good. When do you leave?"

"Four days from tomorrow. We're supposed to have a command performance for the King of Thailand. The word is that he's a swinger. He plays the clarinet or some such. Can you feature the king himself sitting in and wailing, and this little girl vocalizing? A long long way from Nairobi. Wow!"

I saw her plane off at Kennedy Airport.

There was a postcard from Manila, another from Tokyo, and a third letter from Bangkok:

Bwana Evan:

Bangkok is a gas but the bread is running low. It looks as though I'll maybe have to sell my jewelry. As you know I have a very valuable collection. Do you have contacts that will prove helpful? Please let me know.

My first reaction—that Tuppence had lost her mind somewhere between New York and Bangkok—gave way to a feeling of general bewilderment. When one lives in a world of secret societies and underground political movements, and does odd jobs for a nameless US undercover agency, one becomes accustomed to finding meanings in apparently meaningless messages. I read her letter over and over and decided that, if there was any hidden kernel of sense to it, I couldn't spot it for the time being. Tuppence had a pair of long gold hoop earrings, and as far as I knew, that was the extent of her jewelry. I stopped thinking about it.

Until two days later *The Times* ran a story on page five that stated that the Royal Gem Collection of Thailand had been stolen in its entirety, that the thief or thieves had made good their escape, that it may or may not have been an inside job.

And a day after that, while I was still recovering from that one, Tuppence and the quartet made the front page of *The Times.*

Thai Communists Kidnap American Jazz Quartet, Kenyan Singer, said the headline, and the body copy went on to elaborate. The Kendall Bayard Quartet and Miss T'pani Ngawa, in Bangkok for a command performance before His Majesty the King of Thailand, had been snatched from the Hotel Orient. The kidnapping appeared to be the work of Communist guerrillas based in Northern Thailand.

The Times made no connection between the disappearance of Tuppence and the quartet and the theft of the royal gem collection. But I did. I got out my passport...

I went to the Thai consulate to have my passport stamped with a visa. I went to Air India and booked a flight to Bangkok. At Deak and Company on Times Square I turned some American money into Siamese bahts. The baht was holding firm at 4.78 US cents, the clerk told me. On West 45th Street I visited a rare coin dealer and bought a couple hundred dollars' worth of common gold coins, mostly British sovereigns. Bangkok is a center for the illicit trade in precious metals. Gold or silver may be exchanged there for anything—teen-age concubines, opium, guns, anything.

At my apartment I tucked the cash into a flat nylon money belt and fastened it around my waist. The gold pieces, twenty-two of them, fit into the casing of a flashlight battery with just a little room left. I added cotton to fill and put the battery back in the flashlight.

My flight was scheduled to leave Kennedy Airport at 11:35. I took a taxi to the airport...

THE HOTEL Orient in Bangkok was steel and glass on the outside, nylon and plastic within.

I unpacked, had a shower and shaved and stretched out on the bed and watched the ceiling for twenty minutes. I needed a place to start, and Abel Vaudois seemed promising. He was a Swiss who divided his time between Bangkok and Macao, buying and selling almost anything. If anything valuable was stolen anywhere in the Orient, there was a fair chance that he would know something about it.

I put on clean clothes and rode the elevator downstairs to the lobby. Outside on the street I hailed a cruising cab and gave the driver Abel Vaudois' address...

Abel Vaudois was an excellent host. We sat in the comfortable library of his immense estate and drank what was easily the best cognac I had ever tasted. He insisted on my staying with him and sent one of his men over to the Orient to get my bags.

I had told him virtually everything I knew about Tuppence and the jewels. He in turn had known only a little more than I. From what he had heard so far, Tuppence and the musicians were not suspected of being involved in the theft of the gems.

"I had suspected the gems might be offered to me,"

Vaudois said. "It would have been the sort of proposition that might have tempted me."

He rang a bell, and a servant entered silently. "I am sure you will be comfortable here," he said, "and tomorrow will be time enough to see what can be learned about your friends. And the King's gems."

I breakfasted alone the next morning. I was on my third cup of coffee when Vaudois entered the room.

"You had a good night? Good. The breakfast was satisfactory?"

"Very."

"I am glad. And now as to the jewels and your girl friend. I have made enquiries. Not productive, but not entirely fruitless either. First, the gems. The business of the theft, as you may have gathered last night, was carried out in a genuinely professional manner. And yet no local professionals in that line of work seem to have been involved. Nor have any known professional jewel thieves from outside been recognized in Bangkok of late.

"Now, as to the musicians—it does seem very likely that they were taken away to the north. No one to whom I spoke has heard anything about their having been taken out of the country, and my contacts might well have heard of it had it happened. There have been no ransom attempts either.

"So I wonder immediately why anyone might kidnap them, eh? Perhaps they stole the jewels, and the kidnappers then stole them *and* the jewels. But I do not think so. Or perhaps they were kidnapped for political reasons, eh? I would not attempt to guess those reasons, but in the realm of world politics I have found it to be true that anything is possible, anything at all. As long as the motive of financial profit dominates, then a degree of logic prevails. But once political considerations are involved, ah, then lunacy and chaos enter in." He shook his head.

I told Vaudois the plan I'd devised for getting into the north. Obviously I needed a cover. I would not be particularly welcome an American agent. But throughout the remote areas of the world the natives had grown accustomed to the periodic invasions of American scientists, especially of the simpler sort. With just the most rudimentary sort of equipment I could easily pass as an itinerant lepidopterist, chasing net in hand over the rice paddies of Thailand in a madcap hunt for elusive butterflies and moths.

I wouldn't even have to pursue any winged creatures. I could insist that I was only interested in the Bat-Winged Gobbletail or some such, and leave inferior species alone. And, with that sort of cover, I could visit remote villages and mingle innocently with the people, asking all sorts of irrelevant questions

"It is not impossible," Abel Vaudois admitted. "You may make a list of the various articles you require, and I will have them purchased for you. And of course, you will need a car."

I left two days later long before dawn, picking up the main highway north from Bangkok. The first stretch of road was broad and flat, with endless stretches of rice fields on either side. The road was built up high because during the rainy season the lands were frequently under water.

When the road got worse, I began to go into my act. I stopped in the small villages and bought my meals from the people. My equipment drew considerable interest, and the villagers were amused that someone would be foolish enough to spend time and money pursuing the pretty little butterflies. I redeemed myself in their eyes by explaining that I sold the insects at a handsome profit to rich collectors—thus it was these rich collectors who were the fools, and I was merely a shrewd tradesman.

It was at one of these villages, far north of Bangkok, where the rice fields were more and more frequently giving way to stretches of bamboo forest and stands of teak, that I had my first word of Tuppence. Why, yes, an old woman told me, she had seen some people with black skins, a woman and some men as well. It was remarkable—she had not known there were persons in the world of such a color. They had passed through the village a day after Prang's buffalo had calved, just nine days ago.

THEY WERE with the bandits, a man added. They were with the bandits, a man added. But he did not think they were of the bandits but were perhaps their prisoners.

"Bandits? Were they Communists?"

"What are Communists?"

I took a different tack. "How did you know that the captors of the black persons were bandits?"

"They took food," the old woman said, "and did not pay for it, and pointed guns at us. Since they did not have uniforms, we knew they were not of the government, so they must be bandits."

I learned more of the bandits as I moved to the north. There were many groups of them, I was told, and sometimes they fought among themselves and other times they battled the government forces.

I heard scattered reports of Tuppence, nothing too certain but bits and pieces picked up here and there. I left the main road only the engineering marvel that was the Land Rover enabled me to keep on going.

Until at last one fine day I emerged in a clearing and suddenly found the Land Rover surrounded by armed men. They were not in uniforms, so I knew they were

not government soldiers and guessed that I had found
some bandits.

And the next thing I knew I had been stripped naked,
divested of clothing and socks and shoes and money belt,
and tucked unceremoniously into that horrible bamboo
cage.

The sun rose, and the little camp came awake. I wondered if Dhang had been able to carry out the final tasks
I had assigned to him. I had not seen him in over an hour.
He had performed well enough, managing to fetch things
from the Land Rover. I now shared my cage with a jar of
acid from the car's battery, the insect-killing jar, and a short
black bayonet liberated from a sleeping guerrilla.

A voice rose above the hubbub of the camp and began
issuing commands. I watched as a barefoot young man
climbed furiously up the tree from which my cage was suspended. His weight bowed the branch, and the cage dipped
toward the ground. Guerrillas moved to surround it. The
Thai up in the tree cut the rope, and ten pairs of hands
gripped the cage and lowered it gently to the ground.

Another command. Hands unhooked the top of the
cage and lifted it up and off. I scooped up the bayonet, the
killing jar, and the acid. I got to my feet for the first time
since I had first been placed in that unholy prison. My captors gathered around, peering at me over the sides of the
cage. They seemed astonished that I had any possessions
with me, and one, evidently the commander, demanded to
know what these things were.

"What have you? How did you get those things?"

"It is a magic trick," I said. "I am a worker of magic
and would provide you with entertainment."

Some of the younger guerrillas began to chatter
excitedly. The camp wasn't exactly a major draw on the
Orpheum Circuit, entertainment of any sort rare.

But the leader wasn't having any. "A bayonet," he said. "Where did you get that?"

"By a magic entreaty to my gods."

"Give me the bayonet."

I looked at him and at the bayonet and wanted to give it to him between the eyes. I glanced past the bunch of guerrillas clustered around me and caught sight of Dhang hovering beside one of the huts. He smiled tentatively and made a sign with his hand to indicate that everything was all right. I was glad he thought so.

"Come out of the cage."

I couldn't climb over the four-foot cage side without spilling the acid. I gave the killing jar to one of the guerrillas and the jar of acid to another, asked them to hold my magic goods for a moment, and then vaulted the side of the cage. I reclaimed the two jars and began babbling about my prowess as a conjurer and sorcerer. The chief remained unimpressed, but I was earning points with the younger element.

In the center of the camp was a broad section of tree scarred with ax marks and stained with blood. Beside it stood a fat man stripped to the waist, with a massive ax in his hand.

"Go that way," the chief said, pointing at the man, the axe, the chopping block.

"Sacred Leader," I intoned. I bowed my head. "Sacred Leader, you have determined to put me to death. I beg one last request to entertain you with magical visions. If my entertainment does not please you, then I will go willingly to my death."

"It is an imperialist trick."

"But will you not observe it, O Leader?"

He truly was interested in nothing but seeing my head say goodbye to my body, but the group pressured him into it. He stepped back, sighed, and ordered me to get this foolishness over with as quickly as possible. I knelt and unscrewed the cover of the cyanide jar. I took a deep breath.

"Come close," I commanded. "Gather around and breathe deeply of the perfumes of life."

They gathered around. I let them come as close as they could, and I took a deep breath of my own and held it, and then I poured the cyanide crystals into the jar of battery acid.

I held my breath.

They didn't.

And at that happy moment, just as a dozen of them breathed deeply of the sweet perfume of bitter almonds, Dhang picked up his cue. All at once half a dozen huts burst into flame as the gasoline did its work. Blue-faced guerrillas dropped around me, their lungs filled with cyanide gas. The chieftain spun around to look at the burning huts, turned again to look at his men falling like flies. He grabbed at his pistol. I kicked him in the stomach and chopped at the side of his neck and took the pistol away from him.

Across the way a young guerrilla fired at me with a rifle. I saw Dhang loop the butterfly net around his head and knock him off balance. Another man, cursing hysterically, approached Dhang with a machete. I cut him down with a burst from the machine pistol, then spun around to spray a burst of shots at another batch of little men. The pistol was a jerry-built affair; after I'd fired the second burst, it was too hot to hold on to. I threw it aside and snatched up a machete.

The fat man, the executioner, came at me with his axe. He swung and missed, and I flailed at him with the machete. It sliced halfway through his throat.

It's hard to say just what happened after that. Dhang

was off to one side, taking potshots at his erstwhile comrades with the rifle. I was in the middle of everything,
swinging the machete at anyone who got particularly close
to me. Around us the fire had spread to all of the huts.
Evidently one of the huts was used to store explosives, and
when the fire reached it, everything went off at once. That
did it, as far as the remaining guerrillas were concerned.
They scattered like dandelion seeds in a hurricane, racing
through the circle of fire and out into the jungle.

I went to Dhang. He clapped his hands jubilantly. "We
have destroyed them," he shouted. "Like a thunderbolt from
the heavens we have destroyed them, and I shall have a
woman.

"We'd better get out of here," I said. "I'll need some
clothing. Shoes, anyway. And I can wrap up in a panung, I
suppose." I didn't especially want to strip corpses to get my
own clothes back. I took a panung from one of the cya-
nosed guerrillas and wrapped it around my body, tucking
the ends into place. I did manage to find a pair of my own
shoes and put them on.

"We will go to the south now?"

"No," I told Dhang. "To the north."

"The north? But more bandits wait in the north. Why
shall we go to the north?"

"There is a woman there, and—"

"Ah, that is different," he said. "If there is a woman
there, then that is where we shall go."

IT WAS late It was late afternoon. We had been walking
for what seemed like forever, and were making very little
discernible progress. We would have made considerably
less progress if Dhang had not saved me from falling into
a leopard trap.

We were reasonably well equipped for a trek through

the jungle. From the guerrilla camp Dhang and I had each taken a machete and a canteen of water. He had a rifle and I had a machine pistol with a full clip in it. The useless Land Rover had yielded up a few treasures, including my flashlight, which the guerrillas had discarded when it failed to operate.

The first night, Dhang shot three small animals and skinned them while I got a fire going. The creatures were built somewhat like rabbits but had small ears and less powerful hind legs. Dhang hacked them into pieces the size of chicken legs, and we cut green sticks from a tree and roasted the meat *en brochette.* We demolished all three.

"We must keep the fire burning all night," he said. "It will keep animals away, and bad spirits."

"Can't we go any further tonight?"

"It is not good to travel at night. Evil spirits abound. And leopards, which hunt at night. At night the wise man stays in his hut. We have no hut, Heaven (he always had trouble pronouncing my name), so we remain by our fire. Here."

"What's this?"

"Betel. Chew it, and your sleep will be better."

I thought for a moment. Among its other properties, betel nut contains some substance with a mild narcotic effect, and it occurred to me that such an effect might be a help through the long night. Then, too, there was the When-in-Rome aspect

Beside me Dhang chewed solemnly on another piece of betel, sighed, spat, closed his eyes. "Soon we will reach the village," he said.

"The village?"

"Tomorrow or the day after. A village in the north country where they may know of your friends. It is not a camp of bandits but a village that lives at peace. The young men from the village join the bandits, but the others are not molested."

"Why did you join the guerrillas, Dhang?"

He looked intently at me, then arced a stream of red saliva at the fire.

"There was nothing of interest in my village. They said that if I went with them, I would be issued a rifle. I had never had a rifle and could not get one in my village." *Chew.* "I thought perhaps"—*spit*—"that there might be women. My village was small, and of the women in it many were my cousins and sisters. I have never had a woman. Never. I thought perhaps with the bandits—but no, nothing. It was very disturbing."

Dhang sighed, spat out his piece of betel, stretched out on his back, and closed his eyes. I lay down on my side and went on chewing betel nut. My mind wandered, and time slipped gently by, and I chewed and spat and chewed and spat, and waited for the sun to rise and for Dhang to wake up.

We made fairly good time the next day. By midafternoon we reached a large clearing in the jungle, the village Dhang had told me about. Some forty huts were pitched around the perimeter of the clearing. The village came to life at our appearance, with men emerging from the huts, most of them armed with spears or machetes.

Siamese was not spoken here. Dhang talked with one of the village leaders in a dialect of Khmer. I could not follow the conversation completely but managed to catch the gist of it. Dhang explained that we came in peace, that we were not bandits, that we had destroyed a bandit camp to the south and were forced to flee for our lives. This won us a good deal of sympathy. He went on to tell how we were attempting to rescue some black persons who had been recently captured by the bandits.

The chieftain clucked over this and said that he had heard of the black persons and had not believed that they existed. He had never known that there were black persons. He had heard of them only recently and he would be glad to summon the villagers together to find out what was known about them. But in the meantime he suggested we relax and sample the hospitality his humble village could provide. It was to be an evening of feasting; they had slaughtered a calf to celebrate the first night of the Week of Tears and Sighs, which commemorated the death by fire of the infant sons and daughters of the gods. It would honor them that we might participate in their celebration.

"Feasting," Dhang said, translating for me. "And women, one can see that this village overflows with women. Look at that one!"

He pointed at a plump young girl, perhaps sixteen years old, her panung covering her primly from her ankles to her waist, her lovely yellow-brown breasts peering out between silky strands of jet black hair. She looked our way, stared, then giggled musically and ran away. For a moment I thought Dhang might run after her, but he somehow managed to control himself.

For the remainder of the afternoon we had the run of the village. I exchanged my panung, which had grown rather filthy, for a clean one. A villager admired my American shoes. After a couple days of walking sockless through the jungle my own admiration for the shoes was considerably qualified, and I was happy to exchange them for a pair of open sandals. I knew enough Khmer to carry on rudimentary conversations as I wandered around asking about black persons.

No one had the whole story on Tuppence and the quartet. No one had actually sighted them, but various villagers had been subjected to various rumors from men of other villages and other tribes. The result of collating different bits of data was something like this:

Four black men and one black girl had been held captive by a band of notorious bandits. The bandits were not of this immediate region, but had come from the northwest, evidently in Laos.

Curiouser and curiouser, I thought. A kidnapping by Thai guerrillas made a certain amount of sense; Tuppence and the musicians could be used as pawns in some maneuvering between the guerrillas and the Bangkok regime. But why would the Laotians be interested in snatching them?

I was still puzzling it out when the feast began. The slaughtered calf was run through with a spit and roasted over a roaring fire in the center of the clearing. The entire population of the village sat in a circle around the fire. As guests of honor, Dhang and I received one eye and half of the calf's brains, along with a couple of rice cakes and some vegetable stew. I ate everything that was given to me, as a proper guest of honor should, and at the conclusion of the meal I wandered off into the jungle, far out of hearing range, and spent some twenty minutes vomiting.

I returned to the village. Dhang had gone off with the first girl he had pointed out, the plump little topless one. I saw the two of them in the doorway of one of the huts.

"You and I," he said in Khmer. He cupped her breast, kissed her mouth. She seemed puzzled. He undid her panung and pulled it off, divested himself of his own panung and rolled on top of her. She rolled out from under him and screamed—and all hell broke loose.

The elders of the village immediately surrounded him. The girl was led away by an old woman, and the men pointed their spears at Dhang and seemed prepared to kill him at once. I ran through the crowd to his side.

"So this is how you repay hospitality," the old chief said scornfully. "You gorge yourself upon eyes and brains and do thus in return."

Dhang was babbling that he had never had a girl and would die if he did not get one soon. It looked as though he might die regardless. All around us voices rose up in anger. I tried to get through to the chief, but I had trouble making out what he was saying.

It was Dhang who explained it to me. After they had sent us on our way, after they had taken us to the edge of the clearing and ordered us to walk into the night, Dhang translated it all for me.

"It is not permitted," he said. "Throughout the entire Week of Tears and Sighs sexual relations of any sort are forbidden under penalty of death. If we had come at any other time, we could have had any woman in the village. Any one at all, we would have only to choose. Any one of them—"

His voice broke. We walked through utter darkness in utter silence…

CROSSING the border from Thailand to Laos is about as awe-inspiring as crossing from Connecticut to Rhode Island. When you go into Rhode Island at least there's a sign that welcomes you to the state and tells you what the speed limit is and all the terrible things that will happen to you if you exceed it.

None of these formalities are observed when you sneak across from Thailand to Laos. That morning we were in Thailand and that afternoon we were in Laos, and somewhere along the way there had been a border that we had crossed.

We had come a long way, Dhang and I, and it had been an equally frustrating journey for both of us, albeit for different reasons. Dhang was still a virgin, and I was still uncertain as to Tuppence's whereabouts, or whether she was alive or dead.

We had made progress of a sort. We had moved from a portion of Thailand that was vaguely and ineffectually dominated by vaguely Communist-oriented guerrillas to a portion of Laos that was quite thoroughly controlled by the forces of the Communist Pathet Lao. We had, in other words, successfully worked our way out of the frying pan and into the fire.

The jungle thinned out and gave way to level land with a scattering of trees here and there. At a river bank we stopped to drink and wash ourselves. A stranger looked back at me from the water's surface. I had not shaved since leaving Bangkok, and my beard was thick and wild. The sun had done a good job on the unbearded portions of my face, and the betel nuts that I had been chewing more and more frequently of late had turned my teeth quite black.

We pressed onward across the plateau and into the craggy, mountainous country. The path widened into a rude sort of road, and a few miles further on, the road was paved after a fashion with loose gravel. We stopped at a roadside hut to ask directions to the nearest town. The woman who answered our knock looked at our weapons and my beard and shrank in terror. Dhang explained calmly that we came in peace, that we were holy men, that we wished to know the route to the nearest town. She told us haltingly to follow the road for about an hour's time to the city of Tao Dan.

We walked for what seemed like a good deal more than an hour until, from the top of a hill, we saw the town of Tao Dan in the distance. It was a fairly sizable city, a great change from the hut-encircled jungle villages we had passed through. A town of that size meant policemen and sundry officials, which in turn meant that I would draw an uncomfortable amount of attention. It was unsafe to go there, but at the same time the town seemed the most logical place to get word of Tuppence.

We walked about halfway there. Then I took Dhang by the arm. "Leave your weapons with me," I told him. "I'll wait out of sight in the brush. Go to the town and make inquiries. Say merely that you are a Thai and have made a journey from the west. Say that you have heard that black men and a black woman were to be seen in the area and see what you can find out about them."

"And you will wait here?"

"Yes. Find out as much as you can, then come back here. Try to obtain clothing for yourself, and for me if it is possible. At night, when all is dark, then we will both be able to pass safely through the town."

"Evan? How will I obtain clothing? Or food?"

"You have no money?" He shook his head. I had no money, either; the guerrillas had taken my money belt. I still had the flashlight, but the thought of Dhang attempting to pass a British gold sovereign in a provincial Laotian town was somehow disquieting.

I asked Dhang if he thought he could use the machetes and the canteens for barter, and he said he thought he could.

"I'll keep one canteen, though," I said. "Go now. And return as soon as possible."

"Yes. Yevan?"

"Evan."

"Evan. If I find a girl in the town..."

He looked at me, hope in his eyes. He would not find a girl, I thought, and if he did, she would have nothing to do with him. But it seemed less than kind to tell him this.

"If you should find a woman," I told him, "may the

gods grant you enjoyment. But do not dally too long with her, and come back to me when time permits."

I made myself reasonably comfortable in a clump of brush some twenty yards from the side of the road. I popped a chunk of betel nut into my mouth and chewed and spat and chewed and spat...

It was night and Dhang still hadn't come back.

The night was cold and dark and damp and gave every appearance of lasting forever. I did not really have to remain hidden in the clump of brush. I would have been equally invisible in the middle of the road. It was that dark.

It began to rain.

The rain didn't last very long. This was fortunate; a steady downpour like that one would have flooded all of Southeast Asia if it had lasted an hour or so. As it was, I was soaked through to the bone. After a fifteen-minute version of eternity, the rain gave up.

I sat through the rest of the night, shivering, shaking, now and then rending the still night air with a sneeze. I waited for Dhang and for daybreak with the certain feeling that neither would ever arrive.

WHEN DAWN broke, finally, I left my weapons and my canteen in the clump of brush and started down the road with the flashlight. I left the weapons behind because I was fairly certain they wouldn't work anyway after all that rain and mud, and I left the canteen behind because I could not imagine ever wanting water again. I walked off down the road in the general direction of Tao Dan and I stopped at the first hut I saw.

It didn't require any great courage to walk into the little shack. I decided that the worst that could happen was that I would get killed and I told myself reasonably that this was probably also the best thing that could happen. I went inside. An old man sat in a chair smoking a pipe. He looked wordlessly at me.

"I must wash myself and remove my beard," I said. "I require dry clothing. And food. I have not eaten in many hours and must have food."

He merely looked at me.

"I am hungry," I said. I made pantomime motions. "Food, a shave, clothing—"

"You are not of this country."

"No, I am not."

"Parlez-vous français?"

"Oui, je parle français—"

And off we went in French. I don't suppose I should have been surprised. French influence had been considerable in Indochina since 1787, and the French had held the area as a protectorate for many years before Dien Bien Phu. Still, I had been talking and thinking in nothing but Siamese and Khmer of late, and the sudden transition to an Occidental language was jarring. The old man spoke reasonably good French and seemed delighted at the chance to show it off.

"For years I worked for the French," he said. "I was a very valuable man for them. I was chief overseer on a large rubber plantation. I was well paid and performed my work with skill and diligence." He turned sad eyes on the mud-floored hut. "And look at me now," he said. "At what I have come to."

"These are bad times," I said.

"They are. That a man like myself should not be respected in my old age. The Communists and anarchists run wild throughout the country. You are French, my boy?"

"Yes." My head was reeling. *I am whatever you want me to be, I thought. Feed me, clothe me, let me sit by the side of the stove, and I will be any nationality you prefer.*

"I have never been to the beautiful France. It has been my dream, but I have never been there. I live and die in this wilderness." He shook his head. "Once this devastation was a part of France, a part of the French empire. Once it was on the road to dignity, to civilization, to life itself. Now!"

I said, "Perhaps one day—"

Gallic fire burned in his wrinkled brown face. "Ah! I can see it now as I have so often seen it in my dreams. *Mon Général Charles de Gaulle* leading battalions of French troops through all of Indochina, recovering lost territory, bringing my poor country back under the protection of the French flag!"

I stiffened at attention. I began, thin of voice and oddly lightheaded, to sing the "Marseillaise"—*"Allons, enfants de la patrie—"*

He jumped to his feet. *"Le jour de gloire est arrivée,"* he sang out loud and clear, his hand over his heart...

"To share with you my rice bowl and my razor, that is my pleasure," the old man was saying. "But clothing is another matter. My own would not fit you, and I have no other.

"I have money," I said.

"I fear the money of France is no longer of use in this land."

"I have gold."

"Gold!" His eyes brightened. "Gold is another matter. You wish me to purchase clothing for you? To obtain any-thing of quality I would have to go into town—"

"I don't want quality. Just ordinary peasant clothing."

"Ah," he said. He eyed me closely. "You are French and would pass as a peasant. I wonder if you might be working secretly for the French government?"

"Well—"

"Say no more. Perhaps if the day of glory is not too

far away, *hein?* Let me consider. You wish to pass as a peasant, is it so? You are tall for one of us, but that is not so great a difficulty. The Muong tribesmen are men of some height. It is your fair complexion and large white eyes which render you noticeable. In Tao Dan you would be quickly recognized, I fear."

"Perhaps I could ride in a cart or something. The less anyone sees of me."

"Ah, yes. If I had a bullock, you could ride in a bullock cart, and fewer men would look upon your face. But I have no bullock."

"Could you buy one for me?"

"Have you much gold?"

I unscrewed the back of the flashlight and took out the dummy battery. I pried the case open and spilled the gold coins into the palm of my hand. The old man's eyes went wide at the sight of them.

"With this it will be a simple matter to purchase a bullock and a cart," he said. "And clothing as well. There is more than enough."

"You may keep whatever is left for yourself."

"It is not necessary, my friend."

"France rewards her faithful sons," I said. Besides, I thought, leaving the rest with him would keep him free from temptation.

He left. I heated water on the stove and soaked my beard. His ancient straight razor was sharp enough, but it had a particularly difficult job ahead of it. My beard was long enough to be difficult with abundant lather, and shaving it off without any soap at all was quite a problem. Still, I managed to get the job done.

My complexion was still very wrong, the effects of the sun on my forehead notwithstanding. I stuffed a wad of the old man's pipe tobacco into my mouth and chewed it as if it were betel nut. It tasted terrible. I spat tobacco juice into my cupped hands and rubbed it all over my face. I kept repeating the process until I was satisfied with the yellow-brown color I achieved.

A wave of nausea shook me. I went to the stove and picked up the pot of rice. I was ravenous, and it tasted excellent, and even at that I had trouble getting the rice down and even more trouble keeping it down. I felt feverish and weak.

The old man returned. "You have changed," the old man said. "Your whole face, it is very much different. You no longer look like a Frenchman."

I never had, but that was beside the point. I put on the clothing he had brought me, a pair of loose-fitting olive drab trousers, a tan tunic, a pair of more elaborate sandals than I had been wearing. A large white coolie-style hat completed my costume and covered my shaggy brown hair.

Outside, a hump-backed bullock stood hitched to a rickety cart. The cart was piled high with straw. I was still a little feverish. It would come and go, waves of dizziness and nausea.

"Are you all right?"

"I'm fine," I said. "A slight touch of *la grippe*. I guess I'd better go now. I wonder if you have heard any news of five black persons who were brought this way. Perhaps they are now in Tao Dan."

"Five black persons."

"Four men and a woman. They might have passed this way any time within the last few weeks. They came from Thailand."

"I know there are prisoners in Tao Dan. I have heard talk, but no one mentioned their color."

"Perhaps it is they."

"Perhaps. Are they the reason for your presence in this

accursed land?"

"In a way."

I CLIMBED into the bullock cart, sat on the pile of straw, bent forward to keep as much of my face hidden as possible, and let the bullock proceed at his own pace toward Tao Dan.

Tao Dan turned out to be a rather busy little town, the marketplace and seat of government for the surrounding countryside. Ramshackle round huts with peaked roofs alternated with squat buildings of whitewashed concrete block. The streets were very narrow and extremely crowded.

I found one street that was a little less crowded than the others and hitched the bullock at the curb, tying his lead rope to a small concrete pillar erected for that express purpose. I followed a small crowd of men into what seemed to be a cafe. Inside, men were drinking out of small handleless cups of tea. I moved to the rear of the cafe and tried to stay as deep in the shadow as possible. A dozen conversations went on at once around me. I listened to them in turn. The dialect was difficult for me to follow, and most of the conversations seemed to revolve upon the various problems inherent in the life of a peasant in Laos.

Until at length I heard a large, heavy man with a deep voice begin to talk about a criminal event that had transpired during the night. A small crowd gathered around him, anxious for details. I shouldered my way forward and listened to the storyteller.

He knew his trade well, beginning slowly, letting the excitement build. "And so you know the girl of whom I speak," he said. "Her father is the commanding officer of the troop garrison. Just a young thing, she is, with the softest and purest skin, and a waist one could span with one's hands, and breasts exquisitely shaped like cups of tea, and hair like fine black silk…"

He paused for a chorus of oohs and ahhs.

"And this stranger appeared. A young man, crude in his ways, and followed the girl down the street. Some say she did not know she was being followed"—he lowered his voice—"and others say she well knew a man was behind her, and let her hips sway from side to side, eh?

"And he followed her, or perhaps she led him, into the house of her father. The house of her father!" The crowd bubbled at the thought. "And in the house of her father, in the bed of her father, this wayward one prepared to take her."

More hubbub from his listeners. It may not astonish you to learn that I had guessed the identity of the male participant in the drama. Poor Dhang, I thought. I hoped at least that he had attained the object of his desires before they killed him. At least he would have died happy.

But such was not the case.

"Fortunately," the fat man continued, "fortunately her own father arrived in the nick of time, reaching his beloved daughter's side before the culprit could complete his evil mission. With tears of frustration in his beady eyes the criminal was led away screaming."

I could well believe it.

"And the criminal?" someone demanded.

"He shall receive the punishment that is his due."

"Death?"

"What else?"

What else indeed? Dhang, I thought wearily, led a profoundly uncharmed life. It did not surprise me that he had been sentenced to death. But had the sentence been carried out yet?

Someone else asked the same question. "He shall die

this evening," the storyteller replied. "By nightfall"—he pointed off to his left—"his head shall decorate a post at the command headquarters."

Not, I thought, if I could help it.

I slipped unquestioned from the cafe. I stood for a moment on the sidewalk, getting my bearings. Then I retrieved my bullock and led him off in the direction the storyteller had indicated. The streets of Tao Dan were a maze, but at last I turned a corner and stopped in front of a large whitewashed concrete building.

There was no question about it—this was the place. The armed guards at attention on either side of the front doors indicated this, but something else confirmed it beyond question. There was a row of high metal posts off to the side of the doorway, one of which the storyteller had said Dhang's head would decorate.

Four posts were already decorated. I gazed horrified at the four disembodied black heads of the Kendall Bayard Quartet.

I swayed on my feet. Somehow I managed to take my bullock's lead rope in hand and headed him around the corner. A few blocks from the command headquarters I picked out another hitching post and tethered the bullock. I was sweating freely now and had to sit down somewhere before I collapsed. I climbed on top of the mound of straw in the cart, stretched out, and put my hat over my face. I had seen natives resting in this fashion and hoped I would look ordinary enough.

My mind simply wasn't functioning. The stark horror of those four heads atop those poles had evidently had dire effects upon a brain already numbed by a progressively heightening fever. I gave myself a few minutes to loosen up and unwind a bit, and then I tried putting together what I knew.

The Kendall Bayard Quartet was beyond salvation, at least in this world. Tuppence was probably inside the building, but maybe she wasn't. She was probably going to be executed, but that was no foregone conclusion.

Dhang was definitely inside the building, where he would remain until they put him to death for rape. Attempted rape, actually—the poor son of a bitch was going to die without getting the only thing on earth he really wanted.

I had to find a way to get into the command post, had to locate and free Tuppence and Dhang, and then had to get out again. Then I would have to find a way to get out of Laos or at least into the comparative safety of the southern part of the country,

Step One—get in. Step Two—rescue Tuppence and Dhang. Step three—get out.

Fine.

But Step One stumped me all by itself. Get in? How?

I sighed. Everything seemed quite hopeless. My assets were limited: a bullock, a cart, some straw, the clothes I was wearing, and, if I wanted to go back for them, a mud-clogged rifle and a machine pistol, and a flashlight that was missing a battery. I also had one ally: a broken-down old Francophile...

THE OLD man drew on his pipe. He took it from his mouth and looked in turn at it and at me. In his heavily accented French he said, "My young friend, I do not know how I can help you."

Neither did I. I had left Tao Dan to lead my bullock all the way back to the old man's hut, not because I thought he would really be able to help me but because I couldn't think of anything else to do. He took one look at me and made me lie down on his straw mattress and cover myself with his few blankets. While I babbled wildly about Tuppence and Dhang he poured cup after cup of strong herb tea into me. It came out through my pores in rivers of sweat. My stomach calmed down after a while, and finally the fever broke.

I told the old man that a Senegalese princess and a Thai agent of France were under sentence of death in Tao Dan. It was my mission to rescue them and rush them to safety in Paris.

Perhaps, I suggested, he had comrades in the area, other men who had known the glory of French leadership. Men who would help us in our noble task, men who would join with us to...

As rhetoric goes, it certainly went. I don't think I could do it justice in English, but the French language is an ideal vehicle for the expression of such sentiments. The speech fired the old man's blood, but at the end he merely shook his head.

"I am such a man," he said unhappily, "but I know no others."

I sank back on the straw pallet. I had succeeded only in wasting more precious time. It was hopeless, and I should have known as much.

"You say that this son and daughter of the beautiful France are in the command headquarters?"

I nodded.

"If you could gain access to the command post, if you could manage to slip inside, would you have any chance of success?"

"Possibly, I don't know. But the guards—"

"Perhaps I can dispose of the guards."

"How?"

He held up a hand and waved the question aside. An odd smile played on his thin old lips. He was humming the

401

"Marseillaise."

"We must return to town," he said. "Finish your tea, there is time. I will lead the animal, and you must ride in the cart. When you leave the building, how will you flee the town? Have you a plan?"

"No."

"There is a river east of the town. If you had a small boat moored at the bank, it would be a great asset to you, would it not? Gold will buy a boat. There is enough left of what you have given me."

"But—"

"No time, not now. Finish your tea, that is a good boy. Can you get to your feet? I will help you—"

In Tao Dan the old man parked the bullock and took me to a little restaurant. He knew the proprietor and spoke rapidly to him before leading me to a small booth at the rear. Then he pressed a few well-creased little bank notes into my hand.

"I have told him to continue bringing you cups of herbal tea," he said. "I have said that you have a weakness of the brain and cannot speak clearly. Thus it will not be necessary for you to say anything, and you may remain here until I return. No one will disturb you."

I nodded.

"I will be back shortly. I will arrange for a boat."

He left.

I sat and drank endless cups of tea. My time sense was completely shot. When the old man sat down opposite me—I hadn't even noticed his approach, which shows how magnificently I was functioning—I had no idea whether he had been gone an unusually short time or an exceedingly long time.

In French he whispered, "It is arranged. I have purchased a boat. It is small, but I believe it will accommodate three persons. You and the Thai and the Princess."

"What about yourself?"

"Do not worry yourself about me. Now"—his finger traced lines on the scarred table top—"we are here. Here is the command headquarters. You see? The front of the building here, a rear entrance here. Down this way is a street that leads to the river. It runs just so. You follow me? You take that street and do not leave it, and it will lead you directly to the bank of the river. The boat is hidden in the rushes perhaps fifty paces in this direction. The boat is well hidden, I cut reeds and placed them atop it. You will be able to find it?"

"I think so."

There will be very little time. You must hurry into the building and liberate the two prisoners and hurry out again as quickly as possible. You may find this useful."

He put a hand under the table, and I reached to take what he handed me. It was a dagger with an eight-inch blade, razor sharp, with deep blood grooves running the length of the blade on either side. The hilt was covered with tightly wrapped leather. I concealed it as well as I could in a fold of the tunic.

"What are you going to do?"

He looked at me, and over my shoulder, and miles past me. Perhaps he was seeing a parade in the Place de la Concorde.

"I shall do what I must," he said.

"But—"

"It is time." A smile. "The day of glory has arrived. Do not ask questions, young friend. Go now. The day of glory has arrived..."

THE FOUR heads outside the command headquarters stared at me as before, but this time they had no effect upon me.

Perhaps I was prepared; perhaps it was the fever. I looked at the heads, and they looked back, and I walked past them to the side of the entranceway, leaning against the building in what I hoped was a casual fashion.

In the street a jeep made its way through the crowd, the driver driving with a fine disdain for the throngs in front of him. Magically the crowd melted aside just in time to let him pull to a stop in front of the building. Two men climbed out of the back seat. One of them was middle-aged and looked important. The other younger and in a less impressive uniform, hurried to open the door for him. The guards stood aside, and the two men walked on into command headquarters.

Wonderful, I thought. By the time I made my move, half the soldiers in Laos would be inside the concrete structure. I looked around, wondering what the old man had planned. For a moment I had thought he might have organized some sort of riot, with the mob storming the building, but the crowd did not have the look of potential rioters. They were just a mass of bored yokels waiting for something to happen.

Then something did happen.

I didn't even recognize the old man at first, but I stared at him anyhow, just like everyone else. He was a sight. He was riding in my cart, and my bullock was pulling it, and all of that was normal enough, but that was where normalcy stopped. For the bullock was moving faster than it had ever moved in its life, faster, I suspect, than any bullock had ever moved. It tore through the crowd like a bull at Pamplona, tossing its head and snorting, bouncing the little cart on the bumpy roadway, while the old man prodded its rump with fire.

I do not speak metaphorically. The old colonial boy held a long stick like a shepherd's crook, and on the end of that stick was a rag soaked in kerosene or something of the sort, and the rag was burning. He kept poking the flaming end of the stick into the tormented end of the bullock, and the results were spectacular.

All hell broke loose. The crowd stampeded. The animal charged for a mass of onlookers. They broke and ran; some of them got away and some of them did not.

The guards didn't know what to do. They had drawn their guns and were now waving them uncertainly. Through it all the old man prepared for his finest hour. *The day of glory has arrived—*

He was in costume, for one thing. He wore the uniform of a French Legionnaire. God knows where he found it. The pants covered his feet and the jacket's sleeves came down well over his hands. He paused, kept the fire away from the bullock's rear for a moment, and his little voice rang out over the crowd.

"Long Jive King Charles de Gaulle! Long live the beautiful France! Lafayette is here! Long live Napoleon! To hell with Marx! To hell with Lenin! To hell with the Pathet Lao! To hell with Mao Tse-tung! Long live Jeanne d' Arc!"

Singing the "Marseillaise" at the top of his lungs, he began waving a tin can around madly. He splashed something from it, soaking the straw around him, soaking the fine French Legion uniform, soaking the flanks of the unfortunate bullock.

Then, still singing bravely, he brought the day of glory to its peak. He touched his torch to the straw beneath his feet. And, as the straw and the cart and the bullock and the old man burst suddenly into flame, with bullets flying overhead, and with the final death-echoes of the French national anthem sounding around me, I drew my dagger and rushed into the command post.

The entire place was in an uproar, with uniformed men

barking commands and rushing to and fro. I too rushed to and fro, and to as little purpose.

"Outside," I bellowed. "All men to their posts in the streets. Everyone! At once!"

That got rid of a few of them, but there were still too many soldiers around. I looked into one room, then another, but there was no sign of either Dhang or Tuppence. And I couldn't peek into every damned room in the place. There simply wasn't time.

I started into a third room. A soldier on his way out met me with a pistol in hand. I acted without thought, plunging the dagger into his belly. He pitched forward, and I spun away from him and on down the corridor.

And promptly walked into another man. We bounced off one another, and I said "Pardon me," and he said "Who are you?" and I looked at him, and he looked at me. His chest was full of medals and ribbons. He was the important-looking middle-aged man who had dismounted from the jeep in front.

He said, "Seize this man!"

BUT I SEIZED him first. I grabbed him by the shoulder and gave a yank, and he spun like a top. I wrapped one arm around his chest and with the other hand I held the tip of the dagger to his throat.

A semicircle of armed men stood around us, their guns pointed at me. I kept my grip on the important man, and the tip of my dagger stayed within an inch of his throat.

"If you do not cooperate, you will die," I told him, in Khmer. "Tell your men to throw their weapons down upon the floor. Do this at once!"

I pricked the skin over his Adam's apple with the dagger. His voice shaky, he conveyed my order to his men. Rifles and pistols bounced crazily on the bare concrete floor.

"The Thai who was taken prisoner last night," I said. "Where is he?"

"The ravisher of my daughter?"

So this was the commandant. "That's the one," I said. "Where is he being held? Do not waste time." I prodded him with the dagger.

He barked the order and the men led the way to Dhang's cell. A heavy iron door was unbolted and drawn open. At the far end of a dank, windowless room a half-naked Dhang, the upper portion of his body scarred badly with the marks of the lash, stood upon the tips of his toes. His hands were tied to a pipe overhead. He stared ahead dully.

The sight of him infuriated me, and I came very close to ruining everything by killing the commandant then and there. But I snapped out a brace of orders, which he conveyed to his men. They cut Dhang free, and he sprawled face-down on the floor. I shouted at him. He shook himself, looked up at me, then struggled to his feet.

"Heaven! You have come…"

"There's very little time," I told him. "We have to get out of here." I singled out one of the soldiers who was about Dhang's height and build and had the commandant tell him to get out of his uniform. He did this, and Dhang dressed himself in the soldier's clothing.

"I could have had her, Evan. So beautiful she was! And she wanted me, too. They said I tried to have her against her will, but in truth she wanted me. She—"

"No time now," I said. "We have to hurry. Tuppence is somewhere in the building. Go back toward the front door and make sure it's locked. And pick up a couple of pistols from the floor, one for yourself and one for me." I backed off toward the door, dragging the head man with me.

"Tell your men to sit down," I ordered him. "Tell them

407

to seat themselves upon the floor, and remain there until they are called."

He did, and they did. We left the room with the dozen men inside it, and I toed the door shut, then bolted it.

I spun the little man around and backed him against the wall. "The girl," I said. "Where is she?"

"There is no girl."

"The black girl."

"There is no black girl."

I transferred my dagger to my left hand, made a fist of the right hand, and hit him in the mouth with it. He sagged against the wall, wiping at the blood that trickled from his mouth.

Dhang was trotting down the hallway, moving gingerly over the floor: I found out later that they had beaten the soles of his feet. Dhang handed me a pistol and kept one for himself.

"Much is happening outside. Flames and screaming. We must get out of here."

I cupped my hands and shouted. "Tuppence! Tuppence, where are you? Tuppence!"

A muffled cry came in answer from off to the left. Dhang led the way, and I grabbed up the little commander, and we ran. I shouted, and she called out in answer, and we kept running to the sound of her voice until we found the room.

The door was locked. The commander denied possession of a key, and there was no time to find out whether he was lying or not. I called out for Tuppence to stand aside, and put three bullets in the lock before it fell apart. The door flew open, and there was Tuppence.

"Evan, baby! Like where did you come from?"

"Later," I said. "This is Dhang, he's a friend, he doesn't speak English. This is the Lord High Everything-Else, he——"

"I know him," she said contemptuously. "How'd you get here, baby?"

"Later."

"Kendall and Willie and Chick and Niles——"

"I know. Dead."

"You can tell me about it later," I told Tuppence. "First we've got to get out of here. There's a boat waiting. We'll go out the back door and——"

But Tuppence said, "Wait, cool it, Evan. We don't want to leave without the jewels."

"The jewels?"

"The Siamese pretties. This bastard has them locked up in his office. We can't leave them."

"The hell with them. There's no time."

"Won't take a minute."

"I don't even know where his office is."

"I do," she said. "I damn well should. His men dragged me to it once a day, regular as a clock." She glared at the commander. "You little bastard," she said to him.

She led the way through a maze of corridors to another locked door. There was a pane of frosted glass in the door. I knocked out the glass with the butt of my pistol and reached through to unbolt the door.

Tuppence had said. She hurried past it without looking at it and tugged at a drawer of the desk. It wouldn't open.

I let Dhang cover him and went around the desk. I shot the lock off and Tuppence yanked open the drawer and hauled out two leather sacks.

"Wait till you get a look at these, Bwana. Your eyes shall roll in disbelief."

"Later. Let's move."

We moved. Tuppence took one sack of jewels, and Dhang carried the other. I twisted the commandant's arm behind his back and propelled him in front of me, the muzzle of the pistol against the side of his neck.

We located the back door. Dhang thrust the door open, and we went through.

There was no one there. The noise from the other side of the building was deafening—shouts, screams, the staccato snapping of small arms fire. Dragging the commandant along as a hostage, we headed for the river.

The river was dark and muddy, the current swift, forming little whirlpools here and there. The bank was dense with undergrowth. We made our way along the river's edge and found the boat just where the old man had said it was. I would never have found it if I had not been looking for it. It was completely concealed among the reeds.

We removed the camouflage. I studied our craft. It was not the rowboat I had suspected but was more along the lines of the dugout canoes of the American Indians.

Tuppence studied the boat thoughtfully. "We don't need him any more," she said, pointing to the commandant. "He's a good hostage, but we have no use for him now."

"We could take him."

"Really, Evan. There's scarcely room for three of us, and we have the jewels as well. We needn't waste space on a rapist and a murderer. He made me watch when he killed those four boys.

"So?"

"He's had a long life. I think it's time it ended."

I still had the dagger. I handed it to her. "Want to kill him yourself?" I asked. And she, of course, was supposed to do as the girls always do in the movies, clutching the dagger, studying it in horror, and then muttering something like *Oh, let him live with himself, that will be punishment enough for him,* or *Oh, no, I couldn't, I couldn't.*

BUT TUPPEMCE hadn't read the script. "I'd bloody well love to," she said, and fastened her small black hand around the butt of the dagger and advanced on the cowering commandant. He shrank from her, let out a rather pathetic moan, and Tuppence sank the knife into his soft, round belly

I threw up, but I think it was more the fever than the spectacle that caused it. Tuppence and Dhang helped me into the dugout. There was a single oar inside it, and we used it to push the boat free of the bank and out onto the waterway.

I sat in the stern, Dhang perched in the bow, and Tuppence was between us. Dhang had taken the oar and wanted to know in which direction he should head.

"Go with the current," I said, pointing. "We'll go that way whether we want to or not, so we might as well paddle in that direction." Then I leaned back in the dugout and watched birds diving for fish in the river.

What happens now, baby?" Tuppence asked.

"We just keep sailing. I think we should keep moving as fast as we can."

"Uh-huh. Moving where?"

"Downstream."

"Yeah, groovy. What I'm getting at is where does the stream go?"

"Oh," I said.

"I said something wrong?"

"No," I said. I shook my head groggily. I had somehow forgotten to ask the old man that little question.

I had no idea where the river was headed...

My fever grew worse. I huddled in the stern of the canoe while the world went on around me and I paid it as little attention as I possibly could.

I slipped in and out of an eerie waking dream during which periods of fantasy and reality overlapped so that it was impossible to tell which was which, and even now I cannot be entirely certain what was real and what was imagined.

Fragments... Tuppence saying:

"It was a groovy trip until those cats came down on us, Evan. And Bangkok was like the best part of it. The group had this very tough sound, and I was in good voice and all. And the king was too much. He sat in on clarinet for a while. I thought he would be bloody awful, but his technique is good, and he knows where it's at.

"You know I sent you that postcard? That was the day after the command performance. After we played, the king showed us the royal collection, and then he gave us each a present. Chinese jade, he said it was. I got a crazy pair of earrings, and there were cufflinks for the boys. I figured it would say in the newspaper stories how we had viewed the collection and what the presents were, so I wrote you that bit about selling my jewels. I guess it's good I did, huh?"

Our boat is caught in a current and spins madly around. Dhang paddles furiously. On the starboard side a huge log bobs in the water. We paddle over to it, and the log turns and begins swimming for us. It is a crocodile. We try to escape. It swims closer.

Tuppence again. "I couldn't get it was all about. They came into the hotel in the middle of the night and chloroformed us. I guess they had already stolen the jewels. The next thing I knew we were on our way up through Thailand and into Laos. I got some of the drift of what was happening or at least I think I did. They're Laotian Communists, they're hooked up with something called the Pathet Lao, or maybe that somebody's name. The bit was that they were going to make it look as though the five of us stole the jewels from the king and took them to Laos, the part of the country that's not run by the Communists.

And then when we came north, they snatched us and executed us and returned the jewels. They were going to make the United States look bad and they were going to make the other government of Laos look bad, and it was supposed to do a lot of good for them and for the guerrillas in Thailand. Or something like that...

"I was beautiful, and soft and warm and sweetly formed, with golden skin and long black hair," said Tuppence, who had suddenly turned Oriental. "And I wanted Dhang and would have gone with him, and just as he was on the point of making a woman of me..."

"Just as I was on the point of taking her," Dhang said, "just then her father came into the room, and furious he was, and they put me in that room and beat the soles of my feet with long strips torn from old auto tires, and hung me up so that I had to stand on the tips of my toes, and swore they would cut off my head..."

The old man was riding on water skis pulled by a blazing bullock. Fire danced in his hair. He sang the "Marseillaise" at the top of his voice and poured kerosene over himself and burned, and the entire river turned into a sheet of icy flame...

"I think he's coming out of it," a soft voice said. "Him come out of big sleep. Oh, the hell with it."

I opened my eyes. Tuppence was leaning solicitously over me; Dhang was looking over her shoulder. We seemed to be on dry land. I started to sit up, but they both reached to push me back down and told me to save my strength.

"I'm all right," I said. And I was. The fever was gone now. I groped for memory and couldn't get the handle of it. I did not know where we were or how we had gotten there.

"What happened?"

"We almost lost you," Tuppence said. "Baby, you were

in very bad shape. Feverish, and seeing things that weren't there, and talking to people who weren't around. All kinds of crazy languages."

I sat up and looked around at the two of them and the fire and, a few yards off to the side, the river. Our boat was beached on the bank.

"How long was I like that? A couple of hours?'

"Would you believe three days, baby?''

"Frankly, no. Was I—"

"Three days."

"How did you and Dhang manage?"

"Sign language, mostly. You don't remember any of it?"

"Bits and pieces." I drew a breath. I smelled fish baking. I was suddenly ravenous and I turned to Dhang, who had been maintaining a respectful silence. "About that fish," I said in Khmer.

"It will be ready soon, Heaven."

"Good…"

AROUND noon the next day we had stopped the boat and Dhang and I went exploring. We saw smoke off to our right and headed toward it, moving silently through the jungle. Through a break in the undergrowth I saw uniformed men sitting around a campfire, talking and laughing. I listened closely but could not understand what they were saying. Whatever language they were speaking, it was not one I recognized. Dhang couldn't make it out either.

I considered making ourselves known to them, then decided against it. If we couldn't be sure just who they were, things could get sticky. So we slipped away as silently as we had come.

And then, late in the afternoon, we heard a plane flying overhead. We caught sight of the craft and craned our heads upward for a look at it, and the pilot came down for a look at us.

It was a jet fighter. I made out US Air Force insignia on the undersides of the swept-back wings.

"It's one of ours," I said, and Tuppence and I began to wave furiously. The plane continued its downward sweep.

And bullets plowed a furrow in the water beside us.

"Evan! He's shooting at us!"

He missed us completely on that run. He came out of his dive, swung into a graceful turn, and headed our way again.

"Overboard," I shouted. "Swim for shore! Fast!"

We reached the bank, clambered ashore, dove into the cover of an overhang of vines and shrubs. The fighter let us alone and concentrated on the dugout. Bullets tore into the hollow wooden shell, and it filled with water. It didn't exactly sink—it was, after all, wood—but its days of service were over. It was filled with water to the top. It was useless to us, and so were our guns.

The plane finished its run; the pilot banked smartly, headed skyward, and flew away.

"Now he can go back to his base," I said bitterly, "and he can paint a dugout canoe on the side of the fuselage. The son of a bitch!

"Baby, I don't get it. Why?"

"I don't know," I said. "Maybe—"

"Evan—the jewels!"

I swam back to the boat. The two leather bags of jewels were where we had left them, happily untouched by the bullets. I rescued the two jewel sacks and swam back to shore. A US plane, I thought, disheartened. Just what we needed. With friends like him we didn't need enemies.

"Why did he shoot us up, Evan? And what do we do now?"

The second question was unanswerable. But I had the first one figured out and suddenly I knew where we were.

"Those soldiers we saw around noon were speaking Annamese," I said. "And it would have been a very bad idea to join them."

"Why?"

"Because we're in the middle of North Vietnam," I said.

The logical way out of North Vietnam was to head south to South Vietnam. It was also, as I explained to Tuppence and a bewildered Dhang, a good way to get killed.

"But we have to try it. "There's something called the Ho Chi Minh Trail—according to the newspapers, it's what the North Vietnamese soldiers use when they infiltrate into the south. I don't suppose there are any road signs on it, but we head over that way, away from the river, we ought to hit some sort of route heading south. We'll have to travel by night, I'm afraid."

By nightfall we had lost sight of the river without encountering a jungle trail heading south. We had huddled together twice while bands of natives, presumably civilians, passed within a few yards of us.

We reached a southbound trail a few hours later. It was a path about four feet wide, and it couldn't have been the Ho Chi Minh Trail, because it was far too narrow and overgrown to be used by a motorized column. I decided that this was just as well. We made much better time, but it was still very slow going.

Dhang was the first to hear them. He whirled sharply about, dropped to the ground and pressed his ear against the trampled earth. It was the first time I had ever actually seen anyone with his ear to the ground.

I too dropped to the ground and pressed my ear against it. I could hear it then, the thud of vibrations.

"Sounds like a mechanized column," I said. "We'd better get out of the way."

A few miles back our little trail had merged with a much wider path that also was heading southward. This new route was far more open. I hadn't been too enthusiastic over it at first. True, it proved we were on the right track, but new hazards presented themselves. It stood to reason that the route would see heavy North Vietnamese traffic, which meant we would have to be very careful if we wanted to remain undetected. Still more to the point, we were open to observation by US planes and helicopters. The fact that they were on our side didn't do a hell of a lot of good unless they happened to realize it.

We were well hidden in the brush long before the advancing column came into sight. Tuppence and Dhang crouched in silence on either side of me. A trio of jeeps were in the lead, followed by a brace of motorized anti-aircraft guns, a convoy of troop carriers, and, in the rear, four lumbering tanks.

And then, from the south, we heard the cheering sound of American air power.

Tuppence glanced at me, eyes wide with alarm, and I nodded. She pursed her lips and whistled soundlessly. Fly away, fellows, I urged them silently. Fly like birds. Go bomb Hanoi or something. But don't drop anything around here.

They didn't listen to me.

JUST A few yards from us the North Vietnamese braced themselves for action. The column ground to a halt, and the antiaircraft guns readied themselves for the encounter. The troop carriers peeled back their canvas tops and dozens of foot soldiers spilled out, rifles in hand. They scattered in the brush.

The planes droned overhead. The tanks—Russian

T-34's, the same sort I had seen in Korea—pointed their massive guns at the sky. Keep going, I urged the planes. Knock out the oil depots in Haiphong. Do anything, but go away.

In perfect formation the US aircraft peeled off and dived for the trail. A pair of jet fighters led the way, flying directly into the stream of flak, peppering the trail with machine-gun shells. Behind them fighter bombers laid their eggs.

It was what I thought it would be. Napalm.

The jungle burst into flame. "Fall back." I told Tuppence and Dhang. "Don't even worry about the soldiers. They couldn't care less right now. Just get the hell out of the way of that fire."

We scattered like field mice in a burning barn. More planes passed over the trail. Three of the T-34's were out of action in no time at all, two taking direct hits, the third getting the backlash of the bomb that landed square atop the troop carrier in front of it. The ground troops screamed and died in the fire that raged around them.

We missed most of what happened, running crazily through the brush. We outran the napalm, then sprawled at last in a tangle of vines. And lay there, deafened by the sounds of battle, until the last burst of ground fire was still and the last plane flew south...

We had hated the jungle. Slogging through it, through the mud and the snakes and the insects and the treacherous vines, we had personified it and cursed it as an enemy. Now we crept toward the ruined army column and looked upon the alternative of the jungle. Acres of plant growth had been burned out of existence. What had been green was burned black, with little vestigial fires still raging at the perimeter.

I SCANNED the row of ruined jeeps and antiaircraft guns and troop carriers and tanks.

"That's it," I said.

"What?"

"Our passport. They got three of them but one's still operable. All we have to do is get into it and roll."

Tuppence looked at me as though I had gone over the edge. "You rest a minute," she said. "The fever—"

"No fever. I'm talking about the tank. The T-34," I said. "That's our out. It doesn't matter what color you are inside one of those. We'll all be invisible. We can cut right through North Vietnam and across the demilitarized zone without anyone wondering who we are."

"How do we get one?"

"Change places with the clowns inside it."

"Suppose they don't go for the idea?"

"They're probably dead," I said. "If they don't come crawling out in the next few minutes, we can count on it."

"Have you ever driven one of those things?"

"No."

"Groovy."

"I never paddled a dugout, either."

We waited on the sidelines while the uninjured soldiers and walking wounded rounded up as many of their wounded fellows as they could and made their way back north again, all of their vehicles abandoned.

I went to the tank, and the metal hatch was still too hot to handle.

But the next time I checked the tank, it was only slightly warm to the touch. I opened the hood and closed it again in a hurry. The tank had been carrying a full crew of three. They were still inside. I made Tuppence stay where she was while Dhang helped me empty the tank and disinfect it with petrol from one of the troop carriers.

419

We climbed in, bringing along the jewels and a few guns salvaged from dead Vietnamese soldiers. We also collected several cans of fuel that had been aboard one of the troop carriers.

We left the tank's hatch open to combat claustrophobia and asphyxiation, and we made ourselves as comfortable as possible. The control panel was in Russian, which helped. I settled myself behind it and felt like Bogart in *Sahara*. "This baby'll start," I said. "All yuh gotta do is talk nice to her..."

I drove that tank all night. Tuppence and Dhang had dropped off to sleep muttering about food and water, neither of which we had with us. We could get along without food, but water would become a problem before very long. I felt more and more like Bogart.

Somewhere between the middle of the night and dawn we lost the road. This could never have happened farther back, with the dense jungle on either side, but as we moved south the jungle gave way to vast stretches of open ground. By the time I realized what had happened, there was no way to correct the error, so I kept us on a southerly course and hoped it would take us where we wanted to go. By the time the sky lightened, we were far out of sight of the road. When Tuppence woke up and asked where we were, I told her we were in Asia, and she told me nobody likes a smart-ass.

We were still in Asia when the plane attacked us.

We were still in the open, too, surrounded by vast reaches of grassland. We were the only tank around, and he was the only plane, and unfortunately he was one of ours, and the tank was one of theirs. I didn't even see him until he started shooting at us. Then a rocket went off a few yards to our left, and we could feel the impact inside the tank.

"You idiot," I screamed, "we're on your side!"

"Maybe if you got out and waved to him—"

"I don't think so," I said. I had closed the hatch, of course, and now I watched the plane through the tank's sight. He was ready again. He came at us lower this time and fired off two rockets in turn. They were both wide on the left.

"He's a lousy shot," I said. "He's really terrible. We're barely a moving target, and he has all the room in the world to move around in. He should have blown us all to hell next by now."

His next pass brought him even lower, and I cooperated by stalling the tank. This time he scored a near miss, and the tank rocked with the explosion.

He's getting warmer. Evan—"

"What?"

"Can't this thing shoot back?"

I looked up. There was a sort of steering wheel. I turned it, and our gun moved. There was a little door that you opened to insert a shell, and behind me on the floor there were shells. I snapped a command, and Dhang handed me a shell.

"Hey, wait a minute," I said. "I can't shoot him down."

"What's wrong?"

"He's an American," I said. "That's one of our guys up there!"

"This is us down here," Tuppence said.

He came on again, undaunted, diving straight for us. I spun the little wheel and found the gun sights. I zeroed in on him as he swept down on us. He fired his rockets, and I fired the tank gun. He missed completely and so did we.

Dhang handed me another shell. "I don't like this," I said.

"Maybe you can just wing him, baby."

"Sure."

I loaded the shell, put my eye to the sight, and started tracking him. He began his run again, and I had the damnedest feeling that this was the last chance we were going to get. He was coming from our right front. I swung the gun at him and kept it on him, and I fired before he did.

"You hit him."

The tail of the plane seemed to disintegrate. Then the plastic canopy popped open, and the pilot ejected, seat and all. He sailed high into the air, as if shot from a cannon. His parachute opened, and he floated gracefully down to earth.

I watched him land, roll, and come up on his feet. I felt a lot better then. It had been a kill or be killed situation, certainly, but that didn't change the fact that I had felt less than delighted at the thought of knocking American planes out of the sky. I started the engine, and the tank headed for him.

"He'll have flares," I said. "With any luck at all, somebody saw him go down. They'll send a helicopter for him, and we can hitch a ride on it."

"He may not be happy to see us."

"He'll be happy when he finds out we're us. Right now he's getting ready to surrender to a North Vietnamese tank."

Except he wasn't. We had a good look at him as we drew closer. He was a very young Negro airman with a very valiant look on his face, and he had one hand on his hip while he used the other to point a pistol at our tank.

"I think he wants us to surrender," I said. "It's going to surprise the hell out of him when we do."

We drew closer. I flipped open the hatch, and he sent a bullet whistling over the top of it.

"Cool it, soul brother," Tuppence called out. "The natives are friendly..."

THE SAIGON madam was a fat little Vietnamese with gold teeth and a permanent smile. Several soldiers had assured me her house was far and away the best in Saigon. The rooms were nicely appointed, the girls were clean and lovely, and the price was only ten dollars. She bowed us into the parlor and rang a little bell, and seven pretty things in slit skirts and high heels came tripping into the room and bowed before us.

Dhang was drooling, and his eyes were so bugged out that he looked like a frog.

He said, "For me?"

"You're supposed to pick the one you want."

"I want them all."

"Well, pick the one you like best."

"I like them all best."

I counted the girls and recounted the money. Seven girls at ten dollars a girl was seventy dollars. But was it possible that little Dhang could possess seven women one after the other?

Anything was possible, I decided. Anything at all. With what Dhang had been through, it was conceivable that he had built a stock of frustration that all the prostitutes in Saigon couldn't cure. Anyway, he wanted all seven of them, and he deserved a shot at whatever he wanted.

"He wants all seven of them," I told the madam carefully. "They are to go to him one at a time." I paid her.

"He is Superman?"

"Perhaps."

"Seven girls? Ho, boy!"

She relayed the instructions to the girls, who giggled and squealed at the prospect. I sat down, and one of the girls took Dhang in hand and led him away. The madam sat down beside me.

"And you, Joe? What do you want?"

I thought it over. "Do you have any betel nut?" I said finally. She frowned and said that she did not. "In that case," I said, "what I'd really like is a nice cold glass of milk."

Photo by Amy Jo Block

LAWRENCE BLOCK is a Mystery Writers of America Grand Master. His work over the past half century has earned him multiple Edgar Allan Poe and Shamus awards, the UK Diamond Dagger for lifetime achievement, and recognition in Germany, France, Taiwan, and Japan. His latest novels are *The Burglar Who Met Fredric Brown* and *The Autobiography of Matthew Scudder*; other recent fiction includes *A Time to Scatter Stones*, *Keller's Fedora*, and *Dead Girl Blues*. In addition to novels and short fiction, he has written episodic television (*Tilt!*) and the Wong Kar-wai film, *My Blueberry Nights*.

In recent years, Lawrence Block has found a new career as an anthologist, having realized how much easier it is to dash off an introduction while inveigling others to supply the actual stories. *Playing Games* is his nineteenth and most recent effort; his three art-based anthologies, *In Sunlight or in Shadow*, *Alive in Shape and Color*, and *From Sea to Stormy Sea*, have been especially favored by critics and readers.

Block contributed a fiction column to *Writer's Digest* for fourteen years, and has published several books for writers, including the classic *Telling Lies for Fun & Profit* and the updated and expanded *Writing the Novel from Plot to Print to Pixel*; he recently held the position of writer-in-residence at South Carolina's Newberry College. His nonfiction has been collected in *The Crime of Our Lives* (about mystery fiction) and *Hunting Buffalo with Bent Nails* (about everything else), while his collection of columns about stamp collecting, *Generally Speaking*, has found a substantial audience throughout and far beyond the philatelic community.

It is as a creator of memorable series characters that Lawrence Block is perhaps best known, and Matthew Scudder, Bernie Rhodenbarr, Evan Tanner, Chip Harrison, and Keller (respectively, an alcoholic ex-cop, a gentleman burglar, an adventurous insomniac, a lecher in the rye, and a wistful hitman) have won their share of readers' hearts and minds. Ed London, whose three magazine appearances are a highlight of *The Naked and the Deadly*, was arguably the young author's first series character.

All in all, Lawrence Block is a modest and humble fellow, although you would never guess as much from this biographical note.

Robert Deis owns one of the world's largest collections of vintage men's adventure magazines (MAMs) published in the 1950s, 1960s, and 1970s. In 2009, he created a popular blog about the genre, **MensPulpMags.com**. A few years later, Bob and Wyatt Doyle of New Texture launched The Men's Adventure Library, a series of books that feature classic MAM pulp fiction stories and artwork. That series now includes nearly 20 lushly illustrated story anthologies and art books. In recent years, Bob and Wyatt have been featured speakers at PulpFest, and Bob was listed in the book *Who's Who In New Pulp*. Starting in 2021, Bob began working with Bill Cunningham, head of Pulp 2.0 Press, to publish a magazine that features MAM stories and artwork, called the *Men's Adventure Quarterly*. He has contributed articles about MAMs to various magazines and fanzines and also writes two blogs about famous quotations, **ThisDayinQuotes.com** and **QuoteCounterquote.com**. Bob lives near Key West, Florida with his wife BJ (who graciously tolerates his fascination with vintage MAMs), their three dogs, and four cats.

WYATT DOYLE is ringmaster of New Texture, and he edits and designs most releases. His own books include *Stop Requested* (illustrated by Stanley J. Zappa), *Dollar Halloween*, *I Need Real Tuxedo and a Top Hat!*, *Buty-Wave Is Now Closed Forever*, and *Jorge Amaya Doesn't Live Here Anymore*. A retrospective of his photography was presented by Gallery 30 South in Pasadena, CA. With Robert Deis, he edits The Men's Adventure Library series, exploring vintage pulp fiction, illustration art, and history. With Jimmy Angelina, he created *The Last Coloring Book* and *The Last Coloring Book on the Left*, as well as *Be Italian*. Together with Hal Glatzer and Norman von Holtzendorff, he produced *Things That Were Made for Love*, collecting the Jazz Age song-sheet art of Sydney Leff. He assisted in the publication of Georgina Spelvin's memoir, *The Devil Made Me Do It*, and published Josh Alan Friedman's *Black Cracker* and *Tell the Truth Until They Bleed* via his Wyatt Doyle Books imprint. He administers the creative estate of Rev. Raymond Branch, and curates **RevBranch.com**. His screenplay with Jason Cuadrado, *I'm Here For You*, was produced as *Devil May Call*. A member of The Stanley J. Zappa Quartet, a recording, *The Stanley J. Zappa Quartet Plays for the Society of Women Engineers*, has been released.

Weasels Ripped My Flesh!
With guest editor Josh Alan Friedman
Featuring Lawrence Block, Robert F. Dorr, Harlan Ellison, Bruce Jay Friedman, Walter Kaylin, Mario Puzo, Robert Silverberg *and more.*

From the jungles to the deserts to the mean city streets, the men's adventure magazines of the 1950s, '60s and '70s left no male fantasy or interest unexplored. War stories, exotic adventure yarns, "true, first-hand" accounts of white-knuckle clashes between man and beast, and spicy tales of sadistic frauleins and tropical queens hungry for companionship...plus salacious exposés of then-shocking subjects like free love, the Beat Generation, homosexuality, LSD, and the secret horniness hidden in calypso lyrics. This book is your passport to a gonzo world where manly men fought small mammals bare-handed!

He-Men, Bag Men, & Nymphos
Stories by Walter Kaylin

Leaving an indelible mark on three decades of sweat-soaked pulp fiction, Walter Kaylin tackled testoster-one-fueled subjects from Westerns to war, secret agents to sex sirens, Nazis to noir. His frequently over-the-top

plots and characters scaled new heights of ingenuity and
invention, while setting the standard for the kind of un-
apologetic savagery and excess that made men's adventure
magazines notorious, then and now. With reminiscences by
Kaylin, his family, and his former editor, writer Bruce Jay
Friedman.

Cryptozoology Anthology
With guest editor David Coleman
Featuring Arthur C. Clarke, John Keel *and others*

When American men had questions about the Yeti, the
Loch Ness Monster, Bigfoot, and other weird beasts from
the strange world of cryptozoology, they found answers
in the hard-hitting pages of men's adventure magazines.
Here are samples of sensational period reporting and
wild, "true" accounts of savage, fist-to-claw duels between
man and Sasquatch, man and fishman, man and monster!
Plus full-color vintage pulp artwork that accompanied the
stories' original publication, rare archival discoveries, men's
pulp history, expert analysis by crypto authority **David
Coleman**, cryptid-by-cryptid commentary, and much, much
more. Don't leave civilization without it!

A Handful of Hell
Stories by Robert F. Dorr

Aviator, diplomat, and historian, Robert F. Dorr was
uniquely qualified to write for men's adventure magazines,
bringing sweat-and-blood, nuts-and-bolts authenticity to
his stories of risk, combat, and sacrifice. Vivid, gripping
tales of aerial conflict, battlefield heroism and action—
some fact, some fiction, all adrenaline-fueled, white-knuckle
adventure from one of the genre's greatest voices.

Barbarians on Bikes

A full color oversized collection compiling three decades of motorcycle-themed magazine covers and interior spreads from the 1950s through the 1970s, most unseen since their original publication. Biker illustration art at its most savage, a biker movie between covers. **Barbarians on Bikes** is big, bad, and untamed!

THE ART OF SAMSON POLLEN
Pollen's Women • Pollen's Action • Pollen in Print

A series of lush visual archives collecting artist Samson Pollen's most memorable pieces, selected from the hundreds of jaw-dropping illustrations he provided for MAMs from the 1950s through the 1970s. Equally celebrated for his abilities rendering action and movement, as well as his gift for painting beautiful and dangerous women. Illustrating work from authors like Mario Puzo, Martin Cruz Smith, Richard Stark (Donald Westlake), Norman Mailer, Ed McBain, Richard Wright, Don Pendleton, Erskine Caldwell, Walter Kaylin, and Robert F. Dorr, Pollen's immersive illustrations transported adventure-hungry readers from tropical jungles to brutal battlefields to raging seas and mean city streets. Samson Pollen painted it all—spectacularly. Yet almost none of these stunning illustrations have seen print since their original publication. Until now.

Both **Pollen's Women** and **Pollen's Action** are drawn from the artist's own exhaustive archives of his original artwork for MAMs, while **Pollen in Print 1955–1959** is the inaugural volume of a projected series presenting his artwork chronologically as it appeared in the magazines, filling gaps in Pollen's archive and definitively charting the trajectory of a remarkable career.

All three books include reminiscences and autobiographical comments by Pollen.

Eva: Men's Adventure Supermodel
by Eva Lynd

Blonde Swedish countess Eva Lynd's multi-faceted career touches every aspect of 20th century popular culture. A model for leading illustration artists and top glamour and pin-up photographers of the era, she also appeared with some of the biggest names in entertainment on both the big and small screens. Eva shares her story in her own words and pictures. Includes artwork from masters such as Norm Eastman, Al Rossi, Mike Ludlow, and James Bama.

One Man Army *by* Gil Cohen

Exploring the incomparable talent of Gil Cohen via the unique perspective he brought to the Mack Bolan universe as one of **The Executioner** series' most celebrated cover artists, **One Man Army** showcases Cohen's spectacular and original paintings for the bestselling action paperbacks, chronicling his seminal role in establishing the Bolan mythos for millions of dedicated readers.

Mort Künstler:
The Godfather of Pulp Fiction Illustrators

Celebrated for his ability to present large-scale action while never losing sight of essential details, **Mort Künstler** is a master of capturing conflict in paint—both its spectacle, and human cost. At last, here is a stunning selection of his finest pieces from the MAM era in this long awaited collection. A close study of an unequaled career, every page explodes with action, color, and artistry.

Exotic Adventures of Robert Silverberg
Stories by Robert Silverberg

From safari to bordello, from smugglers' cove to opium den, Robert Silverberg's lost pulp exotica returns to print for the first time since its original 1950s publication, presented in bold facsimile re-creations that look fresh off the newsstand, circa 1958. Strap in for illustrated globe-trotting adventures from the imagination of one of speculative fiction's most honored talents, working incognito.

George Gross: Covered

A top artist for pulps, men's adventure magazines, and paperback covers, George Gross's artwork spans decades, and helped establish a visual vocabulary for action/adventure and hard-boiled fiction. A unique talent who led the way for generations of artists, his imagery continues to inspire and influence. Spotlighting dozens of his memorable MAM covers, this full-color collection includes contributions by historian David Saunders and artist Mort Künstler.

The Naked and the Deadly
Stories by Lawrence Block

Spicy detective stories, international intrigue, and bedroom secrets… Before the bestsellers, Block cut his teeth on MAM fiction and nonfiction articles, collected here in their complete and uncut versions for the first time since their original publication. Includes a new introduction by the author.

THE MEN'S ADVENTURE **LIBRARY JOURNAL**

SOFTCOVER AND EXPANDED HARDCOVER EDITIONS AVAILABLE

ROBERT DEIS AND WYATT DOYLE, SERIES EDITORS

I Watched Them Eat Me Alive
Killer Creatures in Men's Adventure Magazines

Cuba: Sugar, Sez, and Slaughter
Cuba and Castro in Men's Adventure Magazines

Maneaters
Killer Sharks in Men's Adventure Magazines

The Men's Adventure Library Journal is a bold and explosive annex of **The Men's Adventure Library**, dedicated to deep dives into some of MAMs' most popular and potent subjects. Titles include **I Watched Them Eat Me Alive**, a hot appetizer sampler of killer creature survival stories, from hungry crabs to flying rodents to a plane crash into a swamp of snakes; **Cuba: Sugar, Sex, and Slaughter** presents torrid ficiton and non-fiction centered on Castro, Cuba, and life under the Revolution in the 1960s; and **Maneaters**, a savage collection of terrifying shark fiction and illustration art paired with mythbusting by contemporary shark experts, including contributions by **Shark Week** creator **Steve Cheskin** and *Mega Shark Versus Giant Octopus* director **Ace Hannah (Jack Perez)**. All volumes are available in both softcover and expanded hardcover editions packed with additional material.

Also from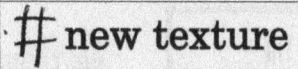

Black Cracker
an autobiographical novel by Josh Alan Friedman

1962, flashpoint of the civil rights struggle. And young Josh is the lone white boy in a segregated grade school. An unflinching funhouse tour of Long Island boyhood, and its now-forgotten poor Black shantytowns. Hilarious and heartbreaking.

Tell the Truth Until They Bleed
by Josh Alan Friedman

Up close and personal with some of the most important and unsung figures in blues and rock 'n' roll: the self-made, the self-serving, and the self-destructive. Illuminating parts of the music business most don't talk about. Show business without the showbiz.

The Last Coloring Book
The Last Coloring Book on the Left
by Jimmy Angelina & Wyatt Doyle

"Images of great movie icons, groundbreakers, and cult movie weirdos…in a pair of VERY unusual works of cinephilia. These are 'anti-coloring books' populated by cult heroes and heroines…" —Ed Grant, *Media Funhouse*

"Truly inspired!" —Steven Puchalski, *Shock Cinema*

"Perfect gifts for the cult movie fan. Crayons not included."
—Laura Wagner, *Classic Images*

Be Italian
by Jimmy Angelina & Wyatt Doyle

People pretending to be Italian and Italians pretending not to be. A one-of-a-kind visual history exploring Italian identity in motion pictures. In compact softcover and oversized deluze hardcover editions.

Stop Requested
stories by Wyatt Doyle; *illus.* Stanley J. Zappa

"A series of rueful, witty and occasionally heartwrenching stories about riding the bus in L.A. Doyle finds consequence in the inconsequential. He's Bukowski without the nasty streak. And he's real good. Highly recommended."
　　　　　　　　　—Marc Campbell, *Dangerous Minds*

nu luna, *a novel by* Andrew Biscontini

After 400 years of colonization, the moon is home to nearly a billion people, living in a crowded industrial police state on the verge of collapse. A deeply personal matinee space adventure, spun through an improbably plausible future history. The future is beautiful and dangerous.

Teacher Tales, *a novel by* Richard Adelman

For 40 years, Mr. Kessler has kept his head down and not made waves. But new acquaintances and bad decisions in his final year before retirement bring his ordered world crashing down around him—tragically and hilariously.

A Day at the Beach, *a novel by* Richard Adelman

Atlantic City, summer of '63. A boy. A girl. And the other
boy, who reluctantly pretends to date her to help his pal.
A funny, nostalgic novel of young love, best friends, and
poetry, deftly and sensitively capturing one 12-year-old's
last great summer as a kid down the shore.

Pop's Cookie Duster
by Don & Lee Doyle; *illus.* Annette Debevec

Rainy afternoons aren't much fun for two lively little girls
who love to play outside. But a hands-on kitchen activity
with their visiting Pop might just save the day!

Nimrodia, *poems by* Eric Reymond

Visual art and ancient history are the starting point for
most of the poems in this collection, as the modern world
intersects with these domains again and again. Though
language, culture, and time may divide us, these are also
the forces that link us together.

Sub-Sub Librarian, Extracts on a, *poems by* Eric Reymond

The title poem imagines *Moby Dick*'s Sub-Sub Librarian experiencing transcendence and illumination through his wide readings. Additional poems find inspiration in texts as diverse as contemporary poetry, vocabulary quizzes, and course syllabi.

Dollar Halloween
Photos by Wyatt Doyle

Off-brand Halloween junk and sparkly death totems, made to be thrown away. Where there's a need, or even a mild desire, a dollar store stands ready to fill it for whatever you've got in your pocket. *"Everything is cheaper than it looks."*

I Need Real Tuxedo and a Top Hat!
Photos and stories by Wyatt Doyle

On the buses, on the corners, in the way. Portraits and stories of the forgotten, the avoided, the ignored. Street people and street life. Life stories scratched out in public, anywhere there's room.

Buty-Wave Is Now Closed Forever
Photos by Wyatt Doyle

Things that are gone, and things that remain. Includes portraits of Georgina Spelvin, Reverend Raymond Branch, Ray Bradbury, George Clayton Johnson, Tura Satana, Ernest Borgnine, Carl Ballantine, Little Jimmy Dickens.

Jorge Amaya Doesn't Live Here Anymore
Photos by Wyatt Doyle

Abandoned places, empty spaces, forgotten faces. Indelible images from across the United States, documenting the wreckage and remnants of the American experience after the parade has passed.

Things That Were Made for Love:
The Songsheet Art of Sydney Leff
Wyatt Doyle, Hal Glatzer,
Norman von Holtzendorff, *editors*

The first-ever songsheet art collection presenting the cream of the Jazz Age illustrator's work on songsheet covers from 1924–1932. A visual feast that playfully captures the moods, elegance, style, and romance of an era.

⧣ new texture Music

I've Got Heaven on My Mind
Reverend Raymond Branch

Sing-Song Songs Stanley J. Zappa

Map of the Moon s/t

Sixty Goddammit Josh Alan

Jimmy Angelina s/t

Cursed Carolina

Continental / International Jon E. Edwards

Live a Little Manzappaczewski

Free / Refuse Hall, Skrowaczewski, Zappa

Crossing Guards Carter, Leffue, Sikora, Zappa

Balloons Carter, Skrowaczewski, Zappa

Turkey Bacon Donuts Bitches
MANZAP REBORN

The Stanley J. Zappa Quartet
Plays for The Society of Women Engineers

new texture

Ingram Content Group UK Ltd.
Milton Keynes UK
UKHW041035190623
423679UK00004B/28

9 781943 444632